FALLING FOR MR. THORNTON

TALES OF NORTH AND SOUTH

TRUDY BRASURE   NICOLE CLARKSTON

JULIA DANIELS   ROSE FAIRBANKS

KATE FORRESTER   DON JACOBSON   EVY JOURNEY

NANCY KLEIN   M. LIZA MARTE   ELAINE OWEN

DAMARIS OSBORNE   MELANIE STANFORD

CONTENTS

ABOUT THIS WORK

This anthology has been a collaborative effort born out of admiration for Elizabeth Gaskell's timeless novel *North and South*. The authors featured in this collection have chosen different styles, techniques, and elements to present facets of the story in new lights.

As a consequence, language usage, spelling, and punctuation styling will vary. Though the short stories represented in this work may employ different strategies and voices, each resonates with respect for the original masterpiece, its characters, and its creator, Elizabeth Gaskell.

OUTLINES

Modern

ONE: On the Island
By Melanie Stanford
Travel blogger Meg Hale doesn't want to return to John Thornton's resort. After all, another visit won't change her bad review.
But the resort has changed—and so has John.
The more time Meg spends on the island, the more she realizes she may have made a mistake. A mistake that could cost John the resort, and Meg her heart.

Time Slips

TWO: *Passages in Time*
By Kate Forrester
Set just before Margaret arrives in Milton. Mr Thornton dies in a devastating fire at Marlborough Mill - or does he?

THREE: *The First Day of Spring*
By M. Liza Marte
Spring this year will bring daffodils, singing birds, and the love of a lifetime.

Humorous

FOUR: *Loose Leaves from Milton*
By Damaris Osborne
A spoof of North & South with a strong twist of tea, the British favoured beverage, and sprang from John Thornton being known as 'JT' in so many forum threads. J Tea was an obvious progression, and

the story follows the television adaptation, loose-leafly, as his love for the haughty Miss Hale with the porcelain tea cup complexion, who looks down upon him upwards, brews until he has to pour out his love, unstrained.

Continuation

FIVE: *Reeducating Mr Thornton*
By Evy Journey
When Mr. Thornton and Margaret arrived in Cadiz for a month's visit with her brother and his new wife, he did not care much about the strange city. Nor did he have great expectations of what Cadiz could offer a visitor like him. But later, what he finds there and who he encounters change his outlook forever.

Variations

SIX: *Mistakes and Remedies*
By Julia Daniels
When John Thornton's sister goes missing, he seeks help from the one woman he can trust—the one who still holds his heart. Saving Fanny is all he hopes for, until a tender friendship begins to flourish between him and the love he had thought lost to him forever.

SEVEN: *Her Father's Last Wish*
By Rose Fairbanks
Two hearts desperately in love divided by her wretched secret, one father's wish to unite them.

EIGHT: *The Best Medicine*
By Elaine Owen
What if Thornton found a way to change Margaret's mind about him earlier in the story? Could helping Margaret's friend Bessy be the way to winning Margaret's heart? This is a short story with more than one happy ever after for more than one beloved character!

NINE: *Cinders and Smoke*

By Don Jacobson

That space between the end of the riot and the new dawn where Thornton faces his demons as Higgins confronts him with questions about his humanity and where Margaret uses her compassion to bring the two sides together.

TEN: *Mischances*

By Nicole Clarkston

When the wrong person discovers Margaret in a compromising position, she is forced to decide who she really wants and just how much she can trust the one man who can help her.

Alternate Endings

ELEVEN: *Looking to the Future*

By Nancy Klein

Starting from Margaret's return to London from her trip with Mr. Bell to Helstone, this story contemplates events solely from Margaret's point of view. Margaret rues her treatment of Mr. Thornton, and wonders if she will ever have a chance to set things to right.

TWELVE: *Once Again*

By Trudy Brasure

A deeper look at Thornton's emotional journey from despair to bliss as he arrives in London to sign the papers to give up the mill.

FOREWORD BY MIMI MATTHEWS

As someone who both reads and writes Victorian romance, Elizabeth Gaskell's *North and South* has always had a special place in my heart. It's a quintessentially Victorian story, and yet one that resonates as much today as it did in the 1850s. It's a tale of evolution, and change, not just in the hearts of the hero, John Thornton, and heroine, Margaret Hale, but in the greater world around them. Within its pages, we find the age-old conflicts of old versus new, country versus city, and long-held tradition versus emerging values and technologies.

These conflicts help to make John Thornton one of the most compelling and relatable heroes in Victorian fiction. He isn't a duke or an earl. He's a working man, who has risen through the ranks to run his own cotton mill. In the process, he's not only saved his family from penury, he's also managed to give his mother and sister security —and the added bonus of an elevated rank in their community.

Mr. Thornton credits much of his success to his formidable mother. She's a strong woman who has instilled an equally strong work ethic in her son. As Mr. Thornton explains early in the novel:

"Sixteen years ago, my father died under very miserable circumstances. I was taken from school, and had to become a man (as well as I could) in a few days. I had such a mother as few are blest with; a woman of strong power,

and firm resolve...Week by week our income came to fifteen shillings, out of which three people had to be kept. My mother managed so that I put by three out of these fifteen shillings regularly. This made the beginning; this taught me self-denial. Now that I am able to afford my mother such comforts as her age, rather than her own wish, requires, I thank her silently on each occasion for the early training she gave me."

As sensible as Mr. Thornton is, he can't help but be bowled over by the grace and beauty of Margaret Hale, a gently-bred vicar's daughter from Helstone. On first laying eyes on her, Mr. Thornton feels not only admiration, but also a keen sense of his own shortcomings. Gaskell writes:

"He almost said to himself that he did not like her, before their conversation ended; he tried so to compensate himself for the mortified feeling, that while he looked upon her with an admiration he could not repress, she looked at him with proud indifference, taking him, he thought, for what, in his irritation, he told himself he was—a great rough fellow, with not a grace or a refinement about him."

Margaret Hale isn't as impressed by Mr. Thornton as he is with her. Indeed, initially, she finds him hardly worthy of remark, describing him as being "a tall, broad-shouldered man...with a face that is neither exactly plain, nor yet handsome, nothing remarkable— not quite a gentleman." Later, however, she comes to appreciate Mr. Thornton's finer qualities. He's plainspoken, sincere, and quite passionate about industry and invention. When he comes to their house one evening for tea, Margaret begins to register the handsomeness of his features, and the brilliance of his smile. As Gaskell writes:

"Margaret liked this smile; it was the first thing she had admired in this new friend of her father's; and the opposition of character, shown in all these details of appearance she had just been noticing, seemed to explain the attraction they evidently felt towards each other."

Of course, the path to true love doesn't run smooth, especially when a hero and heroine of a story are as opposite in background and temperament as John Thornton and Margaret Hale. There are social faux pas, political arguments, business catastrophes, rejected proposals, untimely deaths, and misunderstandings aplenty. Ultimately, it's the slow evolution of opinions about each other, and the gradual acceptance of the changing social order, that lead this unlikely pair to love.

North and South is a thoughtful Victorian romance, filled with strong women and honorable men—flawed but sympathetic characters set against a backdrop of social and technological change. There is much in its pages that twenty-first century readers can identify with. It's one of the reasons it still resonates with so many of us, and why variations of John and Margaret's love story remain so popular.

For me, it will always be a special novel. One that perfectly encapsulates the spirit of the Victorian era—both the pain of change and the earnest hope for a better tomorrow. Who among us can't relate to that?

Mimi Matthews
USA Today bestselling author

ON THE ISLAND

Melanie Stanford

"I know you despise me; allow me to say, it is because you do not understand me." —Chapter XXIV, North and South

J can't believe I'm going back there. Back to the scene of the crime, so to speak. But not my crime. His.

The plane touches down, smoothly despite its teeny size, and then makes its way slowly down the runway to the terminal. It isn't my first time on the island, but I stare out of the window as if I'll see something new.

The view isn't much to look at. Grass a bit too long curling in the breeze. Sky so clear it looks fake. Airport so small it looks more like an office building. It's one of those airports that doesn't have jet bridges connecting the airplane to the terminal. Instead, we walk down rickety metal steps, across the tarmac, and into the building.

While I wait for my luggage, I call my dad. It's his fault I'm here again, after all.

"Meg?" Dad says on the other line. "Is that you?" As if caller ID didn't tell him.

"Yeah, it's me. I made it here safely."

He lets out an audible breath of relief. Dad hates flying. He watches too many shows about plane crashes. "Are you at the resort?"

"No, I'm still at the airport waiting for my luggage."

"Better you lose your luggage than your life."

It's good he can't see me roll my eyes. Obviously dying would be bad, but losing my luggage would be a travesty. There is pretty much nowhere to shop on this tiny island, and I don't want to waste my money on overpriced resort clothes that are better suited for a sixty-year-old lady—one of the things I may have mentioned when I blogged about the resort last time.

"How was the flight? Turbulence? Delays? Shaky landing?"

"It was totally fine." There was a lot of turbulence actually, being such a small plane and all, but I don't tell Dad. He'd freak.

"Okay then." He sounds doubtful.

The luggage starts coming down the conveyor belt. "How's Mom?"

"No change. The doctor said she just needs to keep doing what she's doing."

I grip the phone in my hand. Yet another reason why I shouldn't be on a remote island in the middle of the Atlantic Ocean. If my mom worsens, I won't have time to get home.

My luggage appears, flowery suitcases tumbling from the top of the belt and then spinning away from me. "I better go. Tell Mom I love her."

"Will do. And Meg?"

"Yeah?" I step closer to the conveyor so I'm ready to grab when my luggage goes by.

"Be nice to John, all right? Give him…give that place a chance."

I snatch for the handle of my suitcase but fumble at Dad's words and miss. My suitcase runs away from me. I sigh.

"Sure, Dad."

"Love you, Meg."

"Love you, too."

I hang up and pocket my phone. As I wait for my suitcase to come back around, I resist the urge to call Dad back just so I can yell at him. I don't want to be here. I don't want to give this place—especially John Thornton—another chance. I don't want to be away from Mom again.

This time I grab my suitcase and haul it off the runway with a grunt. I roll it out of the airport, a grumpy and resentful cloud following behind.

"Margaret Hale checking in." I tap my finger on the counter while the receptionist similarly taps on the keyboard. I try not to look, but I'm totally glancing around, keeping my eye out. I really don't want to run into him. I mean, he knows I'm coming, but maybe I'll get lucky and manage to avoid him for my entire stay.

"Meg."

Dang it.

"You're back."

His presence is a weight behind me. If only I could ignore him. Where are my earbuds when I need them? Then again, he'd probably tap me on my shoulder or something. There's no avoiding John Thornton.

I turn halfway. I don't quite look at him. "I'm back."

He doesn't say anything, and it feels like he's daring me to meet his eyes. Hold out, just hold out. You can do it.

I can't do it. The silence is too much, and I finally give in and look at him.

He's not as close to me as I thought, but there's something about him—something that radiates off him like an energy field. Get too close and you'll get hit by the blast.

"How are your parents?"

I blink, not so much at the question but at the softness in his voice. It's so unlike him.

Memories of the moment we met flood into my brain. I didn't want to come to the resort in the first place. My mom had just been diagnosed with cancer, and I wanted to be with her. But Dad asked me this favor. "He's a family friend," Dad said. "Please," Dad said. "Your mother will be fine without you for a little while," Dad said. But what did he know?

Turned out, she was as fine as someone with cancer can be while I was away, but I still resented leaving her. And it just went downhill from there. I arrived at the resort and was told I'd meet the resort manager right away. I ended up waiting and waiting, getting more annoyed by the second. I mean, I know I'm not this huge deal, but when a popular travel blogger with almost a million Instagram followers comes to review your resort, you'd think you'd treat her with a little more respect.

So instead of waiting, I went exploring—in places I'm not supposed to be, but that was the point. Hotels, resorts, they always show you their best sides, but I like to see what's going on behind the scenes. How clean are their kitchens? How organized is the management? How do they treat their staff?

That's how I first found Mr. John Thornton. In his office, yelling at one of his employees. Ripping into him while the poor man cowered before his boss. When John saw me, he yelled at me, too. Screamed at me to get out. Imagine his surprise when he found out I was the daughter of his friend Richard Hale and the blogger sent to review his resort.

It wasn't a good start. He gave me excuses later, trying to explain what that employee had done, but I wouldn't listen. He's the boss, and he doesn't need to treat his employees that way—or perfect strangers —regardless of the situation.

Needless to say, I didn't give the resort a good review.

Now I'm back as a favour to my dad because, for some reason, he loves John and he thinks I treated him unfairly. Me!

"Are you not going to talk to me at all?" John asks.

"I'm sorry," I say, manners automatically kicking in. "I'm tired from the flight. My parents are good."

I don't want to get into my mom's illness with this guy. He probably already knows anyway. It's weird how much he and my dad talk.

He nods. "I'll show you to your room."

He grabs the handle of my suitcase and starts walking away, not waiting to see if I'll follow.

I follow. Grudgingly. I mean, he's got my stuff.

"Last time…" he starts when I've caught up to him. He clears his throat. We both remember what happened last time. "Last time you had a room on the top floor, for the view. This time I thought you might like one of our ocean rooms." He opens the door with a swipe of a key card, then motions me inside.

I forget about his lurking presence behind me as I take in the room. Warm wood floorboards, gorgeous local art hanging on the light blue walls, a king size bed with lush white sheets and pillows. The bathroom is marble and sparkling clean. There's a cushy chair in one corner of the room. And the best part, huge glass doors covered by a gauzy white curtain opening right onto the beach.

I drop my purse on the bed, the ocean beckoning to me. The glass doors slide open, and a rush of warm air blows over me, smelling like salt and something sweeter, like fruit.

"Do you like it?" John asks.

I turn. Swallow at his gaze. "Are all the rooms like this?"

One of the things I criticized in my review last year was the décor, the tacky wall hangings, the cheap bedspreads, the thin and worn carpeting. The whole place needed an update, and it looks like he did it.

"Well, not all of them."

My eyebrows raise. Did he just renovate one room for my benefit, for people like me?

"The whole place was remodelled. I took everything you wrote to heart. But not every room is at this level. This is one of our more expensive rooms."

He remodelled the entire resort…because of me? That must have cost a fortune. How many years will it take him to earn that money back? Will the investment be worth it?

No. I won't feel guilty. He wants a resort people will come back to, will tell their friends about, will remember forever? Then the place has to reflect that.

"Sometime I'd like to check out some of the other rooms," I say. Because of course I can't trust what he said.

"Of course." He's thumbing the handle of my suitcase. He must realize it, because he shoves the handle down a little too hard. "I'll let you settle in. There's an open dinner reservation for you at Bliss. I remember you liked it last time."

The only thing I liked last time. That and the beach. He turns and leaves, closing the door behind him.

Breath rushes out of me, and I sink onto the bed. It's hard to breathe when John is around. I'm exhausted, by the trip, by being near him.

My eyes snag on the ocean again. Nothing makes me feel better than a swim.

The ocean calls.

~

MOST PEOPLE ARE uncomfortable eating alone, but I'm used to it. I've travelled a lot now for work and most of it by myself. So I don't mind at all sitting in a fancy restaurant at a table alone, enjoying the seafood or the steak or whatever local delicacy a starred chef wants to prepare for me. I love to people-watch, musing about who's on their first vacation together, who's been together forever, who's about to break up. Watching people break up over their salmon or get engaged with the old ring in the champagne glass corny bit.

"Another glass of wine?" the waiter asks, and I shake my head. I never drink more than one. I am here on business, after all.

"Dessert will be out in a moment," he says, clearing my empty plate. The ahi tuna was excellent, cooked and seasoned perfectly. The picture is already on my Instagram story. I may have issues with John Thornton, but I never fail to post about good food. The restaurant is definitely getting my top rating again.

I make a few more notes in my notebook about the feelings the restaurant and the food invoke in me. What I love especially this time.

A plate of decadent-looking chocolate mousse is placed in front of me. I look up to tell the waiter thank you, only to meet the eyes of John Thornton.

"How was the fish?" he asks, taking the empty chair across from me.

My mouth tightens. Last year, at this same restaurant, he decided he needed to sit with me while I ate, as if he was daring me to write up something bad. Either that or he felt bad for me, a woman eating alone. I didn't appreciate his company then, and I don't want it now.

"It was excellent," I say, though it doesn't sound like I mean it.

"Good." His smile dies when he sees my face. He clears his throat. "Is there anything you'd like me to schedule you for during the week?"

Why? So nothing will go wrong? "I'll do it myself, but thank you." I can't get a regular experience if I let him manage my whole vacation.

He nods. "Let me know if you need anything."

"I will." Unlikely.

He doesn't get up. I stare.

"Are you going to try it?"

I forgot about the dessert in front of me. I glance at him, but he makes no move to leave. *I don't need an audience, thanks!*

But I pick up my fork and cut through the mousse. Put it in my mouth, the fork slowly sliding from my lips as the chocolate fills my mouth, melting on my tongue.

A hum escapes my lips. My eyes are closed. They pop open when I realize how I must look. John is watching me, the corners of his lips turned up.

Dang, he probably thought I was flirting or something. Playing coy.

"It's…" I clear my throat. "It's very good." I take a selfie with a forkful of mousse near my mouth. An older lady at the table next to mine gives me a look, but I just smile at her. People can judge me all they want, but this is my job. It's what my followers expect.

"I thought so too." John stands. "I'll see you tomorrow, Meg."

I choke on the dessert. *Tomorrow? Why?*

∼

A COOL BREEZE blows over me, and I roll over in bed with a contented sigh. I didn't need air conditioning, just the breeze coming through the screen doors. The bed is soft, and I smush my face into the pillow. I'm too comfortable to get up.

I glance at the clock. Dang. Eleven AM. I never sleep this late.

For a few seconds, I argue with myself about getting up or not. I don't really have to, but I should.

After a quick shower, I knot my hair into a wet bun, put on a bit of waterproof makeup—it's all going to melt off my face anyway—and then head out. I stroll through the resort, snap pictures, make notes of everything that's changed, what has stayed the same. I grab a water and a muffin from a café but don't sit to eat—just keep walking. I pass older couples walking hand in hand. Families with young kids, the parents still yawning while the kids bounce in anticipation of the day. There are sunbathers at the various pools and early drinkers sitting at the poolside bars. The clientele is diverse in age and ethnicity.

It takes me more than an hour to walk pretty much everywhere aside from the floors of rooms. Downing the last of my water and then throwing the bottle into a recycle bin, I start to venture where I don't belong. Into Staff-Only floors, kitchens of the different restaurants. I find John Thornton's office again, but he's not there. Neither is his secretary. Probably on lunch, which means I timed it perfectly.

The office is neat. No papers strewn on the desk, no dust on the bookshelf. I don't rifle through his drawers—it's not like I'm trying to get dirt on him or anything. I already got the dirt last time, already saw the truth. I don't even know why I'm back here again, as if things will be different.

No, I know why I'm here—as a favor to my dad. I stop and check the number of comments on my latest post. People are interested to know why I'm back. *Second chances*, I type, because it's sort of true.

I close the door behind me and continue through the resort.

The sunshine outside beckons, so I walk through the manicured grounds, inhaling the scent of tropical flowers mixed with humidity. Sweat gathers on my hairline, but I don't mind. The heat covers my skin like a blanket.

I round a corner, then stop. There's John, surrounded by a handful of workers who all look like they're in their late teens. His back is to me so I stay put and listen.

"...lack of rain, and we need to keep on top of that. You've done an excellent job this past week. I've noticed how hard you've all worked, and I want to say thank you. Keep it up."

The workers grin at each other, and John gives them all high-fives like some goofy older brother and not their boss. The boss who yells at his employees...

He turns away and sees me, hesitates a moment before walking towards me.

"That was very buddy-buddy of you," I say. I expect him to get defensive. Instead, he quirks an eyebrow at me.

"Despite what you may think, I do my best to treat my employees with respect. I'm firm, but that doesn't mean I can't be friendly as well."

Huh. "Then what about what I witnessed last time?"

He crosses his arms. He's wearing a white button-down that's rolled up at the sleeves, and my eyes go to his tanned arms before returning to his face.

"What you witnessed last time was my anger at a man who was harassing some of our female employees. I admit, I was angry. I couldn't really help it after I heard what he did."

I swallow, speechless.

"You know, Meg, if you want to know anything about me, about the resort, all you have to do is ask. I'm not perfect by any means, but I don't have anything to hide."

I watch him walk away, my gut churning with a very unpleasant feeling.

～

"I'D LIKE to take a tour of the island," I say at the concierge desk. "What's the best way to go about that?"

Last time I was here, I never left the resort. Bad research on my part as a travel blogger. This time I want to experience the island and its people, local delicacies in real conditions, not watered down or jazzed up by a resort.

"We have daily tours which start at 9 am every morning," the concierge—Frances—says. She pulls out a brochure. "The tour stops at a market, a few especially beautiful viewpoints on the island, as well as some food stops to taste local delicacies."

"And what if I wanted to go on my own?"

"You can rent a car, but I warn you they're not usually reliable. You can also take a bus, but the bus schedule is very random and sometimes unpredictable. The tour is the best and most secure way to see the island."

I open my mouth, ready to pick the rental car option—I can always call the resort for a tow if the car breaks down, right?—when a voice stops me.

"I'll take her."

John appears beside me. He leans over the counter and smiles at Frances, who blushes.

"That's okay," I say quickly. This can't be what he meant by 'See you tomorrow'—he'd had no idea what I had planned. Or maybe he's following me. Or having me tailed. I scoff at my own paranoia. He may have had feelings for me once, but he's not a stalker.

I raise an eyebrow and check him out from head to toe just in case. He raises an eyebrow back.

"It will be my pleasure."

Now I'm the one blushing. Dangit. "I'd really rather go on my own. I'm hoping to get an...unfiltered view of the island."

He angles his body toward me. "Frances wasn't lying when she said the rental cars are unreliable. You'll be lucky to get ten minutes from the resort. I'm happy to take you in my car."

I look him square in the face. "You're trying your best to get a better review this time."

He doesn't flinch. "Yes. But I also don't want to spend my day worrying about you."

I blink, surprised by his honesty, especially in front of Frances, who is leaning forward with her mouth open as if she's trying to see what our conversation tastes like.

"It's not your business to worry about me." It comes out harsher than I mean, but I don't take it back.

He searches my face. "If something happens to a writer reviewing my resort, I think that is my business."

Something swoops in my gut briefly, but there's no way it's disappointment. It's gone in a flash, replaced with my usual stubbornness. "I'll really be fine. I have a phone in case anything happens."

"There's barely any service on the island."

I huff. "Is there anything I can say that will convince you to let me go alone?"

He smirks. "No."

"Fine," I bite out. "Let's go."

BEING ALONE in a car with a man I rejected is not awkward at all.

This is what I keep telling myself as John pulls out of the perfectly manicured resort and onto a decidedly less kept-up road. The car is a two-seater convertible, more cute than sporty. What I'd expect a rich sorority girl to drive and not a businessman like John.

He's driving slow, which my hair appreciates, and I can hear the Beatles faintly through the speakers. He doesn't speak, and neither do I. I don't know what to say.

I'm not sure why he insisted on taking me around the island today. Was it really all because he was worried? I don't get why he wants to be around me at all, considering my last visit.

After our rocky introduction, I never could warm up to him, no matter what he did to try and impress me. I thought it was all for a good review.

And then he came to my room the day before I was scheduled to leave. When I opened the door and saw him standing there, I wanted to close it on his face. I didn't like being around him. After catching him yelling at that employee, it felt like everything else he did was an act. The real John Thornton was the one who chewed out his employees—not the guy who personally checked on his guests, or brought them fresh flowers, or made sure they had the best seat at the restaurant or the best view for the Island show. When he came into my room, I was expecting some kind of butter-up for the review.

Instead, he paced around the room for a few minutes. His hair was mussed, and he looked rumpled, almost wild. Not his usual self. He turned to me and blurted, "Don't go tomorrow."

I thought I needed my hearing checked. "What?"

"Stay longer."

He wanted more time to prove how great his resort was. But he'd already missed that chance. Staying any longer wouldn't change my review. My jaw clenched. "I've got what I needed."

"Stay for me."

I think I shook my head, not out of denial but because I couldn't believe what I heard.

His palm hit the wall. He dropped his head. "Is that such a horrible thought?"

"I don't... that's not..." I couldn't get my thoughts in order. All this time, I thought he'd been trying to get a good review out of me. But he liked me?

He stood in front of me, close enough that I could see the lines by his eyes but not so close that he was in my personal space. "I'd like to spend more time with you," he said as if he could hear my thoughts. He cleared his throat. "I know I'm asking a lot but—"

"I can't stay here."

He blinked.

"I can't, and I don't want to."

"I thought... I was hoping..."

"If you're trying to get a good review out of me, this is not the way to go about it."

His eyebrows lowered. He looked dangerous then, but I wasn't afraid—only annoyed. Annoyed that I was in this situation. A situation that I hadn't recognized.

"I'm not doing this for a good review. I like you."

His admission caught me off guard. People didn't usually tell you stuff like that straight up. At least not in my experience.

"I'm not interested." I almost apologized, but I stopped myself. What did I have to be sorry for when I didn't return his feelings?

He shook his head as if he couldn't believe it. Maybe he wasn't used to getting turned down. "You said, on the phone..."

We never talked on the phone. "What are you talking about?"

"I overheard you." His tanned cheeks managed to go red. "I shouldn't have been listening, but you were talking about me."

I think he dreamt that. I had no recollection of talking about him to anyone. "When was this?"

"Yesterday. You complimented the resort, and me." He gave me a wry smile. "You said I was handsome."

I held back a laugh, but my lips still twitched. He must have mistaken my meaning, because he leaned toward me. I pushed my hand against his chest, stopping him.

"Hold up." There's no way I said any of that. Okay, he was good-looking, but I would never admit that out loud to anyone. Especially since his personality made him considerably less attractive.

And then it dawned on me.

"That conversation isn't what you think," I said. His heartbeat pulsed against my palm. I still had my hand on his chest. I quickly lowered it.

"What do you mean?"

I sighed. "I was talking to Mena Boucher. She's a travel writer and an Instagram influencer like me, except she does more opinion pieces mixed with gossip and less about the actual destination."

John was still close, and I was having a hard time organizing my thoughts. I stepped back.

"She wanted dirt on the resort. But I wouldn't talk bad about my worst enemy to her. So when she was grilling me, I..."

He glowered. "You lied?"

"You don't get it. She's horrible. Everything she writes is negative and sarcastic, but people eat it up. I can't stand it."

"So you lied. You don't really think those things."

I swallowed. I knew what a jerk I was going to sound like but, even though I'd lied to Mena and I would do it again in a heartbeat, I wouldn't lie now. "No, I don't really think those things."

He searched my face and, not finding what he wanted, shut down. "Fine. I'm sorry I said anything." He booked it from the room, slamming the door before I could register he was gone.

I didn't expect to see him again after that, but the next day before I left, he appeared while I was checking out, asking in a polite and professional manner if I enjoyed my stay and if there was anything he could do to improve the resort.

"Read my review," I said, uncomfortable at being near him and wishing he was mad at me. *That* would've been easier to deal with.

"I will," he replied, but I'd already turned from him. I was so ready to be away from that resort and back to my mom.

And now I'm back, and alone in a car with him, no less.

The road gradually curves to the coast, magnificent blue water kissing the endless stretch of white sandy beach. I drink in the view. Take in the ocean air, the breeze on my face cooling my skin. Palm trees dot the other side of the road. The wild grass grows a little too high, but I like it. The whole island screams paradise. If only I was with someone else.

But I realize how comfortable I am. Somewhere a few miles back, the awkwardness disappeared. Of course, now that I think about it, it's back.

I glance at John, and he's got one hand on the steering wheel. The other elbow rests on the open window, his hand curling against the back of his neck. He looks perfectly at ease. The wind ruffles his hair. He glances over at me and smiles, and my heart jumps.

It's got to be because he looks good, that's all. Because I don't like this guy.

"Look over there," he says.

I've been staring at him. Great.

I turn back to the ocean. John pulls over while I squint to make out what he's telling me to look at. There's something there, far out in the water. We're too far away for me to tell what it is.

"Here, hold on." John leans over me and opens the glove compartment. I press myself against the chair but that doesn't stop me from smelling the coconut scent of his shampoo. A silver scar crosses his elbow, and I wonder absently where he got it from.

"Try this."

He's close. I never realized his eyes are blue. It takes me a second to register the binoculars in his hand.

"Thanks." The binoculars show me what I couldn't see before—three dolphins leaping out of the ocean in smooth arcs. I can't stop my squeal. "It's incredible!"

I watch until they've swum too far even for the binoculars to make out.

"Was that your first time?"

Even though I know it's totally innocent, a flush spreads over my neck at his question. I keep my gaze on the ocean. "No. But it never gets old."

His hand touches mine, and I flinch before realizing he's just taking the binoculars from me. He puts them away and then pulls back onto the road.

ABOUT A HALF-HOUR LATER, he pulls away from the coast and drives inland. Small, rustic houses appear, some so rundown they look like one stiff breeze would blow them over. Others are well kept up, displaying neat yards, flower gardens, and colorful siding. More appear until we're in town, the only town on the island. Whitewashed shops and open restaurants line the street, but nothing fancy. It's clear this part of the island isn't a tourist hot spot. Local kids play in the street. A group of old men sit in front of a post office/convenience store. They wave at John as we drive by slowly. Some of the kids chase the car, calling his name.

He stops the car beside an open building. "I hope you're hungry," he says, getting out of the car.

The smell of roasting meat and garlic hits me, and suddenly I'm ravenous. Wooden picnic benches sit on the dirt, an awning shading the blazing sun from our heads.

"Johnny!" the woman behind the counter calls out. She rushes to him, her arms outstretched. He smiles and returns the hug, and I can't help but gape.

"You haven't been here in so long," she says, her English accented with the local dialect.

"I know, Alvita, I'm sorry."

"You're too busy—too busy," she says, shaking her head. Then she sees me. "And who is this? You finally got yourself a woman?"

John blushes. *Blushes.* "This is Margaret, a...friend."

"Hi." I reach my hand out for Alvita to shake, but instead she squishes me in a hug. She smells like onions and the ocean and, surprisingly, I like the combination.

"Sit! Sit!" She motions to the tables. "I'll make you the best meal you'll have on the island. Much better than what those fancy chefs make at John's place."

It's funny how she calls it John's place, as if it's his house or a small restaurant and not a gigantic resort.

"It's true," John says, "although I probably shouldn't admit that to you." He grins.

"Why not?" Alvita asks.

I don't know if John doesn't hear or purposely avoids the question, but he turns away to talk to a younger guy behind the counter who's wearing an apron and holding a spatula.

Alvita looks at me expectantly.

"I'm a travel blogger. I travel all over the world and write reviews of the places I've been."

I don't know what I was expecting from her, but it wasn't the knowing look she gives me accompanied by an, "Ah." Did John tell her about me? Are they that close?

"Well, have a seat. The food will be out in a few."

"But I didn't order anything yet," I say.

She laughs as she walks away.

I sit down at an empty picnic table and proceed to do one of my favorite things—people watch. I've always been fascinated by people and places. Sometimes I think I do too much watching and not enough living. Then I remember all the places I've travelled and the fact that I earn a living by being observant.

Two kids are throwing a ball back and forth, a dog darting between them almost like monkey in the middle. A man leans against a tree smoking. He stares at a pair of girls who walk by, their thick hair accented with tied bandanas and skirts flowing in the wind as if they're in the middle of a photo shoot or some kind of hair commercial. I snap about a zillion pictures.

There's a steady stream of people who go by, and almost all of them either wave at John or call out to him or stop by to talk. I watch him chat and smile, and I'm completely flabbergasted by this person in front of me. Who is he, and where did he come from? Holding my phone up, I zoom in on him, snapping a picture before I realize I've done it.

Either he heard the click or he can just sense my stare but, either way, he comes over and sits across from me. A group of guys he was talking to follow him over, cajoling him to introduce us. And then, for a solid twenty minutes, I'm introduced to about two dozen people— names I forget instantly because I know getting out my notebook and writing them down would be weird.

"Shoo, shoo!" Alvita scolds, carrying two steaming plates of something that smells like a thousand calories. She places them down in front of us while the crowd disperses.

I lean over my plate and inhale. Grilled fish and meat and rice mixed with vegetables and sausage. "It smells amazing."

Alvita tsks, and I worry I've offended her. But when I look up, she's smiling.

"Wait until you taste it," John says.

He's right, the smell is right, everything about this food is right. I take a few pictures before digging in. I can't help moaning while I eat.

"Good?" John asks, smiling around his own bite.

I moan some more, and he laughs. I'm not even embarrassed.

When my plate is empty, I push it away from me and then clutch my stomach. "Ooh, I ate too much." I shouldn't have done that to myself, but I didn't want to waste a single morsel.

"It's hard not to," John says.

Alvita reappears and clears out plates. "Did you like it?" John slips her some cash.

"How would you feel if business picks up a little?" I ask.

She's taken aback by my question. There's been maybe a handful of people who came through while we ate. Steady for this little place. But I could make it blow up.

"People like my posts. I love a place, they go there."

She looks at me in disbelief.

"It's true. I mean, you won't become famous, but your traffic will double, at least." Their faces. I wish I'd never said anything. "Not to toot my own horn or anything."

"Consider it tooted," John says.

I can't read his expression, but I can guess his thoughts. Bad review. Fewer tourists to the resort. And all my fault. I mean, I just admitted it.

"Anyway." I decide to ignore him and the uncomfortable feeling in my stomach. I ate too much, that's all. "Just be prepared to get a few more customers than usual."

"Whatever you say." Alvita shakes her head, but she'll see. She turns to John. "See you, sweetie." She kisses him on the head.

I get up from the table and head to the car, but John doesn't make it more than two steps before two women step into his path with warm greetings. I think everyone on the island knows John.

I head to the ocean instead. The beach is covered in rocks, and the water seems to drop off quickly. Not a great place for swimming, but it's beautiful. Wind whips my hair around my head, and my dress flaps against my legs. Waves hit the shore at regular intervals. I close my eyes and listen. Breathe deep. I've travelled a lot of places now, but the ocean will always be my number one.

Looking back, John is still talking to the women, so I slip off my sandals and walk carefully across the rocks and dip my toes in the water. It's cold but not unbearable. I take a couple of steps deeper but that's all. The waves are strong and I don't want to get swept under. Even though I'm a good swimmer, I don't really want to get wet right now. Plus—the rocks.

"Careful, it gets deep right there."

I don't look at John—he'll just see my annoyance. Disturbing my peace, stating the obvious, and that whole twisty feeling in my gut that says I might have been just a tiny bit wrong about him. All of this is annoying me right now.

I walk away from him, following the shore but keeping my feet in the water. I don't have to turn around to know he's following me. Surprisingly, this doesn't annoy me.

The view in front of me is nothing but sand meeting ocean meeting sky. I breathe to the sound of the ocean. It really is beautiful on this tiny island. Is that why John came here—why he decided to build a resort here? I've never asked. It seems impossible to find this place without having some original tie to it.

I spin around and stub my toe on a rock. "Ow, ow, ow!" I lift my foot instinctively and then lose my balance.

John's arms go around my waist. He pulls me up and into him before I can biff it onto my butt.

I'm pressed against him, our faces inches apart. I think I've stopped breathing, so I inhale. It sounds like a gasp. His eyes go to my lips.

I panic. And end up practically screaming in his face. "Why here?"

He blinks and lets me go.

"Sorry. Thank you. Why here?" I'm babbling. My hair blows in my mouth. I turn my head to get it out and to regain some composure. "Why this island?"

Instead of answering, he starts walking again. Carrying my sandals in one hand, I keep pace with him. I don't have much of a choice—he's my ride.

The shore thins out until it's mostly rock. After a few minutes, John climbs onto a big one and sits. He holds a hand out for me.

I could just turn right around and walk back to the car. I could.

I grab his hand and clamber onto the rock. My legs drape over, I tuck in my dress so it doesn't blow up.

"I used to come here as a kid," John says. His gaze is on the ocean, and mine is on him. "I never really knew what I wanted to be when I grew up. Did you?" He looks at me now.

"Yeah. A vet. Until I realized that I really don't like animals much."

He laughs. "I had no clue. But I wanted to live here. Some of my best memories are from here."

I wait for more, but he doesn't elaborate. So I decide to be a good journalist and push. Maybe if I know him better, I'll understand him more. "You decided to open a resort. Did you buy the land? Or was it here already?"

His jaw tenses. "The resort was already here, but it was old, and much smaller. My dad bought it."

"What happened?"

"He died. Before it ever opened."

"I'm sorry."

The only sound between us is the ocean waves.

"How is your mom doing?"

I blink at him in surprise.

"Your dad called me when you were here last year. He told me about the diagnosis." John looks at me. "It must have been hard to be here during that time."

I swallow—can't say anything. Shame makes my skin itch. I rub my hands over my arms.

"Has the chemo made a difference?"

"Who knows? Doctors say one thing but then... I mean, she's fine." I shake my head. "No, that's a lie. She's not fine. I hate that I always tell people she's fine."

"It's because you don't want to talk about it."

"Maybe," I reply.

"I wouldn't have asked if I didn't want to know the answer. The real one."

He means it. I can tell by his expression. Out of everyone I know,

John is the last person I thought I'd talk to about this, and yet I do. I tell him about my mom's illness, how it's affecting her and me and my dad, how much it sucks.

"I shouldn't be here," I say. "Who knows how much longer she has?"

He brings his knees up, drapes his elbows on them. "Then why are you here?"

He's not being rude; he genuinely wants to know why I came back. This is something my dad didn't tell him. "Dad asked me to."

He said I wasn't fair to John. Said I was wrong. Said it was the first time he'd ever read me give a biased review.

So I came back to prove to him I was right. I don't let personal feelings get in the way of my writing. He was the one who didn't know his friend. I saw the real John that day in his office.

"I'm glad you came back," he says softly.

Looking over at John now, I think I might have been wrong after all.

I'M BACK at the concierge desk. Frances—the girl from yesterday who suggested I take a tour and witnessed the entire awkward exchange between John and I—is there again.

"How was it yesterday?" she asks, and I'm sure the question isn't innocent. But I've got some probing questions for her, as well.

"It was good. I got to see a lot of the island. Ate some amazing food. Bought this bracelet." I show her a cuff on my arm engraved with flowers. I fell in love with it at first sight.

Frances grabs my hand so she can examine the bracelet. "That's gorgeous! Where did you get it?"

"From a little market on the north side. Near the bay."

"Oh! Where all the scuba divers go."

"So I heard. In fact, I'd like to book an excursion there for tomorrow, if I can." I had no clue about that place on my last visit.

"Definitely."

After she books me in and explains the details, I linger at the desk.

"Is there anything else I can help you with?" she asks. "Another excursion? We have a very relaxing sailboat—"

"No, I'm not going to book anything else for now." I glance behind me to make sure no one is waiting in line. "I actually have some questions for you about your time here, your job. How do you like working here?"

"I really like it. It's one of the best jobs I've ever had."

I want to pull out a notebook so I don't forget anything, but that usually makes people clam up. Besides, I'm not sure she's being entirely truthful with me right now.

"What did you do before this?"

"I cleaned hotel rooms on the mainland." She shakes her head. "I had to move for this job, but it was so worth it."

"Is pay better here or there?" I ask. She hesitates, her eyes dart. "I'm not asking how much you make, just a comparison."

"Here, definitely."

I lean forward and lower my voice. "What's the worst part of your job?" I give her a conspiratorial wink.

She doesn't return it. "Look, I don't know what you're digging for here, but you won't get it from me. Or anyone."

I lean back. "What do you mean?"

"I haven't spoken to every employee here, obviously, but everyone I do know loves it here. The resort is clean, the pay is good, and Mr. Thornton looks out for us."

"What do you mean?" I repeat.

"He's not the boss I report to, but there isn't a week that goes by where he doesn't check in with me. Makes sure I'm happy, listens to my feedback. He doesn't have to do that, you know? But he does. With everyone. And there are hundreds of employees."

My mouth is hanging open. I snap it closed. "Every week?"

"Every. Week."

That's not possible.

She must see it on my face because she clarifies. "Sometimes it's just a hello, how are things? And I don't take up his time. And I think with some of the younger workers, he talks to them in groups, not individually."

I did see that with a group of groundskeepers.

"But the point is, he cares. He goes above and beyond."

"Wow." I don't mean to say that out loud.

"I know, right? He's open to honest conversations, and he listens when one of us has input. A couple of months ago, I spoke to him about letting us concierges have monthly meetings together so we can keep up on the excursions, talk about the feedback we've received from guests, that kind of thing. And then we go back to Mr. Thornton with anything new we feel needs to be implemented. We had our first meeting almost immediately after I pitched the idea, and we had another last month. This month's is next week."

"That's..." I'm speechless. But I shouldn't be. That's how a good business is run. I decide to change tack. "I have a more specific question for you."

She sighs.

"Last time I was here, there was an employee who got fired." After describing him, I'm about to ask if she's heard about him, but she's already nodding her head.

"You're talking about Earl." She shudders.

"You knew him?"

"Not well. But all of us girls knew to watch out for him. He'd start with flirting—but the creepy kind, where he compliments you on a specific body part, you know? For me, it was my collarbone. Harmless maybe, but it totally creeped me out. And then he'd move on to either asking you out or just saying outright dirty things. One girl actually went out with him. I guess her creep radar wasn't working."

"What happened?"

"Assault of some kind. I don't know the details, but she didn't come to work for a while, not until Earl was fired. Mr. Thornton personally went out to see her, so I think one of her friends here must have told him what happened."

My stomach has begun to ache. For that girl. For every woman at the resort who was harassed by that guy. For my mistake.

I thought John was belittling one of his employees. Demonstrating his power. But he was genuinely upset, and for good reason. If it had been me, I wouldn't have been able to control my temper, either.

"Thank you for answering my questions."

"You're welcome."

I walk away, pressing a hand to my stomach and hoping that breakfast doesn't come back up again.

FRANCES ISN'T the only person I talk to. I interview a handful of employees, all in different departments. Even though they all have different experiences, it all amounts to the same thing—they like working at the resort. John is a great boss. They're happy. Work is still work, but they're happy. For some, like Frances, it's the best place they've worked.

I sit on a lounger outside my room, sweating in the heat but hardly noticing for the turmoil in my brain.

What the heck was I doing last time? How could I have missed so much?

I was so blinded by my disgust. Convinced the small moment I witnessed was the whole truth. Upset at being there when my mom was just starting her battle with cancer, I must have let those emotions—that stress—color my opinions. I never dug deeper. I never even tried to enjoy the resort or find out more about the island, or about the people here.

My dad was right—it was the worst piece I've ever written.

I have to fix the mistake I made.

DESPITE HOW SOFT the bed is, the breeze that blows over my face, the squishy sheets, I barely sleep that night. I wake early the next morning with puffy eyes and a body that feels heavy like a garbage truck. That's what I feel like. Garbage.

So I take an early morning swim. I'm not alone in the water. There are a few early morning surfers and some elderly couples strolling the beach or taking a morning dip like me. I ignore them and swim laps until I'm tired but in a different way than when I woke up. Then I float, letting the sun warm my face while my body becomes weightless, light. If only my mind could feel the same.

The water wakes me up, though, which is exactly what I need. The warm sand of the beach calls, but I know that'll just make me sleepy again, so I head inside my room and shower, get ready. Then I go in search of John.

"He's in a meeting," his secretary says, glaring at me. I'm pretty sure she hates me. She could be lying, except that I can hear voices coming from John's office.

"I'll wait," I say. Instead of sitting, I wander the hallway, pretending to examine the art on the walls but really trying to eavesdrop on the meeting. Old habits die hard, I guess.

"You haven't hit your target in months," a woman is saying. "You were up right after the renos, but after that first couple of months you haven't gotten back to that point."

"I know. We're trying." John sounds harassed. "I've expanded our advertising, introduced new programs at the resort—"

The woman cuts John off. "It's not enough. You're not getting the revenue back from the remodel, and traffic to the resort is down."

"I need more time."

"John, you put too much into the renovations. Realistically, I don't think you'll be able to turn it around."

I'm frozen in the hallway, listening. I wish I could see inside, but I don't dare try to look through the barely opened door.

John did all those renovations in the resort, many of them based on the critique I gave in my blog piece. And now he's in the weeds. Badly.

I focus back on the conversation. John's secretary is still watching me, her eyes narrowed, so I take a step away from the door. Give her an innocent smile. John is saying something, but I can't hear him.

When the secretary turns her attention to the ringing phone, I inch closer again.

"...a few more months," the woman is saying. "I don't see it happening, but I would hate for you to lose this place after everything you've put into it. Surprise me."

John doesn't reply. Instead, the door swings open, revealing a stunning Asian woman in a sleek black suit and heels holding a briefcase. She raises an eyebrow at me while I blush, furiously. Behind her, John sees me, but his face reveals nothing.

"It was good to see you, John," the woman says, shaking his hand before she brushes past me.

John puts his hands on his hips and eyes me. No doubt he thinks I'm up to something. He's got on blue pants and a pale pink buttondown shirt which stretches across his chest. The top two buttons are open, revealing his tanned skin and, for a moment, I wonder if he's naturally that dark or if it's a permanent tan.

"I..." Have no clue what to say. He won't buy any excuse about my eavesdropping, and whatever I had planned to say to him when I was coming down here is completely gone.

"Take a walk with me," he says and strides past me. "I'll be back in an hour or so."

The secretary nods. "Yes, sir."

The elevator dings open. John turns around and beckons to me.

I scurry, lose my footing in my wedge sandal, regain my balance and walk at a normal pace to the elevator. John keeps the door open for me, his face not even cracking at my stumble.

I stand beside him, and the elevator doors close.

We say nothing as the elevator goes down. I fidget with the hem of my shorts while John is a statue beside me. I follow him through the lobby. It isn't until we step outside that he stops and takes a deep breath in.

He sees me watching and says, "I needed some fresh air."

I nod.

His phone buzzes and he turns it off, then shoves it back into his pocket.

"Come on," I say, my mouth finally loosening.

"Where are we going?"

"No idea." I follow the walkway, letting it set my destination. It winds through manicured grass, past beds of native flowers, their smell sharp and sweet in my nose. Over a bridge that covers a meandering stream, through a thick stand of trees.

The walkway takes us to a viewing point which overlooks the beach, tidy with matching lounge chairs and bars in the shape of tiki huts. Looking past the man-made comforts, I see the ocean stretching wild and free into infinity. I love the mix. I'm too pampered to wish everything man-made away, and yet I love to see the earth, the ocean especially, the way it's meant to be.

I snap a pic and post it to my story.

"I really love it here," John says. We both have our elbows resting against the wooden fence. He's leaned over, his face more at my level. "I just wanted to help the island survive." He laughs without humor. "Sounds so pretentious, doesn't it? Like I think I'm some kind of God."

"You're not a God," I say.

He looks at me. "I know."

"But it's okay to be a man trying to do his best. And, when he's trying to do his best for others, that's pretty great."

The breeze ruffles his hair. The sharp angles of John's face soften a little. John—such a plain name for a man who looks anything but. For a moment I think he's going to kiss me. And then he looks away.

"It's not enough, though."

I can help. But I don't tell him so, because I don't know how much it will do. I'm not vain enough to think one article and some Instagram posts will make his problems disappear. But I can make a difference. Publish a new piece on the resort, call in some favors and get it shared on different social media sites, in magazines, on TV. Not to mention gushing about it to my many followers.

He straightens, slaps his palms on the fence. "I should get back to work." He gives me a half-smile and turns away.

"Have dinner with me," I blurt.

He pauses. Doesn't bother to conceal his surprise.

"I have questions...for my new piece. I was going to ask you now but, since you're busy, I thought over dinner maybe, since it's easier. I mean, I have to eat—you have to eat. Then we can eat and eat questions. I mean ask questions. And you can answer them. Maybe."

And now I want to die of embarrassment.

He examines me for a moment, making me squirm.

"How's eight?" he asks. "I'll pick you up from your room."

"Mmm-hmm," is all I say, keeping my mouth clamped shut so I don't say more dumb things.

I die under his scrutiny, only breathing again after he has walked away.

I'M DIGGING into my room service lunch of a green salad and scallops when my phone starts ringing from the table next to me. There's a ton of Instagram notifications but I ignore them and answer.

"Dad?"

"Hi, hon. How is it going there?"

The view from the patio outside my room is perfect. The air is warm, but I'm shaded from the sun. And I've got a plate of good food on my lap. "Fine. How's mom?"

"She's the same. She had a better day yesterday, but today she's pretty sleepy."

"Is that all?" I pick at the spiky green leaves on my plate. "It's not worse than you're saying, is it? Do I need to come home early?"

"No, it's really not. Unless..."

I've put a scallop in my mouth, but I talk around it. "Unless what?"

"Do you want to come home early?"

I straighten. "No, why?" Dad is quiet on the other line. I finish chewing. "Dad, why?"

He hems and haws and doesn't answer my question.

I set my fork down. My heart is racing. "What is going on? Are you sure mom is fine?"

"Yes. Trust me. There's nothing new with your mother."

"Then what?"

"One of my students heard from his friend who heard from their sister who read it online or something."

"What are you even saying right now?"

He lets out a loud breath. "There's some article out about you."

I frown. "Me?" No one writes articles about me. I'm a travel blogger, for crying out loud—not a celebrity.

"It's on a gossip site. There's a picture of you with a man in Florence, I think? He's an editor for some magazine. I don't remember the name of it. Anyway, when did you go to Florence?"

I'm already moving, dashing into my room to the bed and opening my laptop. I hope I didn't spill a scallop. "I haven't been to Florence in years. Four maybe? Five?"

I put my name in the search engine. My own info pops up first, my website and social media, links to articles in different magazines both online and in print. I add Florence to the search engine and there it is. An article with my name in the headline.

"It seemed like a recent trip," Dad says.

The link takes me to a gossip site. There's a clear picture of a man and woman holding hands, walking down a cobblestoned street. The woman's face is buried in the man's shoulder so you can't see it except for a bit of chin. I guess the hair and body type could be mine, but that's not me.

"That's not me," I say to Dad.

"Huh. My student really thought it was about you."

"No, it says my name, but it's not me." I scan through the article and my blood begins to boil. "Dad, I've gotta go. But that's not me, just so you know. The whole article is completely false."

I hang up. My eyes snag on the number of Instagram notifications I have. I open up the app to hundreds of comments on my latest post, most of which have nothing to do with the actual picture—the view of the beach when I was with John this morning. The comments range from congratulations on my supposed boyfriend to trolls questioning my honesty and integrity or just plain hating. The photo from the article is posted and reposted, and I swear I've been tagged in every one.

I read through the article again slowly. It states that I was in Florence just last week. Laughable. I was at my childhood home, playing War with my dad and reading Tolstoy to my mom.

It goes on to talk about the man I'm supposedly with, an editor of a very prominent travel magazine. The article accuses me of using our so-called relationship to further my career, insinuates this isn't the first time I've done that kind of thing. Bashes my writing style, my credibility, and even my fashion sense.

'Meg Hale claims to be a journalist with the highest standards, never resorting to dirty methods or petty behaviors to get a story, but her piece on the Paradise Resort proves otherwise.' The article then quotes me, but it's not what I wrote at all. I even go back to that piece to check. It's my words, but they're manipulated to sound different than I intended.

I scroll back up to the byline. Written by Mena Boucher.

Of course it was.

I almost laugh. She thinks I'm an easy target. That I'll leave this alone and let her write this crap about me. Or that I'll be stupid and comment on the post, trying to expose her lies while just making myself look worse.

But I'm not stupid. I know to go over her head and straight to the owner of the gossip site Mena writes for. But first, I have a call to make to a good friend of mine who happens to be a lawyer.

I'm EXHAUSTED by the time eight o'clock rolls around. I finally had to turn my phone off to stop from hearing all the dings indicating Instagram notifications. I'm mentally fatigued from battling it out all afternoon to get that piece taken down and for Mena to publish a retraction statement. But it worked, thanks in no small part to my lawyer friend Henry who had my back. I'll repay him with an amazing steak dinner next time I see him.

I'm also tired from writing. My fingers are stiff. My eyelids ache. But I finished my new piece on the resort. Sent it to my editor. It should be ready to publish in a few days, if I can manage it.

I glance at the clock. Eight-fifteen. John hasn't arrived yet. Maybe I missed his knock. I check my reflection in the mirror, fuss with my hair before I realize what I'm doing and quit. Then give up and apply another coat of lipstick. I could pretend not to care how I look in front of him, but that ship has sailed.

Eight-thirty and still no John.

And it hits me. The article. Instagram. Maybe he saw it all. Maybe he believes what it said about me. Which—if he does—would make me look like the biggest hypocrite ever.

My stomach sinks. I'm angry all over again, then sad, disappointed. Then surprised. Since when did John's opinion about me matter so much? Not only am I primping for him, but now I'm worried he thinks badly about me. More than worried. It kills me to think he might believe what that trash article said.

I grab my purse and head out, determined to find him and explain.

I hurry down the corridor, my heels clacking on the hard floor. Past the concierge who says something I don't register. Beeline to the building with John's office, but he's not there. Neither is his secretary; she's probably gone home for the day.

John lives somewhere on the resort property, but I have no idea where. I wander the pathways, no clue where I'm going, hoping to run into him, slowed down by my stupidly high heels. *Who brings heels to a tropical resort?* I think as my ankle twists and I almost bail.

I sigh. It's no use. I'll never find him this way. I don't even know how long I've been searching. I open my purse to check my phone, but it's not there. I must have left it back in my room.

I slip off my shoes and head back. It's not the end of the world. I can speak to John tomorrow.

When I make it back to my building, my feet thoroughly hurt and my ankle throbs. Down the corridor, a person sits on the floor, leaning back against the wall. He looks up.

I stop. "John?"

He gets to his feet. I close the distance between us. The number behind his head is my room number.

"I've been waiting," he says. He's wearing linen pants and a baby blue shirt that's casually untucked.

"You didn't come," I say.

"I know. I'm sorry." He looks down at my feet which, I'm sad to say, look a bit dirty. "Where were you?"

"Oh." My face heats. I hide one foot behind my leg—not that it helps. "I went looking for you."

"You did?"

He's leaning over me. Too close. My breath hitches. I step back and wince.

"Are you okay?"

"Yeah, I just... heels! Am I right?" I hold up my shoes as if he can relate. "Anyway, I'd really like to sit down."

He moves away from the door. I swipe my card, and the door beeps. I push it open. "Do you want to come in?"

"Yes."

He follows me inside, and then he takes my hand, leading me out to the patio, nudging me onto the lounger so I can stretch out my legs. He skootches the other chair closer and sits.

"I'm sorry I didn't come," he says. "I was stuck on a conference call and couldn't get away."

"Oh." So it wasn't about the article at all. I'm embarrassed at my earlier panic and that I assumed he saw the article or the comments and tags, as if he follows me on Instagram or something.

And then he says, "I was scrolling through Instagram earlier."

Oof.

"You were in Florence last week?"

And there's that panic, back again. "I wasn't there. That wasn't me."

John turns to face me, sliding his long legs from the chair and planting his feet on the ground. "I know."

"I haven't been to Florence in years. That article—did you see the article? It was completely false."

"Meg."

The way he says my name stops me. Focuses me.

He rests his elbows on his knees which brings his face closer to mine. "I don't listen to Internet trolls. And I knew as soon as I read it that the article was false."

"You did?"

His gaze is intense. "We haven't spent a lot of time together, but I'm pretty confident I know the kind of person you are."

Which is something I couldn't say about him—at least, not before this week. I had no clue what kind of person John was, but I hadn't really looked. Hadn't tried.

"How did you find out about that article anyway?"

"I got an email from a sketchy address. That was my first clue. I shouldn't have even opened it, but I saw your name and..." He shrugs.

"It could've been a virus."

"It totally could've been a virus." He lets out a chuckle. "What can I say? I'm not the smartest when it comes to you."

I swallow. Can't take my eyes from his. "I know how that feels."

The moment grows thick between us. The air charged. Somewhere a bird squawks, breaking the tension.

I fumble in my purse before remembering that my phone isn't inside. I start to get up, but John stops me.

"What do you need?"

"My phone. I'm not sure where I left it, but there's something I want to show you."

He holds up his finger and then disappears into my room, returning a minute later with my phone in his hand.

"It was on the bed." His fingers linger on mine as he hands it over.

I click on the screen to an insane amount of Instagram notifications—probably about the retraction—plus multiple missed texts and calls, all from John. I glance up at him. "Oops."

He laughs.

I turn my attention back to my phone. I've also got some unread emails. I click open the one I was hoping for, the one from my editor.

I scan the email before handing the phone to John.

"Read this."

He glances at the phone, then back at me.

"And the attachment, too. Please."

I wait while he reads what my editor wrote, how she loves the honesty in the piece, although she's worried about how audiences will react to me owning my obvious mistakes in the last review.

Then he clicks open the attachment and reads the first draft of my article. While he does, I watch him unabashedly.

I was so wrong about him, about this place. I know that. What I don't know is how I went from despising him to drinking him in. Being breathless in his presence. Aching to touch him, kiss him. Wanting him to repeat the question he asked me last time I was here. To stay.

When he's done, he puts the phone down and looks up at me. I expect him to say something. Ask me if I believe what I said. Maybe he'll doubt my change in opinion, now that I heard how bad the resort is doing. Maybe he'll thank me. Or maybe he'll tell me he doesn't need this.

Instead, he reaches out his hand and places it against my cheek. He leans in and I sit up, my knees knocking against his as I try to nix the space between us. His lips hit mine. My hands grip his shirt, pulling him closer. Eventually, we end up on the same chair. His hands tangle in my hair. Mine slide along his skin. He smells like coconut and the ocean.

Like the ocean, his kiss—his touch—wakes me up.

But he doesn't ask me to stay.

MY LUGGAGE SITS on the curb. John stands before me, his hands on his hips causing the fabric of his shirt to stretch across his chest. I love it when he does that, and I think he knows because he does it all the time.

"Tell your parents hello for me," he says.

"I will."

He pulls me into a hug. He buries his nose against my head. I think he's inhaling me like I'm inhaling him. Scent memory is strong, and I don't want to forget.

A car pulls up to the curb. My ride to the airport.

"I'll let you know when the article goes live," I say.

"Oh, I'll be talking to you before then." He runs a hand over my hair. "Count on it."

I grin. "Good." And then my heart stutters. My breath hitches. My grin dies. The words I want to say are stuck in my throat.

He kisses me lightly. "You should probably go so you don't miss your flight."

My hands fist around his shirt, not that there's much to grab since it's so tight. "I was thinking..."

"Yes?"

I can't look him in the eye. "I was thinking about coming back. I don't know when. I have to think about my next piece, and my mom, and—"

"You're going to come back?"

In my remaining days here, we never talked about the future, or what would happen between us after I left. He never asked me to stay like he did last time. I gave him no promises.

"I mean, I really like it here," I say. I look up at him. "And I really like you."

He smiles. "I really like you too."

My hands relax against his chest. His heart thuds against my palm. We still have lots of learning about each other to do. And there's my mom, who I can't be too far from. And the resort—my review will help, but we don't know if it will be enough.

The future is uncertain, but the one thing I know is I want to see him again.

John kisses me, slow and sweet. His kiss lingers on my lips as I get in the car.

As the car pulls away, I twist in my seat and look back at him. He waves and I smile, imprinting this last image of him on my brain. Already anxious for the day I can be with John Thornton again.

～

MELANIE STANFORD READS TOO MUCH, plays music too loud, is sometimes dancing, and always daydreaming. She would also like her very own TARDIS, but only to travel to the past. She lives outside Calgary, Alberta, Canada with her husband, four kids, and ridiculous amounts of snow.

MELANIE STANFORD'S other books include: *Sway, Collide, Clash, Then Comes Winter (Anthology)* and *The Darcy Monologues (Anthology)*

PASSAGES IN TIME

Kate Forrester

"Oh my Margaret - my Margaret! no one can tell what you are to me!" -
Chapter XXII, North and South

CHAPTER ONE

*J*ohn Thornton sensed something was amiss as soon as he descended the steps of his home and crossed the mill yard. At first, he couldn't put his finger on what was unnerving him, but something was. He was halfway to the mill office when scuffling to his left caused him to pause and glance into the dark shadows along the mill walls. What had made the noise, he wondered? A rat, probably, scurrying among the wooden crates that were stacked around the yard. The hair at the nape of his neck stood on end, and a shiver that had nothing to do with the cold washed over him. He turned sharply, unable to shake the feeling he was being watched.

He was up earlier than usual – sleep had eluded him these last few weeks, the departure of the woman he loved and business worries fuelling his insomnia. No matter the hour there was always work to be done, and he had taken to going over to his office long before the mill came to life. At this hour of the morning the yard was dark and deserted; sometimes the moon bathed the towering buildings in an incandescent light, but today its welcome light was obscured behind dark scurrying clouds. The wind was lively, cutting through the wool of his suit coat. It was an old one he used for work and he doubted it would see him through another winter, for it was thin and threadbare.

He was almost at the mill office when he saw that the door to the building that held the raw cotton was slightly ajar. How could that be? The overseer would have made sure it was locked last evening when the shift had finished.

"Is anybody there?" he called, entering the store.

The sound of footsteps moving inside was unmistakable.

"Who's there? What do you want?" he called, moving into the dark interior of the building.

A voice cut through the silence. "Thornton, you were warned."

He didn't have time to place the voice before he heard a more frightening noise: a strange hissing pop, a small and insignificant sound that still struck terror in his heart for he was certain he knew what it meant. A second later, his fears were confirmed as flames licked over a stack of bales in the corner.

Fire! It was every mill owner's nightmare. Raw cotton would smoulder for a while but, once well alight, burned fast and furious. The only hope was to stop it before it took hold. Removing his coat, he moved towards the burning bale and began using the garment to beat at the creeping flames. He had barely started when the tell-tale sounds of several other cotton bales burning made him stop. The man had been clever – he'd obviously intended fire to break out simultaneously in several areas of the cotton store, which meant that the blaze would be well alight before it was discovered.

John realised if he was to save the mill, he must get help, but when he reached the great door he realised he was locked in. It wasn't only his mill he was in danger of losing – it was his life.

Knowing that panicking would only make the situation worse, he took a steadying breath before banging on the door and shouting in the vain hope that somebody would hear him.

The fire burned with devastating swiftness, destroying all in its path. His eyes smarted and tears streamed down his face, his body's way of washing them clean of ash and smoke. Smoke was even now scorching his throat and burning his nostrils, causing him to cough and splutter. He suddenly realised the smoke was more of a danger than the flames. Removing his cravat, he tied it over his mouth and nose in an attempt to stop the thick fumes from reaching his lungs.

Looking up through the smoke, he could see flames licking at the roof. The beams were alight now, the heat and flames from the bales causing them to crack and splinter as they exploded into life.

People said that before you died, your life passed before your eyes. His didn't, and yet he felt sure his death could not be far away. His coughing worsened, forcing him to his knees as he tried to get rid of the noxious smoke that burned and clogged his lungs. As he knelt, a thick black veil seemed to descend on him, its tendrils invading his mind and body. His last conscious thought was of seeing a beam fall from the roof and knowing he must move to avoid death.

MJ STOOD IN SILENCE, staring up at the once proud structure; it broke her heart to see the mighty building partially destroyed. Its walls were blackened, the windows blown out by the heat of the fire, and the roof was gone, leaving the whole building exposed to the elements. The mill gates had been thrown open to allow the fire engines access. She walked towards it and stood staring into the yard.

"Please don't come any closer, miss. The building's not safe. We'll be damping it down for several hours yet," a fireman told her as she peered around the corner.

"No, I won't. Was anybody hurt?"

"No. Fortunately, the fire broke out in the early hours of the morning, so the place was deserted. The fire investigator will be along later, looking for the cause. Are you with the press?"

"Oh no, I'm an historian, MJ Hale. I was supposed to meet with the mill's owner."

"I doubt he will be seeing anybody today."

"No, I suppose not. I'll leave a message with his secretary and rearrange our meeting. It's odd – I was seeing him about a fire that broke out here back in the nineteenth century."

"That's an unpleasant coincidence. If I see him, I'll let him know you were here. I must get back to work. Remember, stay well back. It's not safe."

MJ stayed where she was as he walked away, continuing to stare at the destruction before her. It looked like the fire was contained to one building. The large hotel at the end of the yard appeared untouched. It was this that made Marlborough Mills different from other mills. The hotel had once been the mansion home of the original owner, John Thornton – the man who had been killed in the earlier fire and whom she was researching.

Rain began to fall, a gift from heaven to help damp down the still smouldering building. It was pointless standing here getting wet. Matt Slickson wasn't going to see her today. She turned to leave, casting one last glance back at the poor building -- and then she saw him.

It was odd; he seemed to appear out of nowhere. One minute, the yard was practically deserted, and then he was there. Not that she realised at first it was a man; all she saw was what looked like a pile of clothes. It took her a moment to realise that it was someone who'd collapsed on the floor by the door of the mill where the fire had been.

Although she wasn't supposed to be in the yard, she ran across to see if she could help. Fearing the worst, she dropped by his side and rolled him over. The man groaned and began to cough violently.

She knew she should be relieved he was alive but she was too shocked to feel relief. If the portrait she had seen was accurate, the man before her was John Thornton, the nineteenth-century master of Marlborough Mills.

Of course, he couldn't be John Thornton. He must be a tour guide dressed up as the original mill owner, for he wore Victorian-styled clothing. He obviously took his role seriously, for his sideburns were real – no stuck-on mutton chops for this chap. While his identity was a mystery, it was obvious he needed assistance.

She turned and shouted for help before returning her attention to the man on the floor. A moment later, the fireman she'd spoken to appeared at her side.

"Where the hell did he come from?" he asked. "We checked everywhere for people trapped. How did we miss him?"

"That doesn't matter now. What matters is helping him. Call an ambulance! If the fire truck has any oxygen on board, we should use it to help this poor man's breathing."

He nodded and spoke into a radio perched on his shoulder, requesting an ambulance and giving the details of the casualty before running to get the emergency equipment from the fire engine.

When he returned, he heard MJ reasoning with the man, who was trying to stand up.

"Please sir, stay still, help is on the way. Moving around will only make you cough more."

"Here's the oxygen," the fireman exclaimed. "The ambulance is on its way."

Their attempt to place the oxygen mask over the man's face met with violent struggles from the stranger. *He looks terrified*, MJ thought.

"Sir, this is oxygen," she explained. "It will help you breathe – it cannot harm you. Look at me. I will place it over my face so you can see it will cause no harm," she added, seeking to reassure him.

He watched her for a moment. When she was sure he realised it wouldn't hurt him, she placed the mask in his hand and guided it slowly to his face.

"It just feels like a breeze. The strap means you don't have to hold it with your hand. Can I place it over your head?" He nodded.

"My name is MJ Hale, and this is..." She turned to the fireman at her side.

"Henry Bourne. Can you tell us your name, sir, and if you are hurt anywhere?"

"I don't think I am physically hurt." His voice was hoarse, roughened from the smoke he'd inhaled.

"And your name?" MJ asked.

"My name is Thornton – John Thornton, owner of Marlborough Mills. Can someone please explain into what kind of hell I have descended?"

CHAPTER TWO

It was strange, but he was comforted lying in the darkness – the images that the daylight hours revealed scared and disturbed him. At first, when he'd come around in the mill yard, he'd been sure he was gripped by some insanity brought on by the smoke in his lungs. Either that or he was unconscious, and the images were part of some futuristic nightmare. Somebody had been calling to him – a woman whom he now knew as Miss Hale.

He'd opened his eyes, wondering who she was, only for his mind to be assaulted with a scene beyond description. Two huge red machines stood behind her – they had to be some kind of fire tenders, but he had never seen their like before. They were big enough to be traction engines, but he could see no funnels or steam, and the wheels were made of some strange unidentifiable material. All around was activity, but not activity that he knew or understood. Where there should have been mill workers, there were strange men and even a woman – firemen, he was sure, for they had helmets, and all wore a uniform of sorts. But the fabric was not like any he was familiar with; odd for a man who had worked with cloth his whole life.

He'd never seen a woman like her before – Miss Hale, the woman in whose home he now rested. She had told him to call her MJ – what kind of name was that? He'd refused, explaining it would be imprudent of him to call her by her Christian name when they had not been introduced by friends. Unlike others he had met during the day, she alone had understood his use of surnames and had called him Mr.

Thornton as he requested. She unnerved him as no woman ever had. He had never known any female so forthright in manner or speech, not to mention the clothes she wore – trousers and shirts that hugged her body as if they were a second skin, leaving nothing to the imagination. No Victorian lady would have worn such garments. She was kind, though. From the moment the ambulance had arrived, she never left his side.

The vehicle that had transported him to hospital – the ambulance – was not as large as the fire tender, but its blaring siren and flashing lights had him cowering away from it and the people who jumped out from it. Miss Hale had realised how the noise and lights terrified him and had called for them to switch them off.

"They are scaring him – I think he may have hit his head – he seems disorientated."

"What's his name?" a man asked after the siren was silenced and the lights stopped.

"He's insisting it's John Thornton – I think that's the character he is dressed as."

"Okay, John, my name is Brad, and this is Ann. We are paramedics and we need to check you over." He reached out to undo Mr. Thornton's waistcoat.

"My name is Mr. Thornton – only my family call me by my Christian name," he told them, pushing Brad's hand away.

"If that's what you want, Mr. Thornton, but I need to listen to your chest and heart, so you must let me undo your waistcoat and shirt."

"No, there are ladies present – it would be improper."

Brad had laughed. "Well, Ann has certainly seen plenty of naked chests before, and I expect the other women have as well. After all, it is the twenty-first century."

Only Miss Hale understood how that had shocked him. She'd taken his hand. "Mr. Thornton, please let them look after you. I realise that all of this appears unreal to you, but you have my word, nobody will hurt you and I will stay if you would like me to."

He'd not understood why she would do this until she explained that her father had been a minister. "At home in Helstone, he worked with homeless people – I have had a lot of experience helping him," she'd explained.

He'd nodded and, realising he needed a sympathetic person on his side, he'd accepted her offer to stay with him at the infirmary.

He'd had to admit that this strange and alien place was 2019. What his eyes saw but his brain could not understand was confirmed by Miss Hale and the doctors at the infirmary – somehow, he had moved through time. Of course, that was not what the doctors thought; they believed that something had happened to his brain in the fire that caused him to think he'd been born in the nineteenth century. He couldn't blame them for coming up with that conjecture. Even to his own ears, his insistence that he was from 1851 had seemed like the ramblings of an unhinged or damaged mind.

The infirmary had terrified him and not just because the doctors looked at him as if he were mad, though that was bad enough. It was more the lack of anything familiar. He'd assumed he was being taken to the infirmary with which he was familiar, which during his time was new and in which Milton took justifiable pride. However, they brought him to an enormous complex constructed of materials he didn't recognise – well, apart from glass. The place was too bright; large windows allowed daylight to stream in and lamps in the ceiling shone brighter than the sun, but he could not identify the source of their power – certainly it was neither oil nor gas. He was used to dim light and dark shadows. Even during the day, a candle burned on his desk in the mill office. There, the dark strained his eyes; here, the light hurt them.

It wasn't just the light that was unnerving. The noise was, if anything, more frightening. He was used to noise – he owned a mill – but these noises were unfamiliar, coming from machines attached to him and to the other sick people in this place. These machines alarmed shrilly whenever he moved, and several types of bells and buzzers seemed to ring all the time.

Once again, Miss Hale had comforted him by trying to explain these various things and what they did to him. Her hand was never far from his, and he felt himself reaching for it constantly. By far the strangest thing was a type of window on the wall through which he could see people talking. But where were they? Where did they come from and where did they go? The scenes and people he could see changed frequently.

Although he had been told that apart from a little smoke inhalation he was well, the medical personnel would not hear of him leaving. They couldn't just discharge him when he had nowhere to go and no visible means of support. He was told they were waiting for a bed in the psychiatric unit, but that it would be a day or two before one became available. When he'd asked what that was, he realised they were talking about a mental asylum. He couldn't enter one of those places; people didn't ever escape them. His pleas to leave fell on deaf ears, and he'd become so agitated that not even Miss Hale had been able to calm him. In the end, the doctors had given him some sort of medication, laudanum he suspected. He'd read of its sedating effects. He'd fallen into a sleep, but his rest had been tormented with wild dreams and images.

When he woke, he was alone; Miss Hale was not at his side. Before he could panic, his eyes alighted on a note addressed to him. It was from Miss Hale. Her writing was as clear and thoughtful as her spoken word. She wrote that he was not to worry. She had merely left to get some clothing and toiletries for him, and she would return later. He had no choice but to believe her words and rested quietly, waiting for her return.

Relief flooded through him when she appeared at the door to his room. She arrived bearing gifts as she called them: clothing similar to what others in this strange place wore. It was then that he asked – no, begged was a better word – for her help. She had been so kind and sympathetic that he hoped to convince her to help him escape this place before he was committed to an asylum.

At first, she was adamant in her refusal. He was careful not to mention again that he was from a different time, but he implored her to listen to him. "I don't know why or how I am a stranger to this place, but if I am not John Thornton, I need to find out who I am. I cannot do that if I am locked up in an insane asylum."

"Psychiatric units are no longer called insane asylums. That phase died out after Victoria's time."

"Is it not a place where people with sicknesses of the mind are sent?"

"Yes, but you will be treated well."

"Will they be able to explain why I have no understanding of this place or time? Will they seek answers or just sedate me with laudanum?"

"There it is again, the wrong word – that drug has long since gone out of use. Its modern equivalent has a different name." MJ was puzzled by the man's speech and alarmed by his desire to leave. "They would help you, Mr. Thornton. You would receive therapy and medication."

"And if, after all this treatment, I still insisted that I was John Thornton, I would have to stay in this asylum, wouldn't I?"

"Yes, I suppose you would."

"I don't belong here. I need to find out if my family is safe and if any of my workers died. I will have no peace until I do. Please help me leave this place. Once I am beyond its doors, you will never see me again."

"How would you survive out there? You appear to know nothing of this place. It would be dangerous for you – too dangerous."

"Then stay with me – you are a kindly woman. Help me discover the truth."

MJ stared at the man who claimed to be a mill owner, one whose history she knew better than anybody else in Milton. It wasn't possible that he was who he claimed he was – but could she just let him leave without helping him?

He was not sure whether it was kindness or curiosity, but she decided to help him. It had involved lying to the hospital. She told him that if he explained to the staff that he'd remembered his name and where he lived, they would let him go. "Say that you woke and remembered everything. Tell them you are a tour guide at Marlborough Mills. Say your wife is away, but that you have a place to stay with me."

She confirmed with the infirmary staff that she had a room he could stay in (the room he was now in), and that she would be responsible for him. She reassured the staff that he'd attend any outpatient treatment needed, and she would ensure he got safely back home.

The journey to her home brought more horrors – travel in a horseless carriage at speeds he'd never have believed possible, on roads almost as smooth as glass. Was this really Milton? The skyline resembled nothing he had seen before. Where were the soot and grime from the chimneys that powered the mills? Where were the mills? Where were the workers' houses? All he could see were large towers of glass and brick. Rows upon rows of back-to-back houses were gone.

She'd glanced over at him a time or two during the journey, aware of his gasps of fear and horror at what he was seeing. "Perhaps if you were to close your eyes, things would not seem so alarming."

"I don't think so, Miss Hale – while travelling at such speed, I need to keep my eyes open."

By the time they finally arrived at her house, his head hurt worse than it ever had and exhaustion seeped into his every muscle. He was even too tired to offer more than a token protest when he realised that Miss Hale lived alone. He had questions for her, but she suggested that he get cleaned up, eat, and then rest – tomorrow was soon enough to talk.

She showed him the bathroom, where more things puzzled and challenged him. She told him that the glass cupboard was a shower and that he'd feel better once he'd washed away the smoke and grime from the fire. She pointed out bottles of shampoo and shower gel – liquid soap for his hair and body. She also gave him a small brush for his teeth and a tube containing what he supposed was something to clean them with. Finally, she'd placed a large towel and clean clothes on a rail attached to the wall. The clothes, she explained, belonged to her brother Fred. He had left a few things at her home while he was on leave from the Royal Navy where he was a radio operator. He nodded, but had no idea what a radio was, let alone how a person operated one.

Once he worked out how to turn the shower on, he loved it, even if he didn't understand how it worked. The warm pulsating water helped ease the ache in his muscles, and the steam lessened the tightness in his chest. The soap was unlike anything he had seen or smelt before, but it removed all traces of smoke and dirt from his skin.

He dried and pulled on the strangely casual garments she left. They had no fastenings of any description; one just pulled them on – in a way, they resembled his undergarments, but Miss Hale had called the clothes jogging gear. He'd shaken his head at that. It wasn't just everything around him that was different; even the language was unfamiliar. What was 'jogging'? And the only gears he knew were parts for the engines that powered the looms in Marlborough Mills.

The mill! He needed to know how bad the damage was, and if anyone had been hurt. Thank God the fire had broken out early in the morning before the workers arrived; casualties would hopefully be few. What of his mother and sister? How could he find out if they were all right? He'd asked at the hospital, but all they could say was that they had no record of anyone else being admitted to hospital.

He picked up his pocket watch, the only thing he owned that had belonged to his father. Miraculously, it was undamaged by the fire. Five o'clock; he was normally up by now getting ready for the shift to begin. Was it too early to rise? He couldn't help it if it was; he had to find out about his mother and sister. He had to get back to his own time and find out who started the fire. The voice that had called out to him was familiar – he was sure he knew to whom it belonged but try as he might he couldn't put a name to it.

He thought he knew why he had been targeted. His views on worker's rights and conditions were unpopular with many other mill owners whose own workers were demanding the same working conditions as at Marlborough Mills. But, which of them would go so far as to start a fire? He had to find out; as much as the dark and quiet soothed him, he would not find the answers lying here in bed. But how and where should he begin? He supposed his only choice was to return to the scene of the fire – to return to Marlborough Mills.

This decision made, he rose and left the bedroom to head slowly down the stairs, being careful to make no noise and disturb his benefactor. He intended to leave a note thanking her for her help, but as he stepped off the staircase, he realised he needn't have been so quiet, for his hostess was up. She was looking at another of those strange windows he had seen at the hospital, staring intently at something written on it.

She turned at his step.

"Good morning, Mr. Thornton. Did you manage to get some rest?"

"A little. I'm glad you are awake. It means I can thank you for your help instead of just leaving."

"Leaving? Where are you going?"

"I have to return to the mill – the answer to what is going on has to be there."

"Mr. Thornton, you won't get near the mill. It will be closed off."

"I have to get back home. I need to know if my mother and sister are safe."

"Your mother and sister – you speak of Hannah Thornton and Fanny Watson?"

"Watson – so my sister married him then?"

MJ sighed. It seemed her guest still believed he was John Thornton. She wasn't humouring him by going along because she had the power to ease his distress about his family.

"Your mother and sister are safe. Come here, I'll show you." She patted the sofa next to her. He moved to join her but stopped when he realised how immodest her clothing was.

"Miss Hale – I cannot sit in such close proximity to you. While I suspect what you are wearing probably passes for clothes in the twenty-first century, it certainly does not in the nineteenth." He glanced at her bare legs. "Your near-nakedness embarrasses me and should shame you."

"Mr. Thornton, this IS the twenty-first century and my clothes are acceptable, so I feel no shame. However, I can see that as a nineteenth-century gentleman, you are embarrassed and so I will go and change into something less revealing. There is a tea bag in the mug and the kettle has just boiled. Milk is in the fridge--that is the white thing in the kitchen. Help yourself while I change out of my shorty PJs and into something less revealing."

He was so busy trying to work out what a teabag might be that he missed the fact that she had called him a nineteenth-century gentleman.

CHAPTER THREE

MJ wondered if she was losing her mind. It wasn't that she had taken a strange man into her home; her parents, God bless them, had always said she'd been collecting waifs and strays for years. It was that she was even entertaining the notion that this man could, as he claimed he was, be from the nineteenth century. The idea sounded insane, but there were things about him that pointed to his being a man out of time.

It wasn't just his incredible likeness to the image of John Thornton hanging in the Milton art gallery – lots of people had doppelgängers – or his strange way of speaking and his unbending manners; such things could be learned. It was his complete bewilderment at his surroundings and his terror at everyday sights and sounds. Surely even the most feted thespian in the world couldn't be *that* good of an actor. Take now, for instance. He stood in front of the fridge, opening, and closing the door, his expression one of complete confusion.

Those were the things that kept her awake the previous night until she could stand it no longer and got up to study her research on John Thornton. This puzzled her even more — she knew she needed to share this research, and not just with the man in her kitchen.

"It's called a refrigerator. It keeps food fresher longer by keeping it cold. It works better with the door shut," she added as he opened and closed the door again.

"How is it so cold?"

"I'm not a scientist, but it has to do with a gas that circulates throughout it. The motor is electric. And before you ask, that's a type of power."

"I know about electricity; I attended a lecture by Faraday about electromagnetism – amazing man."

"Faraday? Did you meet other Victorian scientists?"

"Several. After my father's death, I had to enter the business and was unable to continue with my studies. But I enjoyed attending lectures. Many scientists give lectures here in Milton, and I am often in London on business."

"Of course you are," MJ muttered.

"Is that sarcasm, Miss Hale? We are not used to that in the North."

"No, it's not. I was just thinking that a businessman such as you would often travel to the capital."

"Indeed, I have only lately returned from the Great Exhibition."

"The Great Exhibition of 1851 at the Crystal Palace?"

"Yes, that one. I suppose you will have seen the great glass palace built to house it?"

"Sadly, no – like the mill, it was destroyed in a fire many years ago now." MJ watched as Mr. Thornton's flawless complexion paled.

"Gone, that magnificent building?" His voice was little more than a whisper.

"I wish I had seen it. I mean, I've seen pictures of it and walked on the ground where it stood. It must have been amazing. Maybe you could tell me about it later?"

"Are you humouring me, Miss Hale?"

"No. I don't know why or how, but I believe that John Thornton, nineteenth-century mill owner, is in my kitchen trying to understand how the fridge works."

He seemed to stagger against the kitchen work surface. "Thank God," he whispered.

"Bring your tea over to the computer, and I'll explain why I believe your story."

"Computer?"

"The machine on the table."

He reached for his tea but paused before speaking. "Do I remove the bag with the tea in it before I drink it?"

MJ smiled. "You do."

Once they were settled in the lounge, MJ decided that the first thing she should do was explain why she had concluded that he was John Thornton, mill owner.

"So many things puzzled me about you and your sudden appearance in the mill yard. Henry Bourne, the fireman, was certain that the mill was empty. It was as if you just dropped to earth. Then, there was your reaction to everything around you – it wasn't that you were merely baffled; it was more that you were terrified."

"I was, but surely that alone is not the reason you believe me?"

"I haven't explained what I was doing at the mill, have I?"

"No, but women have always worked at the mill, so your presence there was not surprising. The startling thing was the way you dressed and the way you spoke and...." He looked down at her elegant fingers resting on the table, his own finger brushing hers lightly as he continued. "And your hands are those of a lady, not a mill worker."

She trembled slightly, suddenly aware of how attractive this man was. "No, I'm not a mill worker nor am I a lady. I'm a vicar's daughter, studying for her Ph.D. in history at the university here in Milton. That is why I was at the mill yesterday. I am studying social conditions in the nineteenth-century wool and cotton mills of northern England. I had an appointment to meet the current owner to discuss its history."

Mr. Thornton nodded, surprised but not shocked by this information. It was obvious that Miss Hale was an educated young woman.

"So you see, I have been studying your mill and its history. I know a lot about you, Mr. Thornton."

"Yes, but even so it is quite a leap to believe that I'm the man you have been studying."

"And I didn't, but I couldn't sleep. So, I got up intending to do some more work. I was going over my notes. It's easier if I show you. First, though, I can answer the question about your mother and sister."

"How?" he demanded.

"This machine is called a computer. Think of it as the biggest encyclopaedia or almanac in the world." She pressed some buttons on the computer and words appeared on the screen. "It contains an amazing amount of information – imagine that not only does it have a brain with a memory, but it is able to communicate with people all around the world. If I type your name," she said as she began pushing the lettered buttons on the machine, "and add 'nineteenth-century mill owner' after it, lots of information comes up about you."

He nodded, looking at the screen where his name appeared many times.

"If I click here..." she said and pushed another button. The individual entries were replaced by what looked like a newspaper article. "This is the report from the Milton Guardian about the fire. You wanted to be sure that your mother and sister were not harmed? Read that part there," she said, pushing some more buttons to highlight what she meant.

"Although Mr. John Thornton appears to have perished in the fire, his mother Mrs. Hannah Thornton and sister Miss Fanny Thornton were both unharmed in the inferno."

"Thank God," he whispered, clutching his hands together in a gesture of prayer.

"The article also confirms that you were listed as missing, presumed dead – no body was found. That piece of information is the reason I am forced to believe your story."

"Why? It seems straightforward."

"Like I said, I have been researching you and your mill. I've read this article before. In fact, I have a copy of it, and I want you to look at it and tell me if you notice anything different about it."

She pushed more buttons and as soon as the article disappeared, it reappeared. Or, at least, he thought it had until he read the line about his mother and sister. The first article had said he was presumed dead. This article said his body had been found by the door of the warehouse.

"I don't understand. This article said they found my body. The other says no body was found. Which of them is accurate?"

"Both, I think. I copied and saved this article several days ago. I think when you moved through time, history was altered; hence, the article changed. When I realised the article had changed, I checked the other articles I had saved. All of them said that your body was found by the door. Now, like the newspaper article on the web, they say your body was never found."

"I don't understand at all," Mr. Thornton said. "Not about the information or what you mean by the web."

"Neither do I about why the information would change, but I have a friend on the physics faculty at the university who might be able to help. She's written a paper on time travel. I called her first thing and asked if she'd see us."

"Wasn't that dangerous? She could have contacted the police and had me committed."

"I didn't tell her that I had a time traveller with me," MJ said with a chuckle.

"And what is this web?"

"The world wide web – it is how information on different sites all over the world is linked and shared. It's too complex to explain in the time we have. The friend I mentioned suggested we meet for coffee. Before we do, though, I want to show you something else."

She typed the words 'John Thornton portrait' into the computer and an image appeared. "This picture hangs in the Milton art gallery. Your mother gifted it to them in her will."

He smiled, recognising it. "It was done for her fiftieth birthday. It hangs in the drawing room of our home, and is one of a pair. The other is of my sister, Fanny. They used to hang side by side."

"They still do – she bequeathed both paintings to the city. When you appeared yesterday, my first thought was of this painting and how like John Thornton you were. Then, you told me your name. At first, I thought you'd sustained a head injury and were confused. However, the more time I spent with you, the more confused I became. There was something that made your story, as implausible as it sounded, seem genuine."

"Are you always so open-minded?"

"I don't automatically rule things out, but I do seek evidence to support what I'm seeing or being told. Hence, the reason I sat up half the night checking my research about you."

"May I ask the reason why you are doing this? Is it to satisfy your curiosity or something else?"

"I'm curious, I won't deny that, but I couldn't bear to see you looking like you did at the hospital. It was like watching a haunted, hunted animal. You looked so confused and frightened. You were actually cowering from everything – I had to do something."

He took her hand in his and shook it in a very formal manner. "I'm very glad that you did. Thank you, Miss MJ Hale."

"I think, Mr. Thornton, you might prefer to use my given name, not my nickname – Margaret Jane."

He smiled, causing crinkles to appear at the corners of his brilliant blue eyes. Something stirred in his mind – familiarity, yet he could not remember any acquaintance of that name maybe it was just the old-fashioned ring to it.

"Margaret – yes, yes, I do prefer it," he said.

CHAPTER FOUR

The building that housed the physics faculty at Milton University was situated in the town centre. Built in the sixties, it had become one of the most prestigious seats of learning in the science world, and had gained tabloid notoriety when pop-star-turned-physicist Professor Brian Cox become a fellow of the university. As a history and politics student, MJ would not normally enter this building; her courses were taught in the Samuel Alexander Building. She'd met the physics professor at a university event celebrating the history of Milton during the Industrial Revolution. Puzzled to see someone from the science faculty at the event, she had struck up a conversation with the young professor that had turned into a friendship.

Mr. Thornton had remained quiet in the car on the way to the university. He didn't appear as terrified as he had yesterday. In fact, he seemed curious about everything around him. The fear in his eyes had turned to wonder. Although he claimed not to have slept deeply, the rest had obviously done him good for his colour was better than when he had left the hospital. It was only when they parked and were walking through the city centre to the university that he spoke. They had passed several Victorian buildings that he recognised, and he was trying to place them in the Milton that he knew. He spoke of buildings long destroyed and what the city had been like in his day, shrouded in smog from the factory and mill chimneys.

MJ explained that she had called ahead to the university and that they were expected.

"What do you mean called? I don't understand."

"On the telephone... but you won't know what that is. It's a way of speaking to somebody who is not right next to you. They could be in New York, Sydney, Paris, or, as in this case, the other side of Milton."

Mr. Thornton shook his head, unable to comprehend how it could be possible to hear someone who was on the other side of the world. "What have you told this professor about me?"

"Not much. I just said that I had by chance met someone who was as interested in the possibility of time travel as she was, and not in a TARDIS or 'Beam me up, Scotty' kind of way."

"A what?"

"Science fiction – did you have that in the early 1850s?"

"You mean stories of fiction that have a scientific element?"

"Yes, but the science is fantastical."

"Yes, we had that." He glanced around. "However, it seems our science fiction may have become science fact."

"I suppose it must seem that way." She squeezed his hand reassuringly.

"I thought things in my time moved fast, in terms of science and invention – what we were achieving and what we believed could be achieved in the future. I never in my wildest dreams imagined this." He gestured with his arm at the streets of Milton.

MJ looked about at the normality of what he was pointing out and tried but failed to imagine what it must seem like to him. "I suppose nobody could imagine all of this. Here we are. This is the main physics building. My friend's office is on the fourth floor. There is a lift, but your breathing seems all right so I think we will be okay using the stairs."

The lift, Mr. Thornton assumed, was the refinement of an invention he had been following the development of in his own time that enabled goods – and now it seemed people – to move between the different stories of a building. Maybe they could use it coming back down. It couldn't be any more terrifying than the vehicle Miss Hale travelled about in.

The office they headed towards was just along a corridor that led off from the stairs. Although they were expected, he still liked the fact that Miss Hale knocked and waited to be called in – some manners, he realised, still existed.

The voice that answered them was female, which was a surprise to Mr. Thornton, as was the broad Lancashire accent. Miss Hale's accent was not from these parts – hers was undoubtedly from the south, but which part he couldn't be sure.

The office was small. Seated at a desk was a fair-haired woman with her head buried in some papers she was studying.

"Morning, Doc. Allow me to introduce the friend I spoke to you about on the telephone, John Thornton."

At his name, the woman's head flew up.

"Mr. Thornton, Doctor..." MJ stopped as Mr. Thornton interrupted her.

"Bessy Higgins," he said in a hoarse whisper.

"John Thornton – Master of Marlborough Mills. My data must be correct; the door must have opened again. But why would you choose to step through it?" she said, her tone incredulous.

"Hold on a minute, do you two know each other?" MJ asked.

"I certainly know Mr. Thornton. I used to work for him at Marlborough Mills, but I am surprised that you know me," Bessy Higgins said, looking at him questioningly.

"Of course, I know you. I employed you. Your father asked me to take you on when I had the wheel installed in the mill. Your chest was bad. Conditions in my mill were better. You disappeared a year ago – your father came to me asking if I'd seen you. You left a note saying that you had gone to a place that could cure your lung problems, but you didn't say where."

"No. Well, it would be hard to explain that the place was almost 200 years in the future."

"You mean there is a cure here for consumption?"

"It is called tuberculosis now, and yes, it is a curable condition here."

"Are you telling me that you are also from the nineteenth century as well?" MJ was incredulous.

"Yes, I'm sorry I couldn't tell you. Even if I could have, I doubt you'd have believed me."

MJ's knees weakened and she sank to a chair. "You'd have been right."

"You wonder why I chose to walk through the door, but I didn't choose to do anything. There was no door," Mr. Thornton said.

"It is not really a door; it is more like a passage in time. Interesting, you must have fallen against the passage as it opened. Do you remember falling?"

"Yes, the heat and smoke from the fire were overwhelming. A beam exploded; I must have rolled out of the way when it fell.

"You're saying this happened at the time of the fire at Marlborough Mills?"

"Yes, is that not how it was for you?"

"No. A man who became my mentor and teacher came through it and offered to take me where I could be cured. I was dying and even though I didn't really believe him, I followed him. What did I have to lose? I arrived here, and he organised treatment for my tuberculosis, and I was cured."

"Matthew Hemmingway travelled through time?" MJ was astonished, recalling the scientist who had died recently. She knew that Bess Higgins had been considered his protégé.

"Yes, he did."

"Why did he not publish his findings?"

"He only travelled through it once, so he felt he needed more proof of what he had experienced. He became the father I left behind. Like any father, he taught me – but not how to walk, talk, read, or write. I knew how to do those things. He taught me physics and all he knew about time travel. He was sure that the passage would re-open, and spent the rest of his life trying to prove when it would. He died last year, but I continued his work – not just on time travel, but teaching physics to a new generation. Working from his data, I thought we must be close to the date the passage would re-open, but truthfully I thought it would occur next week. I don't understand why this has happened earlier than he predicted. Matthew believed the passage is on a loop. He calculated how long it would take for it to return to this point in time."

"Well almost, he was only out by a week," MJ said.

"I don't understand why he was; it doesn't make sense. The maths should work perfectly, unless time in the loop was moving faster than he thought."

"Is that possible?" MJ asked.

"No, I don't see how, not if the loop is elliptical."

"Elliptical--what is that?" Mr. Thornton asked.

"It means oval like an egg, not circular like a ball."

"What if the loop were like a ball, would that make a difference?" Mr. Thornton asked.

As soon as he spoke, a small smiled appeared on Bessy Higgins' face. "Yes, you are on to something there, Mr. Thornton. The loop must not be an elliptical one." She reached for a pad and pencil and began jotting down various complex equations.

"I see you have brains, but I don't see how you learned all of this physics in a year," Mr. Thornton said.

Bessy paused. "I have been here ten years, not one year."

"I don't understand. Your father came to me a year ago. In fact, he remarked only a few days ago that it was the anniversary of your disappearance."

"Is he well?"

"Yes, I believe so. He has formed a union to improve workers' rights – it's not popular with some mill owners, though."

"Are you talking about Nicholas Higgins?" MJ asked.

"Yes. How do you know his name, Miss Hale?"

"He was one of the first union leaders here in Milton. I've come across him in my research. How is it I never linked your name with his, Bessy?"

"Why should you? I think I have worked out why you have fallen through the passage earlier than expected, Mr. Thornton. I think it is on a Mobius loop and the speed inside that would be different from an elliptical loop."

"A what loop?" MJ asked, her head in a daze at all the revelations she was witnessing.

"Think of it as a loop that is twisted, like a figure eight."

"You said you had been here ten years," Mr. Thornton said. "Is that how long I will have to wait to go back?"

"That's what I thought, but if I am correct in my calculations, the passage will reappear seven days from when it first opened because of how a Mobius loop twists. It must have done this last time, but Matthew was unaware of it."

"So I can get back again – is that what you are saying?" Mr. Thornton asked.

"I'm saying that if my calculations are correct, then the passage will open again. I'm not sure whether you can go back through it."

CHAPTER FIVE

Another five days; that was all he had to wait. He just had to be patient. The so-called passage in time would reappear one week from the time it first opened, and he had already been here two days. He had to believe that what Miss Higgins said was correct. It was hard to imagine that his mill worker, Bessy Higgins, was now a Doctor of Physics and Astronomy, but believe and imagine he must, for she was the key to his returning home.

"Mr. Thornton, did you hear what Dr. Higgins said? That although she believes the passage will reopen, she is not sure you can pass through it or that you will end up back at the mill. You may end up back in the fire," MJ said.

"I heard what she said, Miss Hale, but I must believe that all will be well when I return."

"I will spend the next few days doing what I can to check my calculations," Bessy said.

"We have five days, Mr. Thornton. I suppose I should show you around Milton."

"No, MJ, that cannot be allowed. Mr. Thornton must not learn anything more about the twenty-first century than he has already. No physicist is truly aware of how time travellers might alter the future," she said.

"I don't understand. How might his going back alter the future?"

"The things that are happening around us are following a timeline. It stands to reason that if Mr. Thornton takes back something he has learned here and uses it, then the timeline will be altered. What we don't know is how, but you can be sure there would be both positive and negative outcomes."

"Does that mean when the passage opens you will not return with me?" Mr. Thornton asked Bessy.

"No, I cannot. I dare not, for two reasons. Firstly, I cannot forget what I have learned here. It would be impossible, knowing how history unfolds, to remain silent and do nothing. Imagine, Mr. Thornton, going back to the time of the Trojan War. You know of the Greeks' plan to hide in the horse and so have the power to stop the destruction of Troy – what do you do? Do you stand by and do nothing, knowing that Troy will be destroyed with the loss of many lives? Or do you warn them, knowing that you would be changing a future that has already happened?"

"I understand. It would be most difficult to remain silent. Are you saying that terrible things have happened to this world since my time? Surely we have learned that war is not the answer," Mr. Thornton said.

"Mr. Thornton, all I will say is look to the Bible—Matthew, chapter 24, verse 6."

"You will hear of wars and rumours of wars," MJ said. "Sorry, I'm a vicar's daughter."

Mr. Thornton looked at Miss Hale, wondering not for the first time what her father would make of his daughter's decision to entertain a strange man in her home.

"Oh, Mr. Thornton, I can read you like a book – my father would not care that I had a man in my house without a chaperone – you have to stop thinking you are compromising my honour. It was compromised long ago."

Bessy Higgins smiled. "Sometimes, MJ, it is as difficult going forward in time as it is going back. You need to make allowances for Mr. Thornton's upbringing; there was a name for a woman who entertained a man alone in her home in the nineteenth century and it wasn't a polite one."

"I'm sorry, Mr. Thornton, I will stop teasing you."

"And I will try to stop judging you by my Victorian moral compass," he replied. "Miss Higgins, you said there were two reasons you would not be going back with me. May I enquire as to what the second one is?" he asked, turning his attention back to Bessy Higgins.

"I am not who I was when I left. As much as I miss my father – and I do beyond measure – I cannot return to that life. All I would know would be poverty, illness, and hardship – he wouldn't want that for me. It is another reason why you must not get comfortable here – you won't want to leave."

"No, I have to go back. I have to be sure my mother and sister are all right."

"Will the passage open one week later in the nineteenth century, as well?" MJ asked.

"That is my hypothesis, but it is only a hypothesis, one I have no way of knowing is correct."

"I have to believe that you are correct," Mr. Thornton said.

"In which case, please heed my warning. Try not to learn too much about this world, it could be very dangerous."

"Am I allowed to learn things about the world I left?" Mr. Thornton asked carefully.

"Like what?" MJ asked.

"Like who tried to kill me?"

"Kill you?"

"The fire was started deliberately. A man called out to me as the fire broke out. He told me that I had been warned. The fire must have singed more than my hair – I know I should know him, but his name eludes me."

"There has never been any question of the fire being arson," MJ said.

"No, that's not strictly true; a cause was never given. What you must remember, MJ, is that fire investigations were not carried out like they are today – it was a tragedy for sure, but they would be likely to say it was heat from a chimney or something similar. The inquest would open and close. The dead would be buried; rebuilding would begin," Bessy Higgins said, her tone one of weary acceptance.

"Yes, they put the fire at Marlborough Mills down as an accident that happened due to more than one circumstance," MJ admitted.

"Well it wasn't – it was a man. I was lured into the cotton store by seeing the open door, which it wouldn't have been that early. I mean, the overseer wasn't even there," Mr. Thornton said.

"No, that's right. According to newspaper reports of the day, by the time he'd arrived, the fire had already taken hold."

"So, Miss Higgins, would it be all right for me to use the special window Miss Hale has to find out about the fire?" Mr. Thornton asked again.

"Window?"

"He means my laptop," MJ explained.

"Right. Truthfully, I don't know, but I am assuming you will only confirm what you already suspect."

"The future regarding the fire has already changed. It's why I believed Mr. Thornton's story. The newspaper reports online said his body wasn't found, but when I saved and printed them last week, they said his body had been found," MJ said, realising she hadn't explained this to Dr. Higgins.

"That is interesting. I suppose the change is only small since everybody still believes Mr. Thornton died in the fire. I can't stop you doing research, and I obviously did the same. The difference is I never planned to go back. Promise me that whatever information you learn you will use wisely. And, MJ, please keep the research related to the mill. It was the one thing that Matthew worried about – time travel causing a cataclysmic change in history."

"I promise that I will only look at my family and the mill," Mr. Thornton said. "I don't think anybody would accuse me of being frivolous or foolhardy – you must remember how cautious I am."

"Yes, you were a sober man and a fair Master, better than others in Milton at the time. I will continue to work on the calculations for next Monday morning when the passage should reopen."

"I suggest we catch up on Sunday. Come for dinner, and we will discuss what you think Mr. Thornton must do to pass back through the crack in time," MJ said.

She stood to leave, and Mr. Thornton held out his hand to Bessy. "Miss Higgins, thank you for the explanations and for understanding my need to return so I can find out who did this to my family. You have my word that is the only information I will look at."

She took his hand. "And your word, Mr. Thornton, as everybody in Milton knows, is a good deal from you."

CHAPTER SIX

MJ couldn't remember the last time she had eaten at her small kitchen table. It was usually strewn with books and papers. She'd cleared them away, knowing that Mr. Thornton would not enjoy dinner on the sofa. Now, she searched through the kitchen drawers, certain that she had a tablecloth and tablemats tucked away somewhere. She had not made her usual Thai or Italian food, thinking it better to stick with something Mr. Thornton would be familiar with. He'd probably call her chicken supreme a stew, but at least she wouldn't be answering questions about how she was cooking food using ingredients he'd probably never heard of.

They'd spent the afternoon looking at information about the mill and Milton leading up to the fire. The months before the fire had been very unsettled – workers were forming unions and demanding better pay and conditions. She'd been forthright in her opinion in saying how the mill owners must have hated the demands.

He'd smiled slightly and agreed that many mill owners were against the unions – some because they were fools and others because they worried about meeting the cost of the improvements the unions were demanding.

She shook her head and spoke of how pay increases and improvements were disliked for one reason only – they ate into the company profits. He'd responded in his quiet way that not all mill owners behaved like that. Not all mills had large profits; some were barely scraping by. He'd explained how he had made improvements at Marlborough Mills; some were expensive, like the wheel in the carding room that drew the cotton fluff and dust out of the air to prevent it going into the workers' lungs. It was one of the reasons Bessy Higgins worked at Marlborough Mills and not at Hamper's, like her father.

During the course of the afternoon, she'd had to re-evaluate her opinion of the mill owners whom she had labelled as evil tyrants – John Thornton, she realised, was none of those things. Besides the wheel, which would have been a huge financial outlay (as much as five or six hundred pounds), he'd also set up a kitchen where for a penny or two the workers could have a hot meal. At a time when food was expensive and scarce, this was often the only meal his workers ate. He'd built a wash house near the site of the mill so that his workers could have a proper bath for a penny. Since its introduction, they had seen a reduction in skin complaints and diseases. He admitted that these had not made him popular with some of the other mill owners, who couldn't see the sense in improving conditions. "But if my workers are healthier, they work longer for me," he explained.

When she asked if he meant more hours in a day, he looked genuinely hurt. "No, Miss Hale, I meant that my workers do not fall ill as easily and, because conditions are better in my mill, they are less likely to leave my employment. My turnover of staff is the lowest in Milton and my workers suffer fewer accidents."

She apologised, but he became quiet and uncommunicative, so she excused herself by saying she'd make a start on dinner. She realised she'd offended him, but she hadn't expected to like him so much. If anybody had told her she was going to meet one of the Lancashire mill owners whose names she knew almost as well as her own, she'd have said she expected them to be coarse and uncouth, with no concern for the wellbeing of their workers. Mr Thornton was different, she admitted with surprise. His manner, though stiff, was achingly polite; his tone was quiet, and he had obvious compassion for his workers.

She sighed. The table was set, and the meal was ready to serve. She couldn't avoid him any longer. "Mr. Thornton, I am about to serve dinner if you want to come through."

He appeared a moment later in the kitchen. "I hope you have not gone to much trouble, Miss Hale. It seems wrong that a refined young lady such as yourself does not have someone to help with domestic duties."

"I am not a grand lady, Mr. Thornton. I will admit that my parents employed a woman to help with cleaning at the vicarage. She was a part of my life when I lived at home. She had a sharped tongued personality, but she was devoted to my parents – especially to my mother – and of course, like everybody, she adored my brother Frederick. Please have a seat. Would you care for a glass of wine?"

"That would be very nice. Perhaps I could decant it for you, while you serve the food."

She smiled. "There is a bottle of Australian white in the fridge." She pointed to the appliance he had got the milk from earlier.

"You have wine from Australia? I was not aware they produced wine."

"Yes, they are famous for it."

"It must be very expensive."

"No, it's cheap and cheerful."

He retrieved the bottle from the fridge and studied the label. "It seems it is an ideal accompaniment to chicken or fish. Are we having either of those?"

"We are, Mr. Thornton – Chicken Supreme," she said, placing two plates on the table.

"That looks delicious. If you tell me where the corkscrew is, I will open the wine."

"That bottle has no cork. That wine isn't expensive enough for a cork. Twist the top. It unscrews."

If he was surprised, he didn't show it, but just unscrewed the top. "As it is cheap, I presume it does not need to breathe?" he said, his tone humorous.

"Isn't it red wine that needs to breathe? I think you should just pour it."

He smiled, causing crinkles to fan out from his brilliant blue eyes.

Wow, MJ thought, *that smile changed his whole face.* Gone was the forbidding brooding man. She wondered if he realised how handsome he was. He must have been the catch of Milton.

"As the daughter of a parson, I assume you say grace."

"My father would have said not nearly often enough. But I can if you'd like."

"I have noticed how you speak of your father. You use the past tense. Forgive me for prying but..."

Before he could say any more she interrupted. "Has he died? Is that what you want to know? Sadly, yes. Both my parents died in a car accident five years ago."

"I am very sorry – I know what it is like to lose a father."

"Thank you. I am grateful that they were together when they died. They were so entwined with each other; it was fitting somehow. My father's faith was very strong. He had no trouble believing in the concept of heaven. So, let's honour him by my saying grace." She bowed her head. "God, we give thanks for the food and ask you to bless it and those who eat it. Now, eat up while it is still hot."

She held her breath as he took his first forkful. She wasn't sure why, but she really wanted him to enjoy what she had prepared. He chewed and swallowed. "This is really very good, have you had training?"

Relieved it was to his liking, she smiled and thought for a moment. "In a way. Harry Stephens helped me every step of the way – he's a celebrity chef and I have his cookbook."

"Harry Stephens. It's strange, but that name is very familiar to me."

"Well, it's not an unusual name. I imagine it's very possible that you knew somebody of that name in your own time. It could have been a tradesman, another mill owner, a worker even. Chef Harry Stephens' family has always lived locally; he is a well-known Milton boy made good."

As she was speaking, Mr. Thornton paused, a forkful of food hovering between his plate and mouth. His mind cleared and suddenly he knew why the name was familiar. MJ watched as he lowered the fork to his plate, the need to speak outweighing the need to eat.

"Mr. Thornton, is everything all right?"

"Yes, you are right. Harry Stephens is a mill worker – not a very good one, I'm afraid. I had to sack him for smoking in the mill a few weeks ago. To be honest, he's a pathetic idle wastrel. I should have given him his cards months ago, but he has a family. So, against my better judgement, I kept him on. The smoking was one incident too many. He put the whole mill at risk." He picked up his fork and continued eating. It was obvious to MJ that he was thinking deeply about something. She could see it in his eyes. Not wanting to interrupt his train of thought, she too ate on in silence, retreating into her own thoughts.

When he finished eating, he took a sip of the cold wine. "The food and wine have been excellent. I'm sorry my company has not been more congenial."

"You have been fine company. It is I who should be apologising. I had an opinion of mill owners, unfavourable and unfair. I am sorry I offended you earlier. It is obvious that you do have a great regard for your mill workers."

"I do. I am sure the labour market is very different nowadays. Please tell me children are no longer allowed to work."

"No, not in this country. Sadly, in other poorer parts of the world, they still do."

"I wanted to stop all children under the age of fourteen from working in the mill, but their parents were against it. In the words of one, 'mouths that need feeding need to be earning.' Still, reforms are coming, and I won't have them in my mill under the age of ten.

"There you go, enlightening me again about how good a master you were. I understand now what Bessy Higgins meant this morning."

"May I share something with you, Miss Hale? I have not told anybody this."

"I would be honoured if you told me."

"I have acquired some land on the outskirts of Milton where I propose to build a village for my workers. Each house will have a small garden and there will be a school, a church, a doctor, and a hall where they can meet. The workers need to be away from the slums if they are ever to be truly healthy."

"It is a wonderful idea; I wish others from your time had been as concerned about their workers' wellbeing. I hope we can get you back to your time so that you can make your dream a reality."

"I've been thinking about that ever since you mentioned the name Stephens. I am certain that his was the voice that called out to me in the cotton store. That means that the snivelling weasel is working for whoever did this. We must try and find out who he worked for after I dismissed him. We should look now."

"No, Mr. Thornton, we will look tomorrow. It is late. We have done enough today. We are going to have another glass of wine and relax for an hour or two. Tell me, are you a fan of Mr. Dickens?"

"Very much, I attended an evening of his reading when he came to Milton."

"Then I have a treat for you. It is an adaption of his novel, David Copperfield."

"His latest? I have only lately finished it."

"If you open that white door over there, I will do the dishes."

He opened the door and stared. "A machine that washes the plates?"

"Yes, it has taken the place of servants. Take the wine into the lounge. I'll just load the dishes and then we will watch David Copperfield."

When she came in the lounge, she switched on the box that she had earlier called a television. This time, she placed a small flat disc in another machine. "This is a DVD version of the novel Dickens wrote – like a play, but filmed." She smiled at his baffled look. "I suppose it is a major advancement of a Magic Lantern show. I assume you've seen those before?"

"Yes, Miss Hale, I have."

"Well, this is like a play, but the images come up on the screen."

"I think it is best I just watch. I am sure it will be good. When I have time, I enjoy the theatre."

"I'm sure you will enjoy it, but you will see better if you sit over here on the couch. I promise it is all right for us to sit together."

He hesitated for a moment before moving to the other end of the couch where she sat. She had done something to the lighting which was now dimmer than it had previously been.

She pushed a button and images appeared on the screen. The story was exactly as Mr. Dickens had written but brought visibly to life on the screen. He enjoyed it immensely, but it did not hold his concentration completely. How could it, when he sat close enough to Miss Hale to hear her breathing and smell her perfume? Occasionally, their hands touched as they reached for their wine glasses. Did Miss Hale feel the same slight tremor and quickening of heartbeat when their hands met, he wondered? He sighed. He hoped not, for surely nothing could come from the stirring of attraction he was feeling – nothing but pain, and he would spare her that if he could.

CHAPTER SEVEN

It was good to escape the house for the afternoon. They had been holed up in her home for the past three days, researching the mill and the aftermath of the fire in the 1850s. Once Mr. Thornton had remembered the name of the man who had called out to him in the cotton store, they had a starting point for their research. Thanks to MJ's contacts in the city archives, they were able to discover where Stephens had found employment after he had been dismissed from Marlborough Mills. The name of the man who had taken him on had not come as a surprise to either. Joseph Slickson was the owner of a rival mill and a man for whom Mr. Thornton obviously had no time.

"The man is a fool – he cuts corners and uses cheap inferior material, and his mill has the worst safety record. He turns out shoddy work that he sells cheaply. By cutting corners, he keeps his costs down so that his mill makes a very healthy profit," Mr. Thornton had said when he heard the name.

"So healthy that after the fire he bought your mill: Marlborough Mills is owned by the Slickson family," MJ had told him.

"That is not possible," Mr. Thornton had whispered. "My ... my mother's opinion of Slickson is worse than mine." He'd gone on to explain how his mother held Slickson responsible for his father's death. They'd been involved in some scheme that had financially ruined his father – he'd committed suicide shortly afterwards. Slickson had found out that the project was going to collapse and had sold his shares without telling Mr. Thornton's father, unscrupulously making a profit even though he knew the project was doomed. He'd tried to buy the business then, but Mr. Thornton had come home from university and took over the running of the mill, turning it into not only a commercial success but a benchmark for how a mill should be run.

Further research into the sale of the mill shed light on how it had come into Slickson's hands. Initial newspaper reports confirmed that the mill had been bought by a company called the Lancashire Textile Company, a company managed but not owned by a man called Robson. Only later was it revealed that Slickson had been behind the purchase.

On hearing about the duplicitous way in which Slickson had bought the mill, Mr. Thornton had become rigid with shock and anger. She'd watched his fingers curl into a fist, his jaw clench, and his eyes harden until they resembled chips of ice. He had moved away from the computer and walked to her window, staring out over her tiny garden. She had left him for a time as he struggled to contain his emotions, only going to him when he remained unmoving for ten minutes. She reached and touched his arm before taking his cold hand in hers and gently stroking it. She felt his taut muscles relax and his ragged breathing return to normal. He apologised, thinking he'd scared her, but she assured him he had not.

Without letting go of her hand, he returned to the sofa and sat by her side in a way he'd not done since they had watched David Copperfield together. They had been closer that night, for their legs touched – propriety seemingly forgotten.

He spoke of his mother and how important an influence she had been. He wondered what effect hearing that Slickson had got his hands on the mill had had on her. MJ knew the answer, or at least suspected it. She'd not been going to say anything, but he must have read something in her eyes because he asked her to explain what she knew. She told him his mother had died nine months after the sale of the mill, shortly after Slickson's ownership became common knowledge, and one week after his sister's wedding.

His Victorian way of hiding his feelings came to the fore as he merely nodded at the news. His facial expression barely changed, but he couldn't hide the pain he obviously felt from his expressive eyes. MJ reacted to the emotion she saw there, and reached up and touched his cheek.

"We're going to get you home, and there is every chance that the events around the time of the fire will alter," she'd said quietly.

"Do you really think so?"

"Yes. You only know Bessy Higgins as a mill girl – I know her as a brilliant physicist. If she says the passage in time will reopen next week, it will. So, the best thing you can do is consider how you are going to rebuild the mill."

He had smiled then, a sad, quiet smile. "I will have to use the money I have been saving to build the workers' village."

"Then we must find you a partner, one you can trust to invest in the mill."

"I don't trust easily. Anyway, how can I find an investor when I am stuck in the twenty-first century? I wish I knew how Slickson not only bought the mill, but built it up again into a viable business. Even he will not have had the money to do all that. He must have had an investor." No sooner had he voiced this thought than an idea came to him. "Can you use the computer thing to find out who invested in the mill with Slickson?" he asked her. They then spent three days researching the past.

~

"Penny for your thoughts," Mr. Thornton said, bringing her thoughts back to the present where they sat on a bench overlooking the moor.

"I was just thinking about the past few days – how much we have learned, and your plan to use the same backer as Slickson did."

"Yes, let us hope this Mr. Barnes likes my proposition."

"There is nothing to suggest he won't. After all, he is just a gentleman looking to invest his fortune. Now, no more talk of the plan. Today was supposed to be a day out."

"Yes, I thought I knew this place. But Saddleworth Moor looks nothing like it did in my day. That huge lake was not here."

"That is Dovestone Reservoir, the final in a series of reservoirs that run through this place. I think the first of them was built towards the end of the nineteenth century. I thought after we eat the picnic I packed, we could walk down to the water."

"Thank you for this, Miss Hale. I forgot how clean the air is out here on the moors."

"I thought we could both do with a change of scenery, and thought Saddleworth would not have changed much. Of course, I forgot the reservoirs were not started until the 1870s. You'll have to forget you know about them when you return."

He nodded. One thing he would never forget was Miss Hale. His feelings towards this remarkable woman deepened with every moment he knew her. Leaving her was going to be the hardest thing he had ever done.

They spent a very happy afternoon on the moors, walking and watching the wildlife that was so prevalent away from the city. It was only when they returned to MJ's home that the afternoon took on a nightmarish quality

CHAPTER EIGHT

The nightmare began as soon as they returned to MJ's home. She was barely through the front door when she crumpled at his feet. She dropped like a stone: fast, sudden, and straight down. One minute she was talking to him and the next she was unconscious at his feet. He scooped her up and carried her to the couch in her sitting room. He'd never felt so useless before. He was used to being in control, having a solution to every problem, but he didn't even know where to go for help.

He knelt at her side and took her hand in his. She was too pale, but at least she was breathing. "Miss Hale, can you hear me?" he spoke quietly.

She remained still and unresponsive. He brushed a lock of hair from her forehead, noticing for the first time a small scar. Her skin felt cool and soft. At least she wasn't feverish, which had to be a good sign. "Miss Hale, please, open your eyes." Again his quiet plea was met with silence and stillness.

He needed to get help. Something had to be seriously wrong, for several minutes had passed and she did not speak or move. The problem was, he had no idea how to get help. The twenty-first century was a mystery to him. "Margaret, I'm going to get help. I don't know where, but I …." He paused, noticing the device she called her mobile in the pocket of her trousers. She had spoken to Bessy Higgins on this contraption. Could he do that? He hesitated, suddenly aware he would have to touch Miss Hale to retrieve the mobile. He was being foolish. This was an emergency; he would apologise later. He pulled it free from her pocket and studied the small flat object in the palm of his hand.

When Miss Hale used it, she touched something on it and the front lit up. He turned it in his hand and noticed a small button on the side. He touched it and the screen lit up as the time and date appeared. He'd switched it on! Pleased with himself, he studied the screen, trying to recall what Miss Hale had done. She'd wiped her finger across the screen. Doing the same, he revealed several symbols. After frantically pressing several which were wrong, he finally discovered something called her contacts and found Bessy Higgins' name along with several others. As with everything else on this machine, he tapped the screen over her name and some information appeared--a number. He tapped the number and it was replaced with the word 'calling.' Miss Hale had lifted the mobile to her ear, so cautiously he did the same and waited. A moment later, the ringing he heard was replaced by Bessy Higgins' voice – as clear as if she were in the same room.

"Thank God," he whispered, glancing at the motionless Miss Hale.

"Mr. Thornton, is that you? Why do you have Margaret's mobile?"

"IT'S MISS HALE SHE'S—" He spoke so loudly that Bessy interrupted him.

"Speak normally, Mr. Thornton, there is no need to shout."

"It is Miss Hale – she has collapsed. One minute she was standing, and the next she was on the floor. I have placed her on the couch, but she has not come around yet and it has been several minutes since she collapsed."

"Is she breathing – Mr. Thornton?" Bessy said as calmly as she could.

"Yes, but she is not responding to me."

"All right, I will call an ambulance and then I will come to you. In the meantime, try loosening her clothes if they are tight, and place her on her left side. It will help protect her airway."

"All right. Miss Higgins, please hurry! If anything should happen… I don't know…." Mr. Thornton's voice broke.

"I know. I'll be there as soon as I can. I'm not far away."

Her voice went away. He put the phone down and turned his attention to Miss Hale. What had Miss Higgins said? Loosen her clothing. He knelt at her side and undid the top two buttons on the blouse she was wearing, telling himself it was necessary. He also undid the button on her trousers and pulled the blouse free from the waist band. Finally, he gently moved her on to her side as Bessy had suggested.

"Please open your eyes, Margaret, so that I may know you are recovering. I don't know what I would do if anything should happen to you. You have become very dear to me," he said, taking her hand and pressing it to his cheek. "I know that you cannot come back with me when the passage opens, any more than I can stay here with you. Oh, but if it were possible – my dear Margaret! – I would call on you and ask permission to court you, and later I would ask you to spend the rest of your life with me as long as we both shall live."

He turned her hand over and placed a kiss to her palm. "Please wake up, my angel."

MJ stirred. Someone was speaking to her. She was sure it was Mr. Thornton, but something puzzled her – he kept calling her 'Margaret' and, if she was not mistaken, he had just called her 'my angel.' Surely he'd never do that. What had happened? She was so very cold, her whole body felt heavy, and her heartbeat seemed slow and laboured. Had she fainted? She felt the touch of someone's hand brushing her hair from her face. She knew she must open her eyes, but everything was an effort and it was several minutes before her eyes fluttered open.

At first, her vision was blurred, but slowly what she saw came into focus. Mr. Thornton was knelt at her side, her hand clasped in his. His face was a study in deep concern – lines etched his features and his eyes were dark and pensive, staring off into the distance.

"Mr. Thornton?"

His hand tightened around hers and his gaze returned to her face. "Thank God, thank God," he whispered, kissing her hand before he remembered where he was and who she was. He reluctantly released it and placed it at her side.

"What happened?" MJ asked, trying to sit up.

"Stay still, help is on the way – you collapsed. I thought I'd lost you," he said gently.

His face was so close to hers that MJ could feel his breath when he spoke, and his lips were close enough that with the slightest movement he could place them against hers in a kiss. Kissing Mr. Thornton – where had that thought come from? To kiss him, even in gratitude, would be foolish. If his learning about the future was dangerous, then it was reasonable to believe that kissing somebody from the future would be equally as dangerous. But, when did reason ever triumph over emotion? She wasn't sure who moved first, but one or both of them did. The kiss was soft – reverent almost – the lightest of touches, and she gently parted her lips on a sigh of pleasure.

From the first touch, MJ felt warmth flood her frozen body. The leaden weight that had crushed her body moments before lifted and her heartbeat increased. The power of his touch scared her, not because she was frightened of him but because she was afraid of her body's response to him. It overwhelmed her as no other kiss had. It was odd, but she could not shake the idea that he had just given her the kiss of life.

He pulled away slightly, as obviously affected by the kiss as she had been.

"Margaret, Miss Hale – we shouldn't, I shouldn't...."

"I think it is a little too late for that; we already have. Please don't tell me you are sorry. I couldn't bear to hear you apologise – let me keep the memory."

"I couldn't apologise. That would mean I have regrets, but I have none. However, it was probably not wise. If you were a Victorian lady, I would act on my feelings for you. But you are not, and much as I wish to kiss you again, I fear I should not."

Before she could speak, her doorbell rang. Mr. Thornton stood up. "That will be either the ambulance or Miss Higgins," he said.

MJ nodded. "I'm not sure, Mr. Thornton, if we have been interrupted by the bell or saved by it."

CHAPTER NINE

MJ stared at Bessy Higgins in shock. They were in her bedroom. The paramedics had left, satisfied that all she had suffered was a vasovagal episode. Her observations, ECG, and blood sugar were all normal. In other words, as MJ had told them, "I fainted." They'd agreed that it seemed that way. They would have taken her to the Accident and Emergency department, but she declined, saying she'd rest at home.

Mr. Thornton had carried her to her bedroom, lifting her as easily as if she were a feather. He had placed her on the bed and had disappeared to make some tea while Bessy helped her change into her pyjamas.

"Could you say that again?" MJ asked.

"You have to go back with Mr. Thornton," Bessy announced again.

MJ sank back against the pillows on her bed, glad that she and Bessy were alone in her bedroom and that Mr. Thornton had not heard what Bessy had said. "Go back to the nineteenth century?"

"Yes."

"Why do I have to do that?"

"Because if you don't, you will cease to exist."

MJ snorted. "Haven't you just slipped into Back to the Future territory?"

"Most science fiction is based, at least to some degree, on fact. This attack you suffered – I believe it is a sign that your body is failing because of some major change in your personal timeline."

"What change? I am still me."

"Yes, you are, but you have met John Thornton, nineteenth-century mill owner. That is something that should not have happened. Tell me, have you been intimate with him?"

"What kind of a question is that? I would never compromise Miss Hale's honour in such a way!" Mr. Thornton said, entering the room.

"A valid one, given that I suspect that you both have feelings for each other," Bessy Higgins said, not cowed by Mr. Thornton's tone. "Do not deny it, Mr. Thornton – when you rang me, it was obvious that you cared for Miss Hale deeply. And MJ, when I asked that question about intimacy, you blushed."

"You are both right," MJ replied. "Mr. Thornton, you have not compromised me in any way and yes, Bessy, we have been intimate, but not in the way you imagine. We held hands when we walked up on the moors. We've shared meals and movies together. We have spoken of our personal dreams and family. Speaking for myself, I have grown to like Mr. Thornton and I find him very attractive. Were he able to stay, I would hope we could spend more time together, and maybe – what is that old-fashioned word? – court. But there has been no physical intimacy, apart from the most tender kiss he gave me when I came to from collapsing."

"Miss Hale, Margaret – you care for me?"

"I do, Mr. Thornton, but you must know it cannot be. You must go back and –"

"You must go with him," Bessy Higgins said. "You will die if you do not. You almost have once. Tell me, MJ, do you recall what it was like collapsing? How did you feel?"

"I was cold – freezing, actually. I thought I'd never be warm again. My body was heavy and leaden. As I regained consciousness, I found it hard to move. I knew I was alive because I was aware of how slow my heartbeat was."

"Then what happened?" Bessy asked.

"Mr. Thornton kissed me, or maybe I kissed him. Whichever it was, neither of us objected. When his lips touched mine, I was instantly warm and languid, and my heartbeat was normal. But Bessy, I am not Snow White or Sleeping Beauty who needs to be woken by a kiss from one who loves me. This isn't a fairy tale."

"No, it isn't. I have been reading some of Matthew's journals and his theories about time travel. He wrote a theory about what would happen if a person moved forward in time and in doing so missed doing something of great importance in her own time. He called it the missing link paradox. He questioned what would happen."

"But even if Mr. Thornton has missed doing something in his own time, how does that affect me?" MJ asked.

"Do you remember discussing with me how you got interested in the nineteenth century and northern mills in particular?"

"Yes," MJ replied, "I told you how my parents traced their family history and discovered several generations ago that my family had worked to help with social conditions in the mills."

"Did any of the family have Margaret as a given name? Is much known about her? Did she marry, for example?"

"I don't know, there was a thought that possibly my mother's and father's families several generations back were related because my mother's maiden name was Hale as well."

"What are you saying, Miss Higgins? That Miss Hale belongs in the nineteenth century? That the important thing I have missed is meeting her?" Mr. Thornton said.

"You are forgetting that I have come forward in time as well. I not only know you from 1851, but I remember other people from that time. Before I left Milton, a young woman moved there from the south with her family – her name was Margaret Hale. Do you not remember her, Mr. Thornton?"

"No, did I meet her?"

"Yes, I suppose the fire caused you to forget her."

"Are you saying I have moved in time?" MJ said

"I don't know, really. Is it possible for you to exist in two places at once? Matthew had all sorts of theories. What I am saying is that I believe Mr. Thornton was destined to meet you in the nineteenth century, but he has come here instead. As a result, that meeting has not taken place, causing your family line to vanish. I would lay odds on your family tree missing names here and there, MJ," Bessy said.

"So she belongs here and there?" Mr Thornton said.

"Yes, in a way. I came here because I was dying, and this place saved my life. In the nineteenth century, I had done nothing remarkable except to be born and start to die. Nothing I did was of great importance. So, when I came here, nothing seemed to have been affected, except that I lived. Maybe my action of great importance is showing you how to go back and making sure MJ goes with you," Bessy said.

"But that is not all you are saying. You are saying I have to go back and marry Mr. Thornton." MJ said.

"Would that be so terrible, Miss Hale?" Mr. Thornton asked.

"No, I don't mean to imply that. But I barely know you and, while I might fancy the pants off you, that is a mile away from marriage. Bessy, is that what must happen?" MJ said.

"Yes, that and have children. I can offer you no facts or evidence, it is purely my hypothesis. You must go back and be Margaret Hale to save your future self."

"I can't just leave. What about my brother?"

"If I am right and you don't go back – your brother will not exist."

"I hadn't thought of that. So, I'd be saving his life too?"

Bessy nodded. "I really think you would. This is a lot to take in. You look tired, you should rest. I will return tomorrow. If you agree with me then, there will be things that we will need to do. You can't return to nineteenth-century Milton dressed like that."

MJ stared down at her pyjamas. "No, I suppose not."

"Mr. Thornton – come and show me out," Bessy Higgins said. Once they were downstairs in the hallway, she spoke again. "MJ is in danger. She must not be alone, Mr. Thornton. If she collapses again, she may die. Despite what your moral compass tells you, it is important that you do not leave her tonight. She may laugh at being kissed awake by Prince Charming, but I think your kiss may be what lies between her and death. Keep her close."

He nodded. "I want to believe you, Miss Higgins. I would like nothing more than to have Miss Hale return with me – I love her."

"I know you do – I never saw you look at another woman like you look at her. Remember, I know how the women of Milton were after you – all of the eligible gentry and a fair few in the lower classes. Now, go and stay with her."

"Goodnight, Miss Higgins, and thank you," he said, opening the door for her.

"Goodnight, Mr. Thornton."

He returned swiftly to Miss Hale's bedroom. She was leant back against the pillows, her eyes closed.

"Miss Hale?" he said, worried that she had become unconscious again.

"It is all right, I am awake. What did you and Bessy talk about at the door?"

"She said I was not to leave you alone."

"She didn't tell you to persuade me to go with you when you leave?"

"No, Miss Hale. And if she had, I would not do that. Only you can decide if you think what she says is true."

"I don't know what to believe, really. It is strange; even before she said anything, I had the oddest sensation about the kiss – as though it were the kiss of life."

"I didn't think that. I just thought that if it was to be the only time we were to kiss, I wanted to remember every detail of it."

"Is it to be the only time we are to kiss?"

"I don't know – I hope not, but the decision has to be yours, Miss Hale."

"Margaret. When I woke, you were calling me Margaret. If I am to be your wife, Mr. Thornton, you must call me Margaret."

"And are you to be my wife, Margaret?"

"I am still not certain. I am very much of my time. No matter how much I love and know about your time, nothing can prepare me for it, and then I have to forget all I know about my own time." She looked at him, standing so quietly, listening to what she said. It was obvious he wanted to beg her to go with him, but he would not voice what he wanted, of that she was certain. He was an honourable man; in his eyes, the decision had to be hers.

"Perhaps if you were to kiss me again, it would help me make my decision." She patted the bed as she spoke. "Come here, Mr. Thornton – John."

He should have been shocked by her boldness, but instead he was bewitched. "Does this mean you are coming home with me?" he said, lowering himself to her side on the bed.

"Kiss me and then I will tell you."

This kiss was different from the first they had shared, more urgent. If the first had warmed her, this inflamed her. Who would have thought that behind his dignified Victorian image lurked such passion?

"Margaret, my Margaret – please say you will return with me, for you are the other part of me and I cannot live without you."

"If you promise to stay with me tonight, in my world and my time, then I will come with you to yours when you return."

"You mean lie with you in the same bed."

"I do. I need to feel your arms around me. I need to sink into your embrace. I need to be touched by you and in turn be free to touch you."

His mouth went dry at her words. "You wish me to love you – in the most complete way."

She smiled. She would never tire of his strange way of phrasing things. "Yes, John, I want you to make love to me. I know when I return with you tomorrow that society will demand we are more circumspect. So I am asking for this one night."

How could he refuse her when she was giving up the life she knew? The answer was: he couldn't.

CHAPTER TEN

The first thing MJ noticed was the acrid smell of burnt timber and cotton, but there were no flames or smoke. They had not emerged in an inferno. Her eyes moved up towards the roof of this part of the mill. It had been completely destroyed, leaving what remained of the building open to the elements.

They both moved slowly about, surveying the destruction. As MJ walked among the ashes of the cotton bales, she noticed a small clay pipe, blackened with soot, on the floor. Picking it up, she wondered at its importance and was about to ask John's opinion when she saw his expression as he turned in a circle, taking in the damage.

"It can be rebuilt – it will be rebuilt," she said, walking towards him.

He nodded and squeezed her hand. "I know it will. We have made it back – just as Miss Higgins thought we would."

"Yes, we have."

Bessy had returned, as she said she would, that morning. When MJ told her she was going back with John, she had helped find clothing and an appropriate bag so that Margaret should look the part. She had gone with them to the mill and watched as they had walked through the large door to the cotton store. Had Bessy been tempted to return, Margaret wondered. Somehow, she thought not. In her bag was a letter to Nicholas Higgins, to be posted from some warm sunny place, explaining that Bessy was alive and well in a healthier climate. MJ had promised that she and John would travel abroad and post it so Nicholas would know she was well.

"Do you have any regrets, Margaret?" John asked.

"How could I? I have walked through the passage and am here, alive and well. I have to believe this is meant to be. Besides, I am with you – and I love you. I will need your help to adjust to my new life."

"You will be fine – after all, you are a student of this era."

"I suspect reality will be very different from books."

"I will be here at your side." He brought her hand to his lips as he spoke and brushed a kiss against them. "When we leave here, I will not be able to touch you as I wish – not before we are married."

"Best kiss me now, before we leave this place," she said, moving into his arms.

"I never thought I would say this, but you are wearing too many clothes. I cannot feel you as I could yesterday."

"It's the layers, women wear more here. This outfit weighs a ton."

Their kiss was brief, for they knew they must leave the dilapidated storeroom. They pushed the door open and peered cautiously into the mill yard. It was deserted. John pulled his watch from his pocket – eight p.m. – the shift had finished for the day. Taking her hand, he led her towards his home.

"Wait a moment, John. Do I look all right?"

"You look perfect. Please don't worry; when my mother realises that you have helped me, she will think the world of you."

They climbed the steps to the mansion house. "At this time of night, the door will be locked," John said, knocking on the door.

The door was opened by an astonished footman. "Mr. Thornton, sir – you're alive! We thought you had perished in the fire."

"No, I did not. Is my mother at home, Billings?"

"Yes sir, she has just finished dinner – some of the other mill owners are here...."

"Like vultures, they have come to circle the carcass of Marlborough Mills," John murmured to MJ. "We'll go up, Billings. Please be good enough to inform the rest of the staff that I have returned and am safe and well."

"Yes sir, I will."

"I hope your mother is of a strong constitution," MJ said. "The shock of seeing you will be enormous."

"My mother will cope; she is a formidable woman, as you will see."

MJ was not sure if she liked the sound of John's formidable mother, but she had no time to worry about meeting her as he was climbing the stairs.

"Mr. Thornton," she called out, remembering to use his surname as time and convention would expect. "You may want this." She held out the small clay pipe.

"Where did you find this?"

"In the cotton store; it was on the floor by a blackened cotton bale. It's evidence, isn't it?"

"It is."

At the top of the stairs, he paused outside the doors to the drawing room. "Are you ready, Miss Hale?"

"Yes, Mr. Thornton."

"Are you sure of the story that we are giving to explain my sudden reappearance?"

"Yes, I am."

Some events can best be described as conversation stoppers – and this, MJ thought as they walked into the Thorntons' drawing room, was one of them. The babble of conversation stopped immediately. A woman dressed entirely in black stared at them for a moment and swayed slightly. Then MJ saw her stiffen her spine before walking imperiously towards them.

"John, I knew you were not dead – but I must say I did not expect you to return with Miss Hale. I thought you had left Milton, Miss

Hale. After your father died, you returned to your family in London. Your last letter said you had settled in with your aunt, Mrs. Shaw. It explained that although Mr Bell had left you all his holdings, you had no intention of interfering with the running of Marlborough Mills."

MJ recovered first, thinking on her feet about how to explain her reappearance in Milton. "I had some other business in the area. I bumped into Mr. Thornton at the station and he told me about the fire and his suspicion that it was set deliberately – we have been to London to confirm that his misgivings about the fire were correct."

"You think the fire was arson," Hamper, one of the rival mill owners, said.

"I don't think it – I know it," John said, recovering quickly from the news that he had already met Margaret in his own time. "I was in the store when the fire started. A man called out to me – he said that I had been warned. He thought he had trapped me in the blaze, but I escaped."

He pulled the bell to summon a servant, and a maid appeared directly.

"Jane, please ask Billings to fetch a constable."

If the maid was surprised by the instruction, she did not show it.

When she had departed, John held out the clay pipe. "Miss Hale has just found this in the cotton store. With what we have discovered in London about the Lancashire Textile Company – I not only know who started the fire, but who he was working for."

"A clay pipe, Thornton. They're two a penny around here," Hamper said.

"That is true, but I believe when confronted with it and arrested for arson, the little rat will squeal. He will not want to be sent down alone – he will talk."

"Well, as this is family business, we should leave you to discuss it, Thornton," a small man said as he moved towards the door.

"What's your hurry, Slickson? You should stay. After all, this business involves you."

"Involves me? I don't see how."

"As the owner of the Lancashire Textile Company, you are planning to buy Marlborough Mills. You, Slickson, paid for my mill to be torched. You tried to steal Marlborough Mills from my father all those years ago. You didn't succeed then, and you won't now."

A knock on the door was followed by Billings entering with the police constable. "Thank you, Billings. Constable, I want this man arrested in connection with the fire. Tell Inspector Watson I will be along directly, and have some men pick up Harry Stephens for the same offense. He puts up in Mercy Street, I believe."

"Yes, Mr. Thornton," the constable said, for no member of the constabulary would argue with John Thornton, respected magistrate of the district. "Come this way, sir," he continued, placing handcuffs on Slickson.

"You will pay for this, Thornton! You have no proof, no proof whatsoever!"

"You will see that I do, Slickson. You cheated my father and caused his death. You will not do the same to me. Take him away." An uneasy silence descended on the room after the constable led Slickson away.

"We'd best take our leave, Thornton. You have a lot to be getting on with, I am sure," Hamper said, speaking for the other mill owners.

"Yes, we will meet as usual later this week, gentlemen."

When they had left the room, John turned to his mother. "I am sorry to have worried you so, but the inquiries I made had to be made in secret," he said, taking her hand.

Hannah looked at her son and Miss Hale. "I suspect that is not all that has happened in secret. Is Miss Hale back in Milton for good?"

John smiled and took his intended's hand. "Miss Hale has agreed to be my wife, Mother. I could not have got through the last week without her. It is my dearest wish that you should become friends."

Hannah Thornton looked at the woman whose arm her son had taken as he spoke. "We have had our differences. Miss Hale and I have little in common. But you are my son's choice, so I will put aside those differences for his sake."

MJ stared at the woman for a moment. It was odd speaking to somebody who obviously knew you, but of whom you had no recollection. She would have to choose her words carefully. "I can think of one thing we have in common, Mrs. Thornton – we both love your son. Surely that is a good starting point for our new relationship."

"Aye, there is truth in that. I had best go and send a note to Fanny, letting her know you are alive and well, John."

"Yes, Mother. I will see about some rooms at the Grand Hotel for Miss Hale. We plan to marry as soon as the banns are read – so you both best start planning a wedding."

"People will frown at the haste, John, but I'm sure that neither of you will be bothered by that."

"No, Mother. People can talk."

She left them alone.

"So Bessy Higgins was right, we had already met," MJ said.

"I don't understand how I do not remember you, but I am glad we have already met because it means I do not have to wait many months to marry you. Tell me you do not expect a long courtship."

"No, I do not, and a whirlwind marriage is a sign of romance. It seems as if you are marrying a woman of fortune, John – your dreams for the factory, the village, and workers can be realised."

"You would invest your money in those things, Margaret?"

"I would, John, I would. It is time to create your legacy, Mr. Thornton, and to ensure my survival in the future."

"Come, my Margaret, I will walk you to the hotel and then I will deal with Slickson. Tomorrow I will call on you first thing and we will speak to the vicar and arrange for the banns to be called. For only when we are married will I believe this is not a dream."

She nodded. "Only when we are wed will I return to this house. The next time I climb those steps, it will be as Mrs. John Thornton."

"Yes, my love," he said, savouring the sound of her name. "As Mrs. John Thornton."

KATE FORRESTER LIVES IN SHROPSHIRE, one of the most beautiful counties in Britain, with her family and other animals. She has worked as a nurse in the NHS for thirty years. About five years ago she stumbled across the c19 forum and was bitten by the writing bug. Since then she has written two novels Weathering the Storm and Degrees of Silence and is about to publish her third a Nightingale Sang.

KATE FORRESTER'S other books include: *A Nightingale Sang, Degrees of Silence, In the Shadow of the Games, The Best Things Happen While You're Dancing,* and *Weathering the Storm*

THE FIRST DAY OF SPRING

M. Liza Marte

"How was it that he haunted her imagination so persistently? What could it be?...What strong feeling had overtaken her at last?" - Chapter XXXV, North *and South*

⌐∾

*T*oday was the first day of spring, my favorite of all the seasons. The birds were singing, the flowers were in bloom, and the chill of winter was gone. It would have been a perfect day but Mr. Thornton was staying for tea.

"How wonderful such a busy man as John can stay for tea, Margaret, my dear," my Father mentioned yet again.

It was the second time he had made that announcement today. For the past few weeks I had been leery of Mr. John Thornton each time he came to our house to have his philosophical discussions with Father. Of course he was welcomed as Father considered him a good friend, but I was still uncomfortable. Neither Mr. Thornton nor I could forget he was a witness to my brother's presence here in Milton. He may not have said anything to expose him, but he saw.

"Yes, Father," I forced myself to answer him jovially, a pleasant smile fixed upon my face. I was determined to act as normal as possible so Father would never suspect anything was amiss. "I remember, but Dixon did not have the time to make any cakes."

It was true. Of late, our servant's many duties kept her quite busy, leaving me to do the occasional baking or shopping.

"You will have to purchase something at the bakery," Father added, his expression sporting a slight frown. He was dressed in his favorite black suit today, looking just like he used to at the vicarage.

"Worry not. I planned to purchase a butter cake at Fenton's," I told him. His frown disappeared. The smile that touched his lips expanded to his eyes, crinkling them at the corners.

I was glad Father was happy, even if his company was John Thornton. It had been two months now since Mr. Thornton was witness to Fred's midnight departure and the embrace he misunderstood. But it could not be helped. To expose the truth was to expose my dear brother and that I would not do.

On our last meeting, I marshalled my courage and told him I had a higher opinion of him than he did of me. Yet even with that disclosure, he looked disapprovingly at me.

So be it, I thought bitterly.

He drifted in and out of my thoughts as I walked towards the shops, passing a multitude of mill workers on the crowded streets. The large groups no longer frightened me like before and the men and women in turn eagerly parted as I walked among them, allowing me to pass. A few of the men tipped their tattered-looking caps at me. Many of the women wished me a good day.

The same cordial greeting was repeated at Mr. Fenton's bakery. His cheerful, bright disposition helped chase the dour thoughts of Mr. Thornton away.

"Good day, Miss Hale," Mr. Fenton exclaimed, his full, ruddy cheeks looking redder than usual today. A dusting of flour made his white apron even whiter. Only a smudge of what appeared to be raspberry jam broke the expanse of white color. "Can I interest you in the tarts? I added raisins to the apples to make them extra special."

"No, not today, Mr. Fenton, though they do look delightful. A butter cake will do."

"A very good choice, miss," he replied. He disappeared in the back room before I could say another word. As I waited for his return, Mr. Thornton popped into my thoughts once again. I sighed and felt a wave of guilt wash over me though I couldn't explain why. Perhaps it was because I kept thinking of him, while he, I believed, did not spare me a thought.

By the time Mr. Fenton returned with the cake and I paid, I began to feel anxious. The feeling came suddenly, like an unwanted suitor. I tried to hush the feeling to silence as I walked outdoors and the bright morning sun greeted me at the shop's entrance. A wave of warmth brushed over my cheeks, and I could feel my complexion turning pink at the contact. In the next second I smelled a sweet, floral fragrance. It overpowered the scent of freshly baked bread lingering behind me.

"Buy a flower, miss?" An elderly woman suddenly appeared at my side, seeming to materialize out of thin air. I was startled at first, but she looked so ordinary, so very similar to other vendors on the street that my surprise at her appearance quickly vanished.

Inside her basket I counted at least two dozen roses, mostly red, with a few pink blooms. But there was one flower that looked out of place among the roses. It was a single daffodil, its bright yellow color so vibrant that it overshadowed its companions. I hadn't intended to buy any flowers. They always seemed a waste of money for they only lasted a few days before dying but this time I pulled out a shilling, ready to purchase one.

"I would like the daffodil."

She did not take my money right away. Instead she studied me, her expression guarded. I felt she was searching my face for answers.

"Wouldn't the young lady care for a rose?" she asked as she reached in and lifted a red one.

I shook my head. "I prefer the daffodil. Today is the first day of spring." I extended my hand towards her, the shilling held between my fingers. "Daffodils are the perfect symbol for spring."

Perhaps she could sense my eagerness, for her face brightened in the next moment. I thought perhaps she would ask for another shilling, because I seemed so eager but she placed the red rose back in the basket and pulled out the daffodil.

"Take care, miss," she cautioned me, as she placed the bloom in my basket. "Daffodils are special."

All the way home, her words floated in my thoughts. They repeated several times over even as I entered through the back door and walked directly into the kitchen. I placed my purchases on the table, noting with a smile that Dixon had already started the preparation for tea. Cups and saucers were at the ready on the silver tray, which also contained a crystal bowl of sugar and a container for the milk. I unwrapped and placed the butter cake on a plate near the tray.

I ignored the other items I purchased and looked for the small flower vase Mother loved to use. It was small, good to hold just a single bloom. I could hear Father and Mr. Thornton talking as I passed by the study. I suppose I could have knocked on the door and announced my arrival, but instead of intruding on their conversation, I took my single daffodil and brought it to the living room where tea would be served.

It was surprising how quickly the single bloom brightened and lifted the drab colors in the room. Everything took on a glow, as though urged by the flower to reveal their true colors. Once more the flower vendor's cautious words filled my thoughts. *Be careful, miss.*

"Be careful of what?" I cried out loud. "What could she have meant?"

The sweet fragrance of the daffodil grew in abundance. At first I thought I was imagining it, but I could smell it everywhere; on my dress, in my hair, and on the curtains as I walked to the window and tried to open the glass pane. My head grew heavy and I felt dizzy. It became difficult to keep my eyes open. I needed fresh air. My lungs were filled with the sweet, floral scent. As I turned, I saw the yellow color of flower expanding. It looked for a second like a sunburst, sending out sparks in all directions.

Be careful, miss.

I heard the old woman's voice again as though she stood beside me. It was the last thing I recalled before the room grew black and I felt myself falling.

It was that same overly sweet, floral fragrance that pulled me out of the shadows. Groggily, I awoke. I sat up and rubbed my eyes. Then I repeated my actions as I looked around the room. The fear that gripped over my heart was strong.

I recognized the room I was in. It was the Thornton's sitting room in their house at Marlborough Mills. The question that rattled in my head was: *How did I get here?*

The windows were closed, but I could hear the mill workers and the hum of the machinery in the building next door. In a way it felt comforting but it still didn't explain what I was doing in Mr. Thornton's home.

I stood the moment I heard footsteps approaching. My movements were labored and shaky I gripped at the chair for support before looking down.

What I saw caused me to promptly fall down again. A million thoughts raced in my head, from shock to anger, to fear and sadness. I think I must have laughed, too.

I placed my hand at my belly... my very round, protruding belly... and felt movement beneath my fingers. As though burned by the contact I pulled away, placing the back of my hand against my forehead. The movement in my belly continued and I began to panic.

In the next moment a maid entered. I looked at her with such frightened eyes, that she nearly tripped over her feet in her haste to reach me.

"What happened, Mrs. Thornton? Did you fall? Shall I send for Mr. Thornton?" Every question she posed was tinged with true concern. I was angry that she dare call me Mrs. Thornton, but I did not admonish her for addressing me as the mistress of the house.

"Why am I here?" I asked instead. My voice sounded weak and weightless, as though I was starved for words. I knew I sounded confused. I could hear it myself. "I am with child!" I blurted out, stating the obvious.

This time it was she who reacted. She hastily tucked back a loose, blond curl that slipped free of the cap she wore. Her pale, blue eyes danced from left to right while looking at me, and then she turned towards the door as though expecting someone else to enter.

Mrs. Hannah Thornton entered as if on cue looking as stern and unbending as she always did. Strangely enough, she didn't look at all surprised to find me in her home. "Ah there you are, Margaret. John will join us shortly," she told me. She calmly took the seat across from me. "You may bring in the tea now, Susan," she instructed the maid all the while reaching for her needles and yarn.

"Ma'am, something is wrong," the young woman said. She hastily looked back at me, her expression severe, and her hands rubbing together signaling her worry.

"Has the new cook burned the biscuits again?" Mrs. Thornton replied wearily, not even bothering to look up. Her focus and attention remained on her work. "It will be the third time this week. I must speak to her if this continues," she added. She knitted what looked to be a tiny sock, a sock that a baby would wear.

"You are knitting baby clothes!" I exclaimed, and I slumped back in the chair.

Mrs. Thornton stopped her knitting at my outburst and looked up at me. Her sharp, dark eyes looked me over. I was sure the blood had drained from my face, and she must have noticed it.

Instead of rushing at me as I expected her to do, she slowly set aside her knitting and stood. She motioned to the maid, who moved to her side. They were whispering, seemingly unconcerned that I could see and hear them discussing me. After a few nods, Susan exited the room leaving the two of us alone.

"Were you able to rest after breakfast? The doctor said you should as your time draws nearer." She spoke carefully, as though she was trying not to startle me or scare me.

"Mrs. Thornton, I do not know how I can be with child!" I think I sounded like one for my voice felt as small and fearful as that of a child. "How did I get here? I was at home with Father and now I am here in your house." With each word, I felt myself sink further down into the chair until it had engulfed me within its large, leather lined arms.

She had smiled at my words at first, seemingly amused.

Suddenly the door burst open and her son walked hurriedly inside. Mr. John Thornton walked directly towards me and without saying a word, lifted me from the chair and gathered me in his arms.

I struggled against him. I pushed and pushed, uncaring how hurt he looked until he let go and I was free. "How dare you!" I angrily cried out. "I am a respectable lady, Mr. Thornton. This may be your home but you have no right to touch me like that!"

For a moment he looked pale with shock. His mother took hold of his arm, but he brushed her away and turned his attention back to me.

"I have all the rights a husband has, Mrs. Thornton," he replied with harsh tones but they were contradicted by the pain I saw in his eyes. Strangely enough I felt as though this had happened before, dozens of times, where I had rejected and hurt him. His manner and tone softened instantly.

I saw his mother touch his arm again and whisper a few words in his ear.

"I have sent for the doctor, John," she said in a low voice, but I still heard her.

My head hurt, and my eyes, my lips, and my ears all felt so sensitive I was afraid to touch them. I felt the movement in my belly again and placed my hand over the spot where I was sure my baby was kicking.

Two things hit me at once. The first was my acknowledgement that I was with child, my child. The other was seeing the wedding band on my ring finger.

"No, this can't be!" I softly uttered. "I am married!"

"Yes, you are," John quickly added. He moved until he was directly in front of me. It was too close! If he leaned forward, he would be rubbing against my belly. "We were married last year." He spoke as though revealing an unknown event. "Have you forgotten, my love?"

At the endearment, I grew scared again and took a hasty step back, bumping my legs against the chair behind me.

He would not be deterred and pressed forward. "We were married on the first day of spring when all the daffodils were in bloom."

DOCTOR DONALDSON RUBBED his hand across his forehead, and then over his lips. He certainly looked perplexed but he didn't appear worried. I was worried enough for everyone there.

Earlier, while everyone was discussing me, I had looked at my reflection in the mirror, trying to ascertain if this was really me. My hair was naturally wavy and dark, arranged the way I always wore my hair, styled into a loose bun. My complexion was pale, yet a hint of pink had returned to my cheeks.

Yes, I was looking at myself. There was no doubt about that.

I also couldn't argue that I was here in Mr. Thornton's home. Minutes earlier I had been brought to his bedroom. His mother had brought me here after I nearly fainted in the living room. I had tried to protest, but my pleas fell on deaf ears.

I refused to sit on his bed. Instead, I sat at the vanity and found several of my things arranged there. My brushes were placed side by side with an unfamiliar-looking comb. It must be his. Several silver hair combs that I inherited from my mother were also there. A small, crystal decanter filled with what smelled like lemon verbena was placed near a glass vase containing roses. It was my scent.

"I can't be his wife," a frightened voice inside me whispered. But everything I saw pointed to the fact that I was.

"Mrs. Thornton?" I heard Dr. Donaldson say behind me but I didn't answer him. "Mrs. Thornton?" he asked again, this time with more force. I looked up.

"I'm sorry, were you addressing me?" I asked him in return. My heart told me to listen.

He gave me a forced-looking smile. Behind him, Mrs. Thornton and John were watching.

John. His name felt natural on my lips. It was when I addressed him formally that my tongue wanted to protest and go on strike.

"Yes, I was. I am inquiring if you rested after breakfast this morning."

I shook my head. "I'm afraid I don't know." I answered him truthfully.

"Hmm…," he muttered. His gray streaked eyebrows drew together, accentuating his frown. "And what of lunch? Did you have broth with vegetables as I suggested?"

"I don't know. I don't remember." It was true. I didn't know.

Mrs. Thornton came forward then. "I can answer that, Doctor. My daughter-in-law did not want her lunch."

"What?" John cried in a thunderous voice. "You should not be missing meals. You must have the broth now!" he ordered.

I straightened up in my seat, ready to defy him.

"You do not tell me what to do, Mr. Thornton!" I replied angrily. "I shall go home now and speak to my father about all this. You will answer to him, sir," I threatened.

With renewed strength I stood, ready to march out of the room. But his next words stopped me cold.

"Margaret, dearest… your father… Mr. Hale passed away almost a year and a half ago."

His words cut at my heart. I grew angry with him. I wanted to beat this man, I wanted to hurt him with my fists, to kick him with my legs so he would feel the same pain I now felt in my heart.

"How could you say such a horrible thing?" I cried out in anguish. "That is so cruel of you! And to think my father speaks so highly of you!"

My father was not dead. I was just with him this morning. He asked me to buy a butter cake. He was at home in his study reading, waiting for his tea.

"Margaret… my love…" he said softly now, his voice laced with sadness. "Your father is gone. This is your home."

He tried to reach for me but I moved out and away from him. I almost made it to the door when it opened and Dixon came in.

"Thank goodness! Dixon!" I cried. Our long-time servant brought a sense of familiarity with her presence. "Tell them! Tell them Father isn't dead. He is waiting at home for his tea. We must go home, Dixon! I don't know why we are here!"

Instead of doing what I asked, she just stood there looking at me.

"Ma'am, I cannot. I need to… bring your lunch," she uttered.

She left before I could reprimand her. When I turned, the others all looked at me with worried eyes: Mrs. Thornton, Dr. Donaldson, and John.

The room felt so crowded. I ran to a window to open it, hoping the fresh air would soothe and slow the fear growing inside of me. I took a deep breath. The air outside was laced with tiny fluffs of cotton. The voices of the mill workers were so numerous they overlapped, making it difficult to make out a solitary voice. The ordinary sights and sounds did nothing to alleviate my fears.

"Margaret, dearest, please come and have a rest," John said, his voice strangely calm.

"Yes, my dear," Dr. Donaldson added. "We shall have lunch brought up now," he said. He motioned to Mrs. Thornton, who quickly nodded and reached for the bell to call Dixon. "There's no need to worry yourself. A good lunch and rest afterwards will help make things right again."

I let them lead me to the bed. I sat at the edge listening to my rapidly beating heart. I knew the three were watching me, speaking in hushed words that I couldn't hear, unlike before.

Someone knocked at the door and I heard a female voice. It was either Susan, or another servant. I didn't bother to turn around and look. I remembered the Thorntons had several maids. Mrs. Thornton gave her orders to bring my lunch.

She and Doctor Donaldson stayed only a moment before leaving as well. Only John was in the room with me now.

I would not look at him. I knew he looked at me. I could feel his eyes watching my every move. He wasn't saying anything. After a time he appeared at my side. I kept my gaze cast down. For a second I thought I heard his sigh. He would not sway me. I resolved to harden my heart.

Instead of speaking he leaned down and placed a kiss on my forehead. It was the only part of my face he could reach. Then he turned and quietly went through the door.

After he left me alone, I remained where I was for several minutes, just listening to my own breathing and the noise from the mill. At the sound of muffled voices in the hallway, I got off the bed and moved to the door. I opened it a crack and saw the three of them standing there, discussing me.

Dr. Donaldson rubbed his chin, stroking the stubble of gray hairs. "I have seen young mothers become so scared they act in a strange manner. But I admit, I have never seen memory loss as a side effect," he told the two.

"What can we do, Doctor?" Mrs. Thornton asked him. I saw the concern in her eyes. She gripped her hands tightly in front of her obviously worried. I had never seen that before. Mrs. Thornton had always seemed so unflappable.

With a shake of his head, it seemed the doctor was chasing away any dour thoughts cluttering his thinking. His expression had been grave but now looked to brighten. John was the only one whose face I could not see. He stood with his back facing me.

"I believe, with lots of rest and constant reassurance, that all will be well. It is probably just fear of the impending birth." He fixed John with a stern stare. "And it's best under the circumstances not to cause unnecessary worry... of any kind."

Whatever John said in response was lost.

Dixon chose that moment to return. She walked up the stairs carrying a tray. I could almost smell the broth where I was standing. Her destination was the room I was in. Quickly, so as not to be caught spying, I closed the door and hurried back to the bed.

"Here we are," she said cheerfully as she entered. The broth did smell appetizing and I could also detect the aroma of newly baked bread. My stomach grumbled accordingly, but I wasn't ready to eat.

"Dixon?"

"Yes, Ma'am," she replied as she placed everything on the table by the window. She motioned when everything was arranged and remained standing, hands clasped together, waiting for me to sit and eat.

I did as I was bid, I sat at the pulled chair but instead of eating, I turned to her and motioned with a flick of my wrist that she should sit in the other chair. She followed my order easily, wordlessly, which struck me as strange. The Dixon I knew always had something to say, be it pleasant or not.

"Eat, Ma'am, before it turns cold."

"I will eat, but only after my questions are answered," I informed her using my authoritative tone of voice.

"Now there is no need to worry yourself, Ma'am. Tis the baby you should be thinking of," she coaxed, hoping I would comply. "Why Cook made the broth especially for you with bits of ham and carrots."

"I am sure the broth is delicious." I watched as she pushed the bowl closer to me, taking care not to spill the contents. She buttered one piece of bread and perched it on the rim. Dixon brushed off the crumbs from her fingers and wiped them on the apron she wore before standing. Her next destination was the bed. Without being ordered, she pulled down the covers and arranged the pillows. I guess this meant I was to have a nap after eating.

"Is it true?" I asked her, interrupting her work.

"Is what true?"

I steadied my breath, and then let out it in one long exhale. "Is Father dead?"

I saw her hesitate, inwardly sorting out the conflict of whether to say the truth and unsettle me or give a white lie and keep things cheerful.

"Tell me. Hold nothing back," I pushed her to answer.

"Ma'am, you know he passed fifteen months ago. After the mistress, your gentle mother died, he was never the same."

She wasn't lying to me. I knew she wasn't. But how did this all come to pass? A few hours ago I was in my home. I was helping to prepare the tea. I even heard Father lecture and instruct Mr. Thornton in philosophy inside his study. How did I go from there to here?

"I know you are telling me the truth, but I do not remember any of it. I do not remember Father dying. I do not remember marrying Mr. Thornton. When did I fall in love with him?"

At that she smiled, her lips stretching and her dimples in full display. I couldn't recall Dixon ever looking this happy before.

"You told me when, Ma'am." She looked so happy, so ridiculously cheerful I almost couldn't bear to look at her. "It was during the spring. The master and Mr. Hale had been in your Father's study, discussing all those books as they always did on Tuesdays. When they came out for tea, you two and Mr. Thornton were left alone for several minutes. I cannot recall now why exactly you asked him, but you did. You told me you invited him to dinner and he accepted your invitation."

"I invited him?" I asked, incredulous at the notion. I couldn't imagine why I would have done so. In the weeks since he had seen Fred and me at the station, Mr. Thornton barely spoke to me. He looked at me with such disapproval, I felt guilty. Even after I learned he had dissuaded the constable from seeking further into the matter, I still could not approach him. "Why would I invite him? Why did I do that?" I asked aloud.

FOR THE NEXT TWO DAYS, I barely left the bedroom except to join the others at dinner. John and Mrs. Thornton were all politeness, always inquiring after my health and appetite but hearing the same kind inquiries grew tiresome. It was strange how I now addressed him as John. My head was quick to remind me he was my husband, but I continued to fight against it.

His brilliant, blue eyes followed my every movement. No matter which way I turned I saw the hint of blue flash within my line of sight, reminding me he was near and attuned to my presence.

Dr. Donaldson had said I was just scared and unprepared for motherhood. It was a common reaction for a new mother he declared. As I result I became easily flustered. He reasoned that I would eventually come to terms with the way things were. For now, I was to be made comfortable, else my fragile condition would grow worse, and we could not chance that so near my time.

When I came down to dinner on the third night, John held the chair out for me, just as he had the previous two nights. This time however, his fingers lightly brushed against the nape of my neck, and he lingered by my side. His mother cleared her throat and he took his seat.

"Are you feeling better tonight, Margaret, dear?" Mrs. Thornton asked just as the first course of soup was served. "You look well. You do not look as pale."

"I am quite well, Ma'am," I answered. She gave me a look after the very formal address. I had no idea if I had started calling her Mother after the wedding. Perhaps I had and she expected I would resume.

"Hmm," she spoke softly, her voice low. Her expression revealed her worry. Three days had passed but nothing had really changed. I still remembered nothing.

I saw John open his mouth to speak, but he quickly closed it. His eyes were cast down and for the first time I could not see how blue they were. Dinner continued in almost complete silence. The only sounds were of the utensils being used. Voices from the outside drifted in, filling in the long gaps of quiet, but those inside were still.

By the time the excruciatingly long meal was over, I needed to run back to the safe haven of the bedroom. I excused myself and tried to leave without looking at John's fallen expression before rushing out the door. I failed. I suppose I was being a coward, but I couldn't stop myself.

I almost made it to the top of the stairs when I heard his voice.

It was strange how easily I could distinguish John's voice from anyone else's. It drifted from out of the open doors of the dining room and called to me, drawing me back so that I turned and descended the stairs. Outside the open doors, I stood, listening to their private conversation. Mrs. Thornton spoke here and there, but it was John who did most of the talking.

"Mother, she hates me!" he cried in anguish. A wave of guilt struck me and I almost rushed in to tell him that was not true. I didn't hate him. I didn't know *what* I felt.

"She does not hate you," his mother said in my defense. "She is going through a difficult time."

"Why is it that she does not remember being married? I do not understand! My wife can barely stand being in the same room with me."

"I'm sorry. I have no answers," she told him.

There was a moment of silence that followed. I moved a little, trying to get close enough to see them but not be seen. I peered through an opening between the door jam and wall. I saw Mrs. Thornton soothing her son, rubbing at his arm, showering him with motherly love, but John could not be placated.

"I must do something! I can't stand by and let her drift further away from me. We already sleep in separate rooms. But what can I do?"

"Give her more time," his mother advised. "Margaret has gone through a great deal of tragedy, and it was not so long ago. She must miss her parents terribly and wish they were here now that she is to have a child."

Could that be it, I thought? What Mrs. Thornton was saying made sense. I did not realize she was astute enough to see this or acknowledge it.

"Yes, that is true," John admitted, holding back tears I saw forming in his eyes. A big part of me wanted to wipe them away. "Mr. Hale had been gone only four months before we married. Her aunt in London was aghast we married before the year of mourning ended, but neither of us wanted to wait."

We did not wait? What would Father have thought? I know John would have wanted whatever made me happy, but not waiting seemed improper. Could I have been that in love with him?

I did not stay. In my haste to be alone, I walked quickly up the stairs and returned to the bedroom. When Dixon came to help me undress and prepare for bed, I was still thinking of Father, of what he would have said about my marriage.

"Dixon?"

"Yes, Ma'am," she answered. She undid the buttons on my dress and helped me out of it as well as the many layers of clothing beneath. She handed me my night garment next. I also needed help putting it on.

"Where is Father buried? Is he with Mother?"

Yes, of course he must be.

Her coloring altered at that. Her face grew pale, and then her cheeks turned deep pink. She started fussing with my hair instead of answering.

"Dixon?"

"No he is not, Ma'am," she finally replied. She held my brushes in her hand, ready to brush out my curls.

"What do you mean? Of course he is with Mother!" What was she saying? That Father was not buried with his beloved wife? What nonsense!

"Ma'am, he is buried in Oxford." Her voice sounded faint and weak then, as though she was ill. "Do you truly not remember?"

When I shook my head, she sighed deeply, motioning for me to sit.

"Your Father was on holiday visiting Mr. Bell. He was able to meet with so many of his old friends and reminisce about their youth." Her eyes grew sadder still as she related the rest. "He was in such good spirits. The visit had done him a world of good and he wrote often to tell you all the news. Mr. Bell came here just after your Father passed away. He told you Mr. Hale died peacefully in his sleep and that you were in his thoughts to the very end."

"Oh!" I uttered.

What else could I say? Father was buried in Oxford. I could not visit him. I had thought to do just that tomorrow, but now my idea felt foolish.

"And what of our house on Crampton Road?" I asked. "I would not have stayed there alone?"

"No, Ma'am. Your aunt came to take you to London to live with her." She smiled at that memory. I looked at her, perplexed by the sudden change of mood.

"I do not understand why you are smiling, Dixon."

"Tis just that Mr. Thornton told your Aunt Shaw you two were getting married. You were not going anywhere, not without him of course. Your aunt was not happy at all to hear that!"

"But I could not have married John so soon after. The banns would not have been read yet!" I proclaimed.

"That is true. Mr. Thornton and your aunt were in deep discussion for two hours before he agreed you would live in London until a reasonable amount of time passed and you could be married. The banns were read during your stay in London. You purchased your wedding garments and trousseau there."

Hearing this, I felt treasured. I had never suspected the depth of John's feelings for me. But I must have wanted it as well.

"Had I wanted to wait, do you believe he would have waited?" I asked her, confident in my assumption.

Dixon quickly nodded. "Yes. He would have done whatever you wanted, but you did not want to wait."

I do not know how I managed to sleep that night. I dreamt of John, of Mother, and of Father. I even dreamt of our home in Crampton. In my dreams I was still living there and all this was the real dream.

I awoke the next morning wondering who was living in our Crampton home now. The more I thought of it, the more determined I was to go and see for myself if a new family lived there.

After breakfast, I made preparations to go. Dixon tried to stop me insisting I was not well enough yet to go outdoors. When that plea fell on deaf ears she said it would not be good for the baby and that I needed to stay at home and rest. But I would not be swayed.

I waited until John and Mrs. Thornton were fully occupied at the mill. The morning hours looked to be the heaviest in workload.

Dixon stayed at my side; she refused to let me go alone. She unwillingly procured a cab and we went to Crampton. We passed Hamper's mill on the way. The cab traveled down the narrow streets. Seeing Fenton's bakery and smelling freshly baked butter cakes I firmly believed this charade would soon end. It mattered not that my baby kicked at my sides, exclaiming its frustration at being jostled about.

By the time we arrived at Crampton, my confidence that this ruse would be over evaporated. The house was still there but now it was a different color. From out of the front door a stranger in a dark suit with thick side burns emerged. He was followed by a small girl who insisted on one last kiss before being pulled back inside by a servant. I looked up at the same time the man did to see a woman in a second floor window waving goodbye.

Dixon touched a shaky hand to my shoulder, ordering the carriage to drive away.

I couldn't cry. I was too shocked. The truth was staring me in the face.

This was no dream. I no longer lived here. Father and Mother were both dead. I was Mrs. John Thornton and I lived at Marlborough Mills. I was going to have a baby... John's baby. I was.

JOHN WAS furious when he learned of my excursion. I didn't blame him. In his place I would have been angry, too. I had been sitting in the parlor having tea. It was one of the few rooms on the ground floor that did not face the mill and as such, the outside noises could not be heard. It was quiet and peaceful there. I liked the room immensely for it was decorated in pink, cream, and brown, my favorite colors.

Tea had just been served when my husband came through the double doors and marched towards me. It didn't strike me until much later in the day that I should have been wary, but I wasn't.

John spent a good minute glowering down on me. I could see he was trying to control his temper. His lips were so tightly pressed together they appeared as a thin line. He wore only his black vest over his white cotton shirt, the sleeves folded up and stopping just below his elbows. Several tiny fluffs of cotton floated around him. I expected in his haste to return to the house, he had left his coat in his office.

"Why did you go there?' he demanded, his temper still high. His voice was low and deadly calm.

"Who told you I went?" I asked in return, my voice raised.

"Does it matter?" he questioned. His eyes pierced me with such intensity, I should have been branded blue. "Going there always distresses you!"

"What do you mean?"

"My love, you told me your heart breaks each time you tried going there. Why torture yourself, especially now?

I automatically stiffened at the endearment. It was not lost on John. I saw him reach out with a hand only to pull back when I shifted away from him in my seat.

"I had to see," I told him. "I had to be certain this wasn't a dream."

"What are you saying, Margaret?" He shook his head, his expression incredulous. "I do not understand."

"No, you do not!" I countered. "All this, it cannot be real!" I emphasized by gesturing wildly with both hands. "Four days ago I was at home, at my home with Father. You were there, too, in his study, learning about Plato."

"My love, your Father has been dead these past fifteen months." He looked at me with such pity, I almost yelled at him to stop. "I know you miss him, but this is not helping you."

"No! It can't be! I don't know what's happening, but something is wrong. Something happened."

I tried to think again of that day. It began normally enough. I recalled that I had helped Dixon with washing the curtains. I even did the ironing and shopping.

"The doctor said you should not do things that would cause you undue worry. It is not good for you or the baby." His plea fell on my deaf ears.

At that I felt my child kick at my sides again. It was harder this time. I rubbed at the sore spot, trying to sooth the sudden ache I felt because the baby appeared to be fretting.

"What am I missing?" I asked myself. I ignored my husband who grew more worried at my words and behavior. "What else happened that day?"

When the baby kicked again, I stood and walked about the room. It helped. The movements lessened as though the child was tired and needed to rest.

"I remember I had to purchase a butter cake because Dixon did not have time to bake one." I faced John while reciting my steps and activity. "Yes! I went to Fenton's bakery. Mr. Fenton spoke about his apple and raisin tarts, but I told him I wanted a butter cake." I could feel my heart beating faster as the memories returned. "And I also purchased something else. What was it?"

I saw out of the corner of my eye that John had rung the bell for the maid. I supposed he wanted tea. As there was only one cup, he had nothing to use. I expected to see Susan at the doorway, but it was Dixon instead, coming in so quickly she must have been waiting for the summons. I spared them a brief glance. I was still trying to remember my other purchase.

Dixon moved to my side, her expression cheerful but stern. "Ma'am, let me help you to your room," she urged, ready to lead me away.

I saw John behind her waiting. He looked like he wanted to hold me, to carry me in his arms. It was strange how I could sense what he wanted merely by looking at him.

"I'm trying to remember… I purchased something else. What was it?" I kept going over and over in my thoughts what it was I bought after leaving Fenton's. I looked about the room, looking at things on the mantle and tables, hoping something would spark my memory to give up its secrets.

A beam of sunlight came in through an open curtain and shone on the mantle. I saw something twirling catch the light. From where I stood I could not see well enough to tell what it was. When Dixon moved to my side again, I finally remembered.

"It was a daffodil! I purchased a daffodil!" I excitedly told them.

Both John and Dixon looked cautiously back at me. I saw them give each other a look but neither said a word.

"There was something strange about that flower," I explained. "I remember bringing it home and looking for Mother's vase. The fragrance was so sweet it was cloying."

Yes, I was remembering it now. I had arrived home and passed briefly outside Father's study hearing him and John discussing Plato. I was looking for Mother's vase in the living room when the fragrance from the flower grew overpowering. I had felt dizzy and fainted.

Just like before, I smelled the sweet scent of daffodils in the room. I swayed in my steps. For a few seconds I looked at John, my eyes imploring him to listen, to believe me.

My head grew heavy. My neck felt like it couldn't support the weight. I blinked once. The second time my eyes would not open. I heard John call my name, but I could not answer. The last thing I felt was his strong arms as he caught me when I fell.

I DO NOT KNOW how long I slept. By the time I awoke it was dark outside and the household was silent. The only light came from the fire and a small candle. I thought I smelled food and then saw a tray left on the table near the foot of the bed. The contents were cold. The ham and vegetable soup must have been placed there hours ago.

I only managed a few bites before I pushed the plate away. It took me a moment to notice Dixon asleep in the chair by the door, looking very much like a sentry asleep on duty. She was snoring softly, her arms folded across her belly. I watched for a few seconds as it rose up and down. My heart told me it should have been John. Was he in his bed? I was scared to approach him. I knew he slept in the adjoining bedroom. I had heard him often the last couple of nights when he moved about.

It had to be him who had carried me here. Dixon must have helped me out of my clothes because I wore my night dress. Odd that I didn't wake until now. I summoned up my courage, opened the adjoining door, and looked in. The other bedroom was dark. My eyes adjusted quickly to the darkness. I could tell no one was in there.

Where was John?

I walked to the window and looked outside in my quest to seek some answers. The mill was dark except for light coming from John's office. I could just see him, with his back facing me, at his desk. He must still be working I reasoned. I was curious how much longer he would stay there.

I thought about waiting up for him, but my body would not obey. I felt tired, so very tired. Without bothering to wake Dixon, I just returned to bed. I blew out the candle and snuggled under the cool sheets.

I still remembered the daffodil.

Even as my eyes grew heavy again and drooped down I thought about the strange flower. I knew I had smelled its sweet fragrance in the parlor. Did it really change the course of my life? How could a flower bring me into the future? The last thought I had before sleep claimed me again was: *How could something so impossible happen?*

THE GLARE of the morning sun streaming in from the open curtains woke me from my slumber. Strange but I didn't remember dreaming. I recalled nothing, now that it was daytime.

My eyes took a quick turn around the room and I saw I was alone. Dixon was gone and the chair in which she had slept moved back to its place by the armoire.

I looked around again, but this time my eyes were riveted to the unusual looking twirling object at the window.

I had never seen anything like it before. Two extremely thin metal rods were joined at their center forming a cross shape. Four small, intricately carved, wood figurines in the shapes of roses were dangling from the ends of each rod. The carved pieces were so small, so delicate that it must have taken days to carve each one. Several pieces of wood, so thin they could almost pass for paper were arranged in a circular fan pattern between the rods. In the very center was a tiny metal shaped cone. The entire thing was perched on a long and very thin vertical rod attached to a candle holder. The rising heat from the lit candle made the rods spin by pushing at the fan pattern. I thought the wood pieces would burn but they didn't. It reminded me of a merry-go-round or an upright windmill. I remembered seeing the miniature of a windmill at the Royal Exhibition in London.

For several minutes I watched it spin, its pace leisurely. I was amused and enchanted.

"I just finished it this morning."

John had walked into the room so quietly I did not know he had entered until he spoke. I let out a surprised gasp seeing him. I couldn't help myself. It was difficult not to be startled.

"You made this?" I asked, incredulous that he had the skill and patience to create such an intricate piece.

"Yes," he answered. He did not appear angry or perturbed at my question. His manner and tone of voice was matter of fact. "You mentioned you wanted one with flowers. It took longer to carve, but it is what you wanted."

My heart skipped a beat knowing he had done this for me. It was the sweetest gift I ever received.

When John moved closer to where I lay on the bed, I looked to his hands. There were several small nicks and cuts on his fingers, most probably attained from the long hours and days of carving.

How strange that I only just noticed this.

He mentioned that he was still working on one for the baby and promised it would be finished before our child was born, even if he had to work during the nights to finish. I was so touched at this news, I did not say anything when he sat on the bed. For several minutes we both watched his wood carvings twirl around and around, the shadow of the flowers strewn across the walls.

I was so engrossed by the very pretty display that I did not notice my husband moving closer and closer. By the time he was at my side he was close enough to touch me. John started with my hand, placing his on top, letting me feel its weight. The warmth was so soothing, I felt no fear. He grew bolder when I did not pull away.

"Margaret, dearest." He leaned forward, his face mere inches from mine. I could feel his breath on my lips. Just as his hand warmed mine, his breath removed the chill I felt in the air. His warm breath was all I could feel as I stared deeply into his eyes and became lost in their gaze.

I could not help my reaction. Unwittingly I wet my lips, preparing them for the kiss I knew would follow. It was invitation enough for John.

His kiss was slow, soft. He leaned slightly forward, not hurrying me, but letting me become accustomed to the feel of him. For the first time since I found myself here in his home, I did not pull away.

I do not know how long we kissed. I only know I let it continue. I enjoyed the feel of him, the taste of him. John slanted his lips over mine, covering me, his tongue making small attempts to tease mine.

I almost gave in but then he gathered me in his arms. I suddenly felt trapped, the euphoric feelings abruptly stripped away.

"No!" I cried out, yanking his arms down. "Stop it!"

John reacted as though I had slapped him. His stunned expression slashed at me, making me hurt as much as he.

I felt such remorse at my reaction. This man was my husband. Though I did not remember, I should have welcomed his attentions, perhaps sought them. However I could not help my instinctive response, nor take it back.

I wanted to tell him I was sorry, that I was not trying to hurt him. But John had already pulled away. He stood, his eyes averted. I did not have to see them to know they were filled with pain.

"I will leave you to rest," he said, not even looking at me. With his shoulders swooped down, he looked like a beaten man. "I will not disturb you."

"Will I see you at dinner?" I hurriedly inquired after him. He walked so quickly, he was already at the door when I asked.

For just a moment I saw him turn and look back at me. His head was in profile. I could only see half his face. I thought he would say something, but he shook his head instead and walked out of the room, closing the door behind him.

I wanted him to answer me. I thought if only I heard his voice, it might lessen the horrible guilt I felt. I could not stop staring at the closed door. I had almost slapped him, but now, it felt that I was the one who had been slapped.

~

NEARLY EVERY ROOM had a carved wooden, twirling fan. I do not know how it escaped my notice before. Each one was a little different. Some of the dangling carvings depicted animals, one was of boats, and another looked like carved coins. Each was unique and they were all made by John.

I spent the rest of the day looking at them, lighting the candles and watching them spin. It made me wonder what kind of carvings John would make for the baby.

I would have a long wait to discover the answer.

My husband did not join us for dinner. I felt such remorse when I saw his empty seat and unused table setting.

His mother said nothing to me apart from inquiring after my health and making sure I was getting enough rest. The staff followed her lead and kept a round-the-clock watch over me. They walked on egg shells, having been ordered not to alarm me, anger me, or make me overly excited. It grew tedious very quickly.

By the time I went upstairs to sleep, I was frustrated and anxious. Not even Dixon's incessant muttering could calm my nerves. I checked the adjoining bedroom, but John was not there. I could see he was at his office, hunched over his desk working late into the night. I watched him from the bedroom window.

At first, I assumed he was working on mill business. It was only after he stood to stretch tired muscles and walked away from his desk that I saw there were no papers but a pile of wood shavings and different sized knives.

The strongest urge to walk over there and see what he was carving for the baby consumed me. I almost couldn't stand the wait. As much as I wanted to see, I stayed where I was. I feared John would not be welcoming, considering how I had rejected him this morning.

I felt I had to do something. For whatever reason the fates had placed me here, I was here, and by all accounts, I was married to John. I had hurt him by rejecting him, and, in turn, had hurt myself. I did not have any answers, but I needed to make things right. I couldn't bear to see the hurt in his eyes again.

I certainly did not choose to come here, but I would decide what happened next.

OUR COOK DID NOT SEEM ALL that surprised when I walked into the kitchen bright and early the next morning and told her I was making breakfast for my husband. It made me think that perhaps this had happened before and was a common occurrence.

I did not expand on my reasons but quickly went to work, making fried eggs and ham. I toasted slices of bread in the fire and added cheese. There was a basket of apples and I took two and cut them into quarters. Last, I filled a bowl with porridge and placed everything on a tray.

I was smiling down, happy with myself when I realized there was no room on the tray for the tea pot. I expected John had one in his office.

I made it just outside when one of the mill workers saw me struggling with the tray. It was a young girl, barely out of childhood but hearty and strong. She took hold of the tray and inclined with her head that I should lead the way.

By the time we made it to the mill office, she was red in the face and her arms shook. I was truly surprised the child made it this far for it was quite a journey carrying a tray which probably was a quarter of her weight.

"Thank you…?" I inquired as I did not know her name.

"Sara, Mrs. Thornton," she answered. She lifted up the tray, not spilling anything, onto the side board and curtsied. "If you will excuse me, I need to return to the machines."

"Yes, go on."

She was gone before I could say anything more. I did struggle a bit carrying the tray to John's office. It was one floor up. I walked slower than I ever did in my life as I carefully kept the tray balanced while taking the steps at a snail's pace.

John did not acknowledge my presence until I was almost at his desk. He had not looked up when I first entered the room. I expect he thought I was a worker and chose to make me wait. When he did look up, his reaction was loud and angry.

"Margaret!" He quickly seized the tray from me, putting it down with a loud thud on his desk. "That is far too heavy for you to carry!" he grumbled and he fixed me with a hard stare.

He looked angry but there was a sparkle in his eye which gave his true feelings away. He glanced back and forth several times, from the tray to my dress and the spots of food stains that showed who it was who prepared the food. I could tell he wanted to smile, but that he held his emotions in check.

"You were not at breakfast, John." I chanced a look at him and instantly his expression brightened. I could not tell if it was because I addressed him by name, or that I noticed he was not at breakfast. If he was still hurt from my rejection yesterday, it was not showing today.

"I started work early," he explained. He quickly turned the conversation to be about me. "But you have not eaten."

"No," I answered, and I sat in the chair he pulled out for me. "I thought perhaps we could have breakfast together."

Such a simple statement, but it rendered him speechless. His incredulous expression made me smile. It struck me that I had seen John look that way before. I wanted to ask if he recalled a similar circumstance but his hunger took precedence. Any answer he could have given would have to wait.

If I had not taken the first piece of bread and cheese, I believe I would not have had anything to eat at all. John ate like a man starved, which he probably was since he was not at dinner last night or at breakfast this morning. I had doubts he had eaten at all. He certainly was making up for it now. Rather than chastise him for eating nearly everything, I just enjoyed the sight of him eating.

It was true. I did enjoy it. I enjoyed just being with him even if all I did was watch him eat. When did that happen?

He caught me, with a silly grin on my face as I mused about my feelings.

Suddenly our child started kicking, more than usual, acting as excited as I felt. As I sat up in the chair, I could actually see my belly move. It did not hurt, and when I looked to John to tell him so, I saw he was staring. He wanted so much to touch me there. The longing in his eyes was all consuming. He barely looked like he was breathing.

Without saying a word I took his hand and placed it over where our baby was the most active. The warmth of his touch burned through my layers of clothing. I felt him and his touch soothed the child growing inside of me. Neither of us spoke. We looked at each other, the silent message conveyed through our eyes and our smiles.

I do not recall how long we stayed that way. Perhaps it was several minutes; or maybe it was mere seconds, but in that moment, I felt incredible peace. It was the most wonderful feeling in the world. In that moment I finally understood and accepted that I was Mrs. John Thornton.

I wanted to tell John this but the sweet, cloying floral fragrance suddenly filled the room and stopped me. I recognized the scent. I had smelled it before the day I left Fenton's bakery, on the first day of spring.

A streak of yellow dashed across my line of sight. I looked to the window and saw it; a single daffodil in a glass vase absorbing the rays of sunlight. The office had been dim before but now there was so much light I felt blinded.

"John, the flower?" I asked him. I tried to point but failed.

I grew dizzy again. My head felt heavy and my movement grew sluggish. I stood but my legs would not support my weight. My husband was there and took me in his arms, supporting me but all I could think of was the flower.

"What is it doing here?" I asked him. My voice sounded lost, as though it was stolen and I heard it only through an echo.

"Margaret, dearest, what flower? There are no flowers!"

I heard him speaking but I could no longer see. It seemed as though the ground opened up ready to swallow me, and still I could smell it. The sweet scent followed me all the way until I surrendered to my fate and let myself be taken.

THE MOMENT I awoke I knew I was home, not at Marlborough Mills, but Crampton, my old home. I was lying on the carpet, my face touching the coarse fiber. It left small scratches upon my cheek.

I sat up and rubbed at my eyes, then looked down at my belly. It was not round and protruding but flat. There was no baby.

I looked at my hand next. All my fingers were bare. I wore no wedding band because I was not married.

I do not know how long I sat on the carpet, trying to make sense of what had happened. It felt like I was sitting for over an hour. Once again I was confused, wondering how I had traveled while remaining in the same time and place.

As the clock on the mantle struck three, I made myself stand. It was time for tea. There was no tea service yet in the room; no tray or cups; but it wouldn't be long before Dixon brought them in. I almost pulled at the cord to summon her when I saw the vase I had been looking for on the window sill. It was out in plain view. How strange that I couldn't find it before.

The daffodil was not in the vase. I looked around, searching the carpet near where I had fallen, and still I could not see it. I looked under the chairs and table, but there was nothing. I did not imagine buying it. Even now, I could smell a faint trace of the floral fragrance, but it was quickly disappearing. Within seconds, there was nothing left, no evidence it ever existed.

Dixon came bustling in and in her arms she carried a silver tray which held a tea pot, sugar bowl, a creamer, three cups, and saucers.

"Ah, there you are, Miss Margaret," she exclaimed as she put the tray down and moved its contents to the table. "Thank you for getting the butter cake. I did make some sandwiches, but the master always likes butter cake."

I did not answer. I sat in the nearest chair and remembered everything. I remembered in full and precise detail what had happened when I left to buy the butter cake and daffodil. It was as clear as water and not once did my memory feel muddled. I especially recalled the last five days at Marlborough Mills, which in reality never happened.

"Are Father and Mr. Thornton still in his study?" I asked feeling and sounding remarkably calm.

"Yes, but they should be coming out for tea soon," Dixon explained. "I will return in a minute with the cake and sandwiches, miss."

I saw she had arranged everything else on the table. All that was left was for me to pour. As though they knew the tea was ready, the men came in the room seconds later and sat at the chairs around the table. I saw John watching me, and then quickly glancing away when he met my gaze. He seemed almost nervous, as though he wasn't accustomed to being observed.

I served Father first and waited as he used my fingers instead of the tongs to get his sugar. John looked longingly at us and I wondered if I would ever do the same for him. I offered the sugar to him next and he hesitated just a moment before taking hold of the silver tongs.

As close as he was, I was able to see several nicks and cuts on his fingers. I felt myself tremble! I knew how he obtained those injuries! There was the proof that something had happened. I wanted desperately to ask how he came about acquiring the cuts so I could confirm the truth. I chanced a look at Father, but he was busy enjoying his tea. Dixon chose that moment to return with the butter cake and sandwiches.

"Thank you, Dixon," Father said, reaching for the first slice of cake.

He served himself, eating his sandwiches heartily. John took a few sandwiches and chewed slowly. He kept his eyes averted but I could tell he was stealing glances. He was strangely silent.

Dixon looked the table over. Seeing that everything was in place, she left us to enjoy our tea.

"John, help yourself to the butter cake. Margaret bought it fresh this morning," Father explained.

Suddenly, he got to his feet. "Dear me, how forgetful I've become! I forgot that volume of essays in my study." He set his plate down on the table and brushed the crumbs from his lap as he stood and smiled at the two of us. He walked towards the door, not waiting for any kind of response. "Let me get that book before I forget again. I won't be a moment," he told us; and then he walked out.

We were alone. I had no idea how long Father would be away. I expected just a minute or two.

I looked to John's hands again. The nicks and cuts were still there. I knew these injuries were the result of his carvings. The longer I studied his hands, the more I found myself thinking of those five days we spent together.

I remembered expressions that crossed his face during that time. I had seen misery, despair, anger, eagerness, sadness, and ultimately happiness when I brought him his breakfast. I could not forget how the simple act of making his meal brought him immense joy.

I wanted John to feel that again. I wanted to leave him without any doubt about where my affections lay. With my heart wildly hammering away I blurted out a question.

"Mr. Thornton, if you are not otherwise engaged tonight, would you please join my Father and me for dinner?"

As soon as I said it, I almost choked on my words. I instantly wanted to take them back but John's incredulous expression stopped me. Shock was too mild a description. His jaw dropped ever so slightly and his complexion seemed to turn a shade paler than the color of snow. But it was his eyes that revealed the biggest alteration.

Nothing prepared me for the stunned expression swimming in

that sea of blue. He was not just happy; he was beyond that. He looked grateful, as though I had given him the sun, moon, and stars.

Dixon told me I had invited him for dinner. She did not know what it was that pushed me to ask; only that I did it. I couldn't confess to her that it was to show him the turn of my affection.

The silence that fell over us was thicker than January's heaviest snow fall. Father's lingering absence didn't enter my thoughts as I pondered my boldness. Ultimately I decided if I was ever to have the future I was shown, I needed to make the first step.

He finally spoke after what felt like a lifetime of silence, his baritone voice lacking confidence, and his manner shy. I think his hands shook a little, too. I know I heard his tea cup rattle.

"Are you certain you want me?"

John certainly looked like a man in torment, uncertain whether he should be happy or sad. I needed to put him out of his misery. I glanced once more at those cuts on his fingers. I hoped it would not be long before he gifted me with a twirling; wood carving of roses.

I mustered my courage, took a deep breath, and let out the air I held in.

"Yes, Mr. Thornton," I answered. I wanted to call him by his given name, but that would happen soon enough. I could wait.

"I am very sure, I want you."

M. LIZA MARTE lives in Santa Clara, just south of San Francisco in northern California. She currently works in an Accounting corporation. She has written 16 books, four of which have been self-published and can be found on Amazon.

M. LIZA MARTE's other books include: *The Whistle Echoes, A Drop of Red, Above the Roars,* and *More than Words*

LOOSE LEAVES FROM MILTON

Damaris Osborne

She handed him his cup of tea with the proud air of an unwilling slave; but her eye caught the moment when he was ready for another cup; and he almost longed to ask her to do for him what he saw her compelled to do for her father, who took her little finger and thumb in his masculine hand, and made them serve as sugar-tongs.' - Chapter X, North and South

LEAF ONE - A BITTER TASTE

Miss Margaret Hale was thirsty. She was in desperate need of a cup of tea. It had been a long journey from their beloved home in Helstone, around which word a golden glow, the colour of a fine Yunnan golden tip, seemed to have already settled, so that it was said in a voice of sorrowing awe. They had spent one night in London with her Aunt Shaw, who was not just sure, but entirely positive that their removal to The North would end in death, via misery, gloom, and lost consonants. For all that she agreed with her aunt, Margaret felt that the lady could have made an effort and appeared neutral on the matter.

They had spent hours in this compartment, and the beauties of nature, which her father had extolled at length as the train passed through it, had now been replaced by a landscape of industry, and its ravages upon the rural environment. Margaret could not but think of the words of William Blake, a poet whose life did not bear deep investigation, but whose words now seemed far too apt. This was indeed a land of 'dark, satanic mills'. The tall chimneys of the mills and manufactories filled the air with a foggy darkness and a layer of soot that coated brickwork and, she had no doubt, the inhabitants. How could anyone be happy in such a world?

'Are we there yet?' whispered Mrs Hale, holding a lace-edged handkerchief to her lips. She was caught between her tiredness, wanting a positive answer, and her heart wishing they might never arrive in The North at all.

'Very nearly, my dear. This service terminates at Milton, and we have already passed through Grimly, Dimly, Glumly and Darkly, and my Bradshaw's Guide tells me that Milton is next.'

'And does the trusty volume describe Milton, Father?' Margaret was not hopeful of being cheered.

'Er - yes, Margaret. It commends its commercial vibrancy and,' he peered more closely at the printed page, 'its "devotion to industry, regardless of the cost in aesthetic charm".'

'I am not sure anyone in The North knows what "aesthetic" even means, Father. This is not a land where the diphthong could be appreciated. Look at it.' She pointed at a tall chimney, disappearing into a slate grey layer of smoke. 'Is this a place where lapsang souchong is drunk regularly?'

'But you do not like lapsang souchong, my dear,' responded Mr Hale, gently.

'No, but I acknowledge that as a failing upon my part.' Margaret was an honest young woman, except when it came to her brother,

Frederick, about whom she lied whenever his name was mentioned. According to her, he was now growing tea in Darjeeling, though had you asked her mother she would have said he was 'growing' sheep in New Zealand, and Mr Hale would claim he was managing an alpaca ranch in Bolivia. All three believed their inventions were far nicer than the truth, which was that Frederick was on the run from the Royal Navy and living in sin with a female called Dolores, who had enormous castanets and a nice little hostelry in a Spanish port. He had given up tea for sangria, which his family felt was far worse than mere mutiny.

The train began to slow down, and Margaret fancifully thought it was trying not to reach Milton. It drew into a railway station of moderate proportions, and a booming northern voice announced that 'This train terminates here.' Margaret's heart sank. He might as well have cried out that 'Life terminates here.' She and her parents had lived in Helstone, and would exist in Milton. It was very lowering.

MRS HALE HAD FEARED destitution in Milton, but her husband assured her that his friend 'Ding Dong' was a man of means, and owned not only a mill (without getting within fifty miles of it more than once a year) and several likely properties which might be suitable for the Hales at a peppercorn rent. Margaret took this with a pinch of salt, and Mrs Hale, ignoring all forms of condiment, wondered where her husband had formed a friendship with someone who sounded exotic. He had then explained 'Ding Dong' was really Mr Bell of Oxford, a fortunate fellow, and indeed Fellow, of Mr Hale's alma mater.

'He has written to a Mr Thornton, who runs Marlborough Mills for him, and Mr Thornton will show us the houses tomorrow.'

'But none will have roses round the door,' sniffed Mrs Hale. 'I cannot bear to even look at them. You must choose, Mr Hale, and take Margaret with you, for she has an ability to detect woodworm rarely found in one so young.'

'If you are sure, my dear, of course.'

'I was Shaw, but am now Hale, though not, I fear, hale and hearty. I have this cough. . .' Mrs Hale coughed delicately, with just a hint of morbidity to it.

'I will accompany Father, dear Mother, and Mr Thornton will not persuade us to rent any property that has woodworm or, indeed, dry rot. Of that you may be - certain.'

So the next morning, when the morning was sufficiently advanced for the sun to have almost become visible through the layer of smog, the Hales, father and daughter, set out clutching an address at which they were to meet Mr Thornton. They arrived late, having asked directions at a chemist's shop, from a chair mender in the street, and also from a police constable. All three gave answers that were misheard by the soft southern ears, and so they became very lost.

Mr Thornton, a man who was never late, upon the grounds that his father was 'the late Mr Thornton' and he had no wish to be like him, was looking at his pocket watch for the fourth time when Mr Hale hailed him from the bottom of the short flight of steps that led up to the front door of the town house bearing the number one upon the door. He raised his head, though the brooding frown remained.

'Mr Thornton. I do apologise for our tardy arrival. I am afraid - it is not always easy to understand directions when unused to the local dialect and . . .' Mr Hale floundered, in what Mr Thornton decided was an indecisive and very southern manner.

'It was not your fault, Father.' Margaret's tone almost admonished. She did not like the thought of him sounding ineffectual in front of this tall, dark (though hopefully not satanic) mill-master. 'We are in England, and English ought to be spoken in a manner that Her Majesty might comprehend.'

'On a par with the Queen herself, are you, Miss Hale?' Mr Thornton sneered, in a deep and chocolatey voice, looking down his long nose at her as she looked down her small nose up at him, in a strange Möbius strip of nose-looking-downs.

'Of course not, sir.' The word was said as if spelled 'cur,' and she stuck her chin in the air defiantly. Mr Thornton made a small, growling noise in his throat.

'Margaret is in jest, I am sure.'

'No Father, it is Mother's sister who is. . . Ah.' Margaret's cheeks reddened and she fell silent.

'Mr Bell has requested me to show you possible houses to rent, Mr Hale. I shall of course do so, but I have not got all day. Time is money, and I waste neither. If you would follow me.' Mr Thornton took a key from his pocket, and Margaret was conscious of watching his long fingers. She was very glad her blush hid her blush. He opened the door, which had a strangely satisfying creak, as though it resented opening even for such a man as him, and he then stood politely to one side, to allow Miss Hale to enter first. After all, he reasoned, she must weigh a fraction of his own weight, and if any of the floorboards were weak, they would merely sag a little, rather than give way. Mr Thornton was not a man who gave way, nor was he one prone to falling through holes in the floor.

Margaret accorded him the briefest nod as she passed him, and then stood in the hallway and sniffed.

'This property has not been inhabited for the last forty two days,' she announced, confidently.

'Forty three, actually.' Mr Thornton very nearly smirked. Ha, this soft southern lass would not have the last word with him. At this moment, a thought exploded in his brain, and yelled 'Unless it is to say "Yes, Mr Thornton, I accept your proposal".' Mr Thornton spluttered.

'Hmm, but one of those days was Christmas Day, and so does not count, sir.' She looked smug. Deep down, Mr Thornton thought she looked stunning, and so he appeared stunned.

'My daughter has a fine nose, Mr Thornton,' murmured Mr Hale, not without a touch of pride.

Mr Thornton choked back the response that it was not half as fine as her closely confined bosom and lustrous eyes. He focused upon her depressing brown hat, in an effort not to say something impertinent.

She advanced into the parlour, avoiding the long-deceased pigeon in the middle of the floor, and looked about her, sniffing.

'Margaret began turning up her nose at an early age, and her olfactory acuity is quite remarkable.'

So her name was Margaret. Mr Thornton let it swirl about in his head like the leaves in a teapot as the boiling water cascades upon them. He had an insane urge to smile, and repressed it with difficulty. It did, however, cause him to lower his guard and jest.

'Then Miss Hale will settle in very well in Milton, for we have many factories. An "olfactory" will be a fine addition.' The smiling urge triumphed, and he grinned at Mr Hale.

Margaret, who was gazing thoughtfully at a patch of damaged wallpaper at picture rail height above the fireplace, added a snort to her sniff, and sneezed.

'Bless you, my dear,' murmured Mr Hale.

'Hmmm. Upon consideration, the wallpaper is not peeling because of damp, but because of an inferior application using weak paste. And for your information, Mr Thornton, olfactory comes from the Latin and . . .'

'I am well aware of the derivation, Miss Hale. Classics is not taught only south of Oxford. Only circumstance prevented me from continuing the study of Latin beyond my thirteenth year, and it is a matter of regret to me.' Mr Thornton frowned again, aware that he had divulged too much about himself to these soft, southern strangers.

'It is?' An idea hit Mr Hale.

'You need not sound so surprised, Mr Hale. We in The North are not ignorant.' Mr Thornton was offended, and the former parson made haste to explain that he was hoping to take in pupils for Latin and Greek, and that if there were more men like Mr Thornton in Milton, perhaps he might find more mature students seeking improvement, rather than only adolescents being pushed into it by parents.

Margaret, now prodding the ceiling with the ferrule of her umbrella, muttered something unintelligible, and gave an angry shove which brought down a lump of plaster which occasioned Mr Hale rather more pain than the idea. She could not admit her violence sprang from the thought that if there were more men like Mr Thornton in Milton, her life might become complex.

'Is there another property we might inspect? I do not think this will suit us at all. Mother is not to be subjected to precipitation of plaster and loose laths.'

'I think the next house ought to be better suited to delicate southern constitutions, Miss Hale. It is but a short walk away in Scotland Yard.'

'Then lead us there, Mr Thornton, and I hope I detect neither worm, nor mould, nor rot within it.'

LEAF TWO - TEA BREAK

'What are they like, Mr and Mrs Hale?' Hannah Thornton set aside her stitchery, on which she was embroidering the flowers and leaves of camellia sinensis. Tea was her son's favourite beverage, and she felt that he was secretly even more interested in tea than cotton. She had encouraged him in the years after his father's death, for tea was acceptable where the 'C word' was not. 'The late Mr Thornton' had brought ruin upon himself and his family through an injudicious speculation on what he had been assured were coffee beans from Columbia, and had turned out to be jelly beans from Columbus, Ohio. Since such confectionery was already made locally, his imported goods were too expensive to attract buyers, and had lingered in the warehouse right up until his creditors had taken possession of them. Driven to taking his own life from the shame, he had left his wife and two children in penury, from which his son's unstinting hard work had delivered them. None of them ever touched or mentioned the brown beans. Tea, 'the cup that cheers,' had been a solace, to the extent that Hannah fondly called her son 'J Tea.' It was her one concession to softness, which she regarded with suspicion.

'Mr Hale is a mild-mannered man, rather diffident, I should say, and I did not make the acquaintance of his wife, whom I believe to be of an invalid tendency. His daughter, Miss Hale, was with him.'

'And what manner of young woman might she be, J Tea?'

'She is haughty, Mother, very haughty. And she has not one good word to say about Milton and The North.'

'Hmmm. I do not like the sound of her at all. By the way, who is that other young woman I keep seeing in this house?'

'That is your daughter, my sister Fanny.'

'Really? Oh. I did wonder why she turns up at the breakfast table so often.'

The Hales moved into the house in Scotland Yard within the week. Their only servant was Dixon, Mrs Hale's maid, originally from the hamlet of Dock Green, just outside Helstone of blessèd memory. She was also now cook-housekeeper, though a woman whose idea of haute cuisine was a pork chop with apple sauce. Her efforts to find a subordinate, prepared to work very long hours for even less money than the prevalent sum in Milton, proved fruitless. On the bright side, she said, fruit was expensive, so fruitlessness was a good thing. Margaret did not agree. With an ineffectual father and a mother who was permanently listless, having no energy to write any more lists, Margaret took the drastic step of entering the below stairs world beyond the baize door, and taking up duties which would have been unthinkable in beloved Helstone. Her own culinary attempts showed that she could pen a very nice menu card, but actually cooking anything was merely making burnt offerings to some unknown domestic goddess. As the daughter of a former parson, this smacked of idolatry, so she desisted forthwith. Thereafter she applied herself to the laundry, making the beds, and sweeping out the grates each morning before laying new fires. At least the outside world might never know of these demeaning tasks being performed.

It was in the second week that Margaret finally gave in to Dixon's pleading to discover the whereabouts of the key to the silver cupboard. Although the Hales' silverware was limited to a visiting card waiter, a pair of serving spoons, a toddy ladle, and a teapot of melon form that had belonged to Mrs Hale's Aunt Hysteria, Dixon was convinced that they were all going to be murdered in their beds if the silver was not properly protected.

Margaret's argument, which was that if intruders wanted the

silver, they would not need to threaten the family if it was not locked away, fell upon deaf ears. Thus it was that on Wednesday morning, Margaret placed her depressing brown hat carefully upon her head, took up her reticule, and sallied forth to Marlborough Mills.

It was some distance, and as Margaret toiled up the hill through the churchyard, it felt like three hundred miles, not three. This was another northern inferiority. Beloved Helstone was broadly flat, with a slight incline that permitted walkers to gaze upon it from about fifty feet, and without having undue exertion. Milton was all hills, and for every respite of a downhill there was the misery of another uphill.

When she reached Marlborough Mills the gates were shut like some mediaeval fortress. Indeed, the image it brought to mind was from one of the storybooks of her youth, with Robin Hood about to gain entry to Nottingham Castle, despite a multitude of guards.

She was about to knock at the wicket gate set into one of them when there was a creaking sound, and they began to open. Margaret was faced with two Shire horses drawing a heavily laden cart, and a peremptory command to 'Move tha' sen, lass,' which she correctly interpreted as a request to get out of the way. The courtyard was a scene of activity, but Margaret managed to get a response she understood, by way of a pointing finger, when she asked a young woman where Mr Thornton's office might be found.

The office might be located, but Mr Thornton was not there, His minion, who seemed affronted that a young lady should come into the hub of the 'empire,' requested her to wait.

She waited, without even the offer of a cup of tea. She waited, and waited, and eventually gave vent to a huffy exhalation, and decided that she had been forgotten. There was no help for it; she would go and find Mr Thornton for herself.

Having failed to find him in three cupboards, a bale shed and the privy, she climbed the stairs to the upper levels of a large building which thrummed from an unknown source.

She advanced to a door, and opened it cautiously. She was assailed, if not assaulted, by the clacking of the looms and by clouds of cotton fluff that floated about her like a snow shower, and landed like impossibly large flakes of dandruff upon her shoulders. She stood for a moment, open-mouthed, until a piece of fluff caught in her throat and she coughed. Her eyes watered, and as they cleared she saw Mr Thornton, stood upon a gantry, looming over the serried ranks of looms. He was frowning, imperious, and Margaret could not but think him very much the matcha male. Then he suddenly let out a roar, and almost threw himself down the steep iron steps and raced down an aisle, turning a corner, shouting. Margaret followed, and put her hand to her mouth. The tall, dark mill-master was shaking a worker so fiercely his teeth shook in his head, and was yelling at him so loudly that Margaret feared the man's eardrums would burst.

'I saw you, saw you sneaking off early for the tea break, and not outside. You were warned before. Where is it?' The man was shaken again, and a very small cotton bag with perforations fell from a pocket. 'How could you risk every life in this weaving shed for the sake of a swift brew of Heaven knows what? Get out! Get out, and never come back, you . . .'

Mr Thornton became aware of Miss Hale, staring at him, appalled. Whatever intemperate term might have been uttered was swallowed. 'What are you doing here, Miss Hale?' He was still shouting.

'I - I came for the key to the silver cupboard.'

'You came all this way for . . .' He shook his head and the worker at the same time, though the man managed to wriggle from his grasp, and scurry away. 'You have very odd priorities, Miss Hale.'

'Odd to you, sir, but then, you appear to find it normal to mistreat a poor, uneducated man.'

'He might be both, but he is also a very dangerous man.'

'He was pathetic. How unfair of you to . . .'

'I will give you the key and beg you to remove yourself from somewhere you could not possibly understand.'

'I understand cruelty to one's fellow man.'

'You understand nothing, madam. Follow me.'

≈

IT WAS A SHAKEN MARGARET, though not literally, who returned to Scotland Yard. She was outraged and disgusted by what she had seen. This then was the way men of power treated their subordinates in The North. It was too grim even to reveal to Mother and Father, and so Margaret dealt with a large heap of ironing, thrusting the heavy iron upon the linen as though repressing the very thought of Mr Thornton. When her Father asked her about her visit, she told him only of her encounter with a rough but kindly man and his pallid daughter, both millworkers, upon her return journey. Much of what they had said had been unintelligible to her, but the tone had been amicable, and the girl was much her own age. Margaret had arranged to meet the girl, Bessy, to teach her how to hem handkerchiefs, since the one in her possession was somewhat ragged at the corners.

'It was the least that I could do, Father. Bessy Higgins has fluff on her lungs from working in the horrid mills, and I fear that such a condition is very serious. If one has to cough up one's lungs, far better it should be into a well hemmed handkerchief, not some rag.'

Mr Hale agreed most heartily.

LEAF THREE - TEA FOR TWO TIMES TWO

It could not be said that Mr Hale was fending off prospective students from the doorstep, or more accurately, that Dixon was having to do so, although she announced with some pride that she had won the 'person most likely to fend off others' prize in the dame school she had attended in her rather distant youth. There were a few using his tuition as a crammer, being young gentlemen whose ability to pass the entrance examination for The Universities was in doubt. Their doting, or delusional, parents were willing to pay nearly moderate sums for additional tuition in Greek, followed by tea and cakes in the parlour. As Margaret remarked, the amount of cake the crammer boys could cram into their adolescent forms was quite likely to mean that expenditure would exceed income from them. Mr Hale was rather more proud that he had mature students from among the men whose affluence enabled them to dabble in the Classics they had not encountered when young. He did not say he had invested four shillings in flyers, which he had conveniently mislaid when visiting the Cotton Exchange, and the Mercantile Masters' Recreation and Reading Room (Strictly No Admittance To Ladies). He also failed to mention that the advertisement hinted at tales of drapery clad goddesses, and the 'amorous adventures of deities - with illustrations.'

Margaret came downstairs from her bedchamber, where she had changed from her 'I am not a servant in my own home' dress for something more suitable for partaking of tea in the parlour, and entered with a slightly fixed smile, anticipating boredom and adolescent acne. The smile froze, instantly as cold as ice, but not of course, iced tea, since such a thing would never catch on. There, seated, or rather perched, as his tall frame was somewhat too much for the small salon chair upon which he had been invited to make himself comfortable, was Mr Thornton - the man who had dismissed a worker, most violently, for being too eager to have his cup of tea.

He stood rather suddenly, nearly knocking over a jardiniere containing an aspidistra that was finding the grim conditions up north just to its liking, and was threatening to become an obstruction to conversation.

'Look, my dear, Mr Thornton has come to take tea with us after his Latin lesson.' Mr Hale smiled beatifically at his daughter, who sniffed, clearly unimpressed.

'I am surprised he has permitted you to use your spirit kettle, Mama. Mr Thornton objects to tea. Or do you draw the line at violence towards women, Mr Thornton?' Her angry gaze passed from her mother to Mr Thornton, who was taken aback at this verbal assault.

'The situation is very different, Miss Hale, and I am a man who takes tea very seriously. What we have here are comestibles, rather than combustibles.' He indicated a plate of small cakes. They were, he decided, very soft, southern cakes, designed for people who only needed nourishment to sustain them in walking to their carriages, or in lifting their teacups from the saucers. 'What you saw in the mill was both a huge risk to the safety of my workers, and an unforgivable affront to tea.'

'In what way, sir?' Margaret responded, not at all appeased.

'The man's name was Smoucher, and he lived up to it. He has been selling illicit adulterated tea - the worst smouch I have ever discovered - to his colleagues. He puts the mix in small cotton bags and tells them they can make their tea quicker by putting the bag in a tin cup and pouring 'hot water' over it. Fools being taken in by this heresy has resulted in several cases of...' Mr Thornton stopped mid-sentence, and blushed. He could not mention irritation of the bowels in Mrs Hale's parlour.

'"Of"?'

Margaret did not lower her gaze. It challenged him.

'...Of serious indisposition.' He gave her look for look. 'There,' his own look said, 'I did find an appropriate term that will not offend your southern sensibilities.'

Margaret was horrified, but hated to admit that she might herself have slapped the face of a man who suggested she make tea without a teapot and a strainer.

Mr Hale, now frowning at the obvious antipathy between his most able pupil and his daughter, sought to move the conversation onward.

'Mr Thornton did not only bring his intellect to the lesson, Margaret, but has brought us a gift.' He indicated a very thin volume upon the table, entitled 'A Visitor's Guide to the Manufacturing Metropolis of Milton.'

'Timeo Danaos, et dona ferentes,' cried Margaret, scornfully, 'or rather I fear not Greeks but overbearing masters bearing gifts.'

'Oh no! She did it again! What have I told you about showing intelligence in public, Margaret?' Mrs Hale, highly agitated, wafted a thin slice of bread and butter to cool her pink cheeks. 'What will people say? You will never find a husband.'

'I hardly think anyone in Milton would even understand, Mother,' Margaret stuck up her chin, 'and the last thing in the world I need is a rough northern husband, who slurps his tea and drinks it nearly stewed.'

'I understand, Miss Hale,' murmured J Tea, his brows furrowing, and his rather chocolatey voice dropping to a near growl, 'I understand you completely.'

'Oh yes, Mr Thornton, you do?' For a moment her heart stood still. Her outburst was a total rejection of The North, of him, and a little voice inside her was screaming at her for ruining its dream. She admitted to herself that accusing him, by implication, of poor tea etiquette was going too far, so she turned back to his lessons. 'You are studying Vergil's Aeneid, not the works of Catullus? Are you disappointed, or not up to the required standard?'

'Margaret!' Mr Hale was horrified. Not only was Margaret likely to lose him his pupil, but must have been borrowing his books off the top shelf in the book room. 'Mr Thornton is our guest. You will apologise and offer him tea.'

'I am sorry, Mr Thornton, for having the temerity to question your learning.' She did not sound at all apologetic. 'Do sit down and have a small cake.'

He sat, heavily, for the chair was just a couple of inches lower than most, and it groaned beneath him. The plate of cakes was thrust before his nose.

'Would you prefer a queen cake or a madeleine with a cherry on the top?'

J Tea nearly sighed with relief. At least he could now tell one little cake from the other. He selected a madeleine, and placed it on his small, delicately painted china plate. His hand made the plate seem even smaller, and Margaret noted his long fingers. Would he?

Would he not?

'Circumstance, most unfortunate circumstance, curtailed my acquaintance with the Classics, Miss Hale. I find the rigour of Latin an inspiration to serious thought. I am sure we will study Catullus at some point, but I find both the Georgics and the Aeneid very interesting.'

So perhaps he was not just there for the naughty bits. She poured a cup of tea, and leaned a little down to him, sat upon that ridiculous chair. Whether she liked it or not, and her traitorous heart liked it rather a lot, their fingers touched.

'One lump or two?' murmured Margaret, just a little breathlessly.

'Er . . .' His eyes were level with her chastely muslin-encased bosom. He swallowed convulsively. 'Er . . .er, two please.' He did not take sugar in tea. The room felt hotter than a hob with a singing kettle upon it.

The sugar was dropped into his cup with a slightly suggestive plopping sound, and his ears went red. He stirred the tea, the spoon making small clattering sounds like teeth chattering. He gazed at Miss Hale - haughty, high and mighty, looking-down-her-nose-at-him Miss Hale - and he was smitten. He took the cup and set it to his lips. It was too sweet, like her, but had a superb body to it, strong and fortifying. That too was like her, he thought, and his heart missed a beat.

Margaret watched intently, unintentionally holding her breath. Would he? He did - in a way. It was physically impossible for those long fingers to hold the delicate china handle between more than thumb and forefinger, and the other digits floundered somewhat, the middle finger just touching the lower edge of the cup, but the little finger was making an attempt to hold itself in the accepted curve of the 'not near the handle' polite tea drinker. She sighed, and Mr Thornton, still covertly observing the muslin over the rim of his teacup, spluttered, and mendaciously said that a tea leaf had stuck in the back of his throat.

'That hardly seems possible, Mr Thornton.' Mrs Hale was rarely assertive, preferring to suggest without ever, as a well brought up lady, being suggestive, 'The tea strainer was purchased in Mrs Miggins' Tea Shop in Helstone. Her emporium only sells the very best of everything, being in Helstone.'

'Is Helstone so perfect?' J Tea gave a wry smile, thinking he was lightening the atmosphere.

'Absolutely.' Mrs Hale's response was instant, and heartfelt. 'Helstone is as Heaven upon the Earth and . . .' her voice became suspended with emotion, and she dabbed at the corner of her eye with a lace-edged handkerchief, making the tears flow the more as the scratchy bit rubbed her eyeball.

'My Mother is a lady of delicate sensibilities, Mr Thornton, and of refinement. She was presented at Court.'

J Tea, a long-standing magistrate upon the local bench, blinked.

'I am sure that it resulted in acquitt . . .' He stopped, aghast at his mistake. In the confusion of sweet tea and the proximity of Miss Hale's bosom, his brain was scrabbling to work normally, and had clutched at the word 'court' and gone straight to his own regular experiences of it. 'Er, a quite indelible memory.' Whew, he might just have got away with it.

The other three people in the room stared at him for a moment, a long moment. He had not got away with it. 'I fear I have trespassed upon your hospitality too long, Mrs Hale, and . . . is that the time? I really ought to be getting home.' He stood up, almost thrusting his empty tea cup at Margaret, and the teaspoon clattered to the floor. Both bent a little at the knees and attempted to pick it up, with the consequence that their faces were but inches apart. Neither knew whether they ought to let the other pick up the small utensil, and then Margaret took a deep breath, and while J Tea was transfixed by the movement of her bosom, snatched it from the floor.

'A gentleman, a gentleman from The South, never drops cutlery.' The words were uttered to dismiss him, from her thoughts as much as the room.

J Tea, as furious with himself as with this wilful young woman who seduced him, yes, that was the word, with tea and bosomage, said nothing, but nodded to his host and hostess and left, clamping his hat so firmly upon his head as he left that it was a good half inch shorter than when he purchased it.

LEAF FOUR - TROUBLE BREWING

J Tea was unsettled, which he found most unsettling. He was a man who was serious, thoughtful and knew his own mind. At present he knew his own mind was performing feats of acrobatics when it came to the person of Miss Hale; the hoity-toity, look-down-her-beauti-fully-shaped-nose-at-him Miss Hale who despised The North and all things therein.

Their encounter over tea in the parlour at Scotland Yard cast him into alt and despair simultaneously, and copious cups of Assam did not ease him. Should he avoid her, and cease his visits to Mr Hale? He enjoyed the rigour of study, and the fellow was actually less of a mouse when it came to Ovid and fifth declension nouns. Soft and southern he might be, but J Tea could appreciate the even temper of the man, and his patience. Patience was not J Tea's strong point.

Just to add to his frown, which now furrowed his brow almost permanently, there were mutterings of a strike brewing, and with his recent investment in machinery to improve productivity and workers' health, he could little afford to lose money with delayed or incomplete orders. The irony was that the dispute centred upon tea, the best beverage available to man, the beverage that made Britain what it was. Beer and gin inebriated, but tea invigorated. He had actually applauded the inclusion of the clause in the new Factory Act Clause 3(t) subsection 42, which stipulated that mill workers were entitled to drink tea during their statutory lunchtime break, and that it should be made and served not within the weaving shed. However, some Southern parliamentarian with do-good ideas had added an amend-ment, which had been passed, ensuring that each worker might have a biscuit. The Union was now ranting and raving because the majority of mill masters were offering thin, cheap biscuits of no flavour, which immediately became soggy if dunked, and sank to the bottom of the cup (which the worker had to provide). J Tea had his biscuits baked by Widow Murgatroyd, who made a very fine and firm biscuit with just a touch of cinnamon in it, but he knew that Slickson and Hamper were going to Hemmeroyds, who cut them as thin as possible, baked far too many per oven, and then stacked them in piles whilst warm, so that they were inherently soggier. The Union, if it told the workers to walk out, would be taking issue with the mill-masters as a whole, and J Tea knew they would not give a fig roll that Marlborough Mills would suffer for a problem not of its own making.

His mother, revelling in his brooding demeanour, which she saw as a refusal to be soft and weak, was also concerned at the likely industrial inaction, both for its effect and also its timing. She was in the process of writing out the invitations for the annual Marlborough Mills dinner, which was a highlight of the Milton social scene, though she said it herself. She never noticed that nobody else said it, and since she declined all but two other dinners to which she and J Tea were invited each year, she had little with which to compare it.

'Would you prefer me to withhold the invitations this year, J Tea?' She sounded regretful.

'No, Mother. It would show weakness before the other masters, and you never know, we might persuade a few to favour Widow Murgatroyd with their biscuit orders after all.'

'Aye, and Dyspepsia Murgatroyd is an honest and hardworking woman with six mouths to feed on something other than ginger snaps. I admit I doubted you when you went and paid sixpence per dozen for biscuits, but we have no sogginess in Marlborough Mills, and soggy biscuit brings on idleness, as I have always said. I wonder at the Union not applauding inferior biscuits for that very reason.'

'The Union simply wants to flex its muscle, Mother. We shall ride out the storm in a teacup, even if it means getting in workers from Ireland.'

'Oh dear, and they want to dip slices of fried potato in their tea. Can you imagine anything as bad as thinly sliced potato fried to a - well, to a crisp? It must make a noise as one eats it, unless dipped in tea.'

'My thought is that it ruins the tea, but we digress, Mother. Send your invitations, but please add Mr Hale and his wife and daughter. I do not think they leave the house very much, and he has a good mind.'

'But a soft southern head, if he gave up his parish for some whim of libertarian doubt, which is what I gathered when I visited his wife. Besides, the woman is ailing. I have seen ailing, and although it goes against the grain with me to commend a southerner, the woman ails very well, very well indeed. I doubt she will attend.'

J Tea made a mental note to send a basket of fruit to Scotland Yard.

He had no idea why, but baskets of fruit were meant to be beneficial to invalids.

~

MRS THORNTON WAS right about Mrs Hale, The lady was swift in her excuse to her husband that it was her evening to darn socks, since she feared worrying him. She also recommended that Margaret not undertake any ironing on the day of the dinner, since it made her hair fall in damp squiggles.

'Why would I want to attend the Thornton's dinner when I could be darning socks with you, Mother?' Margaret was aware of a fluttering in her bosom, and it was not caused by a small bird trapped within her layers of undergarments. Mr Thornton was a monster, obviously, and she disliked everything about him - other than that voice, those hands, the way he frowned so broodingly, and even the little pock mark above his left eye. Not that she had noticed, oh no. Meeting him whilst wearing evening dress would be disastrous.

'Now Margaret,' Mr Hale remonstrated gently, 'you know that your Mother has always darned my socks, and would never let another at even a single worn heel. Besides, it will do you good to get out of the house. I overheard you talking to the grate in my study only yesterday.'

Margaret could not tell him she was muttering unladylike imprecations at it, involving the word 'blasted.' Nor would she like to admit she called it Herbert, but that was another matter.

'But Father . . .'

'You will come with me and represent your dear Mother, there is an end to it.' Mr Hale tried to sound commanding, and just about managed harassed.

~

THE HALES TOOK a hansom cab to the dinner, since it was pouring with rain and the cemetery hill was very dark on a dark, dark night.

Margaret wore a silk gown cut low across the bosom as fashion dictated, and an expression her father likened to that of an early Christian martyr.

As they trod up the steps into Marlborough House, he whispered that she need have no fear, since there were no lions in Lancashire.

Admittedly, Mrs Thornton arrayed in charcoal silk taffeta and enough jet jewellery to have kept several Whitby makers employed for a month was nearly as scary as a lion. Beside her was Mr Thornton, looking both severe but welcoming to his guests, and a young woman with fair ringlets and a gown Margaret mentally put down as an overblown northern attempt at last year's London fashion.

'And this is -er. . . Anyway, it appears she is my daughter, so I am hoping to show her off to any of the gentleman not currently married, in the hope that she will cease to clutter the place.' Mrs Thornton did not spare the young woman a glance as she spoke. 'Perhaps you young ladies might become better acquainted.' This was Hannah Thornton's bright idea of the evening, though neither Margaret nor Miss Thornton greeted it with unbounded rapture.

'So Miss Hale, do you play the flugelhorn?' Fanny Thornton's voice lacked all chocolate tone, and combined a sense of monetary superiority with a petulant whine.

'Er, no. I am not conversant with the instrument.' Margaret blinked. What was a flugelhorn?

'What a pity. I had hoped that you might, since we might then play duets together.'

'Duets for two flugelhorns?'

'Oh no, for flugelhorn and triangle. I am considered very adept upon the triangle.'

Margaret strove to find a suitable response to this statement, and looked about her desperately, hoping to find her Father. His back was turned to her, but looking at her, almost staring impertinently at her, was Mr Thornton himself, and he was coming towards her, smiling.

'Good evening, Miss Hale. I am sorry that your mother is unable to join us this evening. I hope her indisposition is not serious.'

'Indisposition, Mr Thornton? She suffers from her nerves,

lumbago, plumbago, sago, and occasional vertigo, but other than that, and the constant coughing and pressing a handkerchief to her lips, she is quite well, I assure you.'

'Oh. I apologise, I must have misheard.'

'Lettice Heard is over there, behind the aspidistra, brother, trying to avoid being monopolised by Cosmo Politan. Why do you need her?' Miss Thornton looked puzzled, and J Tea ignored her.

'Miss Hale, when we last met . . .' His voice faltered slightly. 'I think there were misunderstandings.'

'I do not think anyone called Understanding was invited tonight, were they?' Miss Thornton's brows drew together. Both Margaret and J Tea ignored her.

'What I saw in the weaving shed could not be misunderstood, sir. I understand that a worker and mill-master are not equals upon the social scale - I would not expect you to have invited some to dinner - but physical mistreatment . . .'

As Miss Thornton opened her mouth to interject, J Tea took her by the shoulders and turned her away. 'Go and entertain Mr Watson. He is all alone.' He turned back to gaze at Miss Hale with a mixture of anger and hurt. 'When I told you about Smoucher, you focused upon his tea abomination, but that is but half the reason. What you saw was far more than what you saw. It was the culmination of events. Smoucher had been warned three times about his illicit and deceitful sales of 'bags of tea,' which contained but little real tea, and also pretended that a proper cup of tea can be made without a teapot. What was more important was that he was dismissed for setting up a spirit kettle in the weaving shed, which presents a huge risk to everyone inside it. I have seen, Miss Hale, the effects of a fire in a mill, the lines of corpses, men, women and children. I have also seen how 'bad tea' can lay workers low for days, and when they do not work, they do not earn, just as we masters do not fulfil our order books. I admit I am a man whose temper is not mild, whose patience is far from endless, but my "violence" against Smoucher undoubtedly saved those who work for me from illness, hardship, and perhaps even death. Am I so bad a man, therefore?'

'I - a gentleman would not put a lady in so difficult a position, Mr Thornton.'

Margaret hid behind etiquette, being unable to deny that the explanation did put a different perspective upon the incident.

'A "gentleman" in your eyes, Miss Hale, would never be engaged in making something practical and useful, no doubt. A "gentleman" might twist the words of law to ensure the man who pays him is not convicted of a crime, but he never gets his hands dirty, or fails to leave his office by six of the clock each evening. Or are those of whom you speak the idle rich who create nothing and earn nothing by their labours? Miss Hale, if that is the case, I am proud to say I am no gentleman, but an honest Englishman who values hard work and duty.' J Tea paused, aware that the conversation was not one suited to a dinner engagement.

'You must forgive my forthrightness. I ought not to be speaking of serious matters to you upon such an evening. Do excuse me, for I perceive Sowerbutts is trying to attract my attention.' With which J Tea made her a small bow and turned away. He was thus unaware of how her cheeks suffused with colour, and that one hand went to a cheek and pressed it.

MARGARET WAS RELIEVED that her place at the dinner table was some way from that of Mr Thornton, although she was opposite Mr Slickson, who ogled her shamelessly throughout the soup course. The subject that raised its head about the table by the time that desserts were presented was the near inevitable strike. All the mill-masters were in agreement that it was manufactured by the Union to cripple the manufacture of cloth and profit.

'I blame the man Higgins. He is too clever by half, and believes himself even more clever than that.' Slickson, a man of little brain, shook his rather empty head. Cleverness was to be avoided.

'Nicholas Higgins believes in what he is doing.' Margaret spoke up, without thinking of the consequences of her words. A stunned silence followed, broken only by the sound of Mrs Hamper choking quietly upon her syllabub.

'You are acquainted with the man Higgins? You admit to knowing a - a Worker?'

Hamper himself turned puce.

'He does not work for me, sir. He attends Father's lessons on Greek architecture, and I am friends with his daughter Bessy, who is ill.'

'Idle, more like. No good, any of them.'

'The girl Higgins works in Marlborough Mills. I have seen her name upon the lists, but I doubt she will stay long, for she has been exposed to the fine fluff in the carding room elsewhere.' J Tea, whilst agreeing in part with Hamper, was a fair man, and he stared at Slickson.

'Once you changed your machine to reduce the fluff, everyone shouted for it, and it costs a lot. I don't know why we need to worry about workers' health, for there are plenty of replacements available,' grumbled Slickson.

'You ought to care, sir, because they are human beings, God's children as much as you or I.' Margaret's tone was scathing. 'If Mr Thornton shows a care for his workforce, I commend it. If you all did so, perhaps there would be no need to strike.'

'There is no need to strike, Miss Hale.' J Tea's voice held no anger. 'The strike is about the sogginess of biscuits, and could be resolved. The Union takes a little from every member, and needs to prove it is still campaigning for improvements, now the latest Factory Acts have given much of what they wanted.'

'Does not the fact that Parliament has passed the Acts show that the Union was right to seek the improvements?' Margaret put the question more gently. 'Surely worker and master could resolve issues over a nice cup of tea?'

'One day, perhaps, Miss Hale, but at present the tea would be thrown back in our faces.'

'I would not waste even cheap tea on my workers.' Hamper sniffed, derisively.

'No, I do not suppose you would, Hamper. Which is at least half of the - difficulty.' J Tea was aware that Miss Hale was looking along the table towards him, and her expression was one of confusion. Let her be confused, for he was already so far gone along that path that there was no returning.

LEAF FIVE - IRISH BREAKSTRIKE TEA

The strike commenced three days later, right after the lunchtime break, with or without soggy biscuits. J Tea watched the workforce leave, and had a grim look to him which made his mother wonder why every young lady in Milton was not swooning over his deep, delicious grimness. The grimness made men 'ard in The North, 'ard as the Pennine rock, not namby-pamby soft as in The South.

'Shall I ring for tea? It will fortify us in our hour of trial.'

'I think, Mother, that the trial will last a lot longer than an hour, and we had best stock up on Irish Breakfast tea, since I foresee me having to get over the Irish if the strike lasts longer than a week. Confound Hamper, Slickson and their set. They see any expense as waste, rather than encouraging healthy, hard working employees. We can hold our heads up high, Mother, when it comes to the tea and the biscuits which the Marlborough Mills workers enjoy.'

'Then why could our workers not show loyalty and not strike?'

'Ah Mother, that is because loyalty to the Union, or fear of disloyalty, keeps them alongside the "One out, all out" brigade.'

'Hmmm.' It was a very stern and repressive 'Hmmm.'

Meanwhile, in Scotland Yard deductions were being made, and not from the housekeeping.

Dixon was looking permanently worried and Mrs Hale was to be found in a recumbent posture during most of the daylight hours as well as night time. This, along with the discovery that Dr Donal Duckworth was making regular visits, led Margaret to the unhappy realisation that her mother was not a well woman. The strike meant little to Margaret, beyond the gradual increase of underfed children who regarded her most soulfully until she parted with a penny for their grubby palms as the weeks became a month. Dr Duckworth was no quack, but a highly regarded medical practitioner, and when he suggested that Mrs Hale's mind might be given relief by a visit of 'tea and sympathy' from a lady of her own age, Margaret immediately thought of the only other lady with whom her parent had had contact.

She resolved to visit Marlborough Mills the very next day. This proved unfortunate, since it was also the day upon which the angry strike force also chose to pay a call, and they were not merely going to leave a card.

Margaret arrived to find the front gates locked, and had to rap several times before Lipton, the overseer, opened a very small window and peered out at her.

'I have come to see Mrs Thornton upon a very important matter,' declared Margaret, firmly.

'Today of all days,' sighed Lipton, but opened the door just enough for her to squeeze through without damaging her depressing brown hat. 'Best get inside the house, miss, and stay there.'

Margaret was going to say she had no wish to stay longer than absolutely necessary, but the look of worry on his visage kept her silent. She was announced into a small sitting room, though neither Mrs Thornton nor Miss Thornton was sitting. Mrs Thornton turned from the window. Her face was grave, but then it was like that much of the time.

'You have come across town alone, Miss Hale?' Mrs Thornton sounded shocked rather than applauding her bravery. 'Such foolishness when there are strikers about, and they are short of money through their own actions.'

'I had to come, Mrs Thornton, for you are the only lady in Milton with whom Mother has spoken, since she has not been able to get out since we arrived. Dr Duckworth recommended that she have the opportunity to - talk - with another lady of her age and - she is very far from well, in fact nearly as far from well as one could be without not being at all.'

Margaret's voice wavered for a moment, then grew strong again. 'I could not delay.'

'I see. Well, in that case I understand your impetuous behaviour, Miss Hale, but this is the worst possible day on which to visit. My son is currently trying to pacify the Irish workers we have had to bring over, for they are convinced that the Milton men are going to break in and smash their teapots, if not their heads, and -'

'Look, here he comes,' cried Miss Thornton, pointing out of the window, even though it was rude to point at someone. All three ladies looked out of the window, as J Tea ran, his long legs enabling him to cross the yard in but fifteen strides (for Margaret counted them). A few moments later they heard a door shut loudly, and he entered the room, his expression taut.

'I have locked the door of - Miss Hale, what are you doing here?' He blinked at the sight of her.

'I came to ask your mother if - you locked those poor people in? That is imprisonment.'

'It is saving their teapots, if not their bones, Miss Hale. I have had word the strikers are making for Marlborough Mills as we speak. Please stand back from the windows, all of you. I have sent to the militia barracks, so with luck reinforcements will arrive before serious injuries occur. They are a mob, a rabble, and could do anything, even fire the mill.'

'Surely not, sir. They are desperate, yes, for their children lack bread and I doubt not many are trying to get four brewings from a single pot of tea, but they are men, not animals.

Go out and speak with them, as a man.' Margaret's voice shook, not with fear, but with passion. In the face of the passion of Miss Hale, J Tea obeyed not sense but his heart, which throbbed at the only passion he thought he would ever receive from her. He turned, ignoring his mother's command not to be foolhardy, and went from the room. She turned upon Margaret.

'What have you done, you stupid girl? Your ignorance may cause his death.'

'Oh dear,' murmured Margaret, lowering her gaze, 'that would be very, indeed most, unfortunate. I must make reparation.'

Without another word, she too absented herself from the chamber, whilst Miss Thornton cried that they would all be murdered in their beds, despite it being mid morning, and hid in a cupboard, since it was nothing like a bed.

EVEN AS MARGARET emerged onto the open porch at the top of the steps, the heavy bar across the gates began to splinter, and a huge crowd of angry strikers, bearing banners which, owing to incomplete educations, declared 'ARD WORK DEZERVS 'ARD BISKITS' and 'NOWT SOGGY IN OUR TEA'. They looked not only militant but martial. J Tea was suddenly aware that he was not alone, and half turned, horrified, to see Miss Hale bare-headed, for the ribands of her depressing brown hat had come loose as she rushed down the stairs.

'Miss Hale, you cannot be out here. These rough men are seeing you hatless. Go inside, I beg of you.'

'No, sir, even though I breach every code of decency. You are risking your life at my beseeching, and I must therefore take as great a risk. Speak to the men, and -'

Before she could finish, a voice from the crowd yelled 'Look, the shameless hussy has not even a shawl over her hair and is standing with The Maister. It's a Den of Iniquity here as well as full of Irish Potato Dunkers.'

J Tea tried to thrust Margaret behind him, but she resisted, creating what looked like an intimate dance sequence.

'Shame! Shame!' cried voices, and suddenly a cobble from the yard came flying through the air. It missed, but Margaret made every attempt to stand in front of J Tea, in the belief that the men would not throw missiles at a Miss Hale, even if she was hatless. She was wrong. A second cobble executed a perfect parabola as J Tea tussled with her to reverse their places, and it struck her upon the temple. She collapsed senseless in his arms.

'You call yourselves men, and yet throw stones at defenceless women! The shame is all yours!'

'Aye, it is,' a Union man wailed. 'A broken head will break t'strike,' at which moment a clatter of hooves announced the arrival of the militia, wielding batons. Mayhem ensued, but J Tea was aware only of Miss Hale in his arms, and the blood upon her pallid skin, skin broken more than the leaves of an orange pekoe.

'Miss Hale, Margaret,' he whispered, 'I pray that tea will revive you, but in this moment you are all mine, and my heart beats only for you.' He carried her within, calling for assistance, and laid her upon a chaise longue in the drawing room.

'Have a care to her, Mother. I must see to the Irish. And get my sister out of the cupboard. The door is jammed and she is going to run out of air if her hysterics continue.'

When he returned, an hour later, the chaise bore his sister, not Miss Hale.

LEAF SIX - NOT HER CUP OF TEA

J Tea remonstrated with his mother, insisting that Miss Hale could not have been sufficiently recovered to return home, but Mrs Thornton was adamant that all had been done to aid her.

' When her senses returned we gave her two cups of strong sweet tea and a biscuit with currants in it. I was ready to fetch the doctor, but she was determined to go home, and so I sent her in our carriage, once the bruised strikers had been cleared from the yard. What was she thinking, going outside without her hat? Men saw her! She risked her reputation and then - is it true she forced herself upon you, shamelessly?'

'No, Mother, she was trying to protect me from violence. She thought nobody would launch a missile at me with her in the way.'

'Well, it is clear that she is besotted with you, and there is no help for it, you must marry her immediately. Anything less would ruin your reputation as well as hers. I despair of modern misses who let themselves come into but eight layers of clothing distance from a man's torso, but I admit her recklessness was also brave.'

'I shall go immediately, Mother.'

'No, J Tea, go in the morning. Now you also are in need of tea to steady you, and I am sure Miss Hale will have gone to bed with a headache upon reaching Scotland Yard.'

J Tea, coloured, having heard 'Miss Hale' and 'bed' in the same sentence, but sighed.

'You are of course, right, Mother. Er, why is the chaise long wet?'

'I threw a bucket of water over that girl who is your sister. Her hysteria was showing no signs of abating, and she spilled a cup of tea all over the floor.'

'That explains it. I shall go to Scotland Yard tomorrow morning and confess my love, for love it is, Mother, be she ever so southern and proud. Yet I do not feel that she will accept me, for all that you say.'

Secretly, Mrs Thornton also wanted to be wrong for once.

J TEA STOOD with his back to the fire, conscious that his buttocks were getting rather warm, and in what he hoped was the formal attitude of a man about to make a Declaration.

From his frown of concentration it might as easily be a Declaration of War. Miss Hale was pale, and her hand flew to her womanly bosom, which was modestly covered in several layers of concealing garments. Nevertheless, J Tea could not resist looking at that hand, that hand that had passed him the teacup with the delicate curving sides and very fine quality transfer printing. Oh, how he wanted to cup her teacups in his hands. He was stirred, but without the spoon.

'Miss Hale, my feelings for you are very strong, like the tea you make. I never knew a woman who could brew a cup of tea so exactly to my ... needs, even my Mother's tea is ...inadequate in comparison.'

'You have come to praise my tea, sir?' Her voice, like tea-leaves, was a little strained, for no man had ever mentioned his 'needs' to her before.

'No . . .yes . . .to praise all of you.'

'My entire family? Have you even heard of my cousin Marmaduke?'

'Marmalade?' He was now so confused his brain reeled, in fact it did a Highland fling with full bagpipe accompaniment.

'Mr Thornton, are you well? You mention preserves? You are rambling.' She wondered for one brief moment if he had taken strong drink, had let his tea stew to an excessive level of tannins, and with too little milk.

'Rambling,' he mumbled, half to himself, 'like a rose, a yellow tea rose.' He blinked at her. 'I am not well.'

'You bring contagion! Aaaaaaaaaah, and no doubt it is the bizarrely infectious cotton-waste-ing disease that lays my friend Bessy low. And you know my Mother is declining.'

'I would not lay you - low - Miss Hale. And I did not know your Father expected his relations to decline Latin verbs as I do.' He wondered if Mr Hale had become so involved in education that he had forgotten the difference between 'conjugate' and 'conjugal.' 'I always have a problem with touch.'

'Sir!' She blushed, and took a step back.

'Yes. The perfect first person singular is "tetigi" and I always want to say "tacti".'

'Mr Thornton, you make no sense.'

'No, I am sorry for it. I came . . . not in expectation . . .' He hung his head. He had come from an inner compulsion that defied logic. 'My words cannot convey . . .' The polite sentences he had so carefully constructed as he had walked over the hill jumbled in his brain.

'Moio sudno na vozdušnoy poduške polno ugrey.'

'Mr Thornton! What are you saying?'

'Er, my apologies. It is Russian and means "My hovercraft is full of eels".'

Her naturally inquisitive nature distracted her for a moment.

'What is a "hovercraft"?'

'I assume it is some form of Russian fishing vessel, perhaps used in the Black Sea.'

'Ah.' Her brows drew together. 'And you use it to me, Russian, the language of a country where the peasants exist in feudal servitude. That tells me so much, sir.'

'No, no, it is just a phrase I'm going through.' He was so vehement his voice rose. 'Your impression of me is incorrect, Miss Hale.'

'I do not mimic people, sir, for my Father always told me it was cruel,' she paused, 'and I cannot drop my voice to a baritone level anyway.'

'I meant, madam, that you see me as merely a tall, virile, strong willed man, with a voice like melting chocolate and eyes that draw one into my very soul.'

There was this. She fought the urge within her which cried out 'Yes, yes, and what more could I want. Hot chocolate is actually ideal before bed, rather than tea.' She bit her lip.

'It is not enough, is it.' He made it a statement, and sounded defeated. 'I came today to offer you my hand, and all the rest of my body too, not out of a sense of obligation, not even because I cannot imagine life without perfect tea handed to me by those delicate pale hands, but because . . .' his voice faltered, the words becoming a blank in the misery of his brain.

'Mr Thornton. You come inopportunely.'

Deep in the recesses of his mind his desire shouted that he only wanted the chance to prove to her that he could come very opportunely.

'I do?'

'Yes. My friend Bessy is dying.'

'What colours?'

'No, "dying," not "dyeing," Mr Thornton.' She sighed. 'Mother is weak and often in pain.'

'In Spain?'

'I never mentioned Spain.' Goodness, did he know about Frederick, was he here to blackmail her?

She pulled herself up to her full height. He did not notice, since it was still rather short in comparison to himself. 'You - are not the sort of man for whom I could ever pour tea in private, sir. Your attitudes, your demeanour - you think yourself so matcha, like many men, but it is bullying and browbeating, ungentlemanly.'

'I am too northern for you, no doubt. You think me rough-hewn, a jumped up man of trade.' His temper began to fray. He was angry, angry with her, but even more so with himself. 'You strike me with your words, but I shall strike back. Miss Hale, the day will come when you will recognise me for what I am at heart, and then your opinion of me will change. I will not waver. I will not cease from holding you . . .'

She grabbed the doorknob and turned it in haste.

'You shall not grab me at all, sir, or I shall scream for Dixon, and I assure you she has a black belt in macramé. Leave me, leave now, I insist upon it!'

In tumult, he obeyed, striding from the room with barely a nod of his head acknowledging his dismissal. It was several minutes later that Margaret, her bosom still heaving, noticed that he had forgotten his gloves. She picked them up hesitantly, as if they might still have the warmth of his body in them. What she had held within her throughout the interview was that, secretly, though her head told her he was a harsh reactionary, her heart and body longed for mutual tea making. He said she made perfect tea. Ah, and if only he would pour for her . . . the capable hands . . . the spout that would not drip . . . her pot warmed for him.

LEAF SEVEN - MORTALI TEA

Hannah Thornton could not believe her son had been rejected, even though part of her wanted to nip into the small parlour and dance an Irish jig of joy. She limited herself to a third cup of oolong and a slice of lemon drizzle cake, even though it was only half past eleven in the morning. For his part, he wanted to forget what had happened, even forget Margaret Hale completely, but he knew that deep inside he would always remember every moment they had been in close proximity.

THE STRIKE, like J Tea's heart, was broken, and so there was much to do getting Marlborough Mills back in full production. During the long working days the mill itself kept him occupied, but even once the looms began again their chatter, instead of hearing 'we're making cotton, making money,' he could only hear 'she turned you down, she thinks you dross.' He remained in his office late into the evenings and took to drink. He would sit in his office, staring at the ledgers, as a silver spirit kettle came to the boil on the small table by his coat stand, and then sit, morose, with a large pot of orange pekoe, staring into space. Even 'the cup that cheers' failed him, but the act of making and drinking tea kept him from going back into the house, where his mother was in a defiantly buoyant mood. She had begun humming 'Now thank we all our God' as she sat with her sewing, and was too much to face. His sleep, when it came to him, was haunted by a depressing brown hat and accusing eyes that set his love at nought.

IN SCOTLAND YARD, Margaret was distracted from her realisation that Mr Thornton, though obviously not the man for her, was yet such a man that made her heart beat thick. This distraction came in the form of The Grim Reaper, who not only visited her friend Bessy Higgins, but had left his calling card at the Hales' residence, with a promise to return in the near future to see Mrs Hale. Margaret discovered that the doctor was also now calling frequently, as a sort of warm up act for the One with the Scythe. Upon her mother's request, she did not tell her father what she knew, and he metaphorically stuck his head in the fire bucket of sand, and told himself his wife's headache, which had begun shortly after Frederick was born, must be a little worse.

Margaret, both worried and overworked, had as little time for tea as she had exhibited for J Tea, and began wearing her depressing brown hat even in bed. Her mother kept murmuring about her 'poor boy,' and Margaret realised that it would be a huge solace in her last days to have Frederick at the bedside. Despite the risk, for there were very uneven cobbles on the steep incline to the post box, Margaret sent an urgent missive to Cadiz, and hoped he would arrive in time.

Word filtered to Marlborough Mills that Mrs Hale was not long for this world.

Hannah Thornton spared her a nod and a 'poor woman.' J Tea, rousing himself from his misery, added bananas to the list of fruit that he was having sent to Scotland Yard, and tried not to imagine what Margaret Hale would look like in a BBG. After all, most ladies spent years of their lives in Big Black Dresses, mourning someone or other. His mother had taken the decision it was best to remain permanently in one, and had not a scrap of silk, bombazine or lace that was not black, excepting her best dinner gown, which was a daring charcoal grey.

FREDERICK ARRIVED, wearing fake Spanish mustachios, and bearing a large bag of Seville oranges, in case freshly made marmalade might be beneficial. He was slightly put out to see a large bowl of bananas and sweet Valencia oranges on the parlour side table, and rather more so by his mother's imminent departure to The World To Come. Margaret and Mr Hale were paranoid that the authorities might discover him, and provided him with several disguises as an apothecary's assistant, a curate, and a dispenser of religious pamphlets. They forgot to tell Mary Higgins, sister of the late lamented Bessy, and a much needed extra pair of hands in the house, that he was all of these characters and not Frederick Hale.

J Tea visited once, drawn as if by a strong magnetic force, and bearing a basket of fruit of such large proportions that, when emptied, it might be used as a Moses basket for a babe. However, his reception in Scotland Yard was perfunctory and dismissive. Margaret herself answered the door, which he thought odd, and she clearly did not wish to admit him.

Beyond her delectable form J Tea noted a sombrero on the hatstand in the hall, and asked if the Hales had a visitor. Margaret denied this most strongly, just as Frederick, trying to lift his mother's spirits with a rendition of a catchy little number in Spanish, finished with a clatter of castanets and a cry of 'Olé.' J Tea glanced up at the window, and then at Margaret's guilty look. He nearly boiled over, and, thrusting the large basket of fruit into her arms, turned, and strode away with long, angry strides. Margaret, staggering under the weight of the fruit basket, could only gasp 'Oh, Mr Thornton.'

The end came within a few days, and over and above the grief in the house was fear that Frederick's presence had been compromised by his being recognised, even in his curate's disguise, by the Bad Apple of Helstone, a labourer who had spat in the thoroughfare, failed to touch his forelock to the lord of the manor, and been banished to urban life. Mr Hale declared that Frederick would have to leave before the funeral, not least because he did not want his wife's obsequies interrupted by police whistles and the sound of 'I arrest you, Frederick Hale . . .'

Margaret accompanied her brother to the railway station, disguised as an apothecary assistant's sister. The train departed for Liverpool at a late hour, and the station was in darkness but for the gas lamps. They were seen by no one, other than the Bad Apple, who was best part drunk, and then, as Margaret hugged her brother and begged him to make an honest woman of Dolores of the Castanets, Mr Thornton.

~

J Tea, unable to sleep (probably from too much tea) had risen, dressed, and then gone for a long walk through Milton, hoping to take comfort from the dark, satanic mills in darkness. As he passed the railway station at Weaver's End he happened to glance at the platform. It was not a time when many passengers awaited trains. In the pool of light beneath a gas lamp he saw a young woman in black hug a man in black, with some vehemence. The light caught her pale visage, and agony shot through J Tea. It was Her. The man must have his sombrero rolled up in his valise. Margaret had lied to protect her lover. J Tea was desolated, and also furious. All the love his heart had poured out for her had been thrown away like a stewed brew, was unimportant when she idolised a young man with a sombrero and impressive castanets. J Tea sighed, for he was not even very proficient with a pair of spoons.

LEAF EIGHT - LOOK BACK AT TEA

It was three days later when Margaret, who was sat knitting a warm black scarf for her father, was informed by Dixon that there was a police officer in the morning room, wishing to speak with her. Margaret gasped. Was he come to say that Frederick had been detained? She went downstairs with her heart beating fast, but not thick. It was with relief that she heard the sergeant say that he was making enquiries into the death of a man whose body had been found by the Cotton Exchange in Milton, and who had been in an altercation at Weaver's End railway station with a man who was taking fond farewell of a young lady. The young lady had been identified as a witness as 'Miss Hale of Scotland Yard.'

Margaret took a deep breath, of which the police sergeant was appreciative, and denied that it could have been her. The witness was mistaken.

'But the witness was sure, Miss Hale.'

'Oh no, that is impossible. My aunt is Sure, and the entire family live in London and the Home Counties.' If some incident occurred at a railway station, but the dead man was found a mile away, she could not see there would be any connection for the police to investigate in any case.

'The death is as yet unexplained, and the description of the man, who was not local from evidence found upon his person, matched that of the man being disruptive at the station. If it goes to the Coroner, we may yet need you to swear an affidavit that it was not you at Weaver's End, miss.'

'I shall do so if required, sergeant, but I dislike the thought of my name being bandied about in the newspapers. I hope that no inquest is required.'

As the sergeant departed, sharpening his pencil, Margaret pressed her hands to her cheeks. She was going to have to lie to The Law in print as well as word!

J Tea found out about the suspicious death the same day, and when the officer asked if Miss Hale might have been the young lady seen at the station, J Tea instantly supported her. If she said she was not there, she was not there. He also asked the sergeant to leave matters in his hands as a Justice, and went off to the mortuary to see the body. The medical practitioner who had signed the death certificate said that the man showed advanced signs of cirrhosis, and might well have fallen down some steps in a drunken stupor. The injuries upon him would not be such as would occasion death in a normal individual. Armed with this information, J Tea wrote to the Coroner, saying that further investigation and an inquest would be an unnecessary expenditure of the public purse. He had no doubt this was true, but also knew that he was saving Miss Hale's reputation, and he knew that she had lied to protect it, and her unknown lover. His heart hardened against her, at least a little bit, and he resolved to cease his Latin lessons in Scotland Yard.

The police sergeant took Miss Hale the news, which she received calmly, as though it were obvious, but she was suffering palpitations at the realisation that Mr Thornton had been instrumental in keeping her good name safe, and that he knew she had lied and had been at the railway station late at night with a man. He would never know it was her brother, and she could not reveal that to him. She must therefore be damned in his eyes as a woman of low morals, or at best, poor judgment.

~

Margaret was listless, and not from the lack of a notebook. Her father was not listless, but aimless, wandering about the house looking for his slippers even when they were on his feet, and generally acting in the manner of a man who has lost the will to live. It was therefore ironic that it was upon a visit to his old haunts in Oxford, and his friend 'Ding Dong' Bell, that he actually expired. Margaret felt guilty as well as lonely, since she had encouraged him to go to raise his spirits, rather than his spirit to Heaven. She contemplated life as an orphan with misgivings, and was not made happier by the arrival of her Aunt Sure, who was adamant that Margaret must return to the safety of London with her immediately. The thought that struck Margaret was that she would never again see the man she had refused, who was the one man who had ever entered her dreams, and lingered there even when she knew that he despised her. She needed the excuse to say goodbye, and found it in books.

'I understand, Aunt, that the household goods must be sold, for your house can have no need of additional utensils, but I reserve the Minton tea set that was Mother's, and I would have Father's books go to the local public library for the education of all who seek knowl-edge, excepting his texts of Pliny the Elder and his History of Tea. Those I would give to Mr Thornton, for he was Father's friend here.'

'Well we are catching the train at eleven o'clock tomorrow morn-ing, so pack up this minute. We will go to the railway station via this Mr Thornton and his mother.'

All of which meant that at ten o'clock next morning, a hansom cab entered the gate of Marlborough Mills, leaving wheel tracks in the snow that was already lying several inches deep upon the ground. Aunt Sure sniffed at the idea of people living adjacent to their place of work, likening it to a shopkeeper living above his shop, but was impressed by the quality of Mrs Thornton's bombazine, which outshone her own.

Mrs Thornton greeted the news of Margaret's removal to The South with outward calmness, but did suggest they leave as soon as possible, in case the cab was delayed in reaching the railway station in time. She even announced that, in the circumstances, offering a cup of tea was unwise. She secretly hoped that Miss Hale would be gone without encountering J Tea, but he had seen her alight from the hansom cab, and he hastened to the house as soon as he was able.

'I was deeply saddened to hear of your father's demise, Miss Hale. He was a good friend to me, and I hope I was to him.'

'Yes indeed, Mr Thornton, your friendship is - has been - very important to - my family.' Her eyes were declaring 'To me, to me,' but her lips formed the polite phrases. 'Now that I must return south, I would like you to have these, both in memory of Father, and because he would be delighted that you have them.' She took from her reticule the Pliny and the History of Tea, and proffered them, her eyes not leaving his face. His outstretched hands met hers, their fingers touched as once over a teacup.

'I will treasure them,' he murmured, his voice very chocolatey, and, as he saw the titles, he smiled a sad smile. 'Tea. Yes, very appropriate.' He paused. 'So you are going? And will never come back?'

'There is nothing to keep my niece in The North, Mr Thornton,' announced Mrs Sure, loudly. 'She has been here far oolong, er too long, and it has killed both her parents.'

Margaret winced at the harshness and the insult, but J Tea said nothing, and just gazed at Margaret, trying to commit her to his memory as his heart whimpered in his chest.

'You must go, or you may miss your train.' Mrs Thornton would prefer it if Miss Hale waited in a chilly railway station waiting room rather than in her drawing room.

'Yes, we must.' The two older ladies, who knew they disliked each other, shared the same resolve on this. Margaret offered J Tea her hand, and shook his without a tremor. Then she made her farewell to Mrs Thornton and left with her aunt. J Tea followed, and tried to shut out the fervent 'At last' he heard from the drawing room. Upon the very steps where Margaret Hale had clung to his manly bosom to protect him, where she had swooned in those manly arms, his voice nearly unmanned him entirely.

'Come back,' he managed in a whisper, 'come back to J Tea for tea.' His eyes pleaded, and then watered, but that could be put down to getting snowflakes in his face.

LEAF NINE - THE PERFECT BLEND

It felt to J Tea that with Margaret Hale's departure, all the pleasure and good fortune in his life was poured away. Although the strike had collapsed, so had his financial situation, for although he was slowly making up the lost orders, the payments for them were exceedingly tardy and the cash flow was like a spout blocked with leaves and with no mote spoon to hand.

Part of him was bitterly resentful that all his honest hard work had gone for nothing, and he was worried for his mother, though relieved that she had got his sister off their hands to a husband with plenty of money and no interest in unusual interior decoration. For himself, it mattered little whether he ran a cotton mill or became a bank clerk. His life was a pot without the boiling water of passion cast upon the tea leaves of love, and meaningless to him. Mr Bell could find another to run Marlborough Mills, and at least the work force would not become destitute.

It was with some surprise that he found Mr Bell himself in the Master's Office, one Thursday afternoon. Mr Bell had something to tell him, or at least a partial something.

'I am moving abroad for what remains of my health, Thornton. I have no ties now, in England, and enjoyed my youth in South America. I shall enjoy my later days there also, and having no blood relations, have resolved to pass all my English business interests to my goddaughter, Miss Hale.'

J Tea nearly dropped his quill pen, and his fingers trembled for a moment. Mr Bell noted it.

'You need not think she will come and interfere, of course, but you will answer to her, not to me, and the profits, should you manage to make some again, will go to her.'

J Tea grew pale, and it was almost a peremptory farewell that he bade to his now former employer. It was a good thing, he told himself, that he would not be running Marlborough Mills in the near future.

The workforce accepted the news as all news. It was bound to be bad for them because everything was bad for them. Nicholas Higgins, father to the late Bessy, steward to a defeated Union, and chief supporter of the works' kitchen idea, was not seeking revenge.

After all, Thornton had given him work to feed the orphaned Smouchers, when no other would employ him. After the last shift he came to J Tea and shook his hand, man to man. He also asked after 'Miss Margaret.'

'I have not heard of her since she moved south to London,' said J Tea, with a small sigh, 'though she is going to be a wealthy woman from now on, and secure.

'Aye, I 'eard as that were so, but I wondered if she would go to Spain.'

'To Spain? Why? They do not drink tea there, as far as I know. Why on earth would she want -'

'To see 'er brother as came in dead of night to visit 'is dying mother.'

'She has a brother?'

'Oh yes.' Higgins nodded his affirmation.

'Who came here?'

'Oh yes.' Higgins nodded again. 'E 'ad fallen foul of the Navy in some law and is a wanted man in England.'

'It was her brother,' sighed J Tea, and although his heart was still broken, he was eased by the thought that he had not misread her character. What sister would not hug a brother and would not lie to save him?

The two men shook hands, though Higgins dropped the aitch of his.

~

'How dare you.' Margaret slapped boring Henry the Lawyer's face.

'Suggesting I have made money over the course of a night is unforgivable.'

'No, no, Margaret, I meant that your investments have improved drastically overnight, not - not anything unseemly.'

'Ah.' She did not actually apologise, because hitting boring Henry round the face was well overdue. He always talked to women as if their brains were made of sugar lumps and would melt if stirred.

'Yes, and you are several thousand pounds better off, thanks to being involved in Mr Watson's scheme for importing Australian liquorice for sherbet fountains. It was speculative but lucrative. A pity for his brother-in-law that he, your Mr Thornton of Marlborough Mills, did not risk a little. He ceased his running of the mill two days ago.'

'He is not "my" Mr Thornton, Henry, and he had good reason not to enter into speculation. His father was caught in the great jelly bean scandal of 1838.'

'Was he, by Jove! Well, the son ought to have got over the fear of speculation. He is nobody now. He moves out of the mill house next Tuesday.'

'Henry. I need to go to Milton as soon as possible.'

'Why?'

'I have remembered I left Mr Thornton's gloves under the stairs in Scotland Yard.'

She omitted to say that she had gone under the stairs on a daily basis and slipped on the huge gloves for a moment and sighed a sad sigh.

'Can you not arrange for a minion to -'

'No, I owe this to Mr Thornton.'

'Very well, I shall accompany you to protect you.'

Margaret's look spoke volumes. She was going to take a long hat pin in her depressing brown hat, just in case he tried to get too close in the railway compartment.

∽

J TEA SAT in the confined compartment of the railway carriage, tealess and heart-weary. He had gone to Helstone because he could not imagine being within three shires of Her Origins, and not seeing them, feeling the very roots of her. It had been a bitter-sweet day, like darjeeling with too large a slice of lemon. He had found the rectory easily enough, since there were helpful yokels who pointed the way, and a large sign on the gate which said 'THE RECTORY - keep to the path (of righteousness)'. He could see the sprawling house beyond a hedge of yellow tea roses, alas badly pruned, and had parted a few branches, much to the cost of his gloves, to peer at the house.

As J Tea passed the wicket gate that led up to the vicarage, he heard the sound of infant voices, many of them, engaged in some energetic game somewhere behind the sprawling brick building. To the front of it was a small terrace where one might take tea of an afternoon. J Tea shut his eyes after that first glance, and lengthened his naturally long stride, his cheeks suffused. Whilst the clergy were not monastic, he could not but think that vicar's wives ought to be rather more chaste than chased, let alone caught. At which point he stopped suddenly and uttered a mild oath, having walked into a tree. He really ought to have opened his eyes earlier.

So now he was heading back to Milton and Mother, and a mill as empty as a caddy with a rattling spoon in it, heading back to Mother and yet to a solitude. He sighed. The train drew in to a small station and halted. A Woman in Brown passed by, and her brown hat reminded him of Her brown hat. He stretched tired limbs and heard the announcement that the train would depart in five minutes. He looked out of the window onto the platform and saw an apparition. He wanted to see Her so much he was doing so! He shook his head, but She was still there, staring at him. His throat tightened. Breathlessly, he reached for the door handle, stepped onto the platform, and found himself looking down at Her.

'Mr Thornton!' cried Margaret, clasping her ungloved hands at her bosom. 'I have been to Milton, upon business, but you were not there.' She made it sound as if she had searched quite diligently, possibly even under stones.

'You'll never guess where I have been,' murmured J Tea huskily, withdrawing from his pocket a small packet emblazoned with 'Miggins' Fine Teas' and the image of a yellow rose.

'Mrs Miggins' Tea Shop!' Margaret Hale's voice was full of wonder. 'And you have a packet of her Boudoir Blend. I had thought that discontinued.' She blushed, having used the word 'boudoir.'

'I bought the last one. She had to look 'ard' to find it in 'er drawers - of tea.' The brown packet lay in his palm. The Woman in Brown passed again and covered her ears at the words 'boudoir' and 'drawers' being enunciated on a railway station platform. Margaret gazed at the packet, or rather at the hand holding it. Such a beautiful hand, she thought, imagining him holding a teaspoon and stirring his tea, stirring her, stirring, stirring . . . .

'I - I had a business matter to discuss with you, Mr Thornton. We would have discussed it over tea, and perhaps langue de chat biscuits.'

It was his turn to blush. French was a foreign language to him, but he had mastered a little and she had just mentioned tongues. His own tied itself into a neat bow.

'I . . . oh I ought to fetch Henry,' declared Margaret, distractedly.

'Nooooo,' almost boomed J Tea. 'Three for tea is wrong. We do not need Henry. It must be tea for two.'

He grasped her hand, and led her into a tiny tea room, where a medical practitioner was removing a mote of engine-soot from the eye of a well dressed lady who somehow had the air of one wishing it was not just the mote.

J Tea selected a table in the corner and drew back a seat for Margaret before taking his own. His knees touched her skirts, and that alone gave a frisson. She gazed at him, trying to form the words whilst her head was filled with 'Oh my goodness, how much I have missed that brow, those eyes, that commanding nose,' and her heart fluttered.

'As I said, Mr Thornton, I have a business . . .' She was interrupted by a thickset waiter who loomed beside her and looked at Mr Thornton.

'Tea, sir? For two, sir?'

'Yes, please, two for tea.'

'Which tea would you care to imbibe, sir?' asked the waiter, and launched into a list, unbidden, and all in one breath. 'We have black tea, green tea, white tea, bright tea, fruit tea, mufti, tutti-frutti tea, Russian tea, China tea, oolong, brewed-long, lapsang souchong served by me in a sarong, large leaf, small leaf, rolled leaf, light-fingered "tea leaf," Twinings, Tweanings, workers' cooperative with Socialist leanings, First Flush, Second Flush, tippy tea and maidens' blush, and Yorkshire.'

'I did not know camellia sinensis grew in Yorkshire,' remarked Margaret, surprised.

'It does not, madam,' returned the waiter. 'But it is there given a fine northern blending.'

Inadvertently, her eyes flew to Mr Thornton. Oh, the merest thought of a fine northern blending with him!

'We will have the Yorkshire,' announced Mr Thornton, as if half reading her thoughts.

'And a biscuit, sir? We have Nice, spice, Italian baked twice . . .'

'No biscuits, thank you.' Mr Thornton cut off the waiter in his prime, and the man withdrew with a sniff and a mumble about not having got to 'Rook creams.'

'As I was saying, Mr Thornton -' she was still looking at him, her eyes soft, and showing distinct signs of adoration. 'I have a business proposition to make to you. Just that, for you would owe me nothing - except a proportion of the dividend, or something.' She frowned. All that talk of Henry's had bored her stiff. Mr Thornton was looking at her, a half smile of immense gentleness playing about his mouth. She had an idea it was not from his anticipation of a cup of tea. Boldly, she reached the few inches across the table to touch his fingers, fingers that unconsciously wound between hers. She gasped, and looked no more at his face, but their conjoined hands.

'Oh, and I have your black leather gloves,' she murmured, caressingly.

A Woman in Brown entered the tea room and snorted in disgust at the conjoining of hands in a place that sold beverages.

'My financial advisors tell me that I have some fifteen thousand pounds doing nothing in the bank, being just notes and inanimate. I had thought to ask you to use it to restart Marlborough Mills, but - if they can blend good tea in Yorkshire, could we not blend it even better in Milton? Could we reanimate the works producing the finest blend of North and South, Mr Thornton?' Her voice became quite excited. She lifted his hand to her lips and kissed it, as if making a pact.

'You wish to blend with me?' J Tea's voice was barely above a whisper.

'You would give the brews strength and power and a hint of "smouldering chocolateyness," and I, I would give them delicate overtones of fragrance and refinement. It would be a blend made in Heaven, Mr Thornton.'

He had no words. Actions were better. He leaned, one hand teacupping her cheek as he brought his lips to hers. The first kiss was tentative, as if tasting a cup of tea that might be too hot. The second had the assurance of drinking a favoured tea, brewed to perfection.

Over in the corner, the Woman in Brown hit the waiter, who had got as far as 'Chocolate hobnob.'

The station master was calling for passengers for the London train.

'Oh no, my baggage. Henry! I must go!' Margaret rose hastily, and J Tea did likewise, grimacing as the edge of the table hit him in the groin. He paled. She was already by the door. He could not prevent her leaving. He reached the doorway to see her looking up at Boring Henry, a man whom he knew to drink coffee at breakfast. The look between them was not of love.

'Goodbye, Margaret,' said Boring Henry with finality, and handed her the valise she had brought with her. 'You have made a mocha-ry of me.' With which he withdrew into the carriage and shut the door.

J Tea stood at the tea room door, scarcely daring to breathe. The medical practitioner and the lady with the mote passed him, unaware of his presence in their mutual involvement.

'It is no use. I cannot go through with it, Laura. I am leaving for

Africa. I will run a mission hospital in Kenya and start a tea plantation.'

Even in his trepidation, J Tea could not discount business. African tea? It might do quite well. He thrust his visiting card into the doctor's hand. It was a very brief encounter, but one never knew. The man pocketed it without taking his eyes from the woman's face.

'Oh Alec, this is terribly, terribly distressing.'

'Go home and have a nice cup of tea, Laura,' he replied, patting her hand a little sadly, and walked away. She sniffed.

Margaret was turning. She looked a little malformed. The valise was rather heavy and one shoulder therefore drooped. She struggled towards J Tea, who stepped close, holding out his hand.

'You are Keemun home with me?' It was half question, half asser-tion. 'Oh, Margaret, my Darjeeling. I love you.' He beamed at her as he took the heavy valise, wondering what it might contain, and offered his other arm for her to lean upon. They stepped to the Milton bound train. There was no corridor, so no refreshments could be offered, but they did not give a single tea leaf about that. They were going home to Milton - and passionate brewing together.

DAMARIS OSBORNE IS an English author and lover of North & South, whose novella 'North & Spoof' is available from Amazon, and who is the author of a 12thC murder mystery series under another pseu-donym. She says spoofing is her outlet for her 'silly streak', and her literary heroes are Jane Austen, Rudyard Kipling, Georgette Heyer and Terry Pratchett.

DAMARIS OSBORNE's other books include: *North & Spoof*

REEDUCATING MR THORNTON

Evy Journey

"But, surely, if the mind is too long directed to one object only, it will get stiff and rigid, and unable to take in many interests." - Chapter XV, North and South

"Cádiz." Peering into a telescope on the deck of the pilot house, the ship captain announced, at the top of his voice, the pending arrival of the steamship at its destination. It was carrying passengers from Paris to Cádiz.

On the promenade, John Thornton straightened his tall, lean figure and, with his arm around her back, pulled Margaret closer. He could now claim her as his own. They had married six weeks ago. He squinted at the assault of light and wind and strained to catch a glimpse of land in the distance. The strip he saw was awash in white, emerging like an apparition from the cobalt blue Mediterranean.

Mr. Thornton did not have any expectations of what he would find in Cádiz. Nor did he care much to know what the city was like. He was going there to please Margaret, who had not seen her brother Frederick since their mother passed away.

Margaret could not wait to be with Frederick and to meet Dolores, his new wife. She was also anxious for her brother and her husband to get to know each other. When Mr. Thornton and Margaret decided to go to the continent for their honeymoon, a month in Paris and another in Cádiz were their inevitable destination choices.

As the steamship's propellers brought it closer to land, the apparition Mr. Thornton had been watching began to take shape. He spotted two towers and, next to them, a golden dome. They rose above a mass of white buildings topped by turrets and belvederes. He had seen such structures in some English homes, but they were not ubiquitous like they seemed to be in Cádiz. Fascinated, he scanned the scenery. The golden dome seemed the only colored structure against the blue skyline. But a moment later, splashes of bright colors broke the monotony of white buildings. Flowers, he marveled. Red and orange and yellow flowers one rarely saw in the persistently gray and gloomy days in Milton. And it was only mid-June.

His gaze swept back toward the golden dome soaring like a beacon over the luminous city. "Dramatic," he muttered.

"Moorish," Margaret said. "The first mosque, known as Dome of the Rock, has a golden dome."

Surprised she heard him, he smiled down at her. Moorish—that was to be expected. Bewildering Cádiz was, after all, a very old city in Spain, once a rich and powerful empire that had established territories in North Africa since the Middle Ages. The Moors, in turn, had occupied what was now Andalucia in southern Spain.

The idea of travelling had intrigued him as a young man. Educated young Englishmen of means usually embarked on a grand tour of France and Italy for culture and further education. He dreamt of going on that tour. Fate, however, did not will it so. He had to leave school and work to support his mother and his sister. Swindled by a business partner, his father had lost everything he owned and, driven by disgrace, killed himself.

Mr. Thornton let out a long breath as he tucked away the painful memories. He had worked hard to succeed in his trade so he could provide his mother and his sister the good life they deserved. All those years of working had made him a practical man, but he feared that, along the way, he had also outgrown the desire to experience the mystique of a city like Cádiz. He was reasonably content with his lot, at least until he met Margaret.

He put his arm around his wife's shoulder. Margaret held onto her hat and raised her face. Her lips quivered into a smile.

Margaret had taken more care than usual dressing that morning, and he gazed with pleasure at her large expressive eyes and soft generous lips. She always took his breath away. He brushed his lips against her temple and gave her shoulder a tender reassuring squeeze. "You're looking fresh and lovely, Mrs. Thornton."

"These trade winds help," she said. "I am nervous, but I wanted to appear calm and cool, which is rather a challenge when one wears layers of clothing in this heat."

They were waiting for the ship captain to announce that they could board one of the small boats taking passengers to shore. "This is what you've been waiting for. I think your brother will only be too happy to see you."

The night before, she talked about the letters Frederick had written from Cádiz. After he met Dolores, his letters gushed about her mesmerizing midnight blue eyes which he could not turn away from, long thick black hair he could get lost in, and her mix of appealing naiveté and insatiable curiosity that kept them talking. In ending his letters with hopes that his sister and his wife would like each other, Margaret became equally anxious that they should.

Mr. Thornton had his apprehensions about meeting Frederick— apprehensions that kept him fidgeting in bed for the past couple of nights. He had heard enough of Margaret's stories to conjure an image of Frederick as a paragon of a brother. Frederick let her win their games when they were growing up and listened to all her child-hood cares. As a young man, he went to sea, driven by dreams of being captain of his own ship.

After Mr. Thornton and Margaret found each other again, she told him that, years ago, Frederick was among those accused of leading an alleged mutiny against a tyrannical ship captain. The crime was punishable by death, and Frederick had no choice but to be exiled forever from England.

Despite this, it seemed life had been kind to Frederick, now an ardent husband and lover of most things Spanish. A year ago, he found his redemption—Frederick's word—when he met Dolores. Since then, he had been carving a niche for himself in his new country.

Mr. Thornton and Fredrick might not be that different. They both had lofty dreams as well as troubles, despair, and redemption. However, much of what Margaret knew about her brother was from a relatively distant past. And there was that night at the Milton train station when he and Frederick stared at each other, both scowling in unguarded animosity. Would Frederick remember? He himself had been stung with jealousy. He did not know then who Frederick was. How much had Frederick changed? Changes were inevitable, espe-cially when one had been forcibly uprooted and was now living in Cádiz.

AN HOUR LATER, the boat that ferried them from the steamship docked by an opening through the ramparts protecting the city. Mr. Thornton could sense Margaret's impatience to disembark onto the stairs leading to the quay. He grasped her arm and kept a steady grip until they reached the quay, where Customs employees directed them toward the Customs House.

Before they could reach Customs, Margaret raised her arm and waved. She turned to him, her eyes shining. "Frederick. Do you see him?"

Mr. Thornton looked toward where Margaret waved. He had no trouble spotting a young man who stood a head taller than most of the crowd and whose hair shone like polished copper in a sea of dark hair. A pretty petite woman clung to his arm.

He surveyed the crowd waiting to welcome the arrivals, frowning at seeing jacket-less men out in public. But the sight of so many women wearing skirts strewn with bright colors wiped away his frown and brought a small smile to his lips.

How, he wondered, did they weave large red and pink roses or, maybe, peonies into textiles? Had the Spaniards outdone the English? Had they invented new techniques that made such designs on textiles possible? It was so new, unusual, and attractive that it seemed to have become the current fashion, along with the black lace veils adorning the heads of some women. He doubted, however, that veils were of much use in windy, sunny Cádiz. He had only been married six weeks and, already, he was paying more attention to women's fashion.

Margaret tugged at his arm and repeated, "Do you see him?"

"Oh. Frederick. Yes, I do. In this crowd, he does stand out. I only caught a glimpse of him in a dark train station, so I might not recognize him in a crowd back home. Here in this bright Mediterranean light, he's unmistakably English. That must be his wife clinging to him."

"Yes. Dolores. Isn't she beautiful?"

"A real exotic beauty. I expected nothing less after what you told me about her," he said, his eyes crinkling in amusement. He grasped her hand and kissed it. "But for me, no one can compare to you, my love."

Her palm brushed soft and warm against his cheek, and she gazed into his eyes. "I'm so glad you're here," she said.

He kissed her hand once more before he tucked it into his arm. They joined the group from their ship going into the Customs House.

Once inside, they both stood gaping at a crowd that seemed to have taken on every possible shade and color—from black and brown Africans to ruddy English sailors and pale-skinned European aristocrats. They surveyed the motley crowd for a couple of minutes before making their way to the line of arriving passengers going through inspection.

More than a half hour later, they emerged from the stifling Customs House. Relieved to be out among the throng who were free to move about in the salty air and intense light of the harbor, Mr. Thornton said, "The whole world must be represented in there."

Margaret smiled, her eyes round with wonder. "Quite a sight, wasn't it? Do you suppose it's this way every day?"

"Ask Frederick. He is behind you and will be here in a few seconds." Mr. Thornton watched Frederick running toward them, leaving his wife behind. He scowled. He would never have left Margaret standing all alone in a crowd.

He heard his wife suck in a sharp shallow breath. Still scowling, he turned to see her falling into her brother's arms.

Neither said a word. They clutched each other tight as tears rolled down their cheeks. Mr. Thornton stared, drawn into the drama of the reunion of brother and sister yet also astonished by such an open display of emotions. It took a while before Frederick raised his head and held Margaret at arm's length. They gazed long at each other before he pulled her back into his embrace, kissing her cheeks over and over. She returned each kiss mixed with her tears.

Minutes later, her hands trembling, Margaret dabbed her face with a handkerchief she pulled out of the pocketbook hanging around her wrist. Frederick, still holding her, was not trembling any less. He threw his sister's husband a quick glance and swiped his red eyes with the back of his left hand.

Averting his eyes, Mr. Thornton gritted his teeth. *Were they still mourning their parents? Why now? She should have unburdened her grief on me. Why didn't she?*

He sighed. *They grew up together, shared intimate family concerns—maybe even secrets—that an outsider, including me, might never understand.*

"Hello." The hesitant trill of a girlish voice made him turn to peer into midnight-blue eyes on an olive-skinned beauty. Dolores. She stood before him, her abundant wavy tresses cascading over a red shawl draped on her shoulders and down her flowered skirt. Mr.

Thornton arched an eyebrow and failed to suppress a smile that lifted one side of his mouth. Looking closer at the design on the skirt, he realized that it was embroidered, not woven in.

He heard Dolores introduce herself in accented English and, in a move that brought blood rushing to his face, she clasped his shoulders, stood on her toes, kissed his cheeks and offered hers for him to kiss in return. He planted a quick buss on one cheek as words stumbled out of his mouth. "I'm John Thornton, Margaret's husband."

Dolores said, "I know. I've heard much about you."

Bemused at the unexpected warmth of Dolores's greeting, Mr. Thornton shifted his gaze back to Margaret and her brother who had stepped back from his sister. His eyes red and puffy, Frederick smiled tremulously at his wife. "Forgive me for leaving you behind?"

Dolores did not answer. She grasped his tear-stained face with both hands and kissed it over and over as she wiped his face tenderly with her fingers. She pulled him into her embrace. Frederick rested his cheek on her head.

Watching her brother and his wife, Margaret's eyes were once again welling up with tears. She wiped them before they fell down her cheeks. Mr. Thornton took a step towards her to comfort her, but he heard Frederick call out his name.

Frederick and Dolores had broken apart. His face drier and a smile playing on his lips, Frederick approached Mr. Thornton, his open hand reaching out to him.

Mr. Thornton grasped the offered hand. In a quick gesture— another he did not anticipate—Frederick clasped him in his arms. "May I call you John? I feel as if I've known you a long time from Margaret's letters. Welcome to our family. *Muy encantado*, as we say in Spanish. You have met my wife Dolores?"

Having gently extricated himself from Frederick's embrace, Mr. Thornton grinned. "Yes. She has already taught me one of your charming customs."

"Good. You've been introduced to the Gaditano spirit. I hope it doesn't bother you. It's nothing like you'd find in England."

Frederick turned to his wife. He placed an arm around her waist and presented her to his sister.

Margaret raised her face from drying her eyes with her handkerchief and smiled at Dolores. Aware of Spanish customs and predisposed to like Dolores, she embraced her sister-in-law and kissed her on both cheeks. "I feel I know you quite well. Fred's letters are often short and straightforward but when he talks about you, he fills pages."

Dolores blushed. "I hope I meet your expectations."

"You're more beautiful than I imagined, and you make English sound lovelier and more musical."

Her eyes twinkling, Dolores hooked her arm with Margaret's. "Fred—he does not explain well. Like most men, you know. He said, my sister, she is strong and her spirit ...formidable." She hesitated, glancing at Margaret.

Margaret nodded. "Yes?"

"He made me anxious I do not meet your approval. Now I see you. You are sweet and kind, and you have the most beautiful blue eyes I have ever seen, bluer than his."

"I can see we'll get along well, for we're both anxious to like each other."

Arm in arm, the two women started to walk on.

Frederick said, "Shall we join our ladies?"

"Yes, of course." Mr. Thornton strode in step with Frederick. As they kept pace behind their wives, he thought with both wonder and envy: *How easily women make friends. Margaret need not have worried. She and Dolores seemed to have charmed each other.*

He, on the other hand, had been thrown off balance from the moment he set foot on the quay. The sunlight that flooded the city even in late afternoon overwhelmed him. Though diffused, it intensified the vibrant colors all around him and made him more aware of the heat. His cravat was too tight. He tugged at it although he did not dare loosen it. He tasted the salty tang of Atlantic winds, so unlike the metallic effusion of industrial machines, dyes, and textiles he inhaled daily in Milton. He looked one way, then another, his attention riveted by the cacophony of harbor sounds—the rhythmic splashing of waves against the hulls of ships arriving or leaving, the grating shrill of seagulls, and the disorienting buzz of strange tongues that he was sure were not all Spanish.

Frederick broke into his thoughts. "You know we've seen each other before. At a train station at night, I believe, more than two years ago. You looked mysterious, hidden by shadows. Now that I see you better under our Andalusian skies, I have to say I like your smile. A smile says a lot about people."

Uncertain what had passed between brother and sister when they talked about him, Mr. Thornton forced himself to smile. "I'm sure I was scowling at you. But you must understand—to me, you were a stranger embracing the woman who meant the world to me."

Frederick chuckled and laid a hand on Mr. Thornton's shoulder. "I do understand. I hope you weren't left out of our family secret for too long. We all had a difficult time with it, especially my mother."

Mr. Thornton shrugged. "I would have liked to have known about you earlier, not only that you exist but also about the trouble you had at sea. Well, I am here now, and that's all that matters, I believe."

They followed their wives in silence for a couple of minutes before Frederick spoke again. "We're relieved and thankful when difficult times are over and done with. Sometimes, though, their consequences can haunt us forever."

Surprised at his remark, Mr. Thornton cocked his head toward Frederick. He started to ask which consequences Frederick referred to, but the question died in his throat. If Frederick had a new disclosure to make, he believed Frederick should share it freely.

An easy smile had lingered on Frederick's lips since they started to walk together. It faded, and the flush on his face crept back up. His eyes cast down, he said, "I have these pangs of guilt, sometimes agonizing, that I might have hastened my mother's death. You know that she had often suffered from one little ailment or another. What if they worsened enough to kill her because of what happened to me?"

Mr. Thornton reached out and rested his hand on Frederick's shoulder. Frederick glanced at him, a small grateful smile on his lips, though his eyes remained clouded.

It dawned on Mr. Thornton that his brother-in-law had a vulnerable side. Frederick had seen more of the world than he had and endured life-threatening challenges. He had expected Frederick to have been toughened by his past. But this man walking next to him, with his ready smile and confident air, knew the agony of guilt and blamed himself for his mother's death.

Mr. Thornton was acquainted enough with the Hales to be certain that they would never have thought Frederick responsible in any way for Mrs. Hale's passing. However, he was also aware that, in his anguish, Frederick might not be swayed by anyone contradicting his belief.

"You're right about some lasting effects of tragedy and how helpless they make us feel. All we can do is live with them. But surely there are many more good times with people we love that we can celebrate or at least be grateful for."

Frederick's smile widened and his eyes brightened the way Margaret's did when she was pleased. "Yes, surely you are right. I have actually told myself that once or twice. It reassures me, though, to hear you say it."

FREDERICK AND DOLORES lived on Plaza de Mina in a white three-story house topped by a belvedere that Frederick explained was some type of lookout. From there, former merchant owners of the house could look out to sea for the arrival of trading ships from other countries. Its top two floors had narrow balconies—*miradores*, Dolores said—that faced the plaza. Like other houses on the plaza, pots of red and pink geraniums and orange nasturtiums hung on the balconies' metal railings. On the second floor, a large verandah jutted out into a courtyard at the back of the house. It had a large daybed of lacquered mahogany and woven cane, six large matching chairs, and a distressed wooden table with elaborate Moorish carvings on the edges.

The house was nothing like Mr. Thornton and Margaret saw in Milton. It delighted her but, while he had taken his cues from his wife when they looked at art and architecture in Paris, he kept silent throughout their tour of the house. In his mind, he debated whether a house should be this open. It was a house that he was certain would not work well in Milton where, frequently, residents had to close windows to reduce the noise of textile machinery or minimize the smell of dyes used in cotton production.

His silent internal debate did not last. By the second day of their stay, he was convinced that verandahs and balconies were a clever idea and necessary in the hot Mediterranean climate. Frederick and Dolores left the doors to the balconies open day and night, letting ocean breezes flow through the house and out the verandah. Mr. Thornton was grateful for the open spaces that provided welcome relief from the heat.

On that second day, he also saw his wife as he had never seen her before.

Margaret kept wiping her neck and face with her handkerchief throughout lunch. Dolores had noticed Margaret's discomfort. When lunch was over, Dolores turned to Margaret and said, "Come with me. We leave our men to get more acquainted, yes?"

Taken by surprise, Margaret hesitated for a moment. She glanced at her husband before she answered, "Where are we going?"

"Your skirt and blouse, they are too hot for this weather, no? Also, your body—it is beautiful. You do not need the......" She groped for words as she traced her torso with her hands.

"Stays," Margaret said.

"... stays, yes. And petticoats. It is cooler without them, you think?"

"Yes, you're right. I'm burning in these clothes." Margaret pushed her skirt down and agreed with an embarrassed laugh.

"You are taller than me but not bigger." Dolores shook her head as she placed her hands on top of her chest "Spanish blouses—they are loose. My skirts are shorter, but no one will notice."

"They would in England. You can't show ankles."

"Many, many ankles show here in Cádiz. In Andalucía, dancers kick their skirts to dance flamenco, and you must watch how fast they click their heels. So, come with me. You will feel better." Dolores waved her hand toward Frederick and Mr. Thornton. "We join them later."

The two men, glasses of sherry in their hands, got up and went into the verandah to indulge in an after-dinner Andalusian custom. Dolores led Margaret to her bedroom.

When the two women joined their husbands on the verandah, Margaret was wearing a new outfit—a short-sleeved blouse of deep rose through which one could glimpse a shadow of her ivory-colored chemise, and a forest green flowing skirt that clung to her limbs when she moved. She had exchanged her shoes and thick stockings for a pair of sandals.

Mr. Thornton was taken aback. He said nothing while Frederick expressed profuse approval. He had much he could say but judged it best to wait until he and Margaret were alone in their bedroom. She always dressed appropriately, her choice in clothes simple and impeccable. Seeing her in scantier clothing outside the privacy of their home disconcerted him. She did look beautiful in them. They showed her graceful, unbound figure to advantage.

"Isn't my little sister beautiful?" Frederick said, interrupting his musing. He had returned to the seat next to Mr. Thornton's after serving cool chocolate drinks to the two women. "You know, when we were children, Margaret hated wearing petticoats because she could not run fast enough to keep up with me. So she would drag me to the fields away from Dixon's watchful eyes, where she would take them off. Without them, she did sometimes outrun me, partly from sheer determination, I think." Frederick chuckled and finished with another recollection. "Unfortunately, after she was sent to London, she started acting more like a lady, and she was not as much fun anymore."

"She thought you let her win all the time," Mr. Thornton said. "You're right, though. She is quite lovely. I suppose, as her husband, I thought I was the only one privileged to see her dressed so ... casually."

Frederick laughed. "You are on the Andalusian coast. We dress for the public when we leave the house. In here, what you do is between you and your conscience. You make your own rules. Most of the year, we cannot wear those layers of clothes you do in Britain. This climate won't let you. It encourages an informality that is good for the spirit."

"But does not the Spanish temperament figure into it?"

"I can't be sure about the Spanish temperament. The Gaditano's, certainly. Cádiz is ancient, dating back several hundred years before Christ. It has endured and absorbed many influences. Its location is a natural for trade, so you will see all kinds of people when you go out for a walk at the plazas."

"They were all at the Customs House."

"They come from all over Europe, North Africa, and the Americas. Many have set roots here, bringing their own culture. To live here, you can't insist on proper English decorum. You must be open to different things, strange things—learn to accept them."

"You seem to have adapted quite well."

"It took years. I was forced to come here and couldn't accept that I'd probably never return to England. Once I accepted my fate, I saw so much about this city and its people that I liked and admired. I believe there's nowhere else in Europe where you'd find a more liberal outlook. And Cádiz is so alive. It infects you with a *joie de vivre*, though older folk who've lived here a long time insist that, as good as it is now, its most glorious years came and went with the past century. But Cádiz still seduces. It has seduced me. I'm more Gaditano now than English. "

"Meeting Dolores probably helped, too," Mr. Thornton said.

"Yes, indeed." Glancing at his wife, Frederick grinned.

Their wives were standing by the stone balustrade. Margaret was enchanted with the garden, gushing with delight as Dolores pointed to purple bougainvilleas and passion flowers climbing toward the balustrade, large pots of red and deep pink roses whose characteristic damask fragrance wafted up the verandah. Flower beds along the edge of the garden were aflame with bluebells, red and orange poppies, and yellow gazanias. Margaret sighed, voicing her doubts that those flowers could ever grow in the smoky atmosphere and dye-saturated soil of Milton.

"Margaret would have adapted to this society with ease, particularly with you here," Mr. Thornton said with a mix of pride and concern as he gazed at his wife.

Frederick shot him a curious glance. "She would have, maybe sooner than most—sooner than me, surely. She has the advantage of all the letters I've sent her about life in Cádiz. And since she can speak French, she'll learn Spanish in no time at all."

"She told me you wrote and invited her to come live with you after your parents died."

"I did. I worried about her," Frederick said. "She wrote me long letters after our father died. I sensed the silent despair in them, not only because of her grief at Father's loss. I think Margaret faced the reality that she no longer had anyone in Milton whose wisdom she could trust in her bleakest hours."

"But she had her aunt and cousin," Mr. Thornton said. "Her aunt came to take her away from Milton shortly after Mr. Hale's funeral. I understood that she looked after Margaret, and her daughter could give Margaret comfort and affection while she was grieving."

"That's true. Sadly, though, they could not comprehend all that she was going through. Margaret is capable of deeper feelings, and her intellect is superior to our cousin's. Anyway, she considered my offer to live with us, but she wasn't ready to leave England. She said it was a momentous change, and she was right. Anyway, she understood that she would be welcome any time. I did try to entice her, telling her how much I've been enjoying my life here. Later, to my surprise, she sent me a letter telling me she was getting married."

Although Frederick appeared to have more to say, he paused, his brow creased in thought. When he spoke again, his voice was subdued, regretful. "I wanted to come, give her away in marriage. I couldn't wait to meet you, but England is now lost to me. I despaired, worrying that I might not see my sister again, and I spent many sleepless nights after our parents died wondering how she was and what would happen to her, alone in England."

"She wasn't alone," Mr. Thornton said with more firmness than he intended, "and, I confess, I am glad she didn't come here. If she had, I would have invented some excuse to come for her when I found out who you were."

Frederick chuckled. "I do believe you would have. You've been good for her. She has a radiance I've never seen before. And I'm extremely glad you're both here now. I can't thank you enough for coming to visit."

Mr. Thornton went to bed that night trying to recall a Spanish tune Frederick was humming as he poured sherry at the end of dinner. When Margaret joined him in bed, all he said about her attire was "You looked so alluring, my love, that I wanted to take you in my arms and kiss you right then and there, in front of Fred and Dolores."

"Why didn't you? But I'm glad you didn't mind my dress. I worried you might not approve."

He enclosed her in his arms and kissed her. "I was dismayed—for an instant. Anyway, it's how everybody dresses in Cádiz."

IN SUMMER, the Cádiz sun was at its zenith at mid-day, and local people preferred the comfort of indoor spaces. So the city broke for lunch. Frequently heavier than dinner, it could last two hours and was usually followed by a siesta. Were Frederick not on vacation, he would have returned to his office after siesta and worked from about 5 p.m. to past 8 p.m. in the evening.

Margaret remembered siesta from Frederick's letters and was not surprised at the practice. Faithful to the custom, Frederick and Dolores treated the hour or two of repose as a necessary indulgence which they spent in their bedroom, leaving Mr. Thornton and Margaret to entertain themselves.

Accustomed to a schedule of continuous work during the day, Mr. Thornton found it perplexing and could not see himself doing nothing, much less dozing off, in the middle of the day. He thought it yet another quaint Gaditano custom that would not suit Milton. He could never adopt the practice at home.

Earlier he had felt uncomfortable at the casual, demonstrative manner of his hosts. At home, Frederick and Dolores touched, embraced, and kissed each other with unabashed playfulness. He and Margaret felt free to express their affection only in the privacy of their bedroom.

Alone at siesta time on the third day, Mr. Thornton persuaded Margaret to visit the cathedral they had seen on the day they arrived. Inclined to go along with the local customs, she balked at first but relented. He was restless, and she was convinced a brisk walk to Plaza de la Catedral might calm him. Besides, she was eager to see a cathedral that her brother had said was neoclassical while also adapting features of Moorish, rococo, and baroque architecture across the more than a century it had taken to finish it.

The sun sparkled, and the heat hovered just below searing level. By the time they reached the cathedral, their clothes stuck to their skin and their faces were flushed and moist. Mr. Thornton pushed the massive door into the cathedral. But it did not budge.

He said, "I'm sorry to have dragged you on that miserable walk to this cathedral. It seemed so grand, I thought we should see it."

"Oh, no," Margaret said. "I was hoping to sit inside for a while and cool off a bit."

"I was quite impressed with the light in this lively and colorful city. But I must admit that, right now, I'm wishing I was back to the dreary but cool atmosphere of Milton."

Margaret shrugged and said nothing. She stepped into the narrow strip of shade cast by the cathedral.

"Now I understand why they have siestas in the afternoon, but how terribly inconvenient for visitors like us." Mr. Thornton was annoyed. He waved his hand at the sun. "I suppose, in this part of the world, there's nothing much you could do about something you can't control."

Margaret pulled Mr. Thornton toward her. "Oh, John. Relax here for a moment, will you? Cool down a little. Then we'll go back to the house so I can shed off these petticoats and we can have large glasses of pomegranate juice."

The next day, Margaret declared that, for the rest of their stay in

Cádiz, she would devote the siesta hour to reading. She picked a book from her brother's library, the first volume of a series titled *The Whale* by Herman Melville, a writer unfamiliar to her. She returned to their bedroom, where Mr. Thornton was looking out the window.

She said, "How about reading with me? I can read this aloud—it sounds fascinating—or you can pick another. I know you prefer nonfiction. Fred seems to have quite a collection of books, some of which came from Father's library."

He turned toward Margaret and, leaning against the window sill, he said, "I can't sit still."

Looking sympathetic, she approached him and kissed him. "I'm sorry, John," she said before sitting on the couch at the foot of the bed. She swung her legs up on it and opened her book.

Mr. Thornton resigned himself to staying indoors like everyone else. In Milton, the machines would be running, and he would not have to find something to do. He paced around the bedroom until Margaret looked up from her book. She raised an eyebrow at him, and he walked out of the room to wander around the house and the garden. Wherever he found breezy shaded nooks, he lingered a while. When he had gone through every space he could explore, he returned to the bedroom and, gently laying a hand on Margaret's shoulder, he said, "Come with me to the verandah. It's cooler there. You get the ocean breeze."

Margaret closed her book and rose from her chair. "Let's not waste another minute here, then. I am getting a bit too warm, even in these lighter clothes."

In the verandah, she paused for a moment, her gaze darting from the chair to the bed, back to the chair. "How about the bed? Those tiny holes in the cane should keep us cool."

Mr. Thornton shook his head and scowled. "Lie in bed in the middle of the afternoon?"

Margaret shrugged. "Take the chair if relaxing bothers you. The bed beckons to me. It's big enough for two in case you change your mind."

Mr. Thornton chose the chair closest to Margaret and resolved to be content reading the newspaper he picked up in the living room. The paper was in English, although it had come from America, not England. He spent the next half hour reading it with great interest. His familiarity with America had been limited to the textile trade, particularly cotton. The paper, however, had articles on other products like tobacco, sugar cane, silver from the Spanish colony of Mexico, and one product that Cádiz direly needed: ice.

After perusing these articles, he folded the newspaper and tossed it on the table. He watched Margaret. She had fallen asleep with her open book perched upside down on her stomach, one hand on top of it. She looked so peaceful that he was tempted to join her on the bed. Still, he hesitated.

Napping in mid-day had never ever occurred to him. He had been quite content being busy at the mill and rarely did anything unrelated to it until he met Margaret's father, Mr. Hale, who inspired him to continue his interrupted education. And pleasure? To him, that meant an efficient mill that brought profits healthy enough to make life much better for his mother and his sister Fanny.

Margaret changed him, and not only because he fell in love with her. Her influence became clearer to him in Paris, where they had honeymooned before coming to Cádiz. She dragged him to museums and art galleries, cafés, and theaters—places he would not have visited alone. Though this was also her first Paris visit, she had read books and heard stories from one of her father's friends, Monsieur Fleury, a Frenchman. She recognized art pieces and lingered before them, ogling them with a child-like wonder that beguiled him.

She was ambivalent about the structural changes Paris was undergoing. To him, those changes were exciting. They were necessary. Modernization was good. Then, he saw Margaret bite her lower lip, her eyes pooling with tears as she witnessed neighborhoods once teeming with life being destroyed. He placed an arm around her waist. He could sympathize.

Through her eyes and her translations from French to English, he saw a culture immersed in arts and pleasure and the pursuit of both. But that land of Diderot and Voltaire was also progressive. The city was rebuilding boulevards and neighborhoods and revitalizing ancient buildings. While the French dealt squarely with serious and important matters, Parisian society and culture also knew the value of "appearances" and frivolities—delightful though not essential to survival or comfort—and indulged in them. Yes, art fed his soul, promenades on the Tuileries relaxed him, and spirited discussions in cafés fired up his imagination.

Cádiz, though, was not like Paris.

He rose from his chair and sat on the opposite side of the bed from where Margaret lay. How he loved her—so much that sometimes he ached from it. He stared, mesmerized by the book rising up and down with her breathing, and he felt the urge to rest his head on her stomach. But he did not want to disturb her. With utmost care, he extricated the book from under her hand and placed it on the table.

He lay down beside her. She stirred, opened her eyes, and gave him a small, dreamy smile before drifting back to sleep. He turned on his side, gently placed his arm on her waist, and pressed a soft kiss on the side of her neck. Before long, he descended into slumber, his face buried in her hair.

In the following days, Mr. Thornton submitted with less reluctance than before to the exigencies of the weather and this strange custom of siestas. Two days after he began to do so, he banished his cravats and vests into their luggage, rolled his shirtsleeves up to his elbows, and led Margaret to the big verandah bed for an afternoon nap right after lunch. Margaret returned her book to the library.

"I could get used to this," he said one afternoon, shifting his body to find the most comfortable position.

"What?" She feigned surprise, suppressing a smile as she faced him.

"I'm only talking about while we're here. Back to Milton, I'll be at work this hour."

"How could you survive even a few weeks of careless days of ease? I remember you saying how dull that would be."

He gathered her close and planted a kiss on her lips. "How could you remember something I said so long ago? What if I would prefer not to be reminded of it?"

"Really? I rather thought you'd be flattered that I could remember."

"But it offended you at that time, so please forget it."

"It stuck in my mind." She pouted and turned her face away. "It seemed to me you were criticizing life in the South."

"Forget that, too."

"You did redeem yourself when you told us what you had to do and endure after your father died. I was mortified and thought I had been too harsh on you."

"Did you begin to like me after that?"

Margaret did not answer. Instead, she kissed him and laid her head on his shoulder. A couple of minutes later, she said, "I remember another instance when you scoffed at the idea of pleasure. Do you recall when Mr. Bell asked you what you worked so hard for and when you intended to enjoy the fruits of your labor? "

Mr. Thornton groaned. "I ignored him. I was consumed by jealousy, still stung by your rejection, and you sat there looking serene and unconcerned. I told myself I should hate you and ignore you pointedly. Instead, I could not get you out of my mind. Truth be told, I didn't know how to answer Mr. Bell. Was he annoyed?"

"Well, yes, he was. You looked sullen, extremely put upon. Anyway, after you left, I told him you weren't your usual self. Something was troubling you."

He stared at her, his eyes incredulous. "You knew. You defended me."

"I knew by then that I loved you. But I was convinced that you no longer cared for me. How could I possibly have revealed how I felt?"

"Oh, Margaret, my love! All I was waiting for was a look from you so I could show you how contrite I was."

"Things were different then. Anyway, does it matter now? You've been as irascible lately, though. In Paris, you were so agreeable and enchanted with everything. Don't you like Cádiz?"

"I don't dislike it. I do not take to new places as easily as you do, though—particularly one as foreign to me as Cádiz."

She wriggled closer to him. "I forgive you, but you must kiss me and hold me close and tell me again how much you love me."

~

THE NEXT MORNING, Frederick invited Mr. Thornton to a dinner meeting of a club of tradesmen. "Merchants from all over the world will be there, and we often ask someone to tell us about his trade. A few are just passing through on their way to Barcelona—traders and adventurers transporting silver from Mexico. You may enjoy it and learn something from their stories. There might be one or two bringing cotton from America. Cádiz is a way station to England. That should be of great interest to you"

"Thank you for inviting me. I'd like very much to come."

Twenty men and one woman were at the meeting. Many of them were swarthy and unshaven from weeks spent at sea. Mr. Thornton, however, was unprepared for a few who looked more foreign than the others. They were short, had dusky skin, thick straight black hair, and black eyes. They didn't speak much English, and he stayed away from them until Frederick introduced him to the man seated next to him at the dinner table. Benito Hidalgo was the exception, having lived and studied in America in his youth.

Curious about Mexican silver, the club had chosen Mr. Hidalgo to speak that evening. He recounted how the Hidalgo family became rich when silver was discovered in Mexico in the sixteenth century. Generations of Hidalgos searched and claimed mines, which increased their fortune for nearly two centuries until the Napoleonic wars devastated Spain's economy, sending a gigantic wave across the ocean to Mexico. Mr. Thornton was amazed to hear that silver mining in Mexico enriched the Spanish empire more than it did the Mexican economy. In fact, only a few, like the Hidalgos, made a fortune.

Intrigued by Mr. Hidalgo's long and diverse history, Mr. Thornton engaged him in conversation at the table while the rest of the party drifted into smaller groups.

Mr. Hidalgo said, "We lost all but the house we were living in. Do you know the agonizing pain of falling from a tall, steep mountain?

The hopeless anguish from doubting you had the strength and where-withal to climb back up?"

Mr. Thornton nodded. "I do, actually. I was lucky, though. The woman I loved inherited money and continued to love me despite my misfortune."

"Yes, you are fortunate. I've had to work until my hands and knees bled. Then I happened upon international trade, and my experience in America and the other places I travelled proved useful. Sadly, I've only recouped some of the property we once owned. I've learned a lot, enough to kill my illusions that I could get back the old family glory. I have to look to future generations. But they would need to keep their eyes and ears open."

"You must have hopes, then, that silver mining will be very profitable again."

Mr. Hidalgo shook his head. "No, unfortunately. The earth can only yield so much, and wars deplete resources. No, we must learn about or invent new products. Civilization is voracious. It must find things to feed on in order to grow—things people like us must seize before too many others do. We must open our eyes and ears, not just in Mexico and Spain or England, where you live. Going to far-flung places, I've learned not to assume that other people think like me. We all have unique experiences which influence our views of the world and the things which matter to us. Being open to those views can tell us something about what the people we serve need or want."

"Are you still doing business in silver?"

"Some. My ship also transports tobacco and cotton, and sometimes chocolate, fruits, and vegetables. My country's economy is in bad shape, and the government has drastically cut down on international trading. I'm one of the lucky few allowed to continue. One thing I would never do, though, is ferry slaves. That business is lucrative, but inhumane."

Mr. Hidalgo stared straight into Mr. Thornton's eyes, assessing him and, with his jaw clenched, he continued, "Rich Americans and Europeans are greedy for them, but the poor and uneducated deserve to be treated like you and me." Mr. Hidalgo looked away, and Mr.

Thornton could not tell if he was angry or embarrassed by his outburst.

Mr. Thornton wanted to put Mr. Hidalgo at his ease, show him he was not averse to his views. He said, "It amazes me how events happening in one part of the world could affect a country far away. You've opened my eyes. You're a remarkable man, Mr. Hidalgo, and I'm lucky to have made your acquaintance."

Mr. Hidalgo smiled. "Maybe we'll meet again. We could deal in cotton or those precious bugs that feed on our cactuses."

AS THEY CLIMBED into bed that night, Mr. Thornton related his conversation with Benito Hidalgo to Margaret. "I'm ashamed to say I hesitated to talk with him at first. He turned out to be fascinating. I'm sure you'd like him. He's small, muscular, graying, but energetic. And wise. He's sensitive to injustices against the less fortunate. You should see his eyes when he talks about his family and his hopes for the future. They glow and mask the hardships and upheavals he's been through."

Margaret said, "I may never get a chance to meet him, and yet I like him already. I wish him well."

"He regained a quarter of what his family lost and he has ventured into other products. His family had been involved in silver mining. Now his ship also brings in cotton and something very unusual—a bug that produces a type of red color much prized by royalty that brings in quite a bit of money."

"A dye, you mean, that could be used on textiles. Are you getting ideas from what he's told you?"

"I am, though my first goal upon our return is to get the mill back in operation and make it run like clockwork. I'd also explore other ways we can improve our production of cotton. After that, I will look into other products. Maybe I won't be lucky enough to come across a bug like Mr. Hidalgo has, but England is industrializing rapidly, and its needs are multiplying."

"It could all be an exciting adventure."

"I expect it to be," he said as he gathered Margaret in his arms. "Fred is right. You have to be open to new things.'

"So, do you still think Cádiz isn't that special?"

"Of course, it is special. It's as different from Milton as you probably could find in the continent. And you are here with me. If it weren't for you, my love, I would never have come. Never met your brother or Mr. Hidalgo at this crucial time, before we reopen the mill. I've been forced to pause and reflect on what I want for us. And I'll have much to learn."

Margaret purred with pleasure, cupped his face in her hands, and kissed him. "I'll be there, Mr. Thornton. Always."

Mr. Thornton turned off the gas lamp on the night table and gathered Margaret in his arms.

EVY JOURNEY, SPR (Self Publishing Review) Independent Woman Author awardee, writes Women's Fiction, an amorphous category of stories written mostly for women, from a woman's point of view, as varied as that is. They can be romance, chick lit, or literary.

Evy has a Ph.D. in psychology so her particular brand of women's fiction spins tales about well-drawn characters as they cope with the problems and issues of contemporary life. These stories explore the many faces of love, loss, second chances, and finding one's way. Often, they're laced with a twist of mystery or intrigue.

She's also a wannabe artist, and a flâneuse who wishes she lived in Paris where art is everywhere and people have honed aimless roaming to an art form. She has lived in Paris a few times as a transient.

EVY'S OTHER BOOKS INCLUDE: *Margaret of the North, Hello, My Love, Hello, Agnieszka, Welcome Reluctant Stranger, Brief Encounters,* and *Sugar and Spice and All Those Lies.*

MISTAKES AND REMEDIES

Julia Daniels

"You consider me mistaken, and I consider you far more fatally mistaken. I don't expect to convince you in a day...but let us know each other, and speak freely to each other about these things, and the truth will prevail." - Chapter XXVIII, North and South

MISSING

"Margaret!"

Margaret sighed and rolled onto her back but did not open her eyes. She had ignored her father's initial attempt to rouse her, thinking it was simply part of the unsettling dream in which she was deeply entangled. When she felt someone squeeze her shoulder, it became obvious this was no longer part of her dream.

She opened her eyes, squinting at the bright light shining from her father's lamp. "Papa?"

"Margaret, you must get up!"

"Are you unwell?" She sat up so quickly the blood rushed to her head. She had just lost her mother. The sudden thought that her father might be sick too frightened her.

"No, my dear, but you must get up." He put his hand on her back and helped her to stand. "Mr. Thornton is here."

"Mr. Thornton?" She glanced at the clock on the mantle of her fireplace. It was almost half-past ten. "So late?"

"Miss Thornton did not arrive home after seeing you this afternoon," he answered. "Mr. Thornton and his mother are very concerned for her safety."

"Oh. My." She looked around her room for the dress she had worn earlier that day and grabbed it. "Can you help me put this on?"

Fanny Thornton had left the Hale home nearly eight hours earlier. To say Fanny had been despondent and in a state of panic would be an understatement, but Margaret had understood Fanny intended to go straight home.

Once the dress was over her head and fastened, Margaret slid her feet into her slippers and moved towards the door. Her hair was loose and still damp from her earlier bath, but it would have to do. She rushed down the stairs and into the study, where she found John Thornton pacing in front of the fireplace. He came twice weekly to this room to take his lessons from her father, but tonight he looked positively wild. His hair was disheveled. His usual black jacket was off as was his cravat, the top buttons of his shirt flipped open.

"Miss Hale." He nearly lunged for her when he saw her. "Has your father told you? Fanny never came home after seeing you. Do you know where she is?"

"Please sit down, Mr. Thornton." Somehow, she kept her voice steady and firm.

"Do you know where she is?" His loud demand bounced off the walls of the study.

She swallowed and sat heavily on her father's chair, near where Mr. Thornton remained standing. She glanced at her father. He seemed to understand what she had to tell their guest was for Mr.

Thornton's ears alone, as he nodded and turned to go out of the room. Once her father left, closing the door behind him, Mr. Thornton, still vibrating with tension and worry, sat on the edge of the chair across from her.

"Fanny left here just after two this afternoon, Mr. Thornton."

He nodded. "That is what our driver said. Fanny sent the driver home, telling him she would walk home, but she never arrived. Do you know where she went, Margaret?"

He'd never called her by her Christian name, not even the afternoon following the awful strike and mob attack at Marlborough Mills when he'd proposed marriage.

"I may well know where she is, yes." She stared at her hands resting in her lap. "I am not certain how to tell you what Fanny shared with me this afternoon. I fear you will be shocked, John." She had whispered his name so many times to herself, in front of her mirror and when alone. Now, hearing it aloud felt odd.

He leaned forward. "Tell me. Please! My mother is a wreck."

The topic was so improper to discuss, even with female family members; certainly, she had never talked about such things with anyone but her cousin Edith and the one time with her mother just before she had passed from this earth.

"Fanny is carrying." Margaret blurted out the words, unable to think of a gentler way to break the news.

"Carrying?" His brows narrowed. "Carrying what?"

"Oh, my." She covered her face with her hands. Was he as naïve as she?

He reached forward and gently pulled her hands away. "Carrying?" he repeated.

She met his gaze. "A baby," she whispered. Tears began to form in her eyes. She sniffed and looked away.

He stood as if poked with a hot iron. Staring incredulously at Margaret, he yelled, "Impossible!"

He stalked to the window and looked into the dark night. "She told you this?"

The question came out as a roar. Margaret took another deep

breath and remained calm. He was not directing his anger at her but, rather, at his foolish sister.

"Yes," she told him.

He raked his long fingers through his raven-black hair. Was he trying to calm himself? Did he believe her? How awful that she should have to be the one to tell him!

"She thought I could help her," Margaret continued. "She was frightened to tell you and your mother. Because I don't belong to her social circle, she thought it was safe to tell me. She said I had no one to tell whose opinion mattered to her."

How offensive Fanny had been! She had said Margaret was so irrelevant in Milton that no one liked her enough to believe her or would even listen to her if she started such a rumor. Yet Fanny had raced to Margaret for help.

He turned to her, a quizzical look to his brow. "How could you help her?"

Margaret stood and moved close to him. He looked so forlorn. She spoke to him softly, gently. "Fanny thought perhaps my Aunt Shaw could house her until the child arrived. She had concocted a foolish story she planned to use as a cover. She would say she had married a military man who wished her to be in London when he arrived home on leave. When I reminded her that my Aunt Shaw and cousin Edith had met her at the Great Exhibition, she knew that would not be a feasible choice."

"She forgot meeting your family?"

"So it seems." Margaret grimaced. "I do not believe she is thinking clearly at present."

"Nor do I." He sighed. "Do you believe she has run away to London, then, with this story in her mind?"

"No." Margaret shook her head.

"Where then?" he pressed.

"Possibly the Princeton District."

His eyes narrowed again, but she could tell he believed her. "Why there?

Margaret took a deep breath. "Fanny said she overheard two of your maids discussing a woman in Princeton who was able to..." She paused and swallowed, hoping she could force the rest of the words past the lump in her throat. "Who could stop...a baby... from...coming."

"What?" he yelled.

She cringed but was not afraid of him. He would never hurt her.

"The woman is a midwife, Fanny said, who has special tonics and medicines to end the...situation. I have never heard of such a thing, but surely there must be midwives in Princeton, as few who live there can afford the services of a doctor."

"And thus you believe she has gone there? To this midwife in Princeton?"

Margaret shook her head. "I thought she had gone home to you and your mother. That was what I suggested she do. Somehow, she thought I would know this midwife since I visited Bessy Higgins so frequently. When I told Fanny I did not know any sort of person, nor did I wish to, she became very angry. She stormed out, and I stood watching here at the window until I could no longer see her down the street. I imagined she climbed in your carriage and went home to tell you."

"A baby," he whispered. "How could that have happened?"

Margaret's eyes shot to his. Did he really not know how babies were made?

"That is...I know *how* it happened." He chuckled self-consciously as a flush crossed his cheeks. "I simply had no idea my sister was even interested in a man, and certainly not...to such...an extent."

"We should go to Princeton," she said.

"You will come?"

"Yes." She nodded. "Truth be told, you are not well liked there. I might be able to find this person more easily than you could on your own."

"Sadly, I believe you are correct." He nodded. "Very well. If you are willing, I shall ask your father if you can accompany me. It won't help your reputation to be seen with me after dark."

"Fanny's safety is more important than my reputation," she said. "I will come, and Papa will let me."

FOUND

John shifted on the squabs of his carriage seat, anxious to get to Princeton, to find Fanny, and to uncover what the girl had gotten herself into. He believed Margaret. There was no reason not to except, as he'd told her, Fanny had shown no interest in any men and, indeed, John had introduced her to many eligible bachelors.

Margaret sat serenely on the seat across from him, watching the scenery pass outside the window. Her hair was still down, cascading over the front and back of her shoulders. He had never imagined it would be so long or so wavy. Lord, she was a beautiful woman.

"I think we must go to the Higginses' home first," she said, breaking the silence. "Nicholas might be able to direct us to the midwife we seek."

Nicholas Higgins was one of the troublemakers of Milton, one of the union men who had led the strike against Marlborough Mills. John bristled at the idea they would have to turn to Higgins for assistance, but Margaret's closest friend was Higgins' daughter Bessy, and surely he would be willing to help Margaret.

John nodded, conceding she was correct. But would Higgins help if he knew it was to aid a Thornton? "I wonder if you could receive his help without mentioning Fanny?"

"You fear her reputation?"

"That and, if what you say is correct, and I have no reason to doubt your honesty"—*Except for the strange man you were with at the train station*—"she is already ruined."

"Perhaps?" she whispered. "You may well be able to save her from disgrace."

"She will have to marry the father of the child." There was no other option to save her from disgrace and ruin. It was the only solution.

"That is not possible, John." Margaret's eyes were sad in the dim light of the carriage. "She said he is already married."

His stomach dropped. A married man. His sister was having an illicit affair with a married man, had gotten herself in the family way —all under his and his mother's nose. He wanted to roar or to hit something. Instead he clenched his jaw and looked away from Margaret. She was the bearer of the news; however, she did not deserve to be the recipient of his anger. That was best reserved for Fanny.

The carriage came to a halt and, after putting on his jacket, he quickly stepped out, holding out his hand to assist Margaret in her descent. Once on the ground, she continued to hold his hand; indeed, she clenched it tighter as they made their way through the quiet, dimly lit streets of Princeton. Gas lights were sparse in this area. All the decent folk were well asleep by now, preparing for the early morning whistle in a few hours. A baby cried in the distance, reminding him why they were there.

"The Higginses' house is just up this way." She pointed with the hand not wrapped in his. "See the light in the window? That's their home. They leave the light on for Bessy. She sleeps on and off all day long. When she is awake, she is reading the bible, preparing for her journey through the Heavenly Gates."

"Will it be soon?" he asked softly.

She nodded and glanced up at him before stopping outside the Higginses' home. "It is the fluff in her lungs. That was why I asked you about the installation of a wheel in your mill."

He nodded, remembering that conversation. Margaret had been particularly angry that evening. She had come from Princeton just in time to share a pot of tea after his lessons with her father. John had not understood her curiosity at the time, or her fury, but now it made sense. The fluff would kill her friend.

"Perhaps you should step around the corner?" she suggested. "I have no fear of Mr. Higgins' silence and respect for privacy in this matter, but perhaps it would be better if he did not know it was your family."

He nodded, reluctantly letting go of her hand. Did she even realize what comfort that simple gesture had given him?

He stepped around the corner, out of sight but well within hearing distance. Margaret thought she was safe in Princeton, but John was not as confident. He heard her lightly rap on the door and some shuffling inside the thin walls of the house. Soon the door was opened and, after Margaret greeted Higgins, she quickly explained her appearance at such a late hour.

"A midwife?" Higgins' voice sounded incredulous. "Why would ye be needin' 'er, lass?"

"Someone I know came to seek help with a...difficult situation... this afternoon and did not arrive home as expected. The family is worried."

"As they should be." Higgins snorted.

"Please, Nicholas. Do you know of such a woman?"

There was a long pause. John held his breath. What if Fanny wasn't there? What if she had run away to London or elsewhere?

"Aye, I know of the one ye be needin'. She be a gypsy woman an' calls 'erself Vadoma. She ain't too nice, Margaret, but she be the one ye be needin'."

"Where might I find her?"

"Ye want me to go with ye?"

"No."

"Stubborn lass!" After a small pause, Higgins continued. "Ye go to the end of the row and turn right. She puts up in the green house about four doors down on yer right."

"Thank you. I will be here to see Bessy in the morning, but send Mary if I'm needed sooner."

"Aye." His voice had softened to a whisper. "My Bess 'as 'ad a ro'en day. It won't be too long now."

Higgins sigh was so heavy John thought he felt it ten feet away, where he stood.

"Ye might be needin' me name, or she won't tell ye nothin'," Higgins added.

"I'll tell her I spoke with you."

Margaret's dress rustled, and then the Higgins' door clicked shut. A moment later, Margaret came around the corner and joined John.

Without a word, she gave him a quick glance, and together they headed down the dirt path. John didn't question, he just followed, keeping an eye out for any sign of trouble. Once they reached the end of the row of houses, they turned to the right and continued to hurry toward the green house Higgins had mentioned.

It was hard to miss. Painted a bright green, the little shack had lights shining through the windows. Margaret rushed ahead and, with a quick glance his direction, knocked on the door. It took a bit of time, but a haggard old crone, the vision of what John would expect a gypsy to look like, finally opened the door a crack.

"Who are you?" she demanded.

"My name is Margaret. Are you Vadoma?"

"Who sent you?"

"Nicholas Higgins."

The gypsy opened her door a bit wider. "What do you want?" She caught sight of John and then said snidely, "Oh, well, I reckon yer just another couple got themselves in a mess coming to Vadoma to fix it." She clicked her tongue and shook her head. "Well, I'm full up tonight. You come back tomorrow."

John stuck his foot across the threshold, preventing her from shutting the door in their face. "We are looking for—"

"My friend," Margaret interrupted. She touched his hand, and he stepped back. "Tall, pretty blonde girl, about my age."

"Why?" Vadoma asked.

"Why am I looking for her?" Margaret asked. "Because she is missing, and I think she may have come here."

"Why?"

Margaret sighed and, with a roll of her eyes, she reached to open her reticule.

John stalled Margaret's hand, understanding Vadoma required some coins to answer. He reached in his own coat pocket and then placed some money into the gypsy's hand.

"I might have seen 'er," Vadoma answered, after turning the coins in her hand.

A woman moaned in pain behind Vadoma, and Margaret moved forward to go through the door. Vadoma blocked her.

"Is she here?" Margaret demanded.

The gypsy looked at John for more money. A child began to wail inside the small house. He handed her two more coins. "That is all I have."

Vadoma roughly grabbed Margaret's arm and dragged her through the door. She pointed a gnarled finger at him as he tried to follow. "No men. It's the fault of yer kind that I have a house full of women and the foundling homes are full." She slammed the door in his face.

MARGARET PULLED out a handkerchief to cover her nose. The unmistakable scent of blood permeated the hot, stuffy air of the small house. Indeed, this was not a true house but rather just a large, open room with cots lining the walls, all of them filled with women in various stages of childbirth and the aftermath. The sound of grunting and crying came from behind the single door in the room, a closed door. Margaret's stomach tightened and tears burned her eyes. These poor women! Margaret had to find Fanny and make certain she was all right.

"Where is she?" Margaret asked.

"This way." Vadoma pointed to a far and completely darkened corner.

Margaret hurried over, refusing to look at the faces of the women Vadoma was *helping*, but saying a quick prayer for all of them. How horrible to find oneself in a situation where you must hide a child. Fanny was lying quietly in the far corner cot.

"Fanny?" Margaret touched her hand. "Fanny!" She roughly shook her.

"She ain't waking up anytime soon," Vadoma said.

"Is she dead?" Margaret sputtered. "Have you killed her?" She shook Fanny harder. "Fanny!"

"She ain't dead." Vadoma stood behind Margaret, hands on her skinny hips. "She's loud."

"What? Loud? She is unconscious!"

"She were loud. Were hysterical." Vadoma shook her head, her thin, stringy gray hairs hitting her in the face. "I gave her naught but a sleepin' draught." Vadoma peered closer at Fanny. "She were too worked up to do nothin' else to 'er."

Margaret was about to ask what else Vadoma would do to Fanny when a woman behind the closed door, clearly in pain, called plaintively for her.

Vadoma waved Margaret out of her way. "You take 'er home. I cannot abide a cryin' and whinin' girl."

Margaret followed Vadoma to the closed door. "But what is she to do now?"

"Bring 'er back when she knows fer sure what she plans." Vadoma turned to Margaret. "You be a fine-looking girl. Don't be lettin' that man out there touch you without a wedding first. Look 'round this room." She pointed her finger from bed to bed. "None of them were smart enough to fight temptation. You be smart."

With those parting words, Vadoma went through the closed door and slammed it behind her.

It took a moment for Margaret to regain her wits and realize she would need help getting Fanny out of the house. She rushed outside to find John pacing just beyond the front door. He stopped the moment he spotted her.

"Fanny is fine," Margaret assured him. "She's sleeping. Go fetch the carriage. You will need to carry her out."

"Has the deed been done?"

She rested her hand on his arm. "No. We shall talk when we get her away from this place of misery." With a soft squeeze to his forearm, she went back inside to get Fanny ready for her removal.

RESOLUTION

John managed to carry Fanny from inside the midwife's home and into the carriage, despite several women spitting on him and others calling him vulgar names. They seemed to think him responsible for his sister's condition. She was clad only in her dressing gown, but Margaret was able to find Fanny's dress and reticule stashed under the bed. How could his sister have thought she could find aid in such an establishment?

It was decided they would take Fanny to Margaret's home to recover. If they went directly to Marlborough Mills, the servants would talk and, before long, the whole of the town of Milton would know how foolish his sister had been. At the Hales', there were only Dixon and Mr. Hale, and John had confidence they'd keep silent.

Once at the Hales', with the help of Dixon, John and Margaret were able to get Fanny comfortably settled in Margaret's bed. Margaret asked the maid to bring a fresh pot of tea and then excused her for the night. Little had been said between him and Margaret since they'd rescued Fanny—and that was exactly how John viewed their removal of his sister from the midwife's house: a rescue.

"I sent the carriage home with a message to my mother. I said only that Fanny was ill, here at your home, but that Mother would not be needed until the morning," John told Margaret once they were alone.

Margaret had brought in another chair. He accepted the offered seat as well as the hot tea, fixed just as he preferred. It would likely be a long vigil, watching over his sister.

"You may retire, Margaret. I would not have you lose even more sleep over my sister's foolishness."

"I will stay," she said. "She may awaken and need help. I know you are quite capable, but I doubt I would sleep, anyway."

They sat quietly for some time, sipping tea. The only sound in the room was the tick of the clock on the mantle. Of course, he had never been in Margaret's bedchamber, and he was quite keen to look about to discover hidden treasures and trinkets she kept nearby. To do so would certainly draw her attention, invade her privacy more than he already had. Instead, he stared into his cup.

"Margaret…" he started. "As of late, I feel as if there has been a shift of…familiarity…between us." He would not look up, fearful of what expression he might find on her lovely face.

"Yes," she whispered but said no more.

After a moment, he continued, buoyed by her admission. "I would like to know, that is, I have had a question for quite some time that I would like to put to you, if I may?" He did look up then, and was pleased that her face showed curiosity, not censure.

"I will answer your question, if I am able."

He found that to be an odd response. What could she not answer? Then it occurred to him that perhaps she would not like to answer the question he had once posed about the man at the train station. Had she not said at that time she *could not* tell him who the fellow was?

"Since our first introduction at the hotel when you and your father arrived in Milton, I understood you to be raised as a gentlelady, a woman of means, part of London's wealthy society. Your father said living with your aunt for much of the year gave you opportunities to learn about things most in Milton, including myself, could only dream of."

"Yes, that is all true." She nodded. "Is that your question?"

"Not quite." He smiled at her. "I'm getting to it." He set his teacup on the table next to him and glanced briefly at his sister, who was sleeping with her mouth hanging open. "Because you were accustomed to associating with only London's finest families, I would have expected you would wish the same for yourself here. Yet I quickly realized you seemed to despise those of the higher society of Milton —namely manufacturers and their families. I suppose, then, my question would be, why? If we were in London, I could understand, because manufacturer such as myself and other mill men are hardly respected as gentlemen, but here in Milton…" He shrugged. "There are few above our stature in society."

A small smile crossed her face. "I tried to explain it to my mother once, as she posed a similar question." Margaret stood and reached for his cup to refill it from the pot. "When my cousin Edith married, I was given the choice to remain at Harley Street or go home to my parents. As you know, I chose my parents. I was tired." She handed him his cup and went to refill her own. "So very tired of the pretense of London Society, the whirl of it all, the expectations, the gossip." She shook her head and sat back across from him. "I wanted to be a part of the world of common, normal people, not above them."

"And by associating with the poor, you felt...a part of that community?"

"Not as I had hoped," she admitted. "They treated me as an outsider. They were not as accepting as I had wished or expected." She looked down at her cup and shook her head. "At times, I find myself quite lost. I could not understand your theories and the way you conduct business, but neither can I understand why people are unwilling to work to better themselves."

"So you believe what I said about rising above your circumstances?"

"Yes." She nodded. "You are a fine example of how that is possible in the world of business. My father told me you rose from a draper's assistant to a mill master. That would hardly be possible in London for, if you were not born a gentleman, you could never become one."

"Precisely. But I have never wished to be a *gentleman*, not in the sense of your idea of one, anyway. I must stay busy, play a role in some sort of occupation that gives me a return—not only on my monetary investment, but also on my time. The London gentlemen I have been acquainted with spend time idling away at their clubs and strolling in the parks. Even just sitting here makes me feel anxious, as if I should be involved in something more industrious."

She chuckled but not unkindly. "Sleeping, perhaps?"

Her laugh was infectious, and he could not help but answer in kind. It was almost two o'clock in the morning.

"We are much alike in that, Mr. Thornton. I had hoped to be useful to the people of Princeton, to occupy myself doing good deeds for others, but I quickly realized most were too independent to need anything from me except money, which I could not provide. When my father was a clergyman, we had an alms box for the poor, but no longer."

"You have returned to calling me Mr. Thornton? I much preferred hearing John come from your mouth."

She flushed. "I spoke without thinking earlier."

"I wish you would continue to address me as John."

"If you wish." A small smile curved her lips and, although it wasn't bright in the room, John would swear her cheeks flushed darker as she looked away from him.

"Fanny has made a very poor decision, and now we must deal with her ruin." He wanted to kill the man who did this to her. John was not a violent man, but this was a situation he had never in his whole life anticipated. How would his mother react?

"Have you family away from Milton, somewhere you could send her?" Margaret asked.

"No." He shook his head. "My mother's only brother died in Burma during the war. My father's family cut ties with us when he...died." He was not certain Margaret knew how his father had passed, so he decided it was best to be vague.

"How awful. My father had no siblings, and my mother had only her sister, Aunt Shaw." She shifted on her chair. "Have you no friends who would marry her despite her condition?"

He had been considering that, but what did he have in his position to entice a man to marry a girl carrying another man's child? "Perhaps," he finally said. "Mother and I have many details to attend to."

"Forgive me for intruding."

"You misunderstand. I am pleased with your advice, so overwhelmed with thankfulness that you have undertaken this...troubling time with me." He shook his head. "This is the difficulty you and I have always had, is it not? This misunderstanding between us. I believe you think one way when, in reality, you think another."

"Yes. That is true." She took a long sip of tea before continuing. "However, now that I understand you better, your ideas of manufacturing and economic prosperity, I realize you are nothing like the coarse ruffian I expected all manufacturers and mill men to be." She stopped and refilled her cup again. She stood for a moment, looking into the fire before continuing. "I never doubted you cared for Fanny and your mother. In fact, your mother takes great pride in how well you have provided for them. I cannot but think you are a very fine man, despite our early differences and misunderstandings of one another."

If she did have a favorable opinion of him, he wanted to ask her why she had rejected him. He wanted so badly to press the issue and try again, but now was hardly the place for such a declaration. Until he had Fanny settled, he could not think of anything else.

"I am pleased your opinion of me has altered," he said.

"And yours?" she asked. "You told me your *foolish passion* for me was gone."

He opened his mouth to answer that he loved her more now than ever, but the door suddenly opened, cutting him off. Mr. Hale came inside, wearing his dressing robe and carrying a candle.

"Hello," he said. Mr. Hale always provided a calming effect on John. "I thought I would relieve one of you. Mr. Thornton, would you care to go to sleep for a while?"

"Ah, no. Miss Hale should go if she chooses."

"Yes, I think I shall," she said. She glanced at him and then walked toward the bed, adjusting Fanny's pillows and blanket before lifting the candle her father had set on the nightstand. "Papa, wake me in an hour or so. Mr. Thornton could use some sleep, also."

She started toward the door but stopped abruptly and turned. "Papa, Mr. Thornton and I were discussing some misunderstandings between us. I was hoping you... that is, I think we must tell him about Frederick."

"Frederick?" Mr. Hale had begun to settle into the chair Margaret had vacated but stopped in a half-crouched position. "But why?"

"Mr. Thornton was at the train station the night Mama died... when Frederick left."

Mr. Hale's eyes widened, and he sat completely. "Oh. I had no idea. Yes." He nodded his gray head. "Yes, I shall tell him."

THE FALLEN WOMAN

"She is ruined, John."

His mother sank onto the chair closest to where Fanny still lay asleep. Mother's face looked worn and her regular air of confidence was absent. She took Fanny's hand and shook it. Fanny still had not uttered a peep since being placed in the bed nearly eight hours earlier.

"Surely, we can devise a solution to prevent that."

"How?" she demanded, casting a woeful glance his way. "What can be done?"

He had never seen her so downcast, not even during the workers' strike. As soon as Dixon had shown his mother into the bedroom, Margaret had gone downstairs to fetch a fresh pot of tea and breakfast for him. Her absence had allowed them an opportunity to discuss the situation in private.

"She told Miss Hale the man was married, so he is not an option," she said. She fixed her stare on Fanny. "Perhaps we could find a different man to take her, but who and where? Good Lord, I can hardly believe this to be true. How did she get so out of hand without my noticing?"

He had no words, for he had asked himself the exact same question.

"It was smart of you to bring Fanny here. Perhaps before the gossip starts, we will have a plan."

"It was Margaret's idea."

"Margaret, eh?" She turned to him with a quirked brow.

"Yes, Mother." He sighed. "If nothing else good has come from this situation, it is that she and I have become friendlier toward one another. I believe her feelings have softened toward me."

She clicked her tongue. "Both my children have gone soft. What about her lover at the train station?"

"His name is Frederick, and he is her brother. There is much more to the story, I will tell you about at a later time." John sighed. "You want my happiness, do you not?"

"John, do not vex me today. I have enough to worry about with Fanny."

A few minutes later, Dixon opened the door and then shifted the tray she carried to set it on the table. "Do you need anything else, Mr. Thornton?"

"No, thank you, Dixon," John said.

"Miss Hale says if you would like Dr. Donaldson sent for, she will see to it," Dixon told him.

"Not at present but, if that changes, I shall alert you." John stood and walked to the table where his breakfast plate was resting next to the familiar teapot.

Dixon left the room again, closing the door behind her, and he and his mother were alone again.

He dug into the plate of food Dixon had brought him, oddly famished. Ten minutes ago, he would have said he was too upset to eat.

"She's waking up, John." His mother stood and looked down at his sister. "Fanny, wake up!"

He watched her eyes slowly open. The expression on her face reflected her confusion—she no doubt wondered where she was. She opened and closed her mouth and then swallowed.

"Dixon!" Margaret threw her sewing aside and rushed into the hallway outside the sitting room. "Oh, there you are. You have read my mind."

Dixon held two pails, which she handed to Margaret. The unmistakable sound of retching could be heard coming from Margaret's bedroom. She rushed up the stairs and, as soon as she reached the landing, John was opening the door.

"Fanny is ill?"

He nodded, his face looking a bit peaked.

"You go on; I shall help your mother." She held her smile. *A man of such power unable to handle someone retching.*

She walked inside and was shocked by the state of her bedding and Fanny. She quickly handed Mrs. Thornton a pail and retreated into the hallway.

"Dixon!"

The stout maid appeared at the bottom of the steps.

"Can you gather some fresh bedding, please?"

The maid rolled her eyes but, with a hefty sigh, grabbed the banister and climbed the staircase.

When Margaret returned to her room, Fanny had ceased her vomiting. Margaret reached into her wardrobe and pulled out a fresh nightdress for Fanny, who was now lying exhausted against the bed pillows.

"Let's roll back the bedding," Margaret suggested to Mrs. Thornton. The smell was overwhelming. Once the sheets and blankets were in a huge pile on the floor, Margaret said, "Fanny?"

The girl's eyes opened.

"Let's put a fresh gown on, shall we?" She tried to sound as positive as she could despite the circumstances.

Mrs. Thornton helped Fanny pull off the soiled gown, and Margaret quickly pulled the clean one over her head. By then, Dixon entered the room, carrying a fresh set of linens. Before they could change the bedding, Fanny bolted upright again and began to vomit.

"Miss Dixon," Mrs. Thornton said over the sound of Fanny's gagging, "could you please tell Mr. Thornton to go to work and that we shall return home once Fanny's stomach has settled?"

"Yes, ma'am." Dixon nodded and, with a glance at Margaret, left the room to do Mrs. Thornton's bidding.

"Do you think whatever the gypsy gave her to sleep has made her ill?" Margaret asked.

Mrs. Thornton frowned at her but then softened her expression. "Of course, you could not know, Miss Hale, but women are often ill in the early days of pregnancy."

"Oh. I see."

Margaret had very little knowledge about pregnancy and childbirth. Now, with her mother gone, she wondered fleetingly who she could ask should she ever wed and conceive a child. Edith, perhaps?

"It stops after a few months have passed, and generally the sickness only hits in the mornings," Mrs. Thornton said.

Fanny lay back again, and Margaret and Mrs. Thornton covered her up with the fresh linens. The sound of the front door closing pulled Margaret's attention from Fanny. Margaret pulled the curtains aside and watched John walk away from the house. Good for him, she thought. There was little a man could do here and, as upset he was, he'd be better off working and focusing his attention on something more productive.

Dixon rapped on the door and stepped inside. "Miss Margaret, Mary Higgins is here for you."

"Oh, no." Margaret spun around, a hand to her throat. Mary's presence could only mean one thing. Bessy was close to death.

COMFORT & SECURITY

Margaret held her friend's hand as Bessy took her last breath. Long after Bessy's spirit had gone to Heaven, Margaret stayed, holding her friend and allowing her tears to flow. Even though her friend's passing had come as no surprise, Margaret's heart was still breaking.

Eventually Margaret left, teary eyed and a bit weary from the emotional turmoil of losing Bessy and helping Fanny. When she stepped outside the Higginses' house, she realized how long she'd been there. Darkness had fallen. Had she really spent so many hours with her friend?

She walked past the familiar Princeton houses to the main road, which would lead her home. Was Fanny still there, or had she recovered sufficiently to return to her home? If Mrs. Thornton was right about Fanny being sick each morning, surely their servants would gossip about it. Perhaps Fanny should stay at Margaret's house until a solution was devised?

She stopped walking as a familiar imposing figure appeared, walking toward her on the road. She smiled, despite her tears.

"Your father is worried about you," he said. "I told him I would come find you."

"Thank you," she whispered.

"Bessy?" he asked softly.

Her throat closed, and she shook her head and burst into tears. How was it that tears seemed infinite? Just when she thought she could cry no more, more would come.

"I am very sorry for the loss of your friend, Margaret." He took her hand and kissed her knuckles before threading it through his arm and leading her from Princeton.

They did not speak for several minutes. His quiet strength comforted her, as if his hand covering hers was absorbing some of her distress.

When she finally had control of her emotions, she said, "Thank you for coming for me."

"You must know… That is, I would do anything for you and your father."

She did. He had proven himself too many times for there to be any doubt of his true, abiding care for them.

"Thank you," she whispered. "You are a good man."

He ignored her compliment and said, "Fanny has returned home. I am sorry I deserted you this morning." He chuckled. "I'm afraid I felt a bit queasy after seeing her become ill."

She laughed for what seemed like the first time in days. Perhaps it was.

"I pray a solution can be reached," she said.

"I have already sent letters by express to two gentlemen of my acquaintance who may be interested in having Fanny as a bride."

"You told them—"

"Yes, of course." He cut her off, but not unkindly. "I did not wish for any sense of manipulation. They needed to know why she was in such great rush to wed."

"Are they Milton men?"

"No." He shook his head. "One is from Le Harve—an investor I have worked with for many years. The other is a man in Scotland. We met at school when we were young but stayed in touch with each other over the past decade or more. Either would be a good, stable man for Fanny."

"I don't suppose she will tell you the name of the man she's been seeing here in Milton?"

"I will force her at some point. He must be held accountable."

Margaret stopped walking. "Force her? How?"

He chuckled. "Fear not, Margaret. I would never harm my sister, no matter how much I might wish to wring her neck at the moment."

He pulled Margaret along gently, and they completed the rest of the walk in silence. He saw her inside the door, said goodnight to her father and to her, and then departed back down the quiet street of Crampton.

"He's a fine man, Margaret," her father said once they were alone. "It is such a shame about his sister."

"Yes," she agreed.

"Perhaps your aunt would keep her?"

Margaret took off her gloves and bonnet before shaking her head. "Fanny could never stay hidden away and would somehow embarrass herself in London. I would not burden Aunt Shaw with such a situation."

"Yes, I can see that." He nodded thoughtfully. "I have a question I must ask."

"Yes?"

"Have your feelings softened toward Mr. Thornton? Is that why you had me tell him about Frederick? I never had any real concern Thornton would turn us in, even if he is a magistrate, but I never had a reason to tell him until you asked."

"Yes, Papa." She nodded. "I believe our misunderstandings have disappeared as I have come to know him better. I have come to love him, especially after seeing how kind and loving he has been toward Fanny despite her enormous mistake."

"Love, eh?" A soft smile appeared on her father's face. "I was hoping it would come to that between the two of you. I have always longed to see you settled well and comfortable. But Fanny...will her behavior not cause scandal here? Do you wish to tie yourself so closely to a family that has something like this looming over their heads? What would your aunt say?"

"What do *you* say, Papa? Aunt Shaw is not my guardian; you are. If it will not offend you, ought I care what my aunt thinks?"

He chuckled. "Your mother said Mrs. Shaw called me a disgrace when I decided to leave the church. It bothered your mother, of course, but not me." He placed his hands on her shoulders. "I did what I knew was right in my heart and do not regret it but for the loss of my friendships with the parishioners in Helstone."

"Friends… Oh, but I did not yet tell you. Bessy has died."

Silently she walked into his embrace, seeking the comfort only a father's hug could give. Tears began to flow once again. The next few days would be almost as difficult as the days following her mother's passing.

"Lucien Picard will be here Thursday," John told his mother. He folded the letter from his friend and set it on the table next to his chair.

Today was Sunday, his only day free of the constraints of the mill. They were sitting in the parlor, drinking tea and awaiting the arrival of Margaret and her father. He had invited them for lunch following church services that morning. He believed the first bachelor candidate, Scotsman Ewen Stewart, would arrive for Fanny's inspection soon, and it might be easier to have Margaret there to help push the conversation along should they decide to walk out. Besides, he was anxious to see Margaret and sought out any excuse to do so.

She looked up from her stitching and met his eyes. "Can the Frenchman speak English?"

John grimaced. "Some. Enough, I think, for Fanny."

"If she had only behaved as she was instructed…if she had acted like a lady instead of a—"

"Mother." John cut her off with a warning tone in his voice. "It does no good to continue to reflect on what could have been or what should have been. We must hope she will now be on her best behavior and charm one of them enough to secure him."

"Secure him!" She snorted. "And what of Miss Hale? That was a surprise, you inviting her to lunch, but I suppose she's *secured* you, eh?"

He rolled his eyes at her but grinned nonetheless. "As you well know, she had my heart long ago."

She clicked her tongue and then asked, "Have you approached her again or spoken with her father?"

"No." He set aside his cup, leaned his head against the back of the chair, and stretched out his legs. "My attention these past two weeks has been fixed upon finding a comfortable situation for Fanny."

"But you will?" she prodded.

He turned his head to face her. "Have you apprehensions, Mother?"

"I did," she admitted. "No longer. She was a true friend to Fanny, despite Fanny's cruelty to her. I believe she helped your sister because of her love for you. Now that I know she did not behave improperly at the train station, I have no reason not to accept her."

A knock sounded on the door. A moment later, Jane stepped inside to announce Mr. Ewen Stewart, John's closest friend from school.

John leaped to his feet and greeted Ewen with a hug. Many years had passed since he'd last seen his friend, but theirs was a peculiar friendship that continued despite time and distance. John pulled away, laughing and continuing to shake Ewen's hand. Ewen had widened quite a bit around the middle, was still as tall as John remembered, but now, like John, had stray gray hairs in his side whiskers.

"Mother, you remember Ewen?"

"Of course! Welcome, Mr. Stewart."

She held out her hand, and Ewen quickly grasped it. She turned to address the maid who still stood in the doorway.

"Jane, would you get Fanny, please?"

The doorbell chimed.

"Admit the Hales first, Jane, then fetch Fanny."

"Yes, madam." Jane nodded and left the room, closing the door behind her.

"You will now meet Mr. Richard Hale, a man who has kindly taken me on as a student of Greek," John explained. "His daughter is Margaret. They come from the south, from a village called Helstone."

"That is quite a distance," Ewen said. "What brought them here?"

"I will tell you over drinks this evening." John winked.

As Jane announced the Hales, a shiver of familiar excitement race through John at the thought of seeing Margaret again.

She wore the same dress she'd had on at services that morning. For the past two weeks following Bessy's passing, Margaret had worn only black. Now, she had on a dark-blue gown. A few days earlier, she had admitted to him how sad she still felt at her friend's death. He knew her so well. He could see the pain in her expression but doubted anyone else would notice, except her father perhaps.

"Miss Hale, Mr. Hale, may I introduce you to my good friend, Ewen Stewart?"

"How fine to meet you both," Ewen said jovially. He shook both their hands. "Thornton tells me you are his tutor, Mr. Hale?"

"More than a tutor," John said. "Mr. Hale is a mentor and, I would like to think, a friend."

"Indeed." Mr. Hale smiled. "We could not have asked for better friends upon arriving here than the Thorntons." Hale looked between John and his mother.

"I can well believe that! And Miss Hale?" Ewen turned his attention to Margaret. "Do you teach, also?"

"No, sir," she said with a smile. "I keep home for my father."

Fanny breezed into the room, and all attention shifted to her. Ewen had met Fanny years earlier when she was barely grown. John quite looked forward to seeing how she'd react to Ewen now she was a grown woman and, likewise, to learning what Ewen thought of Fanny. The fact Ewen was willing to meet with her despite the secret she carried from the rest of the world was a testament to his character and proof enough of his friendship for John.

"Miss Thornton," Ewen said, "it is fine to see you again."

Fanny being Fanny, she replied, "Although I am told we have met before, sir, I am sorry I do not remember you." She nodded toward Ewen.

Ewen laughed. He was a good-natured bloke. John could never tire of his company, but he worried Ewen might not be firm enough to keep control of John's sister. Of course, who was he to judge? John had failed miserably in that endeavor.

"Shall we go in to lunch?" his mother suggested.

Mr. Hale offered his arm, and he and John's mother led the way. John allowed Margaret to enter the room ahead of him, leaving Ewen and Fanny to bring up the rear. The food was already on the table, and they would eat family style, passing bowls and serving themselves. John raised a brow. He had expected his mother would have ordered a more formal lunch.

"Everything smells wonderful, Mrs. Thornton," Margaret said.

John pushed in her chair for her, which was located to the right of his.

"Indeed, we are very thankful for your invitation," Mr. Hale said. "We have only a single maid, Mr. Stewart, and Sunday is her day off. Margaret is quite a fine cook despite not having a great many opportunities to practice the skill, but I am certain she's pleased to be free of the chore today."

"Thank you, Papa." She flushed a rather becoming shade of pink and stared down at her plate.

John settled into his chair. Why had the compliment embarrassed her so? Perhaps the fact she was expected to cook?

The food was passed quietly around the table. Fanny put much on her plate, while Margaret ate only a little. John was looking forward to walking out with her that afternoon, chaperoning his sister as Fanny did the same for him. But what a ridiculous idea... Chaperoning a woman who had already given up her virtue!

"In what occupation are you employed, Mr. Stewart?" Mr. Hale asked.

Ewen wiped his mouth before answering. "I am a barrister. I work with two others in an office and serve the needs of those planning estates and wills."

"I suppose everyone needs a will," Fanny said between bites. "It must be quite steady work. And rather...dull?"

Ewen chuckled. "Not at all, Miss Thornton! Steady, yes, as every one of any means ought to have a will, but never dull. I enjoy meeting new people, learning their stories."

"You are from Glasgow?" Margaret asked.

"Born and raised but for the few years I came south and attended school with Thornton, here." Ewen clapped John on the shoulder. "We had some good times, did we not?"

"We did." He grinned. "Although I am not so certain we ought to share tales of those times with my mother present." He nodded toward her and glanced at Margaret.

She gave him a warm smile, and his heartbeat increased a bit. Ah, the affect she had on him!

"Nothing so bad as that!" Ewen exclaimed. "Just boys being boys."

The rest of the meal passed peacefully. John spent his time catching conversations between his mother and Mr. Hale and trying to gauge the interest between Fanny and Ewen. Margaret ate silently next him. Was she glad to be there, or had she felt pressured to accept his invitation?

When everyone was finished, John suggested they go for a walk, as it was a fine autumn day. His mother declined and instead invited Mr. Hale to join her in the parlor, where he might find a book to occupy his time while the couples went walking.

Jane was quick to present cloaks, hats, and gloves, and soon their party of four set off. John had given Fanny a few tips on some subjects Ewen might be interested in discussing. Although she had daydreamed through most of his lecture, John hoped she had retained at least some of what he'd said. He shrugged. He could only provide suitors; she would have to capture the men's interest on her own.

John forced his attention back to the woman at his side. He could not allow himself to become so caught up in what was going on between his sister and Ewen. John refused to neglect Margaret in any way, and she deserved his undivided attention. She and he walked on ahead, her hand wrapped tightly on his arm. Since the incident with Fanny, they had shared many cups of tea after his lessons, and he'd even stayed for a meal at the Hales' home. John had every reason to think she was beginning to care for him, maybe not as violently as he liked her, but at least more than she had when he first offered for her.

"Thank you for coming today," he said.

"I was pleased to accept your invitation. Even if it was to chaperone your sister." She glanced over her shoulder. "I am not certain how they will suit. He is certainly gregarious and as social as you said he would be." She looked up at him with a smile. "Were you ever like him, or did he serve as your opposite, drawing you from your shell so you might make friends?"

His brows shot up. "You find me antisocial?"

She frowned. "No. I think this is something you and I have in common. Neither of us have the need to fill the air with useless chatter. I was never very good at making friends, but Edith was and, thus, I always had friends. Perhaps Ewen provided a similar service to you? At least whilst at school?"

"How very perceptive." She knew him so well! "It is true. Then, as now, I would generally choose a book over a party. However, in the position I find myself now, I must socialize."

"Do you despise the theater and musicals?" she asked.

"No. Not in the least."

"I am glad of that, as I greatly enjoy such things."

He chuckled. "What if I had said I did hate those gatherings?"

"I suppose I would have pulled away and gone back to speak with your friend. Although he probably prefers parties to plays."

"Just as Fanny does," he said. "He also enjoys being the heart of society and a part of the whirl of it all."

"Will it not be obvious to his friends, then, that the child will come too soon?"

"I am certain he will contrive a tale all will believe. He is an attorney, you know, and they have a way of twisting lies into truths."

She chuckled. "And magistrates, Mr. Thornton? Do they do the same?"

She was teasing him. How easy it had become between the two of them.

"Not this one. I am too stiff." He straightened his shoulders. "Too proper."

"Papa told you about my brother, Frederick," she whispered.

The sudden change in conversation caught him off guard. He nodded.

"I wish I could have told you but, in your role as magistrate, we were not certain how you would react," she said. "I think had you known it was him at the train station, things between us would be rather different today."

"Would they?" He wanted her to explain what she was thinking rather than simply jumping to conclusions. Before, when he had thought he knew her mind and heart, he had been so wrong.

"I believe so. You would not have thought so poorly of me and, while you supported and continue to support my father so kindly during this mourning period, I think...that is, I hope you would have offered me the same kindness."

He swallowed. Now was the time to come clean and clarify perhaps the biggest lie he had ever told. "That day in your foyer before I joined your father for my studies... Margaret, I lied when I said my passion for you was gone." He stopped walking and turned so he could better see her expression. "You had broken my heart, you see, and by hurting you I thought it would make me feel better. But it did not. I love you. I believe I have loved you from our first argument." He chuckled, recalling just how fiery her temper could be.

Her eyes glistened with tears, and a blinding smile crossed her face. She moved closer, perhaps to hug him, but he blocked her, whispering, "They are coming."

He nodded behind her, and she turned and watched with him as Fanny and Ewen approached.

"Fanny tells me she enjoys playing the piano." Ewen was slightly out of breath. "Perhaps we could go listen for a bit? She's offered to play for us."

"She does love to play," John agreed. He smiled down at Margaret and offered her his arm once again. "Let us return to the house."

If the others had stayed away, what would Margaret have done? Would she have embraced him? Would she have shared her feelings? This time, she'd appeared quite pleased to hear of his ardor.

"Miss Hale, do you play?" Ewen asked.

"I do." She cleared her throat. "When we came to Milton, we had to leave the piano behind, so it has been quite some time since I have had the opportunity. My mother was not particularly fond of the instrument, and I really only played when I was in London at my aunt's."

"Now there's a real city!" Ewen said. "London. Have you been there often, Miss Thornton?"

"Only once," Fanny answered. "John took me there for the Great Exhibition this past summer."

"Ah, well, there's a fine coincidence! I was there for a fortnight during the Exhibition. What was your favorite part of the display?"

And so the conversation shifted to Fanny talking about all the beautiful gems and jewelry she had seen, many of which she had never heard of before her trip to the Exhibition. Margaret had been entranced by the daguerreotypes and even the machinery, which was where they had crossed paths, John recalled.

Of course, speaking of the Exhibition reminded John of how Henry Lennox had stuck to Margaret's side and how her cousin Edith seemed to look down her nose at John, whom she had referred to as "that manufacturer from the north." At least her husband, Captain Lennox, had spoken of investments, and he and John had enjoyed a logical, albeit short, conversation. He remembered feeling out of place within the group but had been willing to feel uncomfortable if it meant being near Margaret.

When they arrived at the mill house, Margaret's father was ready to depart. Apparently he was not feeling well or perhaps John's mother had caused his indigestion. John walked them to the front door and told Mr. Hale he would not be at his study lessons on

Tuesday, as Ewen was scheduled to be there until Wednesday morning.

"Miss Hale, my friend from France is coming Thursday. I have procured tickets to the concert given by John Braham at the Lyceum Hall and was hoping..." John turned his head to address her father. "That is, may I have your approval, Mr. Hale, to escort Miss Hale to the musical?"

"Of course, you may!" Mr. Hale replied. "Do you wish to go, Margaret?"

"Yes." She smiled. "Thank you for the invitation."

"I shall fetch you at six, sharp," John told her. "Thank you for coming today."

"It was our pleasure," she said.

Soon the carriage pulled up, and he helped both Hales inside. He closed the door and stood on the steps as he watched them leave. Would she turn back and look at him?

THE MAN

Margaret believed it took weeks rather than days for Thursday to arrive. She had not seen John since Sunday, but he had sent a note yesterday reminding her he would pick her up for the performance the following evening. As if she needed a reminder! As the days dragged along, she became more and more excited to be with him again.

Thursday evening, Dixon tried something new with Margaret's hair. Together they had raided one of her mother's old boxes of fripperies where she'd kept hair baubles. Inside were glamorous gemstones and pearl clips. Hair pins and ribbons were strewn about inside the wicker basket in no particular order. They found some decorative combs that matched her fanciest dress, the one she had worn to the Mill Master's Dinner. She wished, from a vain perspective, to have a new dress to wear, one John had not yet seen, but this dress was her finest and would be best for the evening.

The chime of the doorbell startled them. They had spent far more time working on Margaret's hair than either had realized. John was always punctual, and tonight was no different. They heard Margaret's father open the door and welcome John inside.

"Do I look well, Dixon?"

"Lovely, miss, simply lovely."

Margaret smiled and picked up her wrap—her mother's wrap, actually—from the edge of her bed and, with a deep breath, she walked into the hallway and stopped at the top of the stairs. John was wearing the formal attire he had worn at the Mill Master Dinner, a suit of black tails with a gold cravat and matching waistcoat. Had she not rejected him, they would likely be man and wife already. Butterflies danced in her stomach at the abrupt thought.

He caught her eyes as she descended the stairs and met her at the bottom. With a formal bow, he handed her a large bouquet of colorful flowers he had been hiding behind his back. She smiled. How thoughtful! And the flowers were truly beautiful.

"They are gorgeous, Mr. Thornton. I thank you."

"You are quite welcome," he answered. "Fanny and Lucien Picard are waiting in the carriage for us."

"Here, hand me the flowers." Her father reached for them. "I shall find a vase and place them in water for you, Margaret. You two go ahead and enjoy your evening."

She kissed her father goodbye and, after putting on a cloak and gloves, led John outside.

"You look very fine this evening, Margaret. Is that not the dress you wore to the Mill Master's Dinner?"

She smiled, pleased he remembered. "It is. Thank you."

John helped her step into the carriage. Fanny sat on one side, Mr. Picard across from her. Margaret smiled at them both and sat beside Fanny. John sat next to Mr. Picard. John tapped on the ceiling with his walking stick, and the carriage pulled off.

"Miss Margaret Hale, please meet Monsieur Lucien Picard," John said.

"*Enchante, Monsieur Picard.*" Margaret held out her hand, and he kissed her knuckles. "*Bienvenue a Milton. J'espere que vous apprereciez votre visite?"* She very much hoped he was enjoying his visit. Fanny must choose Mr. Picard or Mr. Stewart for a husband. Her choices were limited, and time was short. No one knew for certain just how soon a baby might be born.

"*Est-ce que tu parles Français?*" Picard asked if she spoke French.

"*Oui!*" she answered.

"Good, good," Picard answered in English. "My English is a bit... rough, but I must try." He grinned. "Miss Thornton does not speak French."

Margaret glanced at Fanny who was staring out the window of the carriage, seemingly oblivious to the conversation. Was she pouting?

Margaret asked Picard, "Did you have a pleasant trip from Le Harve?"

"Yes," he answered. "The train was late."

"It happens all too often," John said. "I wonder at the purpose of having time schedules if they fail to maintain them."

Margaret grinned at John and nodded in agreement before turning to his sister. "Fanny, you look very pretty tonight."

Fanny glanced at Margaret briefly but then looked back out the window without comment.

Margaret looked at John and raised a brow. He shook his head as if to suggest she not say anything else.

Instead, Margaret discreetly studied Picard, who was watching out the window as they rolled through the streets of Milton. He was older, perhaps even forty years old. He was not unattractive —indeed, he was quite well kempt—but there was nothing special in his appearance. She glanced over at John. Why was he giving her such an intense look? She smiled brightly at him and, with a nod, he turned his gaze back out the window. How odd. The rest of the trip to the concert passed in uncomfortable silence. Her excitement began to dwindle.

What had Margaret gotten herself into?

The carriage pulled up directly in front of the door. John stepped down, held out his hand to help his sister, and then did the same for Margaret. Picard hopped out and straightened his waistcoat and shirt sleeves. Margaret had to look away to hide her surprise. The man was very short! Perhaps an inch or so taller than Margaret but not as tall as Fanny and significantly shorter than John. Fanny led the way with Picard following behind, but John pulled Margaret back slightly.

He bent over and whispered, "Fanny did not want to come this evening. She said she does not wish to be seen in public anymore."

"Oh, I see. She does appear rather out of sorts."

He began walking. "She seems disappointed by Picard. What do you think of him?"

She looked up at him. "Think of him?"

"Aye. You were staring at him in the carriage. What do you think?"

She laughed. Was he jealous? "I think he is quite old," she whispered, "and not nearly as handsome as the man I am now walking with."

He grinned and straightened his shoulders as they entered the main door. Her words had pleased him, obviously. He handed their tickets to the man standing at the entrance and led them inside.

The building was full already, although not nearly as crowded as the concert halls and theaters in London. Having walked by this hall many times, Margaret was excited to finally have an opportunity to see the inside, and it did not disappoint. Margaret had not known what to expect but, for a hall located in an industrial town, the building was decorated very fashionably, in a classical way with murals on the walls and detailed moldings along the edges of the ceiling and circling the chandeliers.

"What do you think, Miss Hale?" John asked. "Do you approve?"

"It's a very pretty place. I like it very well."

"I hope the singer will appeal to you, as well. Braham is quite older than when I first heard him many years ago. His wife was a Milton girl; thus, he performed here often, even before this hall was built."

Margaret continued to look at the pictures on the wall and covertly study the people in attendance. Fanny was not talking to Mr. Picard but was standing by him, and they both looked rather uncomfortable and awkward.

Margaret turned to take in the area behind her just as the Latimers entered the building. Margaret had last seen Miss Ann Latimer walking with John shortly after Margaret had turned down his proposal. Margaret thought for certain he had transferred his affection to the other girl, but here Margaret was, standing next to him, ready to enjoy her first musical in Milton by his side.

Fanny hastily walked away from Picard and disappeared down a darkened hallway. Picard went to follow her but caught Margaret's eye and decided to come instead to where she and John stood. She tapped John's arm and pointed discretely to where Fanny was walking away.

"What happened?" John asked Picard.

Mr. Picard shrugged. "We were talking of the paintings. The young woman there"—Picard nodded toward Ann Latimer—"came in, and Miss Thornton turned white and hurried down the hallway."

John looked at Margaret.

"I shall go see if she is unwell," she said.

She left the gentlemen, stepped around Miss Latimer, who tried to talk with her, and found Fanny sitting on a padded bench in the ladies' room. Margaret sat next to her and handed her a handkerchief from the sleeve of her gown.

"What in the world is wrong?" Margaret asked.

Fanny was breathing quite heavily, as if she had been running. Margaret set her hand awkwardly on Fanny's back and rubbed it in a circular motion. She hoped this might calm her but, of course, she had no idea what had spurred the girl's sudden exit from the lobby.

"He's here, Margaret. He's here." Fanny looked at Margaret with red, puffy eyes.

"Who is here?" she whispered.

Another woman walked in the room and stared at the two of them as she walked past to study herself in the mirror.

Fanny pointed to her stomach. "Him!"

Margaret's eyes widened. "Oh! I see. Do you wish to leave?"

"I must."

Margaret started to rise, but Fanny held her back. She leaned over so the woman still admiring herself in the mirror could not hear.

"I cannot leave while *he* is still out there. I have been crying, and I am certain I do not want him to see me looking as I do. I do not want him to know how upset he makes me. Not looking as I do."

"Of course. Allow me to tell your brother."

"Oh, and Margaret." Fanny's face twisted. "I find Mr. Picard rather disgusting. I cannot be away from him and his foul odor soon enough!"

Margaret moved from Fanny and followed the other woman out of the room, leaving Fanny alone. Margaret did not find Picard disgusting, nor had she noticed any offensive odor. Perhaps Fanny was simply being overly sensitive? She could hardly afford to be exceptionally particular about her choice.

Margaret found John and Mr. Picard just as the ushers were calling people to take their seats. She crooked her finger so John might bend low enough for her to speak without being overheard. Margaret was not certain which man Fanny was trying to avoid seeing, so she had no idea if he was lingering in the lobby or had already assumed his assigned seat.

"Fanny is ill, and we must go," she whispered. "However, we must wait until the doors close for the performance."

His face grew dark. "Are you certain?"

Margaret nodded.

"If we must." His sigh was great. "I shall go flag the carriage, although he may have returned home already."

John's face remained stiff as stone as he stalked toward the door, leaving Margaret and Mr. Picard alone.

"Is it me? Do I offend the lady?" Picard asked in French, likely feeling more confident speaking his own language.

Margaret's heart went out to the man. With a shake of her head she smiled. "I think this has nothing to do with you, sir," she answered.

"That is good. I should feel offended if it were true."

Margaret shook her head again. "It is not your fault."

"Excuse me, sir." One of the ushers came up to Mr. Picard. "Will you be coming inside? They are about to begin."

Picard shook his head. "We will not."

Margaret frowned her disappointment at the young man. He

nodded quickly and moved to close the final door. Once she was certain there was no man lying in wait to pounce on Fanny, Margaret excused herself from Mr. Picard. The orchestra had just begun and, as she went back to the ladies' room to fetch Fanny, Margaret enjoyed the music.

Once inside, she said, "Your brother has gone for the carriage." Her voice reflected her displeasure at missing the concert. "As you can hear, the music has begun, and no one remains in the foyer but Mr. Picard."

"Thank goodness," Fanny said. She sniffed a few times before standing and going in front of the mirror but, as she gazed at her reflection, she moaned. "I want to go home."

This was not exactly how Margaret had expected the evening to end. She had been excited for the concert, excited to be with John and, as they waited at the main entrance for him to return for them, she could hear just how fine a concert she was missing.

John came inside, still wearing a scowl on his face.

"I've hired a ride," he said. "My carriage returned to the mill."

He led them outside and, once everyone was loaded, they pulled away. No one spoke. Margaret rarely felt such irritation toward anyone or anything as she did just now with Fanny. Why had the girl agreed to go, likely knowing that the man she wanted to avoid would be there? Clearly, the two of them moved within the same social circle. Was Fanny really upset over seeing her secret lover, or had the sight of her closest friend Miss Latimer brought on Fanny's panic?

Who had entered the Lyceum about the same time as Miss Latimer? Margaret did not know everyone in Milton or even a mere fraction of Milton's elite. She struggled to recall the moment and frowned. The only people who'd entered with Ann Latimer were her father and mother. Miss Latimer had approached, smiling and waving at Fanny, and then, suddenly, Fanny fled from Mr. Picard.

Could it be Mr. Latimer? But no…that seemed impossible. Although he was a fine looking older man and rich, to be sure, why would Fanny form a relationship with her best friend's father? Margaret swallowed back her disgust at the thought and turned her gaze out the window. They were almost to her home in Crampton already. What a disappointment!

"Miss Hale," John began, "you are welcome to come to the mill house with us. Perhaps we could play cards?"

She turned to face him. "Thank you for the invitation, but I must decline."

Nothing else was said until the carriage stopped, and Margaret said goodbye to Mr. Picard and Fanny.

As John saw her to the door, he asked, "Why will you not come home with me?"

"I believe I have had my fill of Fanny for some time." It was an honest statement if perhaps a bit cruel.

"You have done much for her," he said. "Thank you for that. I wish our evening had ended differently. I was very much looking forward to spending time with you, Margaret."

She nodded. "Good night."

She opened the front door and entered, quickly closing it behind her. As frustrated and agitated as she was, she did not care if John stood there longer or not. Her father was sleeping in his chair in the sitting room, an open book on his lap. She decided to leave him there. She had brought enough turmoil to him the past weeks with Fanny's situation and Bessy's death. He looked content in front of the fire, and she did not wish to disrupt him.

Dixon helped her undress, asking no questions, likely sensing Margaret's dismal mood. Margaret sat at her dressing mirror for quite some time, rehashing Fanny's reaction to seeing her secret man. Obviously she could not remain in Milton if that was how she would behave each time she saw him and, if they did move in the same circles, that would likely be quite often. It made sense, really... Who else would Fanny come to know so well she could succumb to having an affair with but someone with whom she was already well acquainted?

But Mr. Latimer? The father of her best friend? The very idea made Margaret's stomach turn.

NEW BEGINNINGS

John was feeling under the weather and had decided to leave the mill a bit early on Saturday evening. He suffered from a simple cold, but his head was foggy, and he had trouble concentrating on anything but blowing his nose and wiping his watery eyes. There was plenty of sneezing as well—more than the cotton fluff usually caused, anyway.

When he arrived, his mother was situated in her favorite chair near the roaring fireplace. The weather had turned cold suddenly, which may have brought on his sickness. He simply felt unwell and needed to go home for the night.

She was surprised to see him.

"I do not feel very well." He chuckled. "You know I am never ill, but I believe I have caught a cold." As if to accentuate the point, he sneezed.

She set aside her mending and stood. In typical mother fashion, she felt his head for a fever. "You might be a bit warm but not feverish."

"My thoughts exactly," he said. "I am for bed."

"Just one moment. I have two things I must tell you."

All he wanted was to collapse on his bed, but he gave her his attention instead.

"Fanny received a letter from Mr. Stewart today asking if she was willing to come to Glasgow. He is interested in marrying her but wishes her to see the town before she decides if she can be content among his friends."

"Did she reply?"

His mother smirked. "I told her what to write. She wrote that she would gladly become his wife and was certain she could be content in any situation he would provide for her. She added that she would be pleased to meet his friends following the wedding."

He nodded. Stewart was a good bloke—would perhaps not be the best of husbands, but he would not be cruel to her and would provide security for Fanny and the child to come.

"Is she satisfied with this?" John asked. "Are you satisfied with this?"

"Yes to both questions. She did not care for Picard and, as shallow as Fanny is, all she wants to know is whether or not the wedding ring will be large enough to flaunt." His mother rolled her eyes. "I am just relieved to have this settled."

He nodded. "Indeed. This could have ended far worse." He sneezed. "What was the second thing?"

"The servants have begun to gossip about her condition," she said. "The sooner we have the wedding, the better."

"Did you send the letter express?"

She nodded.

"He should receive it tomorrow," John said "We asked for him to apply for a special license so it might be accomplished quickly."

"There is Gretna Green, of course." It would be cheap and fast. "We could meet there, have it done with immediately."

"I had her suggest that, as well."

"I will be interested to see his response." He leaned forward to kiss her goodnight as he always did but thought better of it. "I am ill."

"There is a letter waiting for you in your room. I captured it before the gossiping hoard could get to it."

"A letter?"

"From the Hales'."

"Goodnight, Mother."

As he walked down the hallway, divesting of his coat and then the cravat, a small grin found its way to his face. Had Margaret written to him? Perhaps she thought he had forgotten about her. While that was farthest from the truth, Fanny had consumed his mind so much that, until her situation was settled, he could think of little else except fixing his business, which seemed to be finally resuming its full functioning following the awful strike.

The letter was resting on the top of his bureau. It looked like a masculine hand had written his name on the front, but perhaps that was a ruse to throw off the servants. He wished they could have concealed Fanny's situation a bit longer but, with her sickness each morning, that was hardly possible.

Before picking up the letter, he changed into his dressing gown, already feeling a little better...and cooler. He opened it and noted the difference in handwriting. It was flowery and definitely feminine.

DEAR MR. THORNTON,

I had hoped to see you before now but understand that work duties and family commitments must at this time prevent you from calling upon us.

At the urging of my father, I have decided I must share with you something that has been steadily and uncomfortably weighing on my mind.

I am certain you recall the incident at the Lyceum. I believe it was the arrival of the Latimer FAMILY that compelled the situation. I hope I am not correct in my belief, but I fear it must be so.

Although I do not know if you will agree with me on this supposition, I felt I must share my conjecture with you, for whatever good it might do.

Margaret Hale

HOW ASTUTE SHE WAS. John had thought the exact same thing! Why must it be him? Latimer was John's banker and the only man he was indebted to, owing him the sum of nearly six hundred pounds. *The bastard pig.* No, that was too good a title for Latimer. John had never liked him or his manipulative daughter, and he never, for even a moment, considered that Fanny might form an attachment to the much-older man!

He rubbed his watery eyes again with a clean handkerchief and blew his nose before literally falling into his turned down bed. The maids might be gossips, but they were efficient at their jobs.

Latimer! He should write a response to Margaret, but surely he would see her at church services the following morning. Perhaps by then he would receive confirmation from Fanny herself. Not that it mattered, as there was next to nothing John could do to force the banker to do right by Fanny. Besides, chances were quite good he was completely unaware of her condition.

~

MARGARET and her father were sitting in their normal pew at church when Mrs. Thornton walked past them with a polite nod. Margaret turned to see if Fanny and John followed, but it appeared she was alone that morning. Odd. Fanny, with her morning stomach illness, had been absent for several Sundays, but John always came. Had something happened?

After services, Mrs. Thornton pulled them aside in the back of church.

She began to explain immediately. "John has taken Fanny to Glasgow. She insisted she could not wait another day. She had become nearly hysterical with the concern that she might find herself in the same vicinity as *that* man again."

"So, she will wed Mr. Stewart?" Margaret asked.

"Yes, that appears to be her choice. John and I had both hoped Mr. Picard would have suited her, as John travels there twice a year, but it is to be the Scotsman."

"You must be relieved," Margaret's father said. "What a difficult time. As a clergyman, I was called upon more than once to help in such situations. It appears Miss Thornton has made a fine decision. Margaret thought Mr. Stewart to be a good man."

"John likes him, but I doubt we will see much of him."

"It is not so far to travel, Mrs. Thornton," Margaret said. "Surely, no more than a day's train ride. Why, the trip from Helstone for us was likely longer."

"Perhaps." Mrs. Thornton conceded. "John also asked that I give you this letter." She reached into her reticule and pulled out a folded piece of parchment.

"Thank you."

Mrs. Thornton nodded. "Good day to you both."

Once the two of them were alone, her father asked, "Do you wish to read it now? There is no rush to be home, is there?"

She shook her head. "I will wait until we are home."

They walked through the bustling streets of Milton toward Crampton. All the mills were closed on Sundays, so businesses were open to cater to the people who only had access to shopping on the Lord's Day. John was gone to Glasgow, which meant it would be several days until Margaret saw him again. She had already been missing him just in the few days that had passed since the concert.

They entered the house in Crampton. Dixon had lit the lamps, as the day was quite dreary; rain would surely fall soon. Dixon usually left once they returned from church. They never asked what she did on her day off; it was her own business. She did much for them, and the least they could do was give her some privacy.

She entered the sitting room with a tea tray and small sandwiches. "Thank you, Dixon," Margaret said. "Enjoy the rest of your day."

"I shall, Miss Margaret. Good day, Mr. Hale."

Once Margaret poured her father a cup of tea and had settled down with her own, she opened her letter. Her father busied himself with a copy of the *Sunday Times* they had picked up along the way home.

MY DEAREST MARGARET,

HER HEART BEGAN to thump at a livelier pace at such an address.

AS YOU KNOW BY NOW, *I have taken Fanny to meet with Mr. Stewart in Glasgow. I wanted very much for you to accompany us, as you alone have been my rock through this entire ordeal. Mother, correctly so, thought it would be improper. Thus, I am to take this ride with Fanny alone, as my mother does not—will not—travel from Milton.*

When I return, I am hopeful you will greet me with pleasure. I have tried

my best to convey my feelings for you. Indeed, I have been as open and forth-
right with you as I am in every endeavor I undertake. You can have no doubt
what I will be asking of you. I hope over the course of the following days you
will search your heart and decide if you are satisfied making Milton your
forever home.

Yours most truly,
John Thornton

"Papa?"

"Hmm?" He looked around his paper.

"Has Mr. Thornton approached you about...well, about marrying me?"

"Of course, he did."

"Of course?" She laughed. "You neglected to tell me?"

He folded the newspaper and set it aside. "I suppose I wanted him to surprise you. Women like a little surprise, don't they? Of course, not the kind of surprise Miss Thornton's situation presented but good surprises. Was that within the content of the letter? Has he proposed again?"

"No, but it is rather obvious that is what he intends to do once the business with his sister is settled with Mr. Stewart."

He nodded several times before he continued thoughtfully. "John is a good man, Margaret. He will be a good husband, a good provider, and based on how he has treated his sister, I sense he will make a fine father one day. However, he has much responsibility, and as a businessman he will have many commitments that will likely weigh heavily upon him day to day. It is up to you, Miss Margaret Hale, to decide if you are strong enough to accept that you will not always be the first thought in John's mind each day, and you will have little control over his schedule and often wish for more time with him. You will be required to modify your life and interests to mirror his needs and wishes."

"You paint a rather difficult picture, Papa."

"I do so only to prepare you, my dear. Surely, this is something your mother would have spoken with you about; God bless her soul. Of course, she would have most likely encouraged a match with Henry Lennox, who she liked very much, or a different gentleman of such leisure and flexible engagements. You could live back in London, which I believe you enjoyed."

"Perhaps. But I don't love Henry Lennox."

"Not all marriages involve a love match. Some are made out of duty or necessity, as Miss Thornton will sadly realize. Some are made for convenience to join family fortunes or to provide stability for a woman who might otherwise die an old maid. Not that I fear that for you," he quickly added with a chuckle. "You must decide, beyond your heart perhaps, what would be best for you, what you want for your life. The two choices at hand are here in Milton, which I know you are still not terribly fond of, or London, where you have family and many friends and opportunities you will never have here, but you'd have no John."

"What about you, Papa? Will you be with me wherever I am?"

"Yes, my dear. I will never live away from you again. I am saddened by the many months and years we lost while you were in London. At the same time, I believe you would not be the fine woman you are today had we not allowed your aunt to help educate you."

FANNY WAS WED and settled within three days. John had never anticipated such an easy or quick conclusion. She decided, once she saw the enormous mansion in which Stewart lived, that she could be quite content in Glasgow. Perhaps her shallowness served its purpose this time. Ewen was pleased with the settlements, as was John, and, knowing his friend would care for his sister and meet her needs was comfort enough for John to leave directly after the wedding.

He had gone with his friend to select a wedding ring for Fanny. Of course, Stewart had chosen the most expensive and prestigious jeweler in Glasgow, and the ring's price and elaborate design would definitely impress Fanny and any friends she would gain over the coming months and years.

This morning, before leaving Glasgow, John had returned to the shop to purchase a ring he had eyed while on the trip with Stewart. He'd been unable to meet the expense his friend was able to pay for a ring and, feeling a bit sheepish about being called out as cheap—even in a teasing manner—he had not brought up the idea of purchasing a ring of his own.

He found a band of gold with simple floral etching. There was a matching band with a single emerald set inside the gold. Margaret's eyes were a beautiful shade of green, and he found both pieces perfect for the woman with whom he wished to spend the rest of his life.

As soon as he got off the train in Milton, he hired a gig and headed to Crampton. More than a week had passed since he had seen Margaret. He had sent letters to both his mother and Margaret notifying them of Fanny's marriage and explaining she would send more details in time.

When he arrived, Margaret and her father had just sat down to dinner. Mr. Bell was there as well. Bell usually let John know in advance when he planned a visit to Milton. Perhaps he had tried to reach John while he was in Scotland. Mr. Hale graciously invited him to join them, and Dixon quickly placed a dinner setting in front of him.

"Congratulations, John, on getting Fanny settled," Margaret said. "You made a good choice in the selection of Mr. Stewart and Mr. Picard. I'm glad Fanny was satisfied with one of them."

"Couldn't find a Milton man for her?" Mr. Bell asked between bites. "I am a bit surprised your mother allowed her to go so far away from home."

John smiled. "Mother will visit one day. I believe in time, Fanny will be happy with Mr. Stewart," John answered. "If not happy, at the very least, content. There was no one here in Milton she seemed to favor, so I suggested two men I felt would be worthy of her. He is quite wealthier than I believed him to be and, eventually she will settle and mature."

"Richard mentioned one of the men was Lucien Picard?"

"Yes," John agreed.

"I never met the Stewart fellow, but I should think Picard would have been a good choice." Bell said. "Margaret, what was your thought?"

"Oh…well…I do not think she and Picard had similar personalities. I found him very gentlemanly and polite."

"She would have had to learn French, also," John said. "You know, Mr. Bell, learning has always been hard for her."

"Margaret, do you not speak French?" Mr. Bell asked.

"*Oui.*" She smiled.

"And Italian," her father said.

"*Si!*"

"And German," Bell added.

"*Ja!*" She laughed. "Enough! Let us stay with English, please? The governesses Edith and I shared gave us both nightmares about conjugations and translations."

John almost choked on his bread. What was he thinking? Margaret did not belong in Milton. She was too good for him. Suddenly the food he ate settled like a heavy stone in his gut. Why the bloody hell would she settle for him? What was he even thinking asking her to stay here?

After dinner, he would make his excuses and go home. She was a fine lady, and he was nothing more than an unwashed lackey. She had been raised to marry a man of the aristocracy, not some manufacturer from the dirty, smoky north.

"I am sorry I could not say goodbye to Fanny and wish her well in her marriage," Margaret said.

"You know her well enough by now that if she sets her mind to something, she has no patience to wait for it." He looked at Margaret meaningfully.

"I hope she will be happy," Margaret answered. "I have never been to Scotland, have I, Papa? Did we go when I was small?"

"No, my dear. We traveled twice a year to Oxford to see Mr. Bell.

We went to France with your Aunt Shaw to visit your grandmother's family, but no, never to Scotland."

"Well, Mr. Thornton." Margaret turned to him, grinning. "In a few months, perhaps the late spring, I will go to Glasgow to see Fanny."

"If you wish. I am certain she would be pleased to receive you." That might be a lie. Fanny would not want the reminder of her behavior that seeing Margaret might bring.

"Shall we retire to the sitting room for coffee?" she suggested. "Or perhaps I shall be a good hostess and excuse myself so you men can smoke smelly cigars and talk business?"

"I do not see any need for that," her father said with a smile. "Coffee sounds perfect."

Margaret stood first and led the gentlemen out of the dining room door. As if she had been waiting, Dixon was holding a coffee tray, and she followed them into the sitting room.

"I ought to leave," John said once everyone else was settled, hating every syllable. "I have not been home yet. I came here first. Thank you for dinner." He looked briefly at Margaret, who was already sipping her coffee, before nodding his goodbyes to Mr. Bell and Mr. Hale and heading for the door.

～

WHAT IN THE WORLD?

Margaret quickly set down her coffee cup and rushed from the room after John, indifferent to what Mr. Bell might think.

Dixon was handing him his coat and hat.

"Why are you going?" she demanded.

"I told you," he explained. "I have yet to go home." He pointed to the case sitting by the door.

"Just like that?" Oh, she was mad! "You come here first but leave without even speaking to me?"

"I spoke with you at the table. I told you Fanny is settled and encouraged you to visit in the spring if you wish."

"Please excuse us, Dixon," Margaret said.

Once they were alone, she walked forward and took his hand. "I missed you."

He pulled away. "I do not think... I do not think you should have. Margaret, you and I come from different worlds. You speak five languages, and I have barely mastered English. After meeting me in London, your aunt said I was not a gentleman, nor was I good enough for you. I tried to fight that, tried to be enough for you, but I am not. You were right to reject me."

He spun around and left the house without another word, leaving her standing open-mouthed. She thought about what may have happened to cause his quick departure. He had come to their home first, after leaving his sister in Scotland, leading Margaret to believe he was anxious to see her. He had been in a fine mood until they began to tease her about her education. Then his mood had turned sour.

There had been too many misunderstandings between them already; she was not going to let this pass without acting to make things right. She had waited a week to see him, and enough was enough. She grabbed her cloak from the hook and rushed out the front door, hoping to catch him before he rounded the corner toward the mill house. The street was empty. Either he had walked even quicker than usual, or he had hired a gig.

Mr. Bell's driver was leaning against the carriage, smoking. Knowing her godfather would approve her use of the ride, she asked the man to drive her to Marlborough Mills. He helped her inside and, once on top of his seat, he headed down the road. She closely studied people walking, hoping she would meet up with John before they reached the mill. She did not wish to explain her actions to Mrs. Thornton or be judged by her.

It was not meant to be. Clearly, John had taken a carriage and would arrive just before her. Margaret had never done anything so impulsively and in the end might regret her actions. Mrs. Thornton had never liked Margaret, but she loved the woman's son, and Mrs. Thornton would have to learn to accept that he loved Margaret, too.

The driver hopped down and opened the door, setting down the steps for her to descend.

"You can go back to Crampton," she said. "The Thornton carriage will see me home."

"Very well, miss."

She waited until he pulled away to walk to the door and ring the bell. What in the world was she doing? What if John had changed his mind about her? Had his love died so quickly? If that was true, she did not want him...would go back to London. Her father was right; she did prefer to London to Milton, but she wanted John, and she was confident he felt the same.

Jane answered the door as usual and granted Margaret admission.

"Has Mr. Thornton arrived home?" Margaret asked.

"Yes, Miss Hale. Just ahead of you."

"I wish to see him, please?" Margaret removed her cloak and handed it to Jane.

"Follow me, if you will?"

They climbed the staircase, and Jane led her to Mrs. Thornton's sitting room. Margaret took the time while she was being announced to straighten her shoulders and prepare what she might say.

Jane showed her inside and closed the door behind her.

"John just came from your home, Miss Hale," Mrs. Thornton said. It was obvious she had just been hugging him. She stepped back and glanced between him and Margaret. "Has he forgotten something?"

Yes, me. Instead of voicing that thought, Margaret shook her head. "May I speak with John privately?" she asked.

Mother and son exchanged a quick glance. As Mrs. Thornton walked past her, Margaret never took her eyes off of his. Although she left, Mrs. Thornton allowed the door to remain open. John followed his mother's path and closed the door with a resounding click.

He moved from the door and stopped directly in front of her. She took a step back so she could better see his face.

"Why have you come?" he asked gently.

"I thought we had decided to try to avoid misunderstandings moving forward." she said. "I thought you would want an answer to the question you posed in your letter to me. I expected you would expect an answer…in my own home this evening. Instead, you left me in great, inexplicable haste."

He seemed formidable. Although, over the course of time she had known him, she had become well accustomed to his facial expressions, this one she could not read.

"What question was that?"

"You asked me to consider if I could make Milton my forever home."

"Yes, I did ask that."

She stepped forward and took his hands. This time, he did not pull away. She threaded her fingers with his, studying the rough texture of his skin compared to hers. He had a workman's hands. Indeed, there was nothing soft about him.

"I will only do so if I can be forever at your side," she whispered. She looked up at him. "I have not been given an opportunity to admit my love for you, John. And I do love you, John Thornton, Marlborough Mills mill master, magistrate, and textile manufacturer. I want you, just as you are, just as you always have been, and whatever you may become with me by your side, in Milton, forever."

"Margaret," he breathed. Shaking his head, he pulled away. "It cannot be. You and I…our worlds… We are too different. I saw in Glasgow how you deserve to live. Stewart has an impressive estate, a mansion. Fanny does not deserve such splendor, but you do."

"I want *you*," she said. She placed her hands on the lapels of his jacket. "You. I want to marry for love as my parents were fortunate to do. Aunt Shaw chose to marry for money, and she lived a sad, lonely life. I want love, and that means I can only have you."

She fisted the fabric of his coat to pull his head down to hers, glad when his arms encircled her waist and drew her against him, his warm lips crushing hers. Oh, the joy! The fulfillment she felt in just this single kiss. He cupped her cheeks and continued to ravage her mouth with such tenderness, tears came to her eyes.

When they pulled apart, he simply stared at her as if in a daze. She smiled at him and felt a sense of shock as he sank to his knee and pulled a small pouch from the inside pocket of his coat. Reaching inside, he pulled out two rings. He held up one—a golden band with a large emerald in the center.

"You have taken my heart, Margaret. I ask if you will now take my name?"

"Yes!" Tears welled up in her eyes, and she nodded, laughing through the tears with such happiness.

He took her left hand and placed the ring on her finger and kissed it before standing and pulling her into another embrace. He rested his cheek against her head.

"I love you, Margaret."

"I ought to have accepted you last time." She pulled away to look at him. "I loved you even then. You are the best man I have ever known."

JULIA DANIELS LOVES to write happily ever after stories that warm the heart and make the reader satisfied. From rural and farm romance to historical western romance and even romantic mystery novels, Julia can spin a tale that ends in a happy romance. Her characters come to life on the pages, drawing the reader into the love story, making them want to stick around and see what happens.

Julia lives in Nebraska with her husband and two kids. In addition to writing, she designs counted cross-stitch patterns, sews, gardens and cares for an odd menagerie of animals, including chickens and goats.

JULIA DANIELS' other books include: *Milton's Mill Master, Master of her Heart, Choices of the Heart, The Earl Next Door, Duchess on the Run,* and *Saved by a Cowboy*

HER FATHER'S LAST WISH

Rose Fairbanks

"'Hale! did it ever strike you that Thornton and your daughter have what the French call a tendresse for each other?'" - Chapter XL, North and South

⁓

"*H*e'll be coming tonight," Nicholas Higgins said as Margaret and her father sat huddled around the crowded room in the small home.

His words brought Margaret's eyes to his as her mind had wandered during the visit. "Who is coming?"

"Mr. Thornton, we be speaking of Miss."

Mr. Hale inquired after the schooling of the Boucher children, but Margaret's mind raced. Should she encourage them to leave to avoid seeing Mr. Thornton? Their last meeting had been awkward and unbearable for her. Oh, but she did miss speaking with him. She had a far higher respect for him and understanding of his ways than she ever had before. Only, surely it was not quite proper for her to knowingly be in his path. He took enough care to not come to the house very often. She could not suppose that he wished to see her.

Finally, Margaret suggested they leave, and they bid Higgins farewell. They had rounded the street when Mr. Hale doubled over, gasping for breath. He clutched Margaret's arm, bringing her down to the ground.

"Papa!" She sat on the dirty ground, soiling her gown and eased her father down. Elevating his head in her lap, her eyes searched his face before looking out for help.

"Mr. Hale!"

Margaret turned her head at Mr. Thornton's voice, and he raced to them.

"What has happened?"

"I do not know!" Margaret cried. Her father clutched at his chest. "He had complained of shortness of breath, but never like this."

"You!" Thornton called to a woman who had emerged from her house at the ruckus. "Send for Dr. Donaldson immediately."

Margaret had never been more thankful for his commanding presence and demanding orders.

"No," Hale panted out. "No time."

His breath came as wheezes, his face turning blue from lack of air. "John." He took Thornton's hand and placed it over Margaret's. "Take care of her."

Sobs ripped from Margaret's body as her father breathed his last in her arms.

Thornton's hand tightened over Margaret's and with his free arm, he drew her to his chest. She cared nothing for her reputation or politeness at such a time, even as she knew her tears stained his suit, and he knelt with her on a dirty street. She clung to the comfort he offered, the closest shred she had of her dear father. She may not have always respected Mr. Thornton, but he was a friend to her father and mother both.

In time, she registered that men had gathered to take her father away. "No!" she cried and threw herself on his still form.

"Miss Hale, we must see to the body." Margaret heard from the familiar voice of Dr. Donaldson. "Will you have help with the arrangements?"

"I will be assisting Miss Hale," Thornton spoke from her side. He leaned closer to her and dropped his voice. "Allow them to take your father. I vow no harm will come to him, and everything will be taken care of properly with no anxiety on your side."

Margaret turned her head a little to see Thornton's face. If she could have thought clearly during her father's announcement, she would have expected him to look at her with hatred. She who had previously refused his hand and whom he had avoided as best he could was now forced into his care by a dying man. She had known Mr. Thornton would honour it, but she had expected it to be met with offense and disdain.

Instead of seeing any such malice in his eyes, she saw concern, tenderness, and grief. For a moment, Margaret thought it might be for her sake, but Mr. Hale had been a friend to Thornton. He might even be recalling the demise of his own father.

"Thank you," she murmured to him.

She leaned back and allowed the men Dr. Donaldson had gathered to carry her father to a nearby house. She did not immediately move from her position. When she closed her eyes, she could almost imagine this was all but a terrible dream. She was not alone in the world.

"Margaret," Thornton whispered in her ear as his arm was still wrapped around her shoulder. "I do not mean to trouble you or cause you to exert yourself before you are ready, but a crowd is gathering. I suspect you would wish for privacy. Shall I escort you back to Higgins'?"

She only nodded. Mr. Thornton stood first, the absence of his arm leaving her feeling cold and bereft. She shivered against the chill which now enveloped her. He extended his hand to assist her, and she gripped it tightly, not letting go, even when standing. Again, Thornton's discerning eyes took in her countenance and form. She lowered her eyes from his gaze which saw too much.

Margaret wondered if she would have the strength to walk even the few steps to her friend's house. Squeezing her hand, Thornton placed it on his arm and bore her weight as she leaned into him. Their progress was slow, mirroring the beat of her heart. She did not have to wonder if it were possible to die of grief; her father just had.

The thought struck her just before reaching the door, causing her to tremble and her knees buckled. Thornton caught her to him, and she rested her head against his chest.

"Breathe, now, Margaret. Higgins and Mary will look after you, and as soon as I can manage it, we will have you home."

"You are not leaving me, are you?" Terror gripped Margaret before she could be ashamed of her dependence upon him.

"Only for a little while. I leave you with your friends. I would trust no one else."

He lowered his arms, almost reluctantly it seemed to Margaret, and they trailed softly over her back before hanging at his side. "Can you walk again?"

She placed an unsteady foot forward, but again her legs shook. Thornton scooped her up in his arms, and her arms went about his neck. A shocking memory of a similar position months ago flitted through her mind. Evidently, it affected Thornton as well, for he paused and took a deep breath before moving.

Reaching Higgins' door in a moment, he knocked and carried her inside. He briefly explained all that had happened while she was still in his arms. Mary had gasped at their entrance and then busied herself around the room to make a comfortable place for Margaret.

The young woman brought Margaret something to drink and then petted and nurtured her just as she had done for her elder sister so recently passed. Margaret's eyes swept the place and thought of the dismal town outside the desolate walls.

She had known so much sorrow since coming to Milton. The loss of some things, innocence, and youth might be rejoiced in for it is better to learn the truth of the world. She could never hold with ignorance. The loss of her parents, however, was a different thing entirely.

She wondered if now she would be a wanderer on earth for the remainder of her days.

Time passed unknown to her. She only recognized the late hour when the sun had slipped low, and Mary left her side to light a candle. It occurred to Margaret that the house was unnaturally quiet. The Boucher children had been shuttled to other neighbours, and even Higgins was gone.

Rousing herself, Margaret stood. "I must get home to Papa..." She trailed off, recalling the horrible truth.

"Come, Miss," Mary said and took Margaret by the arm. "Might help if ye ate a bite."

"Oh, but Dixon—"

"'spect the Master sent word to her already. Ye shan't worry 'bout a thing when ye get home. Not a thing."

Defeated, Margaret slumped in the chair and tried to smile appreciatively when Mary put a plate before her. Food held no interest and might not ever again. Her young companion spoke of home, but that house would cease to be a home without father or mother.

Managing to swallow a few bites, Margaret soon apologized for her appetite. She had never traversed home alone from Frances Street so late in the day. She had never wished to worry her father, but there was no concern for that now. Mr. Thornton was taking too long in his return. The truth was, he had little reason to hasten to her side. It was a cruel, unfortunate twist of events which had him come upon her just as her father breathed his last.

Oh, she knew he would assist her in every way he could. He would never shirk the duty of a promise to a dying man. There was too much honour in him. However, she hoped to be of little trouble to him as possible. Seeing him only brought her pain and remorse. He showed enough disdain of her for Margaret to know his previous feelings were long in the past. And now, Mr. Thornton was forced to be of service to her when he must loathe her very sight. Margaret did not doubt that he did. A man with so much to be proud of must abhor that the woman he had loved turned out to be the basest liar by all the facts that he had.

Longing for the comfort of her bed and all the familiar things, she determined to get on with the dreadful purpose of returning to her home without her father. She stood, and the crude chair scraped against the floor.

"Thank you, Mary. Your kindness to me today has meant more than you can know. However, I must leave. The hour grows late."

"Miss, you mustn't."

"Tell your father I appreciate his assisting Mr. Thornton and the disruption I placed to his home and his evening. I know his time is precious."

"You can't leave!"

"Oh, I am not afraid of the streets. I daresay everyone around here knows me by now and is used to seeing me."

"He made me promise you wouldn't leave without him."

"Who? Mr. Thornton?" Margaret's nostrils flared. He had no right to command her comings and goings—and he never would. "I do not see him here. He can hardly enforce his wishes."

Margaret's hand was on the door when Mary cried, "He will sack my Pa if you leave."

Mr. Thornton wouldn't dare! Would he? Oh, he knew her well. It was perhaps the only thing that could keep her contained when she did not wish it. And yet, for as much as he seemed to know her, he had assumed she had some secret lover.

As she hovered with indecision at the threshold, the door flung open and in walked Higgins and Thornton. Margaret moved aside, but she did not shirk back when the latter turned a disapproving eye on her.

"Were you leaving?"

Margaret raised her chin. "I had made up my mind to do so."

"Without me; without an escort?"

"It appeared necessary. I did not know when you would return."

Thornton's eyes flew to Mary. Margaret glanced at her, and the girl took a step back and lowered her eyes. Surely after his visits at the house, Mary knew not to be afraid of him? But, then, Margaret had seldom seen him look as angry and thunderous as he did now. That was not the expression he entered with. It just appeared when she confirmed her willingness to leave without him.

"She stopped when I told her ye would sack my Pa. I tried my best, sir."

Margaret grew ashamed of herself as she saw her friend's lip tremble. She should not have put Mary in such a position.

"Sack me! And after I helped you all afternoon?"

"Forgive me, Higgins, Miss Mary. It was not a serious threat."

"Aye," Higgins said. "I see your meaning. Well, it is not just Milton that breeds up outspoken and determined folk." Higgins' voice had a shred of amusement mixed with admiration in it.

Margaret blushed anew. She now had the reputation of stubbornness even amongst her friends. She stammered an apology.

"There is no need for you to ask forgiveness," Thornton began. "I had not intended to leave you so long. I am sure it is only the grief of the day that clouded your judgment so." He spoke with kindness, but on his final words, his brows tilted down and a strained look entered his eyes. Did he recall the last time Margaret had been full sick with grief and assumed her clandestine meeting at a train station was due to an error in judgment because of her mother's death? That would not explain her lying afterward, though.

"Let us get you home," Thornton said and extended his arm.

Margaret took it, and they walked in silence until just before reaching her house. "I hate to leave you tonight, Margaret. In the morning, I will send round servants and a cart for your things so you can take residence at Marlborough.

"I beg your pardon? Why should I be there?"

"I assure you my mother will be a stalwart chaperone, and no one would dare say otherwise. However, if it makes you ill at ease, perhaps she can stay here until the wedding."

"The wedding?" her voice had become shrill. She raced up the steps and Dixon opened the door. Margaret immediately fell into the old servant's arms, and everything went black.

∼

"WHEN WILL SHE WAKE UP? She did not take this long in coming to when—" John clamped his mouth shut. Dr. Donaldson had been unavailable when he was sent for the second time this day, and a doctor he did not know as well had come to see to Margaret. He did not need to say things to a man that might damage his future wife's reputation.

His wife! How he had scarcely dreamed such a thing would be possible. After her refusal, he gave up the hope entirely. Too soon, the reality of why she would be his would enter his mind. That she could not love him—and never would—and came most unwillingly would be dwelt on another day. He had not meant to think on the sweet gift Mr. Hale had left him until he had reached home. During the day, he was occupied with taking care of matters for the old man. Now, as they waited for Margaret to awaken and he was once more in the Hale residence could he not keep the thoughts at bay.

"She should rouse soon. I am confident there is no physical malady, only the strain of the day. That is, unless her father was ill with anything. I know her mother passed not too long ago."

John furrowed his brow. Margaret ill? The thought of her lying still and lifeless now but pale as if? her heart had ceased to beat filled him with dread. God forbid he ever see the day. He would bargain with his Maker that he be struck down first rather than to see the woman he loved—and one so vivacious and alert as she—in a coffin. It would be the death of him as well. It was no wonder that Mr. Hale did not long outlive his wife.

"No," he answered the doctor at last. "It was his heart."

"Well, there can be little possibility of the same calamity for her."

Not unless she was grieved by the death of her only family and the possibility of marriage to him. That had stung. Once she had been willing to throw herself in the path of danger for his sake. She had said she would do so for any man. Now, the thought of marriage to him had caused her to faint.

Had she put the thought from her mind all day only to be forced to face it prematurely by his words? How could she have interpreted her father's words to mean anything else? How best would a single man care for a single woman than by marriage? John had flattered himself that he was Mr. Hale's only friend in Milton. There had been instant respect and esteem between the two. In Mr. Hale's keen mind, John found the memory of better times when he was young and had a tutor. Now, he could appreciate it more than he had in his childhood when he selfishly did not know what he would soon be missing. Even when he first had to leave school, he had not considered what he would be missing. He rejoiced in the freedom and manfully took up the yoke of providing for his family. It was only in recent years when he tired of the work-driven minds of his fellow mill owners that he desired more.

Despite Hale's gentility, he had to know that John could amply provide for his daughter. It would be better for them to marry and she be provided for immediately than it would be to trust to chance that she would one day find a man she loved who could marry her. John felt his lip curl with the memory of one that it appeared she would most willingly marry. As nothing had ever been said of a betrothal—even from Miss Hale—John could only assume her suitor was of low means even if he was of gentler stock. John shook his head. They would have to talk about it eventually, but he would not let it cloud his mind now.

Margaret's lashes fluttered, and John knelt at her side. He had collected her from Dixon's arms and carried her to the drawing room sofa. It was an all too familiar scene to him, this time he was thankful she had no wound. Again, however, her distress came at his hands.

"Margaret, how do you feel?"

"Now, I won't stand for nothing improper," Dixon said as she hovered, casting John a dirty look.

The doctor assisted Margaret as she attempted to sit up. "Easy, now, Miss Hale."

"May I have some water?" Margaret asked. She had yet to meet John's eyes. Dixon presented a glass, and Margaret drank. "I feel much better now. I am sorry if I worried anyone."

"I should say you did, Miss!" Dixon said and dabbed at her eyes with a handkerchief. "My mistress long gone and the master barely cold, and you go and collapse!"

John glared at the woman, effectively silencing her. He turned his attention back to Margaret. "The doctor thinks your fainting was only caused by the effects of the day. Are you ill? Do you feel unwell at all?"

She did not look at him. "I am sure he is correct. All I need is rest. There is nothing wrong with me."

Nothing save marriage to a man she hated, John thought. It was so like Margaret, to put herself and her interests last. She was an exceptionally loyal and devoted daughter.

"I should like to see if you can walk about," Dr. Reynolds said.

Margaret nodded and slowly stood. She walked around the room with ease. There was no swaying to her steps, no indication she still felt faint.

"Very good," he observed. "Then, I will trust your servant to make you comfortable. I will call on the morrow to see if you have continued to improve. It is imperative that you rest and eat."

"Yes, doctor," Margaret agreed, but John wondered if she had eaten anything all day. He ought to have thought of that before walking her home.

John walked with the doctor to the door before returning to Margaret's side. Dixon stood in the corner but continued to look at him with all the suspicion of an old maid who believed every man a brute and ready to attack unknowing females.

"I must be at the Mill in the morning, and there are a few matters I will have to attend to tomorrow regarding your father as well. When I am finished, I will call upon you."

Margaret's gaze remained steadfastly upon her shoes. She made no reply.

"Is there anyone my mother might contact for you? I believe I heard Mr. Hale mention relations in London."

"No," Margaret shook her head. "My aunt is abroad for her health, and my cousins are in Greece. They are not expected back for many weeks. There is no urgency to write to them. I shall do so when I can manage it."

John watched her for any indication that there was someone she intended to inform or someone whom she hoped to rely upon. There was a strain in her reply, but he was not sure it came from the source he had assumed.

"What of your father's friend, Mr. Bell? I am very acquainted with him and could inform him for you."

Margaret frowned. "He is abroad as well. Thank you for the offer, but I can manage it."

He had no doubt she could. She always did. Mr. and Mrs. Hale had relied upon her too much since their departure from Helstone. Indeed, it was one of the things which he believed had connected them. Who could she rely on now?

John gathered her hand in his, feeling the slight tremble of her dainty hand. "Margaret, you do not need to shoulder this burden alone. In his last breath, your father assigned your care to me, and I will see to you."

She finally met his eyes. Tears shimmered in hers, but she blinked them back. "I know you will do your—your duty to me. I will try to not cause you too much trouble. I know you are very busy and—" she stumbled with her words as though she could not quite decide on what to say next and had begun to reply without thinking entirely of her response. She lowered her eyes. "I thank you for your kindness, but there is no need to overly trouble yourself."

Dixon, who had followed John and the doctor out of the room and then saw to arranging things for Margaret's bedtime ablutions, arrived in the doorway. There was another glare at John and then at their joined hands, but she did not chide him this time. "I have everything ready. Come on to bed now, Miss Margaret. You need your rest."

Margaret nodded and withdrew her hand from John's. Instantly, he felt bereft of her sweet softness. He did not know until then how a small hand in his could make him feel whole. He rose first and assisted Margaret up and to Dixon's side. He watched after as the two ladies went above stairs and waited until the loyal if fierce servant re-emerged.

"She sleeps?" he asked.

Dixon eyed him with continued suspicion. "I doubt she will sleep this night, but she rests."

"She needs to sleep if she is to retain her health." She had seemed too faint and fragile today. Her cheeks had lost their bloom. The fatigue she had tried to hide for months became an open book on her face.

Dixon straightened. "Miss Margaret is as healthy and strong as any of your northern lasses, a good deal more I would say. If she suffers, it must be the unclean air of Milton. My mistress, God rest her, always said—"

John held up a hand. He did not need to hear lectures from this proud woman. "See that she rests as much as possible. If she does not sleep, I will call for Dr. Donaldson. She is to have as much fresh food as she will take."

"I do not see why you are ordering me about or where you think this food will come from! Nor do I like your insinuations that I do not feed her well enough—"

A hard glare silenced her for a moment. "My mother will arrive in the morning. Speak to her about anything you need, and everything will be arranged. She is a most efficient manager."

"I will not have a stranger rule over me or this house. Miss Margaret is the rightful mistress—"

Her attitude bristled, but he considered that she, too, grieved for the loss of her master and cared for all that Margaret had gone through since moving to Milton. "Dixon, it has been an exceptionally long and tiring day. I will forgive your impertinence if you forgive anything I say which seems as such to you. I act in Margaret's best interest. Mr. Hale himself secured me in that office. If he had not, then I would do as much as I could out of admiration for his daughter. Now, I hope we can get along better in the future. I bid you goodnight. Lock up after I leave."

She did not say anything, only tipped her head in acknowledgment before following him to the door. As it closed behind him and he waited to hear the click of locks, he thought he heard her muttering under her breath about not needing to be told how to do her job by one such as him.

He purposefully kept his mind as blank as possible on the journey home. When heavy thoughts began to seep in, he considered how bone-weary he felt after the events of the day. More profound ponderings would need to wait for reflection in the privacy of his chamber. Arriving home, he greeted his mother.

"Is it true what I have heard?" she asked.

"What is that?"

"That Mr. Hale died in the middle of Frances Street after leaving one of those Union leader's houses. The one you took on."

She gave her head a shake of disgust. She had not learned to be content with his decision; she had yet to see the wisdom in it. However, she no longer voiced opposition to it.

"I am grieved to say that it is."

"Then is it too much to hope that it is a pure invention of gossips that you carried Miss Hale all over town in your own arms?" She stabbed at her embroidery.

John came to her side. "Miss Hale fainted."

Mrs. Thornton chucked her embroidery aside at last and hummed. "The tittle-tattle is that alone in the world, she has made a final play at your hand. Some say she threw herself in front of a carriage, hoping you would save her. Others that she embraced you."

"And what do they say of the man she was seen with only weeks ago?" John sneered. "You told me that I was honour-bound to her after the strike. You said her actions proved her love. I suppose they think this does too? Do they think she has no constancy?"

"Her own actions prove that she does not. She loved you one day but by the time you proposed she had changed her mind! Then we hear of this other lover. Now, he is gone, and the father is dead. Of course, she will fling herself at the nearest choice."

"Mother, I will thank you to not do Miss Hale such a disservice. For the grief my heart has known due to her—"

"Aye, I know your grief, Johnny. It is why I hate her so. It is why I must tell you these things—"

"No more." He fell to his knee beside her. "She is to be my wife. My wife, at last!"

A gasp stole from Mrs. Thornton's lips before she covered it with a hand. Her cheeks grew red as though ashamed of that show of emotion. "It cannot be. Aside from all her games, I am sure she is too proud to have you."

"It will be. Her father decreed it just before he died."

"John, no! Not like this. Do not bring me that creature as a daughter and tell me to love her. Not when she is too foolish to love you as well and treats your heart so carelessly. I cannot bear it. Do not be so foolish!"

"I have vowed to look after her, and I will. She is not as fickle as all your gossips say. You ought to know better."

She hung her head a little, penitent in believing the vicious and idle chatter of others. However, no apology formed on her lips.

"She is as alone as you say, but not for us. Tomorrow, I ask that you call on her. Be a mother to her in her grief."

"She would not want—"

"You did not see her sorrow today. Whatever you think you know of her, she is softer than that. Or do you think I could love a hard woman? Do you suppose I was taken in by her charms? I thought you did not believe she had any."

"I would never think so little of you."

"Then listen to me now when I say your Christian duty requires this of you at the very least. Your mothering heart will demand it as well. Every time you speak evil of her, you wound me." John did not wait for a reply. He stood and ascended the stairs, too tired to call for a tray or ask for one to be sent to his chamber.

At last free with his thoughts, he collapsed on his bed still half-dressed. Margaret's pain was like an iron searing his heart. He recalled too easily the grief of losing his own beloved father. The misery of knowing he had made foolish choices and left him alone to bear with them made a prison for John. It was not only the death of Mr. Hale which now weighed on Margaret but the fact that he had moved them to Milton—to the place that took so much from them.

Could a woman driven into a man's arms by such mourning find love there? Would she give up the other man in return for John's loyalty and kindness? He would never want her gratitude, and he thought he could settle for even less than her whole heart. He prayed that she could allow him just a piece of it. He needed only a small fraction to move in. Perhaps when their time on earth was through, she could say with a small smile that if he did not love her best, he had at least loved her the longest. Perhaps that would do for her.

It was all the hope he had, but it shined brighter than a solitary candle in the darkest night. He could not see clearly the path between here and there. He knew not how he would traverse it. John only knew that he would bravely seek that light. Reaching for it would be his guide, and he prayed it would be enough to escort Margaret on the way there and through her heartache.

MARGARET AWOKE WITH A START. The dream had turned too delicious. She was encased in Mr. Thornton's strong arms. In her sleep, she revelled in it in a way that would have brought a blush to her maidenly cheeks during the day. Through the fog-filled thought of sleep, she realized it was no dream. The memory of his heat against hers, the feeling of security, and the desire to lay against his chest forever were far too real to be a conjuring of her most secret yearnings.

Misery and shame assaulted her as soon as her eyes flickered open. How could she think on yesterday with any sort of pleasure? How often had she hoped in the hidden depths of her heart that she might receive another offer from Mr. Thornton? Too late she had realized his value and—oh!—how pride went before the fall! He could not love her. She had shown an unpardonable trait. Not only must he believe her in love with another man, but all she had ever heard about Mr. Thornton was of how highly he valued honesty. The lie of Frederick's appearance at the Outwood train station stood between them as wide as any chasm. He would hate her forever after being trapped in a marriage he did not want.

To find even a fraction of gladness, even to rejoice in the situation she was now in showed more of her wickedness than she ever knew she had. She had sometimes longed for a respite, for a chance to sit and think without caring for a parent. Now, she had such the opportunity but at the highest cost! However, she could not regret all of yesterday.

Pain and joy, misery and hopefulness mingled until she could contain the flood no longer. Bitter tears fell down her cheeks. Margaret thought she could fill an ocean for each regret she had. In this state of anguish, with her knees drawn up to her chin and her hands covering her face as sobs wracked her body, she sat until Dixon entered the room.

"Mrs. Thornton is in the sitting room. I told her you were not up to visitors, but she insisted it was not a social call and to let her pass. I do not know where these Thorntons get their—"

Margaret wiped her eyes with the handkerchief her loyal servant provided. "Please do not let me hear you abuse them, especially Mr. Thornton. He has been incredibly kind to me, and he was so good to Father."

Dixon opened her mouth ready for a retort, but soon closed it and nodded. "We best get you dressed then."

She may not have wanted Mrs. Thornton's presence in the house, but Dixon primped Margaret until she looked fit for the drawing rooms of Harley Street. Margaret stared at herself in the mirror, wondering when her eyes had taken on such a lifeless look.

Steadily, she went down the stairs and greeted her guest. Mrs. Thornton had been standing in the room, looking as though she were critiquing every article her eyes landed upon. Her expression did not change with Margaret's entrance. "Please, do be seated," Margaret said as she made herself comfortable in a chair. "I apologize for the wait."

"I suppose you keep Southern hours."

"I am far more accustomed to Milton than that by now. You will allow me the indulgence this morning."

Mrs. Thornton stared at Margaret, scrutinizing her face. "Keeping to a schedule is for the best, even in your situation. I am not so heartless to criticize you for being so affected by the death of your father, but I have now vowed to two people to see that you are on the path of health and safety."

"You promised my father you would look after me?"

"Of course not; my son."

"Oh." Margaret sat back, stunned for a moment. Then, gathering her courage and hoping to appear indifferent, asked, "And how is Mr. Thornton this morning? I regret that I troubled him so much yesterday."

"He is not ill if that is your worry. He often keeps later hours than he did last night—at the Mill, mind you, not on social practices. I suppose you will want to change that, but I tell you to think better of it."

She was referencing the marriage to which Mr. Thornton had alluded as well. Could Margaret really go through with that? To be the wife of Mr. Thornton—oh!—but to trap him in such a way. He could not love her anymore. Even if he did, she did not deserve him and had not earned the blessing of matrimony. He offered for her now only out of duty to her father.

Unsure what to say, Margaret avoided a reply entirely. "Dixon said you did not come on a social call. How may I assist you?"

"You assist me!" Mrs. Thornton looked her up and down. "I will say this for you, child, you have the gumption needed in the North. No, Miss Hale, there is nothing you can do for me. My son wanted me to come and be of service to you. I understand there are household matters to see to."

"I am sorry for the trouble you took to come, but things are well in hand. I do not know why Mr. Thornton believed I would need your presence."

"I knew you would be too stubborn to allow this. I tried to tell John, but he would not listen."

Despite the insult from Mrs. Thornton, Margaret smiled. He knew her well enough for that. Perhaps all was not so hopeless. Mrs. Thornton stood.

"Well, I will not be made to leave." She glanced around the room. "I suppose we could start with the books. You surely have no need for them now."

"No, I cannot part with Father's books!"

"And you spend much time with Plato, do you?" Mrs. Thornton picked up a volume and then put it down in disgust.

How could Margaret hope to explain it to this woman who was so hopelessly unsentimental? The books made her feel closer to her father. "Might Mr. Thornton have use of them?"

Her soon to be mother-in-law's lip curled. "Aye. Perhaps he might, but I do not know that he will have reason to continue his studies. I do not know of any other gentlemen tutors in Milton." Something softened in Mrs. Thornton then. "I regret it keenly. Your father was a good man and a good friend to my son. He has not had many. He cannot befriend the workers, and he cannot trust the other masters."

"My father, too, greatly enjoyed Mr. Thornton's friendship."

"Very well. We will allow John to choose the books he wishes to keep. Where shall I begin, Miss Hale?"

For a moment, Margaret considered refusing again. Her sense of independence did begin to rally, but in the end, fatigue won out. "I have no attachment to anything in this room, save the desire to keep some of Papa's books."

"Now that I have my instruction, there is no need for you to wait upon me. Please, go and rest for the remainder of the day."

Margaret wondered at the suggestion given her earlier words, but she did not question it. Once in the quiet confines of her room, Mr. Hale's Plato in her hands, she leafed through the familiar pages.

"I wish you were here, Father," she murmured to herself. "Why did you tell Mr. Thornton to take care of me? Did you really mean for him to marry me?"

She may have always been the dutiful daughter, but she would not violate her principles on marriage to please her father. It also was not enough that she loved Mr. Thornton. She was now sensible to the differences in their stations in different ways—ways that mattered more in the North. More than this, she did not want a man to feel honour-bound to her. It was even more repugnant to her now than it had been the day after the riot at Marlborough Mills.

Casting her eye about her small room, she wondered what she would take with her when she left this house. If she chose not to marry Mr. Thornton, she must go somewhere. Edith was still in Corfu, and Mr. Bell was on the Continent as well. She could find a home with Frederick in Cadiz, but did she wish to leave her Mother and Father behind? Could she start life anew in an even more foreign land? Could she leave Mr. Thornton behind?

She had almost resolved that she would when a new consideration made her change her mind. She could refuse Mr. Thornton and trust that one day they might be on more even ground. However, how could she trust that he would ever extend his hand a third time? How would time bridge the rift between them due to her dishonesty?

Leaving her chamber, Margaret crept into her father's room. He kept a few books in there, and she may as well go over his more private things without the peering eyes of Mrs. Thornton or Dixon. The matron was correct. She could not wallow in pain and misery indefinitely. She longed for industry.

Pulling her father's long-held favourites off the shelves, she carried them back to her room. Next, she found his personal letters. They would need going through. Margaret rummaged through them, looking for letters of business and set aside his private correspondence. They would be consigned to the fire.

Suddenly, her eyes alighted on her name. In her father's neat, familiar hand was a letter dedicated to her. Nay, it was not a letter, more like a benediction, proof that the clergyman remained in him even in his days of doubt.

My Margaret,

May the Lord grant you peace and comfort during this trying time in your life. I see you as a woman of faith, as an Abraham sojourning in a strange land and among strange people. You do not question why we are here, although I am sure you must wonder at it. You do not grumble and complain as we are left in darkness, unlike the Children of Israel.

Can I suppose you are willing to sacrifice everything you hold dear and your most beloved to prove your faithfulness? You have lost your mother already, and your father is sure to soon follow. I pray thee, my child, do not sacrifice more for the sake of duty. You have proved your devotion to Frederick and us.

As our Heavenly Father sees the smallest sparrow, I have seen how you wrestle with it. You have attempted to hide it from me, but I have learned enough from Dixon to piece together the facts. If I do not summon enough courage to ask you face to face, then I will do so now. Why do you not tell Mr. Thornton the truth of Frederick? He is too honourable to use his position as magistrate against us. He loves you most devotedly.

You must marry John. In Mrs. Thornton, you will have a mother again. Did not the Lord say he would comfort the motherless? In my pupil, I think you will find enough of my qualities—as many as you would wish in a husband and not a father, at the least.

You must marry John because I see evidence that your heart is attached to his. You covet news about him. You smile at the mention of his name just for the pangs of regret to make it vanish. I do not know all that has passed between you, but I know nothing is impossible with God. Let Him lead you, if only you would have a bit more faith.

The Lord bless you and keep you; the Lord make his face to shine upon you and be gracious to you; the Lord turn his face toward you and give you peace.

YOUR LOVING father

MARGARET PRESSED her father's words to her heart. Recalling her Bible lessons, she knew God had told Abraham he would be a father of many nations through his son Isaac. Then, years later, He ordered Abraham to sacrifice his son to prove his faithfulness. Obediently, Abraham set out. At the last moment, an angel appeared and commanded Abraham to stop. Another offering was provided for the sacrifice.

It was an oft-quoted passage used to illustrate the force of faithfulness in dire times. Margaret had attempted to live it week after week, and month after month of life in Milton. She could hardly understand her father leaving his parish, let alone choosing Milton as their new home. It had damaged her mother's health and given seemingly nothing but heartache. Everywhere she looked, she saw unkindness and unhappiness except in a few shining examples in what some would call the least likely of places.

Now, a weight lifted from Margaret's heart. Perhaps there was some purpose to Milton after all. Maybe even the loss of her mother and father might have a divine order. She would know soon if she could face her fears and talk with Mr. Thornton truthfully about Frederick. Her father called on her to have faith, and she did not wish to disappoint him.

"Take heed, little heart. If a sacrifice must be made, one will be provided."

Choosing to stay occupied in her current task, Margaret continued to clean her father's chamber until she heard Mrs. Thornton and the servants she had brought leave. She ate a little and rested at Dixon's command; then when she knew it was the most probable time for Mr. Thornton to arrive, she awaited him in the drawing room.

JOHN'S ERRANDS regarding business and Mr. Hale were finished, but his feet did not find their way to Margaret's home. Instead, he found himself lingering at the mill and inviting Higgins into his office on some fabricated subject of importance.

"You been wrestling with it, I see," the sharp-eyed employee observed.

"What do you mean?"

"With marrying Miss Margaret. More than one person heard the old parson say it. I thought you liked the girl, but you have the look of a man who would rather hang than wed."

John shook his head. He would gladly marry Margaret tomorrow if only she came to him with love or even esteem. Did not he know her low opinion of him and all manufacturers? All that before seeing the proof with his own eyes that she loved another. Indeed, he would much rather face the gallows than have Margaret only out of duty.

Only, why could she not have loved him? Why did time and distance not separate her heart from the handsome young man whom she clutched so desperately and yet seemingly had no future with? He knew the answer. When Margaret loved, it would be for her whole life. She was not the sort of fair-weather sweetheart who would lose affection for a man, regardless of his income or fortunes, due to circumstance. He could at least do her that justice. Indeed, even if she had been like the least reputable of her sex and her heart so changeable, it could never look on him in favour.

"Mr. Hale ordered me to take care of her. He likely did not mean for me to marry her, and if she has a mind to refuse, I will not press my case." He had thought about it all day. No matter the glimmer of hope he had last night, he could not force his hand like this. She could regret forever what she agreed to in a moment of weakness.

"Take care of her! Why, she is not alone in the world."

"Her London relations and friends are abroad."

"Well, London, you say. But, I had thought the young master who went to Spain—" Higgins abruptly stopped speaking. "Perhaps I should not say more."

"The young master—what—do you mean a young gentleman?"

"Aye, he was. Younger than me, at least, and I reckon younger than you as well. For sure, he was older than Miss Margaret—her older brother."

"Her brother!"

"That is what I am saying, if only you would listen. She could go and live with her brother, the old parson's son. He lives in Spain and was only in England when the mother was dying. Some big secret with the law."

"Her brother," was all John could echo.

Without so much as a farewell to Higgins, John was out the door of his own office. He had not stopped to gather his hat or gloves. He thought only of Margaret. She had a brother!

As he tramped about town to her door, he thought little even of his own relief. That she might not be in love with another man brought some comfort. However, it was not a vindication of her approbation for him. No, what he considered most was that Margaret had been ripped from a brother at some point in her life. That even now, as they mourned over another parent, he was not present to share in that pain with her. On top of all her other anxieties, she had to wonder about a brother and his welfare!

John had no right to claim her. She ought to be with her brother. He would do everything in his power to bring about a reunion of the siblings and gain her passage to Spain.

He knocked on the door and stepped inside before the servant could even say two words. He showed himself to the drawing room, without paying attention to the woman and whether she said Margaret was prepared for his visit or not.

He entered the room and saw Margaret staring out a window with her back to him. She had not been looking out the window when he approached the house. She must have heard his knock and anticipated his arrival. Her choosing to stand so far from him was only further proof of her disavowal of him.

Indeed, John was struck with a memory from another encounter in this room. She had quietly entered while he stared out the window, pondering what words of love he would tell her. It was the day his heart had been sliced open. Releasing her of Mr. Hale's wishes could not further harm it than it had been done that day. Still, he stood and watched her in silence for a moment. This would be the last he would see of her—he could not bear to see her again when her choice was made clear to him. He took in every shape of her figure, memorized every hue of her hair and the path of each curl and braid, her queenly posture, even the proud hold of her shoulders and head. He would never forget her. He knew it now as he had known it on the day he first offered his heart. She had saved his life, and now his life would be lived for her, in memory of her. Each beat of his heart would serve as a monument to the one woman he could ever love. While she might soon wish to forget her time in Milton, he never could forget Margaret Hale.

Finally, determined to break the spell, he stepped forward. She heard the noise and turned. Just when he opened his mouth, she fell into his arms, crying.

"Oh, Mr. Thornton. I am not good enough!"

"Not good enough! Not good enough for what?" Mr. Thornton's arms tightened around Margaret as his voice was filled with wonder and surprise.

She pulled back and dropped her eyes. Immediately, he lifted her chin, and she had no choice but to see his luminous dark eyes full of softness and tenderness. Her heart rallied. Was this for her? Could he have even a morsel of affection for her still?

"You know I have lied, but you cannot conceive as to why. I know I have lowered myself in your eyes. I have no excuse."

Mr. Thornton led her to the sofa, where he did not relinquish her hand. "What are you attempting to tell me? Is it to do with your brother?"

"My brother! I did not know you knew of him. Did Father tell you? And yet he never told me you knew."

"No, Mr. Hale never told me he had a son. I learned of it only a few moments ago from Higgins. He had not meant to tell me new information. He meant to save you from the misfortune of marrying me."

He began to withdraw his hand, but Margaret tightened her hold. "It would be no misfortune."

"You know my heart, Margaret. I have spoken of it to you once before, but never again without your welcome. I will not force you into matrimony with me or see you marry any man for the sake of a home and security. Say the word, and I will send inquiries about a ticket for you in passage to Spain."

It was too much. She had been pressed to her breaking point and could contain herself no more. He spoke of sending her away, and her heart should shrink back in fear. However, he also spoke of the time when he claimed to love her. This was the hope she had prayed for, the little ray of sunshine in her gloom.

With eyes focused on their entwined hands, and with a trembling chin, she said, "I do not wish to go away. Please, Mr. Thornton—John —will you not let me stay and love you?"

"Love me?" he cried in astonishment. "I had not dared to hope— but is it true? Do you really love me? Margaret!"

Slowly, she lifted her eyes to meet his, her affection for him filling them and threatening to spill over. "I do," she whispered. She could not speak louder, not now when her heart was so full and her thoughts tossed about like a ship on a stormy sea.

Words were unnecessary, as John—her own John!—pulled her into an embrace. Her head nestled against his chest, hearing the steady beat of his heart. The comfort and rapture she felt in his arms, she had never thought possible. How could he still love her? She had spurned him so callously and gave nothing but a reason for offense for much of their acquaintance.

There was a sound at the door, and Dixon emerged. Instantly, they sprang apart but not before Dixon cried and ran away. Margaret looked into John's eyes, laughing. The expression she saw on his face stole her breath. A rare, genuine smile had relaxed his features, and nothing but sheer joy could be emanating from his eyes. By instinct, she placed a hand on his cheek.

He turned his face and pressed a kiss into her palm, making her gasp and her breath come quickly. Turning her hand over, his lips next met her knuckles. He said nothing; he did not need to. His head dropped to hers, touching their foreheads together for a moment. Then, he drew back and sought her eyes for permission. She nodded a little and shyly smiled.

So slowly she thought she might die from holding her breath, John leaned toward her until finally their lips touched. It was full of all the tenderness she had come to expect from him, and behind the first meeting lay an inherent strength.

His hands came up to hold her face, his fingers caressing her cheeks. She had no wish to leave, and her fists clung to his lapels. Again, and again, he met her lips, his slanted this way and that to change the angle and pressure. Each new touch sparked the joy of discovery in her, resulting in the sure knowledge that she would have a blessed marriage indeed.

Margaret had lost all sense of time in the bliss known in John's arms, but eventually, he ceased his ministrations. Pulling her head to rest above his heart again, she smiled to hear its rhythm matched her own racing one.

Margaret was in his arms and accepted his kisses. John had thought he could die a happy man sheerly for knowing her. Now, he knew the folly of an inexperienced man and the real pangs of unrequited love. Now, he understood the wretched pain Mr. Hale must have felt at the death of his wife and the loss of her these last months. How could he ever return to a life without the sweet temptation of Margaret in his arms and the joy of her lips on his? To think he must leave her this night! But soon, he need never go without her again.

They sat together, her cuddled in his embrace, for many minutes while their breath slowed. "My love," he said, at last breaking the silence that had been between them for so long, "what did you mean to tell me about your brother when I had come in?"

"Oh," Margaret attempted to straighten, but he held her fast in his arms. "I had forgotten about it," she said as she settled against his chest again.

"You said you were unworthy and had lied but had no excuse." He wondered what she could have meant. He could well guess that she meant lying about her presence at the train station the night of Leonards' injury just after her mother's death. Certainly, if her brother had some reason to hide his identity, then she had a very good excuse to lie.

Haltingly, she told of what she called a sin. She explained about Frederick and his part in the mutiny. She regretted that she had panicked and lied. She had forgotten entirely that John had witnessed her at the station and thought only of saving her brother.

He had no difficulty in believing her or excusing her. The son of Mr. Hale could never be the worst sort of man that would resort to the overthrow of a sane captain. John even doubted that the young man would have been the primary conspirator. Having been a magistrate, it was no news to him that the law might have wrong information and would set an innocent man as the guilty party.

"What I regretted most of all, though I would scarcely admit it even to myself, was that I knew you must have hated me for lying. What must you have thought of me!"

"I will not deny that I was sorely tempted to hate you. My heart was still in agony from your rejection, and here I thought I had proof of some weakness in you. I could not do you the injustice, though. I could not reconcile it with the lady I had known and loved. Perhaps wiser men would determine they had been fools and loved falsely to spare themselves the misery and torment I inflicted upon myself in quiet hours, but I have always known what sort of man I am. I am not the sort who would love a woman with so little honour."

A tear trickled down Margaret's face. "It is exactly that which makes me so unworthy. Where was my honour when I lied for Frederick's sake? I had faced down a rioting crowd not many days before. I argued with you about business and workers, and I know not what else I scarcely have an understanding of, but before that officer, I shrunk back and lied. Where were my honour and bravery then?"

"My Margaret!" John cried and pressed a kiss to her hair. "You have been brave for so long, the champion of so many. It is only right that you would have a need to rest. Do not forget that you were overwrought by your mother's demise, and the fear for your brother was genuine. I hate to say it, but I think it very unlikely that Frederick would ever get a fair trial in England. It is best that you kept everything quiet until he was safely abroad. Anything but a flat refusal would have continued the questioning, and then everything would have been at risk."

"But the lie! I cannot forgive myself for the lie."

"Do we not all make mistakes, dearest? Do we not all have regrets? What matters is how we move forward with our knowledge of a better way. I have no doubt that you will turn away from such things. You are not now enjoying that you have hidden a thing and got away with it."

"Surely not!"

"Then let us talk no more about it. I am grateful for this test in our love. I would not deserve you if I threw you off for such a thing. You might not have discovered your feelings for me if not for the issue. Indeed, I shall be as thankful for it as I am for your father moving you to Milton and for his final wish. I would not have pressed you into it, but I had no hope of a second chance without it."

"Do not say that. Somehow, our hearts would have come to an understanding. I am exceedingly grateful for Father and his wisdom. I had doubted him when we moved from Helstone, but it proved the perfect plan in the end. I will not consider what I have lost here. Mother was never strong, and Father would never live long without her. How should I have found you in any place but Milton? How would I have understood you if I had?"

"Perhaps it is not for us to know, my love. The Lord's ways are mysterious, indeed. Do you really understand me?"

"I think so. Although, perhaps not as well as I will after I have been Mrs. Thornton for many years," she added shyly.

"Margaret Thornton of Milton! How well that sounds!"

Margaret did not reply. Instead, with a smile on her face and a gleam in her eye, she pulled John's head down for a kiss. Mr. Hale's final wish had been the unspoken desire of their hearts, and John would forever remain grateful for the gentleman and the woman he now held in his arms.

∾

BORN IN THE WRONG ERA, Rose Fairbanks has read nineteenth-century novels since childhood. Although she studied history, her transcript also contains every course in which she could discuss Jane Austen. Never having given up all-nighters for reading, Rose discovered her love for Historical Romance after reading Christi Caldwell's Heart of a Duke Series.

After a financial downturn and her husband's unemployment had threatened her ability to stay at home with their special needs child, Rose began writing the kinds of stories she had loved to read for so many years. Now, a best-selling author of Jane Austen-inspired stories, she also writes Regency Romance, Historical Fiction, Paranormal Romance, and Historical Fantasy.

Having completed a BA in history in 2008, she plans to finish her master's studies someday. When not reading or writing, Rose runs after her two young children, ignores housework, and profusely thanks her husband for doing all the dishes and laundry. She is a member of the Jane Austen Society of North America and Romance Writers of America.

ROSE FAIRBANKS' books include: *The Gentleman's Impertinent Daughter, Letters from the Heart, Undone Business, No Cause to Repine, Love Lasts Longest, Mr. Darcy's Kindness, Once Upon a December, Mr. Darcy's Miracle at Longbourn, How Darcy Saved Christmas, Sufficient Encouragement, Renewed Hope, Extraordinary Devotion, Mr. Darcy's Bluestocking Bride, The Secrets of Pemberley, Pledged, Reunited, Treasured,* and *A Sense of Obligation*

THE BEST MEDICINE

Elaine Owen

"Similarity of opinion is not always—I think not often—needed for fullness and perfection of love." - Chapter XXVIII, Ruth

ohn Thornton sat moodily in his office at Marlborough Mills. Last night had been the annual dinner he and his mother held for the most prominent families in Milton and, by most accounts, it had been a success.

The only downside had been his spark-filled conversation with Margaret Hale, the fiery daughter of Thornton's tutor. Miss Hale made her opinion of Thornton and the other masters clear. She thought he was a monster who cared more about profits from his business than the well-being of his workers.

Thornton and Margaret held utterly opposing views of how to resolve the current disastrous strike taking place in Milton, where hundreds of families were facing starvation while the wage earners in the families refused to work. The union leaders would not come to the bargaining table until the masters agreed to an unreasonable pay raise, while the masters refused to negotiate without some sign of sincerity on the union's part. The fastest way to solve the situation, according to Thornton, was to let the workers feel the result of their stubbornness. When their little ones started to cry with hunger, the leaders of the strike would begin negotiating in good faith.

Margaret, however, was determined to give aid and comfort to the families of the strikers by delivering baskets of food to them. Thornton had tried to convince her that her actions would only prolong the strike rather than stopping it, but that was not her concern. She could not turn away from the suffering she saw all around her, and Thornton could not quite suppress a twinge of guilt when she urged him to think of the children.

Their difference of opinion would not have mattered to him, of course, had it been anyone but Margaret. The rest of Milton could go to the devil, he thought. Margaret's opinion was the only one that mattered to him. That was a shame, because her opinion of *him* was not favorable. And he had no idea how to change it.

A knock at the door interrupted his thoughts. In response to his call, a slim man about his own age pushed the door open and cautiously peered inside.

Thornton had to think for a moment before the gentleman's name came to him. Then he leaped to his feet and held out his hand in warm welcome. "Lawson, my friend! What a pleasure to see you again!"

"Good day, Thornton." The newcomer gripped his hand firmly. "I always knew you'd run the world once you got out of school. And now here you are, the master of half of Milton!"

"You are mistaken, my friend. You were the one determined to change the world."

"We were both ambitious fellows, but only you have succeeded in making your mark. I am still waiting to make mine."

Thornton invited Lawson to sit and took a seat opposite, pouring a glass of brandy to welcome his unexpected guest.

The years had not changed Lawson much. He still had thick blond hair and classic features that ladies would probably consider handsome. Lawson had been two years behind him in school, but their friendship was not affected by the age difference. Thornton had finished school and gone straight into business, while Lawson had gone to London to study with a physician. Over the years they had fallen out of touch.

"Are you back in Milton for good," Thornton asked, swirling the brandy in his glass, "or is this simply a visit home?"

"I plan on staying here permanently. I am a doctor now, you see. I finished my training last year, and now I am opening a practice in Milton."

Thornton raised a surprised eyebrow. "Congratulations. But why Milton? Can't you make more money in town?"

"The need is greater here. Milton is in my blood, Thornton, and I decided that this is where I can make the most difference. I may never change the world, but I can at least change a small part of it."

Thornton eyed the younger man respectfully. Lawson had always had a quietly noble, self-sacrificing quality, and it seemed his medical training had only enhanced that part of his character. "Very good of you, I'm sure."

"I was hoping I might count you among my patients, once my practice is established."

"I would like nothing better, but you know my constitution. I am never ill."

Lawson was unruffled. "What about your family? Children are always coming down with something or other."

"Thank you, but I am a bachelor, and my mother and sister are attached to their doctor."

Now it was time for Lawson to raise an eyebrow. "Still unmarried? I wouldn't have thought it. You could have had your pick of any woman in town."

Any woman but one, Thornton thought. "I have been too busy to fall in love," was his terse reply.

Lawson shrugged. "Well, perhaps you will keep me in mind when there's an injury in your mill. I would be glad to be of service."

"I will do that." Injuries were common in cotton mills due to the heavy machinery all around. Having ready access to a doctor with the latest training could help Thornton's workers recover from their injuries more quickly and would help his business be more profitable in the long run.

Lawson stood and took up his hat, preparing to leave; but as he did so, Thornton thought again of Margaret. She was a fierce advocate for anyone in distressing circumstances. Hadn't she mentioned having a friend whose lungs had been damaged by the white cotton fluff that infested the cotton mills?

"Wait, Lawson," he said, frowning as he tried to recall what Margaret had said. "There is one case I am aware of, a young woman you might examine. But I warn you, it is likely to be hopeless. She used to work in the mills and now she has the white fluff in her lungs."

"The white fluff? I thought you masters put in blowing wheels to get rid of all that!"

"Most of us have. But this young lady had the misfortune of working for a less scrupulous master."

"Hmm." Lawson frowned thoughtfully, considering. "I will be glad to take a look. There are some new treatments I learned in town which may help her."

TWENTY MINUTES LATER THORNTON, flanked by Lawson, stood on Crampton's front step and lifted his hand to knock. But the door opened before he could complete the action.

"Mr. Thornton!" Margaret Hale stood in the open doorway wearing her hat and coat, an oversized wicker basket hanging on one arm. It was clear she was leaving the house on some errand. "I did not know you had a lesson with father today. If you will come inside, I will call him for you."

Thornton shook his head, thinking how lovely she looked with the dark hat and coat framing her delicate features. "My business is with you, Miss Hale. I wish to introduce my friend Arthur Lawson to your acquaintance."

Margaret looked surprised, but she accepted the introduction graciously. Thornton noted with pleasure that she shook hands in the Northern way, following the custom Thornton had shown her.

"Lawson is a friend of mine from school who just finished medical training in town. He wants to establish a practice in Milton, so I told him about your friend, Miss Higgins. He has expressed a willingness to examine her and see if he might be of some assistance. I wonder if you might be so good as to tell us where to find her."

"Oh!" Margaret's lovely green eyes opened wide in surprise as she looked up at Thornton. For a moment, she floundered for words. She glanced uncertainly from him to Lawson and then back again. "You are very thoughtful, Mr. Thornton, but I doubt if she will accept Mr. Lawson's services. Her father is not a wealthy man. There is no way for her family to afford a doctor."

"I will be happy to accept the bill on your friend's behalf," Thornton offered. From the corner of his eye he caught a quick look from Lawson.

Margaret's face changed from surprise to delight, and then to suspicion. "Why would you do that?" she asked, her eyes flashing. "She is my friend, not yours. You do not even know her. And her father is one of those rabble-rousers you are so eager to starve into submission!"

"That is precisely why I wish to help, Miss Hale," Thornton answered, using his best persuasive tone. "Last night you accused me of being indifferent to the plight of the strikers and their families. Allow me the opportunity to prove you wrong." Margaret still looked unsure. "Come, Miss Hale, you must give me this chance."

"Nicholas – Mr. Higgins – would not want to accept charity from you. He blames you and the other masters for causing the strike by not accepting their demands."

"The masters would say much the same," Thornton answered gravely, "except that we blame Higgins and the other union leaders for not negotiating to begin with. But surely we can set aside our differences in a good cause."

Margaret hesitated, but she finally stepped out of the house and pulled the door shut behind her. "I was just on my way to Princeton now to see Bessy. If you would like, you may accompany me." As Thornton and Lawson fell in behind her, letting her lead the way, Margaret spoke over her shoulder. "You may wish to keep your head down, Mr. Thornton, and try to not make your presence obvious. You are not a well-liked person in Princeton at this moment."

"BESSY? I've brought someone to see you."

Bessy struggled to push herself up in bed when she heard the gentle voice of her unlikely but most cherished friend, Margaret Hale. She had to stop halfway through the motion as a violent cough racked her body. "A visitor? Yo' never said nothing 'bout bringing a visitor here."

"He is a doctor, Bessy. He is here to help you." Bessy felt Margaret's strong arm go around her shoulders, helping her to a sitting position.

"Don't want no doctor. Can't pay f' one." Another spasm of coughing prevented her from saying more.

"You are not to worry about that, Miss Higgins." Bessy's head whipped up at the sound of the new voice. She would have recognized the deep, commanding voice anywhere, but she still had to look to make sure.

"Master Thornton? What're ye doin' here?" *And hoo be that 'andsome man next t' yo?* she wanted to ask.

"Mister Thornton is the one who thought of bringing a doctor to you, Bessy," Margaret said brusquely, adjusting the pillows behind her. "This is Mr. Lawson. He was trained in town, and he might have some new ideas of how to rid your lungs of the white fluff."

"Now I know I'm a'dyin,'" Bessy commented as she re-adjusted her bed covers. She ran weak fingers through her thin hair, trying to make herself presentable. "They say the dyin' have strange dreams just afore the end. But I never thought I'd have a dream as strange as seein' Master Thornton in me own 'ouse!"

～

"WHAT DO YOU THINK, LAWSON?" Thornton asked his friend some time later, after Lawson had examined Bessy, asked numerous questions, and taken careful notes in a little book he carried inside his jacket. Margaret remained with Bessy as the two men began to walk back to Marlboro Mills.

Lawson peered up at him, his shorter strides struggling to keep up with Thornton's quick pace. "What does that girl mean to you, Thornton?"

Thornton shrugged. "Miss Higgins? She is a worker, or she was until she became ill. Her father is one of the strike organizers, but I never met her before today."

"You know that is not who I meant, Thornton. What is your relationship with Miss Hale?"

"We have no relationship," Thornton answered immediately, and scowled.

"You volunteered to pay the costs of her friend's medical care without even being asked," Lawson pointed out.

"This is not something I wish to discuss." Thornton's scowl deepened.

Lawson could not help giving a little chuckle. "So that is how the land lies! You are attracted to her but she does not care for you. You asked me to help one woman in order to impress another." He shook his head. "You are far gone, my friend."

Thornton did not change expression, but Lawson knew he had surmised correctly. In his profession, he was accustomed to observing symptoms, finding a pattern, and quickly confirming a diagnosis. In this case, he already knew what bothered the other man: severe lovesickness. Unfortunately, this was one illness for which he had no medicine. They continued to walk together in silence.

"Just tell me if you can cure the girl, Lawson," Thornton finally growled.

"It is not an easy case," Lawson answered, his mind instantly returning to the frail girl with the strong spirit. "The fluff has worked completely into her lungs, and the disease is far advanced. Without proper treatment, she will die. But my mentor in town has had success in treating several of these cases. I am going to come back tomorrow with medicine and a treatment plan."

"I would like to come with you." The words were a command, not a request.

Lawson noticed several rough-looking men with balled fists staring at Thornton as he walked by. "You may need my services if you do."

"MISS HIGGINS, you will need to drink a tablespoon of this three times a day."

Bessy sniffed the opening of the dark glass bottle Lawson held out to her and winced. "Eh, that's 'orrible stuff!"

Lawson could not help smiling at the face she made. "It is called an expectorant. It will stimulate your coughing and loosen the fluff so it can be expelled from your lungs."

"What's that yo' say? What's it to do?" She looked up at him wide-eyed.

Lawson chose his words more carefully. "It will make you cough harder, and more often, so that your lungs can bring out the fluff. You must take it every day."

"Just the smell o' it would be 'nough to make me cough up 'most anything!" But she obediently swallowed the prescribed dose. Lawson waited until she had finished another fit of coughing before speaking again.

"My other prescription is simpler, but it will be harder for you to carry out."

Bessy looked up at him expectantly. "What is it?"

"You must get up out of your bed and walk every day."

"Walk!" Bessy exploded in disbelief. "Ye must be daft! I've nowt been out o' this bed in weeks. I haven't the strength. The last time I tried, it wored me out just crossing the room."

"I have seen many of these cases, Miss Higgins, and it is always the people who lie abed who do not survive. Being still so much is unnatural, especially in one so young, and it opens the body to infection and further disease. Besides, getting up and moving around will also stimulate your lungs to take in more air, helping to further expel the fluff. You must walk!"

"I will try," Bessy said doubtfully, "but I canna do it on me own."

"I can help you," said Margaret, moving from the shadows at the edge of the room to stand by her friend. "Let's try it now."

"Here? In front o' all these people!" Besides Margaret and Lawson, Thornton stood by watchfully, observing in silence. At Margaret's encouraging nod, Bessy swung her legs over the side of the bed. With Margaret holding her around her waist, she managed to put weight on her feet for the first time in weeks. She took half a dozen hesitant steps forward before her strength gave out and she began to slump over.

Thornton was at Bessy's other side before Margaret even realized what was happening. "Here, Miss Higgins, allow me." He grasped Bessy's elbow firmly but gently, keeping her from collapsing any further. "Lean a bit towards me so that your weight is more centered. If Miss Hale can hold you up on her side and I do my part on this side, we might be able to take you all around the room."

"Just t' the door would be 'nough," Bessy answered, her usual tart tone softened by a note of longing. "It's been so long since I seen me the sun. And I'd love t' see me a bunch o' roses one more time. We used t' have a bush growing just outside."

In unspoken agreement, Thornton and Margaret steered her towards the front door. When they reached it, Bessy put out her hand to grasp the door frame as she looked outside. Luckily, the sun was out from behind the clouds. She closed her eyes and inhaled deeply as its rays hit her face. Bessy smiled.

At that moment, with the sun creating a halo on Bessy's fair hair and with her face displaying an angelic smile, Lawson felt something inside him lurch. He turned away hastily, making notes in his ever-present notebook. "That is excellent progress for today, Miss Higgins. Tomorrow I would like you to try to walk out of doors, if possible."

Once Bessy was safely back in bed, Thornton offered to walk Margaret back to her home, but she declined. "I have errands to carry out before I go back to Crampton, and I am sure you are busy with the strike. Do not allow me to detain you."

Thornton unhappily watched her walk away. When he turned back to Lawson, he found the doctor's eyes on him. "You might try telling her how you feel about her, Thornton," he advised knowingly.

This time Thornton did not bother denying his feelings for Margaret. "You do not understand, Lawson. If I thought I had a chance in the world, I would throw myself at her feet. But she is from the South and does not understand our Milton ways. She thinks me rough and crude."

"Nobody would call you rough or crude after seeing the way you were with Bessy--that is, Miss Higgins--today. Her own mother could not have taken greater care with her. Let your young lady see more of that side of you, and her opinion is bound to change. It seems to me," he added with a sly smile, "that Miss Hale cannot possibly take care of Miss Higgins by herself every day. She will need help."

"I will come every day," Thornton vowed, "as long as the girl's father will allow it."

"Yo'd must be outten yo' mind, girl!" Nicholas Higgins exploded at his daughter that night when she told him of the visits from Thornton and Lawson. "Any friend o' Miss Margaret's is welcome here, o' course, but the sight o' that Thornton vexes me! So proud and lordly, thinkin' he owns whatever he sees!"

"Hoo very nearly does, father," Bessy pointed out, but Nicholas was not in a mood for humor.

"How'll it look t' me union brothers, havin' a master 'ere in me own 'ouse during a strike?" he fumed. "I'll not allow it! Find help somewhere else. We don't need charity fro' Thornton nor any o' his kind!"

Betsy took a deep breath. "Father, I'm a-dyin'," she said.

Her simple proclamation pulled Nicholas up short, and he turned to stare at her. "Yo' know it's true. I've got the white fluff just like mother 'ad and just like all t' others we've known 'fore and since. This doctor is my only chance at livin'. And I do want t' live, father. I want t' get better and grow older and maybe get married and 'ave me own children someday. Would yo 'ave me throw away that chance?"

Nicholas sighed, frustrated by his conflicted feelings. It was impossible to picture Thornton here in this house, helping his own daughter get better. What did the man mean by it? Was he trying to relieve his guilty conscience for the misery he'd put his workers through? On the other hand, Nicholas was in no position to refuse anything that would help his daughter. He turned and stalked away from Bessy, his heavy footsteps pounding like thunder as he went.

The next day, Nicholas stood suspiciously in the doorway as he watched Margaret and Thornton walking Bessy around the room. Lawson, as was his custom, sat at the table, watching and taking notes. Thornton and Margaret were concentrating on their patient and did not notice Nicholas' presence. It was Bessy who looked up, saw her father, and stopped in her tracks.

Before he could say anything, Bessy smiled a radiant smile he had not seen from her in months. "Father! Just look what Mr. Thornton brung me!" She gestured to where an arrangement of flowers stood on the kitchen table – the one and only table in the small house.

"Roses," said Margaret, in a tone of disbelief. "Just like Bessy mentioned yesterday."

"It was the least I could do," Thornton answered, looking not at Bessy but at Margaret, who flushed slightly.

Nicholas was silent, standing with his arms across his chest. He noted that Bessy's color was better, with more red in her cheeks than he had seen since she was first ill. She looked exhilarated, not exhausted by the short walk around the room. Her coughing the night before had been considerable, but at least it had been productive. And best of all, she was walking! Nicholas had given up on her ever rising from her sickbed, certain that her days were numbered.

"Thank ye for lookin' after my girl," he finally said, nearly grunting the words out. "I'd be here meself, only there's a strike on, in case yo' hadn't noticed."

So that's where she gets her sense of humor, Lawson thought. He had come to appreciate Bessy's droll remarks and amusing observations, so different from the reserved ladies he met everywhere else.

The dry humor eased the tension in the room noticeably, and Bessy finished her steps around the room with help from her two companions. When she finished her circuit, Margaret and Thornton again led her to the doorway of the room.

This time she stepped all the way out the door, shielding her eyes from the afternoon sun. "Ach! Never thought I'd see the plain day outside like this again! 'Tis almost as good as medicine, bein' out in the fresh air!"

"Fresh air is the best medicine for the white fluff, isn't it, Lawson?" Thornton asked, still supporting Bessy.

Lawson shook his head. "The best medicine for any ailment is love."

FOR THE NEXT WEEK MARGARET, Thornton, and Lawson continued to visit Bessy every day, and every day they saw more improvement in her symptoms.

The strike, however, only worsened. And as Bessy spent more time out of doors, walking longer distances up and down the sidewalk outside her house, Thornton's presence began to draw attention. A half dozen or so union men gathered across the street from Higgins' home one afternoon after Thornton had gone into the house. They waited impatiently for him to emerge.

They did not have to wait long. After several minutes, the front door opened, and the usual trio appeared –Bessy in the middle, Margaret on her left, and Thornton on her right. All three stopped upon spying the small crowd across the street. It was Margaret who spoke first, hesitating in the doorway. "Perhaps we should stay inside today."

Bessy answered, defiant despite her illness, "I guess I've a right t' walk down me own street if I want wi'out bein' bothered by the likes of 'em!" Margaret and Thornton exchanged a look of concern, but the girl's determination was hard to resist and they allowed her to step over the threshold, supporting her on either side.

Nicholas Higgins had just turned the corner of his street when the pending confrontation caught his attention. His sweeping glance took in the whole scene – the angry men standing with their fists clenched, glaring at the little trio across the street that happened to include his daughter. Without hesitating he crossed the street and confronted them directly. "What be ye doin' 'ere?" he challenged, putting his hands on his hips and drawing himself up to his full height.

The men were abashed by his unexpected presence. After all, he was one of the union leaders, the main one holding the strike together. And he was a large man – not tall, but rough and big boned. "We mean t' talk t' Thornton, Higgins," one, bolder than the rest, finally answered. "Tisn't right for him t' be paradin' about 'ere in Princeton with all 'is fine clothes and 'is fine friends while we sit 'ere starvin'."

"Where else is hoo supposed t' be, with no work t' look after at the mill? Hoo's 'ere t' help me daughter, as ye can see, and I don't see no 'arm in that," Nicholas countered.

"But yo' be a union man!"

"Aye, I'm a union man, but I'm a father first. If yo' attack Thornton we'll all go t' jail, and then who'll feed the families we leave behind? If yo' want 'omething useful t' do, go t' the better parts of town and beg money for the strike fund 'stead o' standing here lookin' like mischief. Least that way, people'll 'ear 'bout our cause."

The men considered Nicholas' words briefly, shuffling their feet and looking at each other uncomfortably before drifting away.

Watching them retreat, Nicholas knew he had not seen the last of them.

"Ye'd better not come here anymore, Master Thornton," Nicholas advised. He entered his house just after Bessy and the others finished their short excursion. Lawson waited for them inside. "The longer this goes on, the more dangerous it gets fo' ye. For all o' us," he added soberly.

"Do you wish to keep coming to Princeton, Miss Hale?" Thornton turned to Margaret, who nodded. "Then I will, as well. Your father would not like it if I let you put yourself into harm's way."

"There be no need fo' all this trouble on account o' me!" Bessy exclaimed. "I can get around on me own just fine now!" A fit of coughing belied her words.

"No, you cannot," Margaret contradicted. "You are getting stronger, but you still need help. I will keep coming as long as you need me to."

"And I, as well," Lawson added, "though there is no danger for me. If the men know I am a doctor, then they know I am here to help."

"Ye been seen with Thornton so much it won't matter t' 'em," Higgins told him. "Make no mistake, if there be trouble or mischief it'll touch all o' us. Master Thornton, yo'll need t' watch yo' back."

"If only the masters and the workers could sit down together to talk over their differences!" Margaret exclaimed. "There is no need for such violence and danger. I feel sure they could come to an agreement if they would just listen to each other."

"Do you, Miss Hale?" Thornton asked. He pulled his gaze from her eager, impassioned face to Higgins' more sober one. "What do you think we should talk about first?"

Higgins' eyes glinted sharply and he pulled his chair closer to the table. "We might start wi' the profits the masters been makin' the last few years, profits 'at ne'er make it t' the worker's paychecks."

Thornton did not flinch. "And I think we should start by talking about the rising costs of production, something you unionists do not wish to discuss!"

"Please, Mr. Thornton, Nicholas," Margaret pleaded. She looked imploringly between the two of them, but it was the gentle hand she laid on Thornton's arm that did the trick. Thornton looked down at her hand for a moment and then pulled his own chair closer to the table. He directed his sternest master's gaze at Nicholas.

"For the sake of all the workers of Milton, let us make a beginning."

Bessy drew Lawson's attention as Nicholas and Thornton began to talk. "Mr. Lawson, what'd ye mean when ye said yo' are 'ere t' help? I thought ye were only looking after me because Mr. Thornton brought yo' 'round."

"I am here to give aid to whoever needs it," Lawson answered firmly. "In fact, I am looking for rooms to rent right now. I plan to hang my shingle in Princeton if I can."

"In Princeton! Who'd come t' Princeton when they could set up a practice anywhere else? Yo' could make more money in some other part o' town."

"I intend to make a living, but my mission will always be to the poor. There are some things in life more important than making money."

～

SEVERAL DAYS LATER, after their regular visit to Bessy and her father, Margaret finally gave Thornton permission to walk her home for the first time. He was nearly overwhelmed at the thought of being allowed to claim her attention for the time it would take to walk to Crampton. "What do you think of the discussions Higgins and I have been having together?" Thornton asked her as they began to walk.

Margaret looked up at him with her eyes glowing. "I think it is splendid that the two of you have been able to talk over the complaints between the masters and the workers. Nicholas finally understands how the rising costs of supplies have affected your profits, and you now appreciate how hard it is for workers to support a family on the wages they earn."

"I wish we had had these talks earlier," Thornton answered, gratified by her response. "Perhaps this whole ugly strike could have been avoided had we sat down together earlier in the process. You have taught me an invaluable lesson, Miss Hale. I shall not be so hasty with my workers again."

Margaret flushed. "And perhaps Nicholas can convince the other union leaders to be more reasonable now. There has been too much suffering. By the way, I have been meaning to ask about the yellow roses you bring Bessy. There is a new arrangement almost every day. Where do you find them?"

Before Thornton could respond, he heard a whistling of something flying past his head. Fragments of stone bounced off the brick wall behind him and fell to the ground around his feet. Looking frantically around, Thornton caught sight of a group of rowdy men in rough clothes coming out from between two buildings a little ways ahead of them. Another group emerged from the opposite direction, and Thornton heard a second projectile strike the building, sending shards of stone through the air. He tried to push Margaret behind him, out of danger's way, but she moved too quickly.

"Mr. Thornton, take care!" she cried. Before Thornton could react she flung herself in front of him, throwing her arms around his neck, using her body to shield him from the onslaught. Just as she did so, a third stone approaching its target struck her on the temple. With a little gasp, she loosened her grip and began to sink down to the ground. Thornton realized, horrified, that the blow had rendered her insensible. A trickle of blood made its way down the side of her face.

Thornton gathered the unconscious Margaret up in his arms, cradling her against his chest, and turned to face his attackers. "Are you satisfied now?" he cried. "Will you let me take this woman to get help, or will her death be on your conscience? Kill me if you want, but for God's sake let me get her to a doctor first!"

Even in his agitated state, Thornton could see the pale faces and looks of dismay on the men who had attacked him. They had not intended this turn of events and could only stare in horror now.

Thornton did not wait for them to recover their faculties. He charged towards them with Margaret in his arms – passed through their very ranks – and left them behind as he carried Margaret back to Princeton, Higgins' home, and Lawson.

Thornton laid Margaret down on the makeshift bed at Higgins' house and stood gazing down at her lovely face, so pale and still in the dim light of the small room. Lawson had wiped the blood from her temple and face and was examining her closely while Thornton stood next to her, oblivious to the rest of the world.

She had been so light in his arms, so delicate. How could such a frail body absorb the blow she had suffered? And she had done it for him. She had thrown her arms around his neck to protect him from the onslaught. For one delicious moment, she had clung close to him, her head nestled against him, his arms around her – and then she had been struck down.

"Margaret, oh Margaret!" he murmured, leaning next to the sweet, pale face. "No one can know what you mean to me! I may be rough and unpolished, but no one will ever love you with a truer heart than mine. I would give up my very life blood to heal you from this hurt!"

In his fevered state, he forgot the presence of the others in the small room. They did not hear his passionate declarations. But words were unnecessary at such a moment. His feelings were evident in the anguish on his face, the clenching of his fists, and the silent watchfulness he maintained over her.

Lost in his thoughts, Thornton did not hear the sudden banging at the door nor see how Higgins lunged at it in fury for the disturbance to a sickroom. He did not hear the quick discussion on the threshold nor notice when Higgins left the house without explanation and returned minutes later, coming straight to Thornton's side.

"Master," he said urgently, "Master Thornton, 'ere's some men outside as want t' speak t' yo."

"Men?" Thornton echoed. He shook his head as if to wake himself from some deep dream. "What do they want with me?"

"It's the union men, master. They want t' end the strike, and they want t' do it now."

"Now?" Thornton scoffed. "Now that they have nearly killed a woman? Now that they have seen what their intransigent attitude has brought about, they want to make amends by negotiating an end to this madness? Let them speak to one of the other masters. I have nothing to say to them."

"They won't talk t' nobody else. This is the time, Thornton!" Higgins said, his voice low and compelling. "Now, while they're ashamed a' what they did, when they realize what'll happen if the law goes after 'em. Yo' must speak wi' 'em!"

"I cannot leave her," said Thornton despairingly, because Margaret's eyes had not opened, and she had remained motionless from the time he took her up in his arms.

"But if yo' turn them away now, hoo knows what'll 'appen next? Go t' them and help put an end t' this!"

Lawson looked up quickly. "Miss Hale will live," he assured Thornton. "She has a concussion and she should not be moved tonight. Let a message be taken to her family advising them of this. But she had only a little blood loss and no permanent damage that I can see. She will live!"

"See, Master Thornton?" Higgins urged the man. "Yo' are needed elsewhere. Come with me. Let's speak t' the other union masters and put an end t' this. Have good news for Miss Margaret when hoo wakes up!"

Thornton stood, irresolutely looking down at Margaret. It was his fault that she lay on this bed now, seriously injured, instead of safely at home. If he had reacted more quickly, he could have taken the blow meant for him rather than Margaret absorbing the hurt.

But wouldn't Margaret want him to go speak to the union leaders if he could? Wasn't ending the strike one of her dearest wishes? He could do nothing to relieve her pain or help restore her to health, yet he could do this one thing for her: he could make her glad and proud of him once she regained consciousness. Throwing back his shoulders, he turned away and went with Nicholas out the door.

"Oh, Margaret, it's that much of a scare ye've given us!" Bessy's voice broke into Margaret's mind as she began to open her eyes. She felt as though she were emerging from under great depths of water, her head twisting and turning in the currents. A great light pierced her brain.

"There now, sit up slowly, Miss Hale." This time it was Lawson's voice, and his face hovering above hers came into focus. She pushed her arms underneath her and found herself reclining on the bed normally used by Bessy.

"Where is Mr. Thornton? Is he all right?" she asked, trying to reconstruct events in her head. She had vague, dream-like memories of arms around her, of a tender voice speaking words of affection, and of a long, deep sleep.

"You have been unconscious most of the night," Lawson told her. "Thornton brought you here after you were struck on the head."

Margaret's hand instinctively went to the lump on her temple. "Was Mr. Thornton hurt too?"

"Nay, lass," came Higgins' reassuring voice. He was seated at the humble kitchen table just a few feet from her. Bessy sat at the foot of the bed. "Thornton wasn't hurt at all. Hoo brought ye here and made sure ye were safe, then went out t' deal wi' the union men. The strike is over."

"He didn't call the soldiers, surely!" Margaret gasped. "Tell me he did not! The men were driven mad by all that has happened with the strike! They didn't deserve to have the soldiers set on them!"

"Ye're nowt understandin'. Thornton went out t' speak wi' them, not t' have them punished. They were ashamed o' themselves after ye were struck down, and they were ready t' see where they'd been wrong afore. They all sat down at t' union hall fo' the better part o' the night – them and Thornton together – and they managed t' make a bargain. The strike is over. Everyone'll be back t' work tomorrow!"

"The strike is over!" Margaret nearly fell back against the pillows in relief.

"Aye, and Thornton and the other masters'll be back in their mills. Don't suppose he'll come around 'ere much anymore."

"I wonder if I shall ever see him again," Margaret murmured, more to herself than to anyone else, but Bessy heard her. She laughed harder than Margaret had ever heard her do before.

"Hoots! God bless ye for an innocent, Margaret Hale! Yo' don't think Thornton's been coming to Princeton every day just t' see me, do ye?" Margaret flushed self-consciously at her friend's open laughter, which did not stop until it was cut off with a fit of coughing.

TWO DAYS LATER, Margaret was back at Crampton, fully recovered from her ordeal. She had not yet been back to see Bessy, nor had anyone been to see her. She was in her bedroom writing a letter to her brother when the housekeeper, Dixon, announced that Mr. Thornton was asking to see her. Tremulously, she rose and made her way to the drawing room, wondering if he had come to say what she hoped he might. She knew there was a conversation that had to take place.

"Miss Hale," he began, "I was very ungrateful three days ago when you—" But he could not finish even one sentence before Margaret nervously interrupted him.

"You had nothing to be grateful for," she said, looking down, afraid to meet his eyes. "You mean, I suppose, that you believe you ought to thank me for what I did."

"For what you did, for what you are, for what you mean to me!" Thornton exclaimed, moving closer and taking one of her hands in his. "I am a better man because of knowing you. All gladness in life, all honest pride in doing my work in the world, I owe to you! To the one whom I love as no man ever loved woman before!"

Margaret trembled. She shook, she quaked, and she nearly fell insensible again with the force of his emotion and her own feelings in return. "Mr. Thornton, I am not good enough—"

"Not good enough!" Without hesitation, he pulled her close, seeking again the delight of feeling her nestled close to him, and she followed his lead. She laid her head against his heart and rested it there, more content then she had ever been. For long cherished, tender moments they kept silent as they clung together. Then he murmured, "Put your arms around my neck, love, as you did three days ago."

She shyly complied; and when she dared to look up at him, her eyes at last meeting his in confirmation of his greatest hope, he dared to bring his lips to hers in a gentle kiss. He let go of her long enough to withdraw a small yellow rose from the pocket of his waistcoat. "Do you recognize this, dearest?"

"It is a rose from Helstone, is it not?" she asked. "I recognize the deep indentation around the leaves. You brought these for Bessy!"

"I brought them for you. I will give you a bouquet of them on the day we marry, if you will consent to be my wife!" Margaret sweetly lifted her face to his and gave him the only possible reply she could.

Two months later, Bessy smiled as she read Margaret's letter from Scotland, where Margaret and Mr. Thornton were on their honeymoon. Then she sighed deeply. She was glad that Margaret and the master were so happy together. Nobody deserved as much joy as her dear friend, who had been the means of saving her own life and helping the workers of Milton.

Bessy was deeply grateful that her own recovery continued so well. She was startled to realize that she had gone from being bedridden to being active and useful in just over two months.

Oh, she had a long ways to go yet. Walking a great distance still wore her out, and the persistent cough would stay with her for months to come. But nobody doubted any more that she would one day be a useful member of society again. Eventually, she would learn a new trade, find work, and contribute to the household once more.

Yet, with her return to good health, Doctor Lawson called on her far less often than he had before. He was busy with his other patients, she supposed. And he was still trying to find a suitable location for his office. He did not have the time for a sickly, uneducated factory girl who could make little difference in his life. That dream, she supposed, was over.

Her melancholy was interrupted by a knock at the door. When she opened it, the doctor himself smiled engagingly at her, the sun gleaming on his bright hair. "Miss Higgins, I have come to make sure you are still getting your daily exercise. Have you been out of doors yet today?"

Bessy drew herself up. "There is no need," she answered, unconsciously imitating Margaret's educated manner. "I can walk quite well on me own now."

"Yes, well, there is someplace very particular I would like to show you," he persisted, not put off. "Will you come with me?"

Curiosity overcame her reluctance, and she fetched her heavy shawl. Lawson offered her his arm and they walked together down the street, just as if she were a regular lady entertaining a caller. Bessy wondered if this was how fine society ladies felt when they were out with their beaux – proud and embarrassed and happy and shy all at the same time.

Eventually, they stopped outside a small house that appeared to be unoccupied. Cobwebs covered the ancient window that opened out to the street, and the front door creaked when Lawson opened it. Lawson led Bessy inside. "My new home," he announced with pride. "This is where I will set up my practice."

Bessy looked around approvingly. "This is a first rate place!" she announced. "And so handy fo' a doctor!"

"This first floor area is where I will see my patients when I am not making house calls," Lawson told her.

"It'll do nicely fo' that. Yo' can put a desk in this corner, and set up chairs along this wall. The back rooms can be where ye'd see yo' patients." She used a corner of her apron to dust off a nearby piece of furniture. "Look! Yo' can put medicines and such right 'ere in these cabinets." She moved from room to room, examining each one eagerly. "Where do these stairs go?"

"Upstairs, to the living quarters," Lawson answered, watching her carefully. "There will be room for as large a family as I could want."

"A family," Bessy repeated flatly, her heart sinking. She stared down at her shoes. "So you'll be wantin' t' get married, then."

"Yes. Miss Higgins, will you share this with me . . . as my wife?"

"Yo' wife!" She whirled around to face him. "Yo' can't mean that! Yo'd want someone educated, someone hoo knows the right way t' speak and act in front o' all yo' fine friends! Yo' dinna wan' me!"

"I want someone to help me manage my little practice. My wife must be someone with a compassionate heart. She must know poverty and illness first hand. She must understand the people of Princeton and be someone they can trust. Above all, despite the hardships she will see on every side, she must be ready with a joke or a laugh at any time. Miss Higgins, will you marry me?"

Bessy's eyes were wide. "What makes yo think I can do all those things ye just said?"

Lawson laughed. "What makes you think you can't? You've been doing them as long as I have known you."

"If I didn't know better, I'd think ye've gone clean out o' yo' head!"

He crossed the room quickly, reaching out to take her hand in his. "I have fallen in love with you, Bessy Higgins. Tell me you will be my wife and make me the happiest man on earth."

Hearing those words, Bessy smiled and put her hands on his shoulders, feeling that she might burst from a sensation she'd never experienced before: pure joy. "Aye, I will marry yo', if yo' insist on it."

"Oh, I do indeed." Lawson bent his head and kissed her soundly. "Doctor's orders."

WHEN MARGARET and Thornton returned from their wedding trip, she found that Thornton had arranged for bouquets of yellow Helstone roses to be delivered to her new home. There were displays on every table downstairs, and a vase filled with the delightful flowers welcomed her to her new bedroom. She sank down onto the dressing table chair to inhale the scent.

An envelope sitting on the table caught her eye. She opened it eagerly while her husband supervised their bags being brought into the house.

When Thornton came into the room he found Margaret sitting as if in a daze, holding the note in front of her. "My love, are you all right?"

Margaret looked up at him with the starry glow that he loved so much. "You will not believe me if I tell you."

"Tell me what?"

"Bessy has sent me a message. She and your Doctor Lawson – they are getting married!"

"Married!" Thornton took the note from her and scanned its contents for himself.

"To think how ill Bessy was when they first met!" Margaret exclaimed as he read. "And not only is she much better, but she is getting married soon. Did you have any suspicion that Doctor Lawson cared for her?"

"I suppose I should have," Thornton answered, putting the letter back on the table. "It is not really so surprising, when you think of it. He must have been suffering from the same illness that affected me."

"Illness! Whatever do you mean?"

"I mean that I was sick with love for you, my dearest."

"Oh! I thought you meant a real illness, one that a doctor might be able to cure."

"There is no cure, but there is a treatment." He looked down at her roguishly.

"What cure might that be?" Margaret asked, with a teasing smile. Thornton pulled her to her feet, heedless of whatever servants might be nearby.

"You have the only treatment for my condition, Mrs. Thornton," he whispered in her ear, just before soundly kissing her. "Love is the best medicine of all."

ELAINE OWEN WAS BORN in Seattle, Washington and was a precocious reader from a young age. She read Pride and Prejudice for the first time in ninth grade, causing speechless delight for her English teacher when she used it for an oral book report. She practiced writing in various forms throughout her teen years, writing stories with her friends and being chief editor of the high school yearbook. She moved to Delaware when she married.

In 1996 she won a one year contract to write guest editorials in the Sunday edition of The News Journal in Wilmington, Delaware, and she continued her writing habit in political discussion groups and occasional forays into fiction.

In 2014 she began to write Pride and Prejudice fan fiction and decided to publish her works herself to see if she might possibly sell a few copies. Thousands of books later, the results have been beyond her wildest hopes, and she plans to continue writing fiction for the foreseeable future.

When she's not writing her next great novel, Elaine relaxes by working full time, raising two children, volunteering in her church, and practicing martial arts. She can be contacted at elaineowen@writeme.com.

ELAINE OWEN's other books include: *Common Ground, Duty Demands, Mr. Darcy's Persistent Pursuit, One False Step, Love's Fool,* and *An Unexpected Turn of Events*

CINDERS AND SMOKE

Don Jacobson

"...every pulse beat in him as he remembered how she had come down and placed herself in foremost danger, —could it be to save him?" - Chapter XXII, North and South

⁓

The full moon had vanquished Milton's perpetual oily haze. The cobbles in the mews below, scummed with cinder slurry, were cast into gritty relief. Empty now, the space had been filled only an hour before with angry sounds and desperate faces.

This was his aery, his high point where he always had kept solitary post. The dormer jutted out above slates steeply cascading down toward the great courtyard that was the basin between the master's house and the mill. Not much more than a windowed catwalk, this was where he watched over his kingdoms, both inner and outer.

One set of panes looked back into the factory, giving a bird's-eye view of the shop floor. Here was his safety, his security, his place of comfort. Words like *spindle, warp, woof, and yarn* formed the placid surface upon which he floated. Like a mallard, he paddled in this growing pond known as Milton, always moving with a degree of majesty above the waterline despite the fury with which his feet and legs moved below. Even the complexities of the hulking dobby looms with their mighty Jacquard devices rising toward the rafters did little to challenge his confidence. Their rumbling power spoke of his dominion over forces which once had been reserved to the Almighty.[111222333]

However, as with silvery shillings, what was heads on one side demanded that a tail exist on the obverse. While philosophers long had insisted that the back of a coin needn't represent the opposite of the front, humanity and its myth-making explainers had always reveled in the binary: *up and down, in and out, left and right, known and unknown.*

Assurance and doubt.

And if there was anything an acquaintance could say of the Master of Marlborough Mills was that he was a man blessed with an uncommon amount of self-assuredness. That observation would have been the result of his carefully curated efforts undertaken in the rough-and-tumble arena characterized by innovation and wealth, stagnation and failure. What he presented to his fellow manufacturers was as similar to his true self as was the HEIC mark on the outside of an antique tea chest to the aged product inside.

There were those–his mother and perhaps Bell—who might have offered a different character sketch of John Thornton. His intimates would have added daubs of ochre beneath his eyes and lightly shaded his jutting cheekbones with antimony, thinning his face with a lean look. Hannah Thornton and the old Oxford don would have darkened features that may have been left deceptively bright by Thornton himself. Their canvas would portray a young man forced into his majority before his time, revealing the hidden forces that drove him.

Those influences lived beyond the outward-facing transparent fence, formidable yet fragile in its silica simplicity. The glassy sheets prevented him from falling—*leaping*—into the mews four stories below.

This was the world where Thornton had no control.

He had tried to exert his authority to compel the men and currents outside of Marlborough's walls to respond in the manner he wished.

Thornton had failed before…as he had tonight.

Old Hale would have laughed at my inability to grasp that which the Greeks had known of so long ago…the sin of hubris. My pride combined with my arrogance has ripped and crushed the most delicate of flowers.

Thornton rested his forehead against the window, its surface cool against his fevered skin. The night frost deepened as the overcast vanished. His breath, inhaled and exhaled in gulps, fogged the glass. He had not been able to regulate himself and calm his tremors since she had been slapped to the ground as if by a giant's invisible hand.

One moment she was appealing to the mob. The next, Margaret Hale was a pile of rags at his feet.

After-images flickered through his mind. Those memories were not transitory wisps, but rather were profound impressions that echoed down the corridors of his awareness.

How positive he had been in his ability to break the strike. How convinced he had been that the workingmen of Milton were weak and undisciplined, that they would willingly accept his actions as being as inevitable as a fire's heat.

Hubris!

Once word of the Irish arrivals had reached the Frances Street warrens, the crowds boiled out in their hundreds, angry and restless. Thornton had watched the black wave approach from another outpost, the upper floor of his house. The women were safe behind iron-strapped oak shutters…or so he thought.

Hands and arms rose from the dark mass as it restructured itself, roiling inexorably against lesser edifices as it coursed from source to the delta of its discontent. Torches and lanterns flickered within the mob, illuminating disparate features until they coalesced to become individual men. So, too, did the rumbling outcries eventually resolve themselves into articulated grievances. Any questions of interpretation were thrown aside as words were framed by the distorted expressions that reshaped the faces of men whom he had been aware of, if not actually known, for years.

This was an anger which Thornton recognized, although he was surprised that these men possessed it. He had always believed this primal emotion to be that which had fueled his rise from the obscurity of a draper's assistant. He had proven his mettle by dint of the fact that he had scaled the heights from which he had been thrown by his father's disgrace. Others would have failed.

He was different from those men who had marched to *his mill, his monument*. He had to be. If they had possessed the same impetus, the same innate urge, would they not have risen from their *lesser* status to fight for space higher up the ladder? Or was it something more, something which prevented them from taking their place much as he had? And, if outside influences were holding these men back, what would happen to him, John Thornton, should these powers choose to pay closer attention to him, upstart that he was?

Anger and fear are handmaidens. We do not react in anger toward what we do not fear. This is a survival instinct as old as Adam. Our ancestors feared the lion and, while they would run from one to climb a tree, if they were faced with a parlous crossing of a featureless plain, they would use anger, much like the Norse berserker, to work their will when resisting the big cat.

The men were angry, but they were angry because they were afraid.

There was a darkness that surrounded all who worked the mills in Milton. The cloud, mostly hidden, but sometimes taking the form of choking, cinder-filled smoke, was freighted with a foreboding that told all who passed through its mists that exposure spelled a doleful outcome. This was a miasma that sucked men and women dry. This after they poured their lifeforce into those caverns from which men like Hamper, Slickson, Watson...and Thornton...extracted their wealth.

But, John, too, was frightened...

Of being found out, of being judged as not being up to the mark.

Cold terror tinted with anguish gripped his guts. He felt more fear now than ever before in his life. More than when he found his father slumped atop his desk, bloodstained certificates his final bed. More so than in that same moment when he realized that his labor was the only way that his mother and little sister would survive. Even more than when he took it upon his young shoulders to repay his father's debts.

At each step, he had transformed that fear into the anger which led to his perseverance. He could not turn what he now felt into anything productive.

The threat of the strike to the mill–that manifestation of his intangible *self*–only served to strengthen his resolve.

Each time, he had known he had the power to prevail. His fear had been forged upon the hard anvil of his life into a billet radiating fearsome intent, scorching all who dared resist.

Thornton wielded his anger against all and sundry. And they would buckle, if not out of respect, then when their own anger was weakened by rising tides of fear like impurities in a poorly-furnaced bloom. When the world was measured in feet and yards, pounds and pence, orders and shipments, he was in his element and could force any outcome he desired.

At this moment, in this time where the Irish were locked into the work shed, bent above looms filled with delayed orders, the mill's future was assured by his ingenuity yet again. Much as old Watson had decamped to London to petition the entire Government for assistance after the Great Meryton Fire had leveled his mill back in the Year Eleven, Thornton could have –should have, perhaps – looked back upon his efforts with pride.

But Thornton was undone by fear.

He could rail against the unfairness of the Universe. He could mount angry protestations to the Almighty. He could smash the very windows against which he rested his head.

But not one of those outbursts would undo that which had been done.

Margaret Hale had interposed her delicate body between his and those who would have avenged their situations upon him.

Her selfless act showed her compassion for both him and the mob. Thornton she would protect from physical harm as the brickbat flew from the night. As for the rioters, that inchoate crowd of snarling faces, she demonstrated that she was a vicar's daughter and sought to prevent one or all from being stained by the sin of violence.

She succeeded in the first and failed, although one might argue that a martyred saint who did not prevent her murderers from completing their crime was equally successful, in the second. Those who raised their hand against the purest of hearts would be condemned forever.

Thornton absently rubbed a bruise darkening the back of his left arm. How he had received it, he did not know. Whatever its source, this was no badge of honor, for she had been laid low within inches of his protection.

His miserable attempt to exercise the sheer force of his will to prevent the marchers from breaking through his gates had illustrated just how thin was his influence over the broader affairs of men.

He was a fraud.

All that he had believed in...that bare-knuckles was the way of business and, thus, life...was counterfeit. Where he had attempted like King Canute to hold back the tide, she had floated above those cobbles like Eve, Venus, or Mother Mary, her hands lifted toward the crowd in the eternal gesture of supplication.

He had shouted in anger, in possession, grounded in his rights as Master. She had barely lifted her voice above the roar, begging men who had been subjected to the worst cruelties to rediscover their humanity.

A tiny woman proved, in a minute of indescribable courage, as she leaped from behind his protective bulk that a life without love was thin porridge. Her ardor was not the idealized romances of men and women but rather of that unique charity that had resonated through every organized faith for the past eighteen centuries.

For her efforts, because of her love for all who that night had crowded the mews between factory and house, she lay small and help-less on the divan in his office, her blood staining her dress.

His life was in tatters. His anger did not flutter high above his putative turrets. Rather it lay in the gutter, cast down after its shaft had been snapped by other weapons. His unworthiness in the light of her towering perfection left him bereft of any anchor in the swirling tides that pulled against his limbs.

If Miss Hale's actions alone were not enough of a punishment, his preconceived notions had taken another telling blow. For all his pretensions of superiority, he, John Thornton, the man who had lifted his family back into Milton's first circle and had made Marlborough Mills a mighty force, was not the one who saved her from falling beneath the trampling boots of enraged workers.

No, that honor was reserved for Nicholas Higgins, the arch-nemesis of Milton's *laissez-faire* manufacturers. They most desired for the government to stay out of all their affairs, to *leave-them-alone*. They were outraged that the Factory Acts had limited the number of hours they could force their child employees to work in a given day. They found it radical and dangerous that working men and women would demand higher wages rather than accept the cuts that would expand mill profits. Yet oddly, for all their protestations about Parlia-ment's long nose, they found comfort in being able to call upon the militia when their laborers objected too strenuously.

Nicholas Higgins was the one Milton man whose iron-strapped backbone would not let these 'Christian' gentlemen have their way without resistance.

As the first man in the union, Higgins was hated with a fervor akin to that heaped upon the Prophet Elijah by Ahab and Jezebel for his presumption in pointing to the industrialists' original sin. And, if one believed, as Thornton did, that every man could be his own master if he had only the gumption, Higgins would serve as the cardinal example of the weakness of spirit and greed ascribed to all who worked for wages by those who profited from that labor.[444]

Yet, contrary to his presumed grasping nature, when havoc was exploding all about, Higgins was the man who had kept his head.

Unlike Thornton, who had been paralyzed, the grizzle-haired man had effortlessly scooped Margaret into his arms as she slid toward the coal-slimed cobbles, the trickle on her forehead glistening chocolate brown in the full moon's watery light.

But the crowd's taste for blood was slaked at the sight of Margaret's, perhaps proving that they only had been seeking vengeance upon one of their oppressors. After Higgins, trailed by Thornton, vanished through the mill's swiftly-bolted portal, the mob evaporated as if Milton's ash-grey April snows.

Thornton was ashamed of himself. The niggling sense that much of his worldview had been built upon shifting sands tried him, as well.

And the frigid glass against his forehead did not cool his fever.

HIS STEPS REVERBERATED as he climbed the stairs into the high gallery.

The bass beat hearkened to his childhood when the Darkshire Regiment would march through town on its way down to Liverpool. Back then, the enemy had been clear: the Beast, the Tyrant, the damned *crappauds*. Men knew then that signing up meant you were out to kill those in Frankish blue, stinking of garlic, and mouthing heathenish words in order to keep them on the other side of the Channel.

The workingman's enemy is well-disguised. His grand'da may hae been your grandsire's best friend. He speaks the same language and eats the same food as you. While he may hae servants, they shop for his needs in the same markets as your woman.

The only difference? He hires. You toil.

So many of them act like they be the Duke of Devonshire, pissing rose-water and shitting sovereigns.

Higgins' shoulders were bowed as he traced Thornton's path up and away from the scene in the master's office. The physician Donaldson had arrived about twenty minutes before, dragged there by Miss Hale's woman, Dixon. When the trouble began, she had been below-stairs while her charge had sat to dinner with the Thorntons.

How that hard woman had found her way through the crowds of muttering men still clustered in the streets to Donaldson's quarters was beyond Higgins' ken. What she said to gain safe conduct back to the mill was less of a mystery. Nicholas Higgins had encountered her when Miss Hale would attend to Bessy. The thought of her taking on work-hardened men and giving better than she got buoyed his battered soul.

Nay, there is little to find in this night, let alone this world, about which to smile.

At least the doctor is hopeful. He thinks the stone only grazed Miss Hale.

But while the lady may be out of danger the cause of all who tend the looms and their families, is more perilous than ever before. The fine folks of Milton, the ladies who use acts of charity to ease their consciences and the men who relieve their guilt by supporting the vicars and preachers with the blunt they need to feed the bairns, will turn their backs on us if this violence against one of their own goes unpunished.

No, this could be the death of the union. All of us will be painted with the same brush as that poor, broken fool.[555]

I will, and must, give him up. There is nothing more to be done.

One short and one long flight led him up through the building's eaves to an area that may have begun its life as a place where workers looped block and tackle arrangements above the factory floor. Sometime in the past twenty years, though, one master or another had walled and windowed the inner side while punching through the roof on the other. Masters could now ascend into the factory's heavens—fittingly, thought Higgins—for a *God's eye view* of the ants toiling among the gigantic machinery.

As his head cleared the final stair, Higgins was able to scan Thornton from the ankle up, his eyes gradually moving from legs to head. He was surprised to see this tall, proud man bent as though he were an ancient gaffer. The Master's posture bespoke of great weariness—both of body and soul.

◊

AT THE SOUND OF HIGGINS' footfalls, Thornton pulled away from the outer window and turned to face Higgins.

"Well, man," Thornton challenged, "how is she?"

Higgins nodded in respect for the man's position and his obvious distress at Miss Hale's injury. He replied, "Better'n we might 'ave 'oped. Th' doctor…"

"Doctor?" Thornton snapped, "Donaldson? Who sent for him?"

Higgins snorted, "Yes…Doctor Donaldson. Miss 'ale's woman, Miss Dixon, somehow got through th' crowds…both ways…to fetch 'im here."

Looking skeptical, Thornton shot back, "Really? How did she manage to get past those men down below—the ones I see lurking about the gates, house, and the very doors to this building? Is she in league with them? Are we to expect an assault? A massacre? How can you stand there, man? I know you care for Miss Hale, I do! She told me about her friendship with your daughter. What if those animals breach our doors? What if they drag her out and ravage her? They will not get to her again! I swear it."

By this point, Thornton's voice had ripped itself ragged on the edges of his despair. He made to dash down the stairs, but Higgin's shoulders blocked his progress. The older man planted a meaty hand on each of Thornton's arms, holding him until he stopped struggling.

"Ye asked o' the men you see in the courtyard, Master Thornton. They be union men. They lissen ta me. Long as we 'ave breath, no wrecker will impose on Marlborough Mills," Higgins said.

He continued, "While the factory be yours an' Mr. Bell's, each o' us…wull, not me as I don' work for you, don' work for anybody…sees this place as 'is. You may buy th' machines, but 'tis our sweat that keeps 'em runnin'.

"I tol' them ta stand guard, not ta let any 'o those 'ot 'eads near th' 'ouse nor th' mill. T'would never 'low 'arm ta come ta any 'oo call Marlborough 'ome, 'specially Miss 'ale. She is dear ta my Bessy."

Thornton calmed at the other man's declaration, thought for a moment, and then levelled an accusatory glare at him.

"You know who did this, don't you?" he coldly quizzed.

This was a test, Higgins realized, that would prove his honesty to a man who doubted any workingman's veracity.

He shrugged and walked to the window and looked down into the factory, "I do."

Thornton pressed him, "And..."

Higgins turned back, sadness pulling down his face, "A blue story, that 'un. Th' man lost 'is job, 'is bairns be starvin', an' 'e is lookin' at life through the bottom 'o a bottle 'o penny gin."

"That is no excuse. Those pennies could have bought bread," Thornton dryly preached.

"Aye, sir, I know that" Higgins replied," But, t'it goes a long way ta explainin' why 'e can't see any way out but throwin' a rock, feelin' a bit like King Davey fightin' the giant...'opeless, ya know."

Thornton was relentless. He leaned in and breathed, "Who?"

One word, "Boucher."

The betrayal of Higgins' long-held principles placated Thornton. He could slip back into his traditional role of magistrate to launch the manhunt.

His musings were interrupted as Higgins spun to face him.

"I know what ye be thinkin'. An' afore ye go any further, ye'll be lettin' us, 'is comrades, find 'im. No need ta turn Milton on its 'ead. Yor bully-boys'll scare th' women and bairns. Rather than locatin' one troublemaker, you'll end up making a hundred more," he cautioned.

Then he added, "If I know Boucher, 'e's gone ta ground, prob'ly down by th' river, drownin' 'imself an' 'is sorrows in 'nother bottle."

Thornton easily granted this concession because his trust in Higgins had been growing over the past minutes. Nicholas Higgins and his animosity toward what Thornton saw as inevitable—that there would be those who built and those who worked—confused the industrialist. The idea that the men who toiled at his looms believed that they were forced to do so by circumstances rather than choice was foreign to him. He could not conceive of any man choosing to undertake that which he despised.

Rather he fell back onto the entrepreneur's code about employees: *If they do not like it, they ought to find another job or move to a place where they might find employment to their liking. My responsibility is to pay them not to coddle them.*

Memory is particularly short in the young, although John Thornton was well past his first bloom. He gilded the recollections of his time as a draper's boy, preferring to recall the gratitude in his mother's eyes when he dropped welcome shillings and pence into her outstretched hands. Of his anger at his father and the men who would exploit his family's desperation, he recalled little except to hold it up before himself as a shame he would avoid at all costs. He conveniently ignored the fact that there were no spare ha'pennies to purchase a carriage ticket out of Milton.

A mote of thought about his earlier trials and their similarity to those of Higgins and his men rose up to disequilibrate Thornton's certitude. There was something in his next question that demanded a response beyond brutal economic realities.

"Why do you hate us so?"

Higgins was a better man, a stronger one, than many who fought to rise to his position. He was a true believer and not in the fray for his own enrichment. So many others had sold out their members to the bosses, secure in the knowledge they could flee town with the £100 payoff and vanish behind a new name on the other side of the country.

Thus, Higgins paused when he understood that Thornton was expecting more than the usual screed about low wages and awful working conditions. Thornton wanted to know *what these elements of Milton's status quo meant to the workers.* Nicholas Higgins was uniquely qualified to offer such insight, as he had seen both sides of the Industrial Revolution.

A child of Yorkshire cottager parents, Higgins had watched them spin the raw wool into yarn and weave it into cloth on the loom that dominated one room of their cozy home. The draper's men would come to carry away the finished stuff and settle up. His mother had her kitchen garden while his father would work his strip of the commons.

Nicky and his sisters lived as children of the countryside do: fishing, picking berries and picking up fallen fruit in the orchards that carpeted the hillsides beneath the crags and moors. Between their parents' efforts and the children's foraging, the Higgins family lived as had their ancestors for generations. The sun was their clock and the church calendar told their year and lives.

Then came the enclosures.

With the new century, great wealth sloshed about the shires. Sterling poured in from sugar plantations and India. Men who had bought and sold for a living overthrew the delicate balance that had governed English life since the Fifteenth Century. Peasants and yeoman farmers who had worked the lord's fields and their own strips, paying their rents in produce, now faced demands for cash rents and the abrogation of traditional privileges long believed sacred writ. The new reality was all about the money, and these new landowners were flush with cash and bought favorable treatment in Westminster. Little could be done in the face of shire militias, which were moved from town to town in a show of force designed to cow the population.

Faced with the question of starvation on lands that had supported them for hundreds of years, families pulled up stakes and moved to the newly rising industrial towns, drawn by the promise of ample work. Yet by seeking to escape from the new face of agrarian exploitation, they simply exchanged oppressors. Feudal masters, whether on the land or in town, now sought to control their labor through force of arms, starvation, or other coercion. Thousands huddled in rapidly exploding slums, finding themselves oppressed again.

Now one of those men sought his view on what—to Higgins— seemed patently obvious and the natural order of the world.

Higgins took the time to gather his thoughts, to offer his reply in a clear, strong manner that would not be discounted because he spoke like an uneducated man. His wife used to chide him for his laziness of speech that grew from his fellow-workers. Higgins had been taught at parish day schools, both in his home town as well as during the early years in Milton.

He recalled that his wife would task him, arguing that, because he could read and write as well as perform the mathematics needed to set up the giant looms, he could have feet in both camps. Each would respect him because he used the King's English as a tool, not a bludgeon.

He framed his reply without the laziness of tongue that had become his norm and stunned Thornton in the process.

"You must forgive me, sir, if I speak slowly. 'Tis been some years since I took the time to say my 'haytches' and the like.

"To your question... I am at least a third-generation loom-man. My father and grandfather before him took in work from the drapers at our home over in Yorkshire. Guess you could say I have wool in my blood.

"But we had to move off the land when corn prices fell after the Duke beat that bastard. T'was lucky for me that the early days saw experienced men like my da getting a good wage. He started out at Old Mr. Watson's—that would be the da of Miss Fanny's Mr. Watson —mill.

"I was able to continue my schooling over at St. Mary's. My folks hoped I could become a mechanic and design new machines for Mr. Watson and some of the other mills that were showing up across the valley.

"But t'was not to be and, by the Year Nineteen, I had to go into the shops with the rest of the Higginses. The greater Milton's population, the more wages dropped. Eventually, it took every one of us in the mills from five in the morning until eight at night to pay for two rooms. Not much left over to feed two grown-ups and three bairns.

"And you ask why we hate you?

"Remember, I am talking thirty years ago when I had to leave school and go with my sisters and parents onto the loom room floor.

"I am the only one left alive.

"My folks lasted the longest, the girls only a few years. Fluff got them, just like it's goin' ta get my Bessy," he broke off as his voice clouded.

A few throat clearings and coughs later, he picked up his litany, "You ask why we hate you, and I'll tell you.

"All men have dreams. I had mine. Because I had more education than most, I could see that working the machines was not a winning proposition. I knew, though, that without money, without an angel, I would never find my way to the office with windows. I could have been a room boss or even an overseer.

"The world had different ideas. Maybe I picked the wrong owners to follow. I should have fingered men who could land on their feet and not throw everybody out onto the street.

"Dreams die hard, Mr. Thornton, but they do and, when they expire, they leave behind foul-tasting ash.

"Dreams die, but the need to feed your family and put a roof over their heads does not.

"You work your fingers to the bone, and you wear your labor like a badge of honor, aware that your only reward is another day in these mills where the overseers demand unconditional obedience and punish grown men like they are misguided bairns.

"Oh, there is another reward: that we may earn just enough to starve slowly while watching our wives and children cough up brown gore. Their bodies are so wasted that they cannot fight to survive!

"We are at the mercy of men like you who would see us as nothing but cogs and wheels in your giant money-making machine. Your underlings see us as beasts and treat us as such, tossing us out the door when we break down.

"You say you are building a better world. I ask you, for whom? I would imagine 'tis for the likes of you, not us. Woe betides any who gets in the way of you and your dreams.

"And I must ask you, of what do you dream? A golden city or piles of gold?

"You and your ilk are blessed with the riches wrung from our very bones, the muscles of the damned.

"You see us as nothing more than the animals you need to make the cloth you sell to pay for your houses and drink. You would cast us off in an instant and damn us for being lazy if age and injury kept us from working all out.

"*Miss Hale considers us men.*"

Thornton was staggered by the way that Higgins' voice dropped from the ferocity of a Dissenter preacher crying out eternal damnation into a reverence akin to when Papists speak of the *Holy Mother*. The memory of Margaret's sanctity–her compassion–curdled his insides as he recalled her responses to the trials of Milton's workers and their families.

Higgins was not finished. He flared back to life, but his ire was subdued, seeking to illuminate rather than indict.

"I have lived in this town for more than thirty years. Little has floated down the canals that I know nothing about. So, I have a fair idea of your story. You were not born into scandal. That came to you later.

"You, Master John Thornton, fought and reclaimed your honor, your family's good name. You paid your da's debts.

"Yet you cannot tell me that you did not ever want another penny or shilling from the men who controlled your time and sweat. Is that not the way of things; men who labor seek a tiny bit more daily bread?"

Thornton fought back if only to try to salvage some of his pride, "Then find a second position. I did. I ran deliveries for other shops before my day at the draper's began, then I would grub a few more pence after hours!"

Higgins appraised the younger man, pursed his lips, and sarcastically replied, "And who might you be to suggest that a man who works fourteen out of twenty-four on your looms ought to find ways to fill the other ten hours with more labor?

"How might you react if I fell asleep down below and ended up destroying machinery worth hundreds?

"Who are you to despise us, to say with conviction that we are trying to steal what is yours? Exactly what is that? The yarn will not spin itself. The fabric will not miraculously fly finished onto the rolls. Without men at the stations, women replacing the spindles, and bairns crawling underneath, you would have nothing.

"You mill-masters accuse us of stealing what is yours? What might that be? The price you get after you conspire to gouge the middlemen, who then must jack up their prices to merchants? The goods become so dear that workingmen cannot even afford to buy a shirt cut out of the cloth they themselves made?

"What about your theft of what is ours?

"You are so proud that you 'reclaimed your family's honor.' Yet what have you done with that good name?

"Have you raised it up so that men like Slickson and Hamper will settle at your table, all the while plotting to destroy you?

"Are you like the slave masters of old, profiting from those without choice, only different in that your conscience is clear of the stain caused by owning another human?

"Or have you tried to find a way to uphold your principals—and I know them to be upright, for if they were otherwise you could not work with Mr. Bell and Reverend Hale—to improve the lives of all in Milton?

"Have you been a good steward of your wealth, or have you simply used it to pursue your own pleasure?"

Thornton heard out Higgins while unsuccessfully seeking to ignore thoughts of the woman who lay injured downstairs. But Margaret Hale, even unconscious, would not allow him that luxury. He listened with new clarity, and Thornton was ashamed of himself.

He had drunk deeply from the gospel bruited by self-righteous vicars nurtured by the ruling classes. These *holy men* were imbued not with the Holy Spirit but rather with the lust for mammon that echoed that of their well-heeled masters.

For the first time, he understood Mr. Hale's rejection of his cleric's living.

Thornton, in his rush to eradicate his incipient shame, had lost his way. The path that led him from his father's study on that awful day was bending back around to deposit him in that blood-stained seat of power with the muzzle planted against his temple.

He had become like Hamper and the others, marking his success, not in the bridges he had built, but rather, by the number of digits in his bank account. Thornton was treading the trail of moneyed men like Marley and Scrooge. His end could be as dire.[666]

He had seen his past. He knew his present. He was terrified of the future.

Somehow, he understood that he had been offered an opportunity to alter what he feared might otherwise become a foregone conclusion.

He whispered, "What must I do?"

Higgins replied simply, softly, *"Exagoras Agapis."*[777]

Thornton squared on Higgins and stared, shocked that this rough-edged man knew Greek, let alone Greek that he, Thornton, was only just beginning to learn in Hale's bookroom.

"What did you say?" Thornton asked.

Higgins suppressed a smile, secretly enjoying the discomfiture of the young man, so full of himself, as was the nature of men without snow in their hair.

"I said *Exagoras Agapis.* That is, sir, the love which causes us to redeem ourselves, to become the best version of who we are. 'Tis something I heard the Countess of Matlock say when I was in the company of my uncle, the old Bosun over at Selkirk Castle," Higgins answered.

He added, "I know something about you, Master Thornton. You have never dealt unfairly with any man—either another master or workingmen like me. If you can be accused of pride, t'would be over this. You always believe you are treating one and all decently, as you would expect yourself to be treated.

"After all, would you not hold yourself in disdain if you complained at your lot or blamed others for your situation? You measure every man with the same stick.

"And the difficulty lies in the fact not all men measure up to your standards. Your pride thus becomes something worse: a prideful nature that leads you to scorn those who may not have your drive.

"You need to find your way back to that caring man with justifiable pride in his accomplishments, but also one who is more tolerant of his lessers. You have lost your way and are seen as a proud man who cares only for himself and his reputation.

"You will have to find the right trail, or you will never convince Miss Hale that you are the type of man who has a place in her future.

"You have to redeem yourself and become the good man I know you can be."

Higgins' fatherly advice sent Thornton back into a deep study. Nicholas left him in peace.

Then a sensation—one that had been unnoticed in its absence—resumed. This was the constant of every textile mill that had been missing at Marlborough for several days.

The vibrations of machinery tremored the floorboards.

Higgins noticed that Thornton snapped into his professional guise as the building shivered. The Master first leaned against the windows overlooking the files of looms lining the floor below. Then he freed a latch which allowed him to swing the frame inward.

The roar of wheels and pulleys drowned out the clicking of shuttles flying between strands of wool and cotton.

Higgins acknowledged his look and slipped back into his deep Darkshire cant as his recent life stepped into the forefront. "Buh-leve me, I am nay scab, but t'it seemed foolhardy to hae ye paying all these men and feedin' their women and bairns in the bargain—and hon'r'ble man ye are, ye be payin' 'em a full wage—an' not hae them do naught to earn their own bread.

"Ye hae a fact'ry full 'o yarn, an' attic full 'o workers, an' a desk full 'o ord'rs. I foun' their lead man an', once't I were sure 'e'd not break the mill, tol' 'im ta git ta work. Th' machines were still set up from when the boys turned out.

"Think 'o this as a one-time-only situation, an act 'o mercy. They be runnin' only what wuz al'rdy goin'. Should be 'nuff ta cov'r their keep for a few days 'til we git this sorted.

"Our argument is with ye, nae with them. They be 'ere because they be starvin' o'er their looms by Dublin Castle. Me da and uncle wouldn'a allow that. They'd be o' the thinkin' that food was part 'o th' answer, but work, too.

"The ol' Bosun would've talked with 'is *betters* up at Selkirk and down at Netherfield, the *May-zon* the Rochets call it. The Earls and Countesses wouldn'a 'lowed any ta starve.

"Ol' Darcy and even his boy, that new hopped up Earl 'o Pemberley, would'a open'd their granaries to feed th' Irish, if only 'cuz Mrs. Elizabeth, may God rest her soul, would have insisted on it.

"I met the Darcys back in the Twenties when the place I wuz workin' closed up 'cuz the owner refused ta switch from water ta steam. The Bosun dragged me up ta Selkirk's stables and tried ta put me ta work shovelin' horse dung.

I tell ya this now, Master Thornton. I be a power loom lead man. I 'ad a big 'ead, but I vow that t'was fur good reason. Knew whut t'was doin', I did. Standin' behind the southbound end o' a northbound 'orse was no way, fur as I was concerned, ta live."

Thornton smiled at the thought of the grizzled weaver as a youngster trying to fit in as a groom on one of the great Derbyshire estates. He heartily agreed with Higgins that life as a stable hand was no way for a town-bred boy to exist.

Further conversation and thoughts were disrupted when Dr. Donaldson joined them in their lair.

MARGARET GRIMACED. She evaluated her appearance with her eyes closed. The pain radiating from her temple sketched itself across the planes of her face. No expression she bore could be pleasant, she mused, so she settled upon defining her countenance as *grimacing*.

She began a swift inventory of her body parts, amusing herself with a vision of John Thornton sorting through the components of a disassembled spinning mule spread out upon the shop floor–picking up one piece and then another, inspecting each for wear. Oddly, that picture left a warm glow in its wake. Margaret began by wiggling her fingers and toes and, later, her limbs. Her head, however, persisted in plaguing her with a dull ache. Movement of that member was not to be borne!

Sound became more distinct as her hearing improved.

"Doctor...doctor! I thin' she be comin' 'round now!" That was dearest Dixon, the maid's strident tones colored with worry and relief rolled into one.

A cool cloth laved Margaret's face, soothing away some of her discomfort. She cleared her throat.

"How long?" She was surprised at the croak that broke free in place of her normally well-modulated alto.

The active cloth was replaced by a cool compress across her forehead. Margaret could imagine her family's old retainer kneeling next to her, squeezing out excess water into a basin. The soundscape was vivid with the subtraction of her sense of sight.

Dixon replied, "'Nigh unto two hours, Miss Margaret. But the doctor says that t'was ta be 'xpected."

Her eyes fluttered open in time to see Dr. Donaldson arrive, hovering above her, while Dixon scooted a few inches closer to the head of the sofa upon which Margaret reclined. Donaldson was focusing on a spot near her left temple in her hairline. He asked a few questions about her symptoms, the date, the monarch, and the city. Then he adjusted his manner from inquiry to caution.

"This may hurt a bit. If you would be so kind, Miss Dixon, as to hold Miss Hale's hand..." he said before gently probing with his fingers, pushing Margaret's hair to one side.

Margaret gasped as a wave of pain scorched across her nerves.

Donaldson pulled back and said, "There now. Finished. My apologies for causing you any discomfort."

Then he became all business. "Normally I would not burden my patients with weather reports, but knowing your history with your mother's illness," at this he lifted his head to include Dixon in his ken, "I feel that you will take my diagnosis pragmatically.

"Physicians always find head injuries, particularly those involving violent impacts, worrisome. For the layman, such wounds are all-the-more terrifying because scalp lacerations bleed—pardon my frank language—like the devil. Such was the case with yours. I fear your gown is ruined. And I think your incapacitation overset your Mr. Thornton, at least according to Mr. Higgins."

My Mr. Thornton? Why would Nicholas know what bothered John?

"Now, as for your condition: from what I can tell, you were struck a glancing blow by either a brick or a paving stone. Either weapon might have done serious—fatal—damage if it had scored a direct hit. However, something deflected the trajectory enough to lessen the impact.

"Your head is laid open for about an inch right within your hairline. With a cut of that nature, I would usually stitch it closed. However, as the skin is stretched tightly at this location on your head, embroidery would be dicey at best. I have decided to allow the cut to heal naturally. I cleaned it, applied some of Maturin's blue mold salve, and covered it with a plaster. Miss Dixon must do the same every day: clean, ointment, fresh plaster. You will have a scar, but only those closest to you will notice: your father, Miss Dixon, and your husband."

My husband?

Donaldson concluded, "I do not believe you are concussed. Your pupils are equal, and you do not seem to exhibit any sort of mental impairment. The headache will subside after a brief period, maybe two or three days. Miss Dixon can visit the apothecary for a powder that I have prescribed. My final injunction is that you move slowly, take your rest, and drink plenty of liquids. No gamboling around, young lady. Allow Miss Dixon to fetch as needed."

The servant vigorously nodded in agreement with the doctor's orders. Donaldson stood tall, tugged his waistcoat, shot his cuffs and smoothed the wrinkles from his suit.

"I will go tell Mr. Thornton and Mr. Higgins that you have rejoined the land of the living."

An unaccountable thrill coursed through Margaret. While the men were absent, she fussed to organize her gown until Dixon carefully rearranged a blanket around her, decently covering her legs and feet. However, short of mummifying her from chin to toe, nothing could be done to hide Margaret's blood-stained collar.

The rumble of heavy footfalls drowned out the mechanical *thrum* that had pervaded the office. Thornton was the first to emerge from the stairwell followed closely by Higgins and the doctor. Upon seeing

Margaret stretched out on his couch, he skidded to a halt, full of conflicting emotions.

In other circumstances, his heart would have soared to see her taking her ease in *his* office. Only two other women in his life— Hannah and Fanny—could presume to recline in so intimate a manner, although his sister was unlikely to cross the mill's threshold. Miss Hale, though, was supine because he had failed in his one duty... to protect those most vulnerable.

Thornton also was immediately overset by the ochre and carmine that besmirched the material of her evening wear. How had she survived?

Again, his copybook was truly blotted.

He ceased his recriminations when his eyes were dragged into the vortices that centered upon her large brown eyes, burning out of the pallor that was her complexion. Those pools took in his being and, he was certain, weighed his sins and failings against a feather. If he were in the Egyptian halls of Ma'at awaiting judgment, John Thornton was sure that a serpent would snap up his soul to extinguish his existence, so heavy was his heart.

Margaret Hale knew the contours of his inner man. Of that, he was convinced. She peeled away all his puffery. He stood naked before her; such was her power over him. He feared her perception, her insight, for it led him to the place he dreaded...where he had to tell himself the truth.

The memory of his father, the suicide, the destruction of what was, rose unbidden to reaffirm the path forward. Thornton had few recollections of his father, so ruthlessly had he purged images that could bring nothing but pain.

Yet one bit of wisdom, seemingly saved until now, chased away every shadow that had plagued Thornton. The gift, only appreciated in the current circumstances and not recalled for at least a decade, had been spoken bare months before the family's world crashed down around their ears. Whether uttered by design or unintentionally, his father had bequeathed it to him one warm summer Sunday as the two walked together upon the moor above Milton.

Hannah had remained behind resting on the family picnic blanket while Fanny played. As the Sun began dropping toward the Irish Sea, Mr. Thornton stopped and looked down upon Milton's smokestacks, somnolent for the Sabbath. He assayed a pensive look before offering his soliloquy.

The women we love the most, John, are the ones who know our darkest secrets without asking. They perceive our transgressions without judgment and find gems lying within the dross that is everything we ourselves value. They do not hector us, nor do they sermonize. Rather, my boy, they use their infinitely better natures to point us toward examples of acceptable behavior and those traits they would encourage within us...and ones they would have us leave behind. This is a difficult task, John, for it demands that we hew tightly to principle rather than expedience. There are few men who could achieve that which would elevate them above the grasping crowd. I fear the price of failure for that would bring unbearable shame.

Such good women would have us work to become the best versions of ourselves so that we may be worthy of our name and their love.

Thornton's eyes widened as the scales fell away. The man his father had been and Higgins, who was now the age his sire would have been, had come together on this dark night.

He exhaled, *"Exagoras agapis."*

Margaret flashed him a quizzical look, a smile lifting the corners of her lips. Her eyes bright, she reached out to both men. Thornton and Higgins shuffled forward to take her hands. Each man felt sheepish that this gentle lady had been laid low by their dispute.

She intoned, "Mr. Thornton, Mr. Higgins, you and I have much to discuss. I fear that the events of this evening are but a foretaste of further trouble if we do not act, even in this small corner of Milton, to find a way forward. It is time for two men I have come to deeply respect to set aside their pride and work together for the good of Marlborough Mills, its employees, and Milton!

"Doctor, could you move a second chair by my side? I find that I agree with you that I should not be rattling about until I have recovered more. I would speak with these two gentlemen but will remain resting here.

"Normally I would ask you and Dixon to withdraw. However, I fear that it might be considered improper for me to be alone with two unmarried men, however honorable. Might you both retreat to the opposite side of the office to bear witness?"

Dixon looked mulish but allowed the doctor to escort her to a seating area surrounding a small table, upon which rested a stack of sample books. He settled next to her to watch the next act.

The field thus cleared, Margaret continued, "Mr. Thornton, Mr. Higgins, I am not above using my sex or my infirmity to have my own way. I have offered us as much privacy as we can reasonably expect. You may feel free to air your dirty laundry without curious ears.

"However, you must cease staking out your territory. Neither of you impresses me as being so insecure that you must mark every lamp-post in the area.

"Begin considering yourselves as joint stewards of Marlborough. Without the mill, Mr. Higgins, the workers will have nothing. Without the workers, Mr. Thornton, the business will cease to exist, eradicating your dreams and throwing your family into penury yet again. Given where matters stand right now, a day's delay can result in disaster.

"Both of you believe that you have the resources to outwait the other.

"You are woefully incorrect."

Her glare speared them, and she added, "While I find much to admire about you, I also appreciate that the traits that made you the men you are can also become barriers to finding a route which leads to the greater good.

"Your stubbornness will be your downfall...that Achilles Heel which will break more than just yourselves.

"You seem, however, to trust me. For that I commend your excellent judgement.

"I submit to you that you ought to plead your cases to me—both grievances and demands—and consider me an impartial arbiter. You ought to allow me to craft a compromise that will meet the needs of owner and worker alike.

"Sadly, whatever we decide upon here will be binding...and only after Mr. Higgins' men approve the agreement...solely upon Mr. Thornton and Marlborough. The other mills will have to deal with their own employees as they wish. That will have to be enough.

"I can only hope that both of you will find something about which to complain because then I will know I have found the middle ground."

Throughout this extraordinary speech, Miss Hale had not released either man to settle back into his chair. She did not free them until they had offered their grudging acceptance of her terms.

What immediately became apparent was that both men toiled under hidebound illusions of the bad intent of the other. Higgins was convinced that Thornton wanted to push his workers to the breaking point. Thornton, in his turn, was convinced that the workers wanted nothing less than to work fewer hours for greater pay.

On top of that, Higgins objected to the universal practice of not paying workers if the machines broke down, even though those workers were required to stand around and wait while mechanics bent to their repair. Thornton responded that the owners believed that workers would sabotage their looms simply to take paid breaks. Higgins growled back that wrecking was at the very least a transportable offense, and most loom-men could not foul a machine in a manner to avoid detection, thus ensuring arrest and conviction.

Margaret stopped them here.

"As I see it, John" (she had determined to use Christian names to eliminate any *lessers and betters* bias) "justifiably fears the drain upon resources and income if workers are paid for not working. I will set aside the somewhat specious argument that employees would be inclined to damage the equipment to avoid working while still being paid.

"Nicholas, with equal justification, worries that his members are being penalized when the machinery fails because owners refuse to maintain the apparatus, preferring to milk as much profit as possible out of old looms.

She paused and looked up at the ceiling, worrying her lower lip in a manner that utterly captivated Thornton. Then she delivered her verdict.

"Nicholas is correct in that no reasonable man would risk his family's welfare by damaging any equipment. However, John also has a point when he bridles at paying for idle hands. As I have come to know John to be a responsible man, I doubt if he would allow any of the machinery for which he has paid dearly to deteriorate to the point where it fails. The best defense against both of your concerns becoming reality is to ensure that machinery is producing cloth throughout an entire shift. That way John would be secure in his income without bearing undue costs for laborers being paid without working. And for the workers, they would be confident that they would not be punished for owner greed.

"However, I do not believe that a worker should be paid his entire wage for standing and puffing his pipe while mechanics work. Half pay seems sensible.

"Perhaps a competent overseer or foreman who knows the equipment and could be trusted to reassign workers to other tasks in the event their primary employment is temporarily unavailable..." She sent a knowing glance at Thornton.

Thornton squirmed. Would allowing Higgins into Marlborough be akin to permitting the camel to stick her nose under the edge of the tent? What would the other owners think?

A revelation stuck; he had never cared what men like Hamper really thought of him...only in how their opinion might affect his ability to raise capital. Yet Mr. Bell had been a gilt-edged reference whenever Thornton had stepped outside of Milton's clannish banking community. In the past, those fat-fingered, beady-eyed City gentlemen gently smiled upon his pleas whenever he had handed over plans endorsed by Mr. Bell.

If Hamper, Slickson, and Watson decided to combine and try to drive him out of Milton because he acceded to Higgins' demands, it would only be a convenient excuse. Thornton knew he already was a threat to their curated status quo. The other manufacturers would gladly try to shutter Marlborough simply for being too successful. It was a matter of time.

He was not concerned about this threat. Thornton realized he had beaten their likes before. They had been at the top of Milton's social pyramid for so long that they had become fat and lazy. Thornton was the lean and hungry cheetah sowing terror in the herd of slack-bellied antelopes that spread across the mercantile savannah.

And a working Marlborough Mills pouring money into his coffers and stealing orders from factories owned by less enlightened men was the supreme defense against his competitors' shenanigans.

He became aware of both Miss Hale and Higgins staring at him. Thornton coughed into his hand and cleared his throat before saying, "You have distilled the question, Miss Hale," he stopped at her quelling glare, "...Margaret...to its essence. I can find nothing objectionable here.

"I will accept the half-pay provision with the caveat that *Nicholas* agrees to become that foreman/overseer you described.

"However, he would have to resign his position with the union, as he must be either fish or fowl—worker or manager. I do realize that this will complicate his life. However, this is an alienation which he must accept, or the employees will refuse to follow his orders....and I will refuse to move ahead in this conversation.

"I have become convinced that Marlborough Mills can become the greatest producer in the Midlands only if it persists in attracting the best employees. That starts at the top with a man like Higgins being at my right hand.

"Yet, an idea just crossed my mind. What do you, Margaret and Nicholas, think of allowing the union members to elect their lead men? That way they would feel empowered in the operation of the mill. Nicholas and I would meet to determine the orders to be run. Nicholas would meet with the lead men to parcel out the work."

Higgins chimed in, "I could see it workin', but only if there be an incentive, something which would ensure that the best man and not the most popular win."

Margaret added, "Linked to quality and efficiency!"

The three looked at each other and nodded as one. The dam had been broken.

Higgins' tacit acceptance of Thornton's job offer led to productive and far-reaching negotiations. Thornton agreed to the union's role in the mill, instinctively understanding that he could not hold back the tide. Work conditions, safety concerns, a dining hall, and a school were all explored and negotiated, in addition to wage scales. Performance bonuses and even some modest profit-sharing were to be implemented on trial to learn if they would encourage greater productivity and attract competent workers.

Dixon had busied herself in the small kitchen below the master's room. She had been shuttling hot tea and coffee onto the small table set for that purpose between Margaret's divan and the two men's chairs.

As the conversation died down, the question of the Irish remained.

Higgins was worried about the idea that the newly-arrived workers would be so desperate if they were abandoned to the streets of Milton that they would instantly cross other picket lines.

He addressed Margaret with an eye on Thornton, "The Paddies are a problem. I canna see how ye can keep any o' 'em, let alone a portion. I am no fool. Ye canna pay two workforces."

Margaret's aura, a halo of compassion, enveloped John and led him through the cracks in his prejudices.

"The idea that I would throw men, families, into utter privation makes me ill.

"True, in the past, I would have waved Liberalism's flag and allowed that they should find employment at other mills or simply move on to another town. Yet I know that Hamper and Slickson...I have contrary hopes for my soon-to-be brother Watson...would take advantage of their dire straits.

"I could pay their fare back to Ireland. Of course, that would be *false compassion* as I would be sending them home to starve like so many others. Other men might find their consciences resting easy not having to watch grieving parents lower tiny blanket-wrapped bodies into the ground.

"I brought them to Milton. Thus, I must find a solution," he said, looking hopefully at his partners.

Higgins shrugged. He had no suggestions.

However, Miss Hale reached into her intuitive mind and offered, "Might you put on a second shift? Is it not the case that between eight o'clock in the evening and six o'clock the following morning the Mill is shut down except for maintenance? Could you absorb some of the Irish in this manner? Making cloth to fulfil your orders in less time?"

Both Higgins and Thornton smiled at one another, surprised at Miss Hale's naïveté about the nature of the textile industry...Their amusement lasted a few moments, swiftly disappearing when she continued.

"I understand that Marlborough's order book is strained. The strike has forced customers to consider other sources, especially the Manchester mills. However, this is a problem faced by every single Milton facility. They cannot fill the orders they have on their books. But they *do* have orders, ones they will lose if they do not find a way to deliver.

"I recall hearing a merchant captain with the Gardiner line, a Captain Keith, who dined at the Parsonage when he passed through Helstone a few years ago. He was Canon Benton's friend. Papa was Mr. Benton's student at Oxford back in the Twenties.

"Over dinner, the Captain explained how the India and China trade works through factoring where one merchant in India may close a deal with another in London to deliver a certain amount of porcelain. That merchant might not have any china in his warehouse.

"But the order itself is a commodity just like the tableware. Another tradesman could purchase that order at a discount, and then he would undertake to deliver the goods at the India Dock and collect the full amount originally agreed upon. The customer wants the goods and cares not who fulfils the contract.

"That, said Captain Keith, is what is called factoring," Margaret stated.

She continued, "You could expand your production if you offer to purchase, to factor, unfilled orders from the other owners. I would imagine that they would take between 40 and 50 percent of their moribund orders' values instead of getting nothing but a cancellation. Maybe Mr. Bell could offer some financial guarantees.

"This would offer two advantages. First, you would make a limited profit, but a profit none-the-less, while utilizing your second shift's capacity and keeping the Irish workers employed.

"And second, the customers would be beholden to you for honoring the original terms of their deals and preserving their margins. Even if you only converted five or six of these from Hamper, Slickson, or Watson customers, Marlborough would be far ahead.

"Only one mill needs to crack. Perhaps Mr. Watson, as he has designs on your sister, may be willing to repave his bank account with an influx of Marlborough cash."

Thornton and Higgins were astonished at her sophisticated analysis. They scrambled for pencils and paper to run the figures. After two or three minutes, the second shift was implemented. However, even the most generous of calculations accounted for only a bit more than half of the imported hands. The Council of Three agreed that this was unsatisfactory.

Thornton had wandered over to his desk as he pondered the conundrum of what to do with the surplus. Something nagged in the back of his mind. Then it was no longer hidden.

A chance meeting at the Lambton station when Thornton was changing to the London train laced his mind.

Thornton had been a little worse-for-wear because the Milton line offered indifferent service at best. He had been delayed and already had missed two southbound trains.

He had been standing on the platform waiting to climb into his carriage when an elegantly-dressed couple strolled up. Perhaps the dark-eyed lady took pity on his weariness. Perhaps the well-tailored gentleman recognized something in Thornton which he himself possessed. Whatever the roots of the exchange, the three had engaged in polite conversation while they awaited the coupling of a private car to the back of the train.

Soon enough, though, all was in order and farewells began.

Thornton and the older man exchanged cards. The couple moved off and boarded their exclusive sleeper, the *Oakham Mount*. Thornton was impressed and curious but did not consider the gentleman's calling card until he was settled in his second-class bench seat.

The words were potent then. They were even more so now.

Thomas C. Johnson
  Managing Director
  Darcy-Dingley Enterprises

THORNTON NOW GRABBED a fresh sheet of paper and scribbled a wire to the man who ran Great Britain's largest industrial conglomerate, an empire spread across a dozen industries and three continents. Higgins agreed to dispatch one of his watchers to the railway station's telegraph office.

When Marlborough's new overseer returned, Thornton explained what he had been about.

"I have presumed upon a very limited acquaintance with the man who runs DBE. I have explained to Mr. Thomas Johnson that I have a difficult problem with excess labor. I wondered if he might be able to employ any of our Irish workers who are surplus to our requirements and would be willing to move on to Manchester to work in DBE's mills. I told him I would happily pay their train fare and one month's housing allowance.

"I am not certain how Mr. Johnson will reply but, by all accounts, DBE is a benevolent employer and is constantly expanding. I hope that he will listen to my appeal."

Margaret looked slightly troubled and asked, "What about those who do not want to work in a factory but, rather, wish to return to farming? What can be done for them?"

At this, Higgins straightened, "Wull, Miss Margaret, while Master Thornton seems ta hae some connection with one side of th' Derbyshire lot, I might 'elp with t'uther.

"You may recall my stories about my days at Selkirk. T'wasn't all shovelin' horse manure, ye know. Got to know Mr. Tomkins, Selkirk's steward...'e was not much more than an 'opped-up footman then...and I would wager that 'e might 'elp find some tenant farms at Selkirk, Pemberley, and Thornhill."

Thornton continued, completing Higgins' thought, "And I am sure that Marlborough might find a way to cover one year's reduced rent."

Higgins looked offended, "Nay, Mr. Thornton, the estates' masters would never presume on your good nature. I am sure they would follow old Mr. Bennet's practice after Mr. Watson's mill burned down in Meryton back in the Year Eleven. 'e let sever'l families live on 'is estate rent-free until their first 'arvest came in."

Another telegram was composed and dispatched to Matlock.

Watching the exchange between the two men, Margaret's heart softened. She had always seen Nicholas as a kindly uncle, perhaps even a bit of a father because his bluff nature was so different from her own bookish parent. Now, as she watched him interact with John, she could see the young man soaking up the fatherly direction. Thornton's need for an older man in his life had never been more apparent than in the last hours. And his open acceptance of Nicholas tipped something deep inside of Miss Hale. She looked more closely at the Master of Marlborough Mills.

And saw something which disturbed her.

Her left hand shot out and grasped Thornton's left wrist, turning it so she could confirm what she had observed.

Thornton winced—not at the idea of her touching him but rather at the absolute fact that her grip was...

He winced and inhaled sharply.

"John," she urgently prodded, "what is this?"

Upon her release, he lifted his arm and turned it, looking at his forearm.

An ugly bruise covered three inches of skin, purpling where it was not green and yellow.

John shook his head, "I have no idea. I noticed it earlier. I must have banged it upon something..."

"Something quite hard, I would imagine, young sir," rumbled Donaldson who strode over, "If you would allow me a moment here." After appropriate manipulations accompanied by *'hmmms'* from Donaldson and small yips from Thornton, the doctor carefully lowered the young man's arm. Then he looked at Margaret.

"You may recall, Miss Hale, my opinion that your head injury would have been much worse but for a fortunate deflection of the missile."

He pointed at Thornton's arm and continued, "The size and shape of Mr. Thornton's contusion tell me that he became aware of the danger and instinctively protected you. He was unable to prevent the impact entirely but, like the Duke said, 'It was a close-run thing.' As Wickham at Hougoumont did for the nation, Mr. Thornton undoubtedly saved you.

"I fear, sir, that you are beginning to pay the price for your heroism. I do not believe your arm is broken, but you can surely expect considerable swelling."

Margaret teared up at the idea that Thornton had suffered for her audacity in stepping forward to address the mob. At the catch in her throat, Thornton leaned toward her while Donaldson busied himself padding and wrapping the bruise.

John whispered, "Now, none of that, Miss Margaret...none of that. Your bravery was inspiring to see. That I was too slow to join you on the front line will be to my everlasting shame. You began this night as a gentleman's daughter, so far above my aspirations yet, to my mind, still within reach."

Then he gulped and looked down, his native insecurity overtaking him.

"Then the realities of my life harshly imposed themselves upon your person.

"How can I hope to raise myself in your regard? I am naught but a glorified mechanic and a suicide's son. You are Milton's treasure."

His humility and despair broke Margaret's heart. She gripped his right hand, stopping his recriminations.

"John Thornton: to use your own words, *none of that!* The question of station is utter foolishness. I may have been born to a man and woman of gentle birth. That fact does not confer any greater goodness upon me than Mr. Higgins' darling Bessy.

"*There* is a young woman in full possession of the virtue to which I would aspire. She looks not at her lot in this world but instead to the place she will occupy in our Father's kingdom. She should be the vicar's daughter, not me.

"You and I are two persons passing through this world doing the best we can and hoping that we will not have to do it alone."

Her last sentence was accompanied by a meaningful squeeze unnoticed by anyone but Thornton. His heart soared and he looked deeply into her eyes, two pools in which he desired to swim for the next several decades.

Donaldson finished his work. Noticing both of his patients locked in their own world, he cleared his throat, causing them to break apart.

"As dawn now is upon us, I suggest that Miss Hale and Miss Dixon make their way home. I am sure her father is concerned," he said.

After a degree of hurly-burly, Margaret was wrapped in a blanket and carried down the stairs by the doctor. A hackney had pulled all the way into the mews. A guard of honor made up of Irish workers created a path door-to-door. She leaned on John and Nicholas as she walked between the files.

Once she was safely settled in the carriage and Dixon had fussed over her, Margaret looked at the two men who, oddly she thought, had become dear to her.

Thornton found the courage to speak first, "If it would be convenient, I would ask if I might accompany you to assure myself that all is well and offer some explanation to your father."

Margaret smiled to herself. *How typical of a man! Once the ice is broken, the male of the species, who before had strutted and demonstrated to attract the female, is at her mercy, insecure and bashful. Best to help him along.*

"No, dear sir, not now, not at this moment. Rather, you may call upon me tomorrow...oh, *this*...afternoon.

"I must, though, ask Mr. Higgins to join you. My father would wish to thank him for his role in saving me.

"I insist that you, Mr. Thornton, be the one to convey him to our house in Crampton. You know the address. I fear that Mr. Higgins may not.

"I would not be deprived of the companionship of the two men whose company I crave," she archly said, "one the father of my dear friend, the other my father's student. Both I have learned are the best of men and are also the most stubborn and bull-headed of creatures.

"Yet I have learned to deal with determined persons," at this, she held a little more tightly to Dixon's arm, "and, I have, in my own way, learned to express *my own determination.*"

"So, Mr. Thornton, you may call upon me this afternoon. However, sir, do not appear at my door without Mr. Higgins at your side. You two will need to learn to abide one-another for my sake and that of this town."

Her speech finished, Miss Hale, still pale, leaned back upon the worn squabs. Higgins' men circled around the cab like frigates guarding the flagship. The vehicle pulled away, moving along at a walking pace to avoid jostling its cherished cargo.

Thornton gulped, his Adam's Apple bobbing between open collars, and quizzed, "Where do you live, Higgins? I would not dare offend that woman, not if I hope to have any chance with her."

Higgins chuckled, "Ach, Master Thornton, dinna defy her. I hae come ta admire ye with all yore 'ide. But ye remind me 'o meself when I was a'courtin' my wife.

"Don'cha look at me lak that. I seen meself looking back from the glass in me Da's 'house. If'n I couldn'a see mah gurl thut day, I t'would drag around lookin' like one o' th' Old Gen'ral's 'untin' dogs if'n one 'o th' grooms 'ad given 'im a swift kick...deserved or not.

"Ah got a feelin' that you'd look the same.

"So, Frances Street 'bove the Golden Dragon. Meebe 'bout 30 minutes afore teatime?" He clapped Thornton on the shoulder and finished, "An', ah do believe you 'ad best hie yourself ta the 'ouse. I see two faces peerin' out from 'hind the drapes waitin' for yor story."

Thornton smiled and shook Higgins' hand before turning and striding purposefully across the courtyard to explain his desired future to his mother and sister.

AUTHOR'S NOTE: John Thornton and Margaret Hale regularized the accent of the working classes with whom they communed on a daily basis. Hence Nicholas Higgins' modified tone, although he slides between more cultured English and heavily accented Darkshire speech. I also employ the concept of solipsism where the act of writing fiction creates the universe within which that story is real. Elizabeth Gaskell wrote about forty years after Jane Austen and, thus, could easily have positioned her characters within a universe (in this case that of the Bennet Wardrobe) with foundations laid down by Austen.

DON JACOBSON HAS WRITTEN PROFESSIONALLY since his post-collegiate days as a wire service reporter in Chicago. His output has ranged from news and features to advertising, television and radio. His work has been nominated for Emmys and other awards. Earlier in his career, he published five books, all non-fiction. As a college instructor, Don teaches United States History, World History, the History of Western Civilization and Research Writing.

Don turned his passion for reading The Canon into writing #Austenesque Fiction. He has published eleven works in the genre since late 2015. As a member of The Austen Authors Collective, Don joins (and he is modestly bowing his head to admit that he is the knave in this deck of Queens and Kings) other Janites who seek to extend the Mistress' stories beyond the endings she so carefully crafted.

DON JACOBSON'S BOOKS INCLUDE: Miss Bennet's First Christmas, The Bennet Wardrobe: Origins, The Keeper: Mary Bennet's Extraordinary

Journey, Henry Fitzwilliam's War, The Exile (Pt. 1): Kitty Bennet and
the Belle Époque, Lizzy Bennet Meets the Countess, The Exile (pt. 2):
The Countess Visits Longbourn, The Avenger: Thomas Bennet and a
Father's Lament, The Pilgrim: Lydia Bennet and a Soldier's Portion),
Lessers and Betters Stories, Of Fortune's Reversal, The Maid and The
Footman

MISCHANCES

Nicole Clarkston

"Yes! he knew how she would love. He had not loved her without gaining that instinctive knowledge of what capabilities were in her. Her soul would walk in glorious sunlight if any man was worthy, by his power of loving, to win back her love." - Chapter XXXIII, North and South

"Thornton, I'd have a word with you."

John Thornton glanced up from the desk in his office, his pen hovering in the air. "Good afternoon, Hamper. What can I do for you?"

"Oh, aye, civil as you please," snorted the other. "I've come about the contract you stole from me."

Thornton raised a brow. "If you are referring to the Regimental contract, I did nothing more than quote a fair price per bolt."

"You knew very well that you were undercutting me. How am I to keep my mill solvent when you quote ten shillings less per lot?"

John set aside his pen and folded his hands on his desk. "Everyone was asked to bid on it, so the contract was not yours by right. I do as is right by Marlborough Mills. We are all suffering after the strikes, but they are ended now, largely at my expense."

Hamper shook his finger. "If you're looking for gratitude, Thornton, you'll not find it from me. You brought the Irish on yourself, and I had nothing to do with it."

"You benefited as well as the next mill."

"So that's how it is!" cried Hamper. "Cutting other mills to fill your own sheds? You think we owe you?"

Thornton sighed and rose from his desk. "I cut no one. It was merely business, and you said last week that you were behind on orders."

"No more than you are. You know as well as I that a contract like that is easy profit. No man in his senses would run small custom lots through his looms first when he could bring in nearly a quarter's earnings with a large plain one. You did this on purpose!"

"And you know very well that I never bid what I cannot do. My hands are better trained, and my looms are newer than yours. I can afford to cut price where I see fit, and I am not to blame if you cannot."

Hamper stepped close with a sneering growl. "Damn you, Thornton. You've been as charming as a bull with a hornet on his back since the riots. What's got into you? We mill owners have always stuck together."

Thornton turned away, resting his hand against the frame of the window and looking out over his looms. "I do not have breath to waste on the matter, Hamper. I regret that you feel slighted over the affair, but I daresay there is enough work to keep us all busy."

Hamper gathered his hat with a hiss and a clatter of the hat tree. "High and mighty now, are you? I see how it is. You think you own this town, but you're no better than the rest of us. You deserve to be put back in your place—*boy!*"

"Boy!" John spun back, glaring at his associate. "Take care, Hamper. My mill would make two of yours. And who is it you turn to whenever you have troubles with the Union?"

Hamper was quaking now in rage, and he shook his hat at John like a stick. His voice, when he collected himself to speak, was dangerously low. "I'll warn you this once, Thornton. Don't do anything you will regret." The door slammed a moment later, and John turned slowly round to survey his now-empty office.

Hamper could not know that his warning had come too late. Regret and the searing agony of failure already haunted John's steps and darkened his thoughts. Yet, it was not in business where he had met his greatest ruin. No! Not on his own turf, which had been his to master and command these eight years.

It was in the only area of life that truly did matter—that core of self that found breath and hope in the being of another. That sliver of *him*, always before unacknowledged and undervalued, was now decayed and rotting his frame from the inside. And yet he carried on, working as he had ever done, and hoping that no one would notice there was no life in him.

Some hours later, dusk heard his clipped and measured strides sounding at his own threshold. His mother looked up at his entry, then set her needlework aside. "You are home very late."

"Forgive me, Mother," he said as he hung his hat. "I trust you kept a tray for me?"

"Jane will bring it. John…" She waited for him to turn back at the hesitant tone to her voice.

"Yes?"

"Dr Donaldson was here this evening. He had just come from the Hales."

He went to her and lowered himself into the chair just opposite. "Is it going poorly for Mrs Hale, then?"

Mrs Thornton looked down. "I cannot imagine anyone recovering from her kind of ailment."

John leaned forward. "I took fruit this morning, but I was not invited in. I understood that to mean that matters were grave, indeed."

"The matter has been grave from the beginning, I understand."

"But she has not refused company before. You saw her only a few days ago. You told me that she asked for you."

His mother stiffened, and a mask fell over her features. "Nothing to concern yourself about. She only wished to commend that daughter of hers to my good offices. I told her I would advise the young creature as I saw fit, but I promised no more."

"Mother—"

"Nay, John, it is enough that I was able to comfort the woman somewhat in her last days."

He was silent a moment. "What did Donaldson say?"

Mrs Thornton sighed. "She has lapsed into a death sleep, and dawn will have settled it."

"Then I am very sorry for her!" he cried and covered his mouth with a trembling hand.

"Sorry for her! She feels no more pain and shall be more blessed than we when she awakens again. To be sure, she was too young to go in such a way, but many are younger. Grieve for her, certainly, but she is not to be pitied."

His cheek flinched as he raised his eyes to his mother's in faint annoyance. "I *do* pity Mrs Hale, but it was not she who...Mother, I am going upstairs."

"What of your supper?" she protested as he rose abruptly away.

"Have Jane bring it up. I have work to do," was his distracted answer.

In his own room, he cast his coat on his bed and sank into a chair. His mother's tidings were hardly a surprise, but he had hoped...no, that was not right. He had willed, in vain it seemed, but such was the strength of his resolve that it had rarely been challenged in his adult years. Fortune, commerce, public opinion and sheer luck–he had held all these in his sway. But the almighty hand of death would not be denied, and now one dearer to him than life would mourn.

His forehead fell to his hand and, if his eyes blurred with feeling, the darkness blotted it out. *Margaret...*

There had been some terror in her that morning—more than the hushed tones, the fragile way of moving—as if any sound would disturb the sufferer two floors above. No, it was something in her eyes —a gathering doom, a desperate apprehension. He had seen it, and wondered at the cause, until he saw a man's hat by the door. Not Mr Hale's worn felt, nor Donaldson's brown silk.

She had flinched at his notice—he was sure of it. Perhaps it belonged to someone she did not want him to see. A relation, he wondered? Someone come to bring the family comfort? But there were none in Milton who would trouble themselves to call nor be welcome above himself in that house of death. His understanding was that there were precious few elsewhere, either.

The fearful and distracted way Miss Hale had greeted and then dismissed him troubled him more than he cared to confess. It had hovered over the rest of his day, and now it would rob him of sleep. His hand strayed over his desk, touching the cover of Mr Hale's copy of Plato.

He would not be the only sleepless soul this night.

"FRED, have you never been to bed?"

Margaret paused at the doorway of the sitting room. The coal was long spent; the curtains drawn against the dim morning light, but her brother's white shirt glared from the darkness. He stirred, lifted his head, then dropped weary eyes to knead them with his fingers. "Margaret? I'd no idea you were up. Have you slept at all since the day I came?"

"A little," she confessed. "When Father finally went to his bed a few hours ago, I tried to sleep."

Frederick Hale moved aside on the sofa to offer his arm, and Margaret sagged into his embrace. "It took him long enough. I was afraid at first that he would not permit the undertaker to—"

"Please!" Margaret whispered. "Do not say it."

He lapsed into silence, his arm settling comfortingly round his sister's shoulders. "I wish to heaven I had been here sooner."

"It was wonderful of you to come at all."

"Little good it did!" was his bitter retort. "What had we, a few hours at the end of her life? That little to make up for the last ten years? And now I must leave again when I have scarcely arrived. You heard what Dixon said about Leonards. He would be sure to recognise me if he saw me."

"Then you must not go out. Not even to the funeral tomorrow. Who can harm you here? It is not as if Leonards will force his way through our door."

He shook his head. "Every moment I spend here in England kills Father a little more. Leonards may talk, or ask questions, and...no, my dearest sister, it will not do. Father will never sleep until he knows I am safely away from these shores. I doubt he will sleep even then, but I will not prolong his suffering. How shall you bear up? It all falls to you, I fear."

She wetted her lips and looked away. "Dixon and I shall manage."

"You could come to Spain. I have a good place there, and I know that Father would—"

"He would never leave Mother," Margaret breathed. "He has already said it—he wishes to be buried beside her."

Frederick sighed. "What of you? You cannot do it all alone. And what of your happiness? I'll not see you sacrifice everything in this filthy excuse for a city. Come to Spain, Margaret!"

"You know I cannot leave Father. And besides, I...I do not mind Milton so much as I did."

"Not mind it! It is everything frightful and dreary. I cannot think how you bear it. How can you possibly be happy here? Father cannot last another year in such a place. How can you be content to stay unless..." He narrowed his eyes. "You have not some secret beau, have you? Some entanglement that keeps you here?"

"Of course not!" she gasped, but her cheeks were unaccountably warm. "No, it is enough for me to remain with Father for as long as I may. I shall not think of the rest."

He subsided rather unhappily, and a morbid silence fell over the siblings. At length he said, "I'll have to leave this evening. Dixon says there is a train leaving Outwood at eleven."

She nodded. "I will walk with you to the train."

"Margaret, who is that man looking our way? Over there, on the horse." Frederick pulled back from what had been a tender farewell embrace and gestured behind her.

Margaret felt a leaden drop in her stomach as she looked in the direction her brother indicated. A rider had drawn up his mount, seemingly arrested by something. Good heavens, it was *he*. His dark top hat was pulled down low, and he wore a high-collared coat against the evening damp, but a shaft of lantern light struck his face. She would know those eyes anywhere...and just now, they were staring at her.

"It is Mr Thornton," she managed in a strangled tone. "He is the friend Father told you of."

"I jolly well wish I could have known him," Frederick lamented. He gave a tip of his hat to the other man, and Mr Thornton made a stiff response in kind. His rigid jaw set, and he turned his horse away— back towards Marlborough Mills.

"Well! Not a very friendly chap. If I did not know better, I would think he believed me to be some enemy," Frederick huffed.

"Do not be hasty to judge. Something has displeased him, for that is not his usual bearing," Margaret apologised. "You would find him more than agreeable if you had seen how gentle he was with Mama." Why she found it necessary to defend *him* to her brother she could not say, but she could not be easy allowing Frederick to think the worst of him.

Frederick grimaced. "Then I am sorry to have insulted your friend. I do hope he remains a friend so you have someone in this God-forsaken city."

"We are far from alone."

He studied her in the weak glow of the gas lanterns, then shook his head. "I hope you are not deceiving yourself, Margaret. Come, it is nearly time for my train. My ticket—"

"I will fetch it," Margaret insisted. "Stay out here in the dark, so no one sees you."

Before he could protest, she was hastening to the office. She pressed through the few scattered passengers warming themselves by the stove and made her way to the counter. There were more than she had expected at this time of night, and she glanced about uneasily. None seemed to care that a lady had entered their midst until her gaze fell upon one among them who seemed familiar.

He removed his hat, revealing a thinning patch of hair and a face she could not help but recognise. "Miss Hale!"

She blinked, and her breath caught raggedly in her throat.

He came forward, offering a smile that was more than welcoming. "You may not recall, but we have been introduced. Hamper, Benjamin Hamper at your service. I believe we met at the Thorntons' dinner party."

She curtsied numbly. "I remember, Mr Hamper."

"Ah, if you are waiting for a passenger from the London train, Miss Hale, I believe everyone has already got off. I only waited because there was some mishap and my bags were damaged. The cargo master is speaking to his supervisor just now."

"That is unfortunate," Margaret answered neutrally. "Good evening, Mr Hamper."

She paid for Frederick's ticket, glancing only once over her shoulder before she turned away and hurried back out of the office. She found Frederick standing on the platform near where the baggage handlers were skulking about their duties.

"Margaret, what is the matter?"

"I encountered someone I knew, that is all. But he would not know you, and…and I do not see him any longer," she added with another cautious look backwards. "Please, Fred, you must hurry. Have you got your bags?"

"Yes, here. Margaret, I—"

"Hale!"

Frederick whirled about, but Margaret saw his eyes in that fleeting instant of recognition. It was a baggage handler, and he was pushing her aside, almost knocking her down as he reached for Frederick. *Leonards.*

A sickening sort of delirium washed through her as she watched the assailant dragging her beloved brother back on the platform, locking him into a fighting grip, and crying out his condemned name to all and sundry. But Frederick was taller and more fit—moreover, he was not the worse for drink as Leonards clearly was. He rallied, he wrested from the other's grip, but then Leonards thrust out his leg and both tumbled together.

"Fred!" she cried.

The two men grappled still more, and it was Leonards who was on top, Leonards who gained his feet first. But when he bent to reach again for Frederick, the latter rolled away and gave a mighty shove against his attacker. Leonards, off his balance and already swaying, staggered headfirst off the platform. They heard him groan, saw him rubbing his bruised crown, but he did not rise at once.

"Fred, you must run!" she urged.

He nodded, his face white with shock and terror. The train whistle blew, and the conductor cried out for all remaining passengers to board. "Margaret, are you well?"

"Yes, yes, but you must go. Now, Fred, before he rises!"

"But I cannot leave you after this! Suppose he—"

"Fred, the train is rolling. You must go now!"

Frederick gazed at her for a long second, then hastily kissed her gloved knuckles. "God bless you, Margaret." He dove for the door, caught it, and leaned out the window. "I will write as soon as I can!"

She pressed her fist to her mouth and waited anxiously as the train rolled out of sight. Only when the lantern from the last car turned out of view did she permit herself to breathe, and she discovered that her hands were shaking.

She had not stirred from that spot where Fred had bid his adieu—had forgotten in her moment of blind terror exactly where she was standing, but a muttered oath caught her ears. She stilled, then watched in horror as a hand reached over the platform. A head followed, and then Leonards' stained, leering smile.

"Ain't you a pretty piece. You must be the Hale wench. Come down here—" His hand locked around her walking boot and he pulled.

Margaret screamed, her arms wheeling back as she sought her balance. She tried to pull her foot away, but he gave a jerk and she fell backwards, her petticoat showing and her other ankle well within his reach. She kicked at his face with her heel, felt it connect, and gasped in frantic relief when his hand fell away.

"Miss Hale! Miss, are you well?"

Margaret rolled to her hip and looked dazedly over her shoulder. Mr Hamper ran to her and bent low, offering his hand up. She took it without thinking, and he helped her to her feet.

"What are you doing out here still, Miss Hale? Were you attacked?"

"I...I fell," she mumbled.

He gave her a dubious look. "I saw you fighting someone. Come, Miss Hale, who was it? I will have the blackguard taken up by the authorities! I'll call the magistrate this very night."

"No! It was nothing—I slipped, sir."

"Well, now, if you will not say, then I...who is that?" Mr Hamper pointed, and Margaret could see Leonards' dark uniform as he stumbled off. He was clutching his side and moaning faintly, but he was leaving.

Mr Hamper turned back and regarded her in heavy silence for a moment. "Miss Hale, permit me to escort you home."

She agreed, not knowing what else she could have done. Not five minutes later, she wished she had asked to remain in the rail office.

"There will be talk of this," Hamper was warning. "Mark my words, Miss Hale. Too many people saw—oh, I fear I may have pronounced your name a bit too loudly. But never fear, Miss Hale. I am quite willing to set matters right. Why, it has been lonely these last two years without my Clarabelle. A man likes to have a wife about to keep up some idle chatter, you know."

"I suppose he must," she answered reflexively. Her thoughts were still with Frederick. Would Leonards give him up? Would he pursue him to London? Or worse—would he find her, follow her, and try to attack her again to learn what he wished? Frederick's life was worth a hundred pounds—a fortune to such a man!

"Did you know I had a son, Miss Hale?"

"Hmm?" She looked up to her escort.

"Seventeen he is, but he was his mother's son. I'd like to set him up in business, but the lad has not been the same since he lost his mother. Addle-brained boy! But I think he would like you very much, Miss Hale. It might be just what he needs to put him right."

"I thank you for the compliment, sir." Her thoughts turned inward again. Was Leonards much hurt by Frederick? He could claim assault—there might be an investigation if...

"I presume I might call on your father on the morrow, Miss Hale?"

"I beg your pardon?" she asked. "My father is in deep mourning, sir. He is not receiving guests."

"Then I shall wait two days, but I dare not let it go longer," he decided.

She blinked and stopped. "Let what go longer?"

"Why! Your reputation will be greatly injured. Surely..." He gestured expansively and shook his head, a bewildered smile on his middle-aged features. "You must see, there is nothing else to be done."

She flushed. "Mr Hamper, I assure you that no such gallantry is necessary. I thank you for the escort home, but—"

"But you have your cap set for that strapping lad who boarded the train?" he asked knowingly.

Margaret's pulse nearly stopped. "For...wh-whom?"

"Has he broken your heart, Miss Hale? 'Fred,' was that his name? Oh! I care not if you are pining after another man, so long as you have no real expectations of him. The heart forgets in time."

"I do not know what you are speaking of!"

"Come now, at least two or three others saw you with him, and they all heard your name. You cannot escape it now, Miss Hale. That, coupled with the attack I witnessed, will be sure to cause you some difficulties. Have no fear, I do not doubt your virtue and would be quite willing to overlook a trace of gossip. You are a clever girl, from what I hear. A bit too outspoken, but at least you are not ignorant. A parson's daughter, is that not right? You must be proper and chaste, so that is something. And a handsome woman you are, as well! You would make a fine mistress for my home."

The blood from Margaret's head was pooling somewhere around her middle. "Mr Hamper, I must protest! I scarcely know you, and I have done nothing improper!"

He raised a brow. "And who was the gentleman you were walking out with after dark? Not your father—I saw him clearly enough to know that."

Her throat closed; a great darkness fell over her eyes. It was like that hideous day at Marlborough Mills when blackness had claimed her and she had fought to see, to move, but found herself helpless. Except this time, it was not Mr Thornton who bent over her with gentle words, who carried her to safety. It was Mr Hamper claiming her arm and directing her steps. She could speak nothing; she knew nothing more until her own door loomed and Dixon's figure appeared.

"I will escort your father to the funeral," she heard, but only vaguely. "Until then, Miss Hale."

She managed to turn, to watch him away, but the next moment she was stumbling into Dixon's motherly embrace. "There, there, Miss," clucked the old serving woman. "I told you it was too late for a lady to go out. Is Frederick safely away?"

"Y-yes." Margaret felt her way to a chair, her eyes still glazed and nearly sightless. "Frederick is safe." *But I—oh! What have I done?*

MRS HALE's funeral passed with little notice or grief by most, but not for John Thornton. The dead woman's husband had come meekly to pay his respects, but with him also had come his daughter. The circumstance was unusual but not unexpected. In fact, John had offered the use of his carriage for the family to protect Miss Hale from prying eyes, but the offer had been politely declined.

The reason, as he discovered later, was that Hamper had arrived to escort them first. He puzzled long and fretfully over this and could not recall any particular friendship between Mr Hale and Hamper. Still, he was silently grateful to his colleague for showing kindness to a family sorely in need of it. Hamper had nodded his greeting and taken a pew beside John, and no words passed between them.

John scarcely saw Margaret's face, draped in her black veil as she was. Once she accidentally caught his eye as she was turning to comfort her father, then she quickly looked away. He regarded her closely, wondering if shame had clouded those living eyes, but he could not see them. What the devil could have made her walk out with a stranger, and in the dead of night?

He would not have his answer this day. Hamper had closed in on them, stepping neatly behind Margaret's black figure as the small assembly filed out of the church. There was some pause as the grieving family stopped at the door to solemnly acknowledge the fellow mourners. Margaret gave her hand to the parson and to a neighbour or two, but him she allowed to pass with a mere dip of her shrouded head and a whispered recital of his name. Then she coaxed her bereaved father into Hamper's carriage, and he saw her no more.

At least not her person. Her image he could not erase from his mind. That shameless public embrace, that handsome youth who clung to her! Was he a cousin, a friend…a lover? The thought made his stomach roil.

John's head was hanging and his steps frenetic as he marched to his door. He intended only to dress for work again and return to the mill, but a curious tittering noise from the drawing room raised his notice. He glanced as he walked by and found Fanny cloistered with three other young ladies—each sillier than the last, if memory served. Odd giggles, flushed cheeks and fluttering fans were sufficient to inform him that their conversation was not one to interest him and he meant to pass on.

"Oh, there you are, John," Fanny called from the room. Her voice carried an amused lilt that he recognised as her particular way when she thought to make a spectacle of him before her friends. He sighed and stopped.

"You have just come from Mrs Hale's funeral, have you not?" she asked.

"I did not know you took an interest in Mrs Hale," was his deadpan retort.

Fanny cast a significant look at each of her friends. "And I heard that Miss Hale meant to attend? Did she really do so?"

"With no other family to comfort Mr Hale, I expect she did not wish for her father to attend alone."

"Oh, to be sure, Miss Hale never shrinks from venturing forth. I never saw anyone who did not fear courting scandal, but our dear Miss Hale seems not at all troubled by such a worry."

John narrowed his eyes at his sister. One of the other young ladies lost her composure and was obliged to conceal her mouth behind her handkerchief. He glanced curiously at each of them, then brushed it off as spiteful frivolity—a thing he was not unaccustomed to from Fanny or her friends.

An hour later, he was back in his office after making his rounds at the mill. He had scarcely taken his seat when a knock sounded on the door, and Hamper walked in. John braced himself for another argument about that blasted Regimental contract. However, behind Hamper came Mason, a young police inspector with whom John had worked before. Perhaps it was to be a new subject today.

"Thornton," Hamper began without preamble, "we've a delicate situation, and you are just the magistrate for the job."

John pushed aside his ledger and drew out a blank sheet of paper to take notes. "What is it, Mason?"

The inspector flipped open his hand book and began to read off the details. "Sir, this morning a body was brought in and identified as a Mr Leonards—a former baggage handler at Outwood train station."

John's cheek flinched as he wrote. *Outwood...* "Yes? Go on."

"We have multiple witnesses who testify that last evening, they saw Mr Leonards struggling on the platform with an unknown man. Leonards fell, and the other man boarded the London train. Leonards was seen later to stumble away and was found dead at five-thirty this morning by the tracks."

"You believe this other man delivered a mortal blow?"

"The coroner is still examining the body, sir. I can tell you more when he is finished."

"Leonards was a diseased drunkard, and everyone at the rail station will tell you so," Hamper interrupted. "What we need help with, Thornton, is that a lady's reputation has become entangled with this. I was a witness to most of the events—well, not the scuffle that Mason here told you of, but much of the rest—and I am here to see that her name is not harmed further."

John blinked; his hand frozen on the page. "A lady? At Outwood station in the middle of the night?"

"Now, we did not say it was the middle of the night," Hamper pointed out. "But you have the right of it, for it was the eleven o'clock train that the gentleman boarded."

The pen was somehow locked in his knotted fingers, and he could not release it. "The name of the lady?"

"Why, you saw her only this morning—you were at the funeral. Margaret Hale. I thought, since you are a friend of Mr Hale, you would be just the chap to help us."

"Miss Hale?" he breathed.

"Yes, well, she had her reasons for being out. I assure you, Thornton, the lady did no harm, and I will personally vouch for her."

John tilted his head up to peer through haze-covered eyes at his old business rival. "Personally vouch for her? How do you intend to do that?"

"Well! I saw her home and out of—may I say—a dreadfully compromising position. I shall refrain from telling more of the circumstance in which I found her, but I have just come from speaking with Mr Hale. She is to be my wife."

Mason was speaking again and Hamper still trying to talk over him, but John's ears were drumming with another kind of torment. *Margaret! Married to Hamper!* It must be a falsehood; he must have misunderstood!

"You needn't trouble yourself interviewing Miss Hale," Hamper was announcing. "I will ask again the name of the fellow she was with and then inform Mason here, but truly, Thornton, I am sure the man did nothing but perhaps hasten Leonards' death. The bounder was sick before he attacked Miss Hale."

"Attacked Miss Hale!" John staggered to his feet, his figure heaving.

Hamper changed hues. "Not Miss Hale, I meant 'before he attacked the other fellow.' Look here, Thornton, I've no idea who the other was, but it is best for us all if little inquiry is made over the affair. I am sure it was only a matter of insult and youthful brashness—you know how young men can be. Miss Hale does not regret him, I am sure of it, and I would have this scandal swept aside as much as possible before our wedding."

"Wedding!"

"Well, that is how a man marries a woman, after all. I'm to speak with the minister after I leave here for, with the bride in mourning, I would like to request special dispensation and a quick and quiet ceremony. I am sure he cannot object. You'll see to the investigation, Thornton? I should hate for the lady's reputation to be harmed in a legal proceeding. Today's gossip is quite bad enough."

"Mr Thornton," Mason added, "if you please, I shall be ready to meet you at the coroner's office at your leisure."

He said not a word, merely watched the other two as they collected their hats and left. Then John Thornton, magistrate and master, collapsed in his chair.

MARGARET LIFTED her head from the edge of the chair when the voices sounded in the outer hall. Dixon had opened the door to someone and she distinctly heard, "Miss Hale is unwell today and is not receiving company."

There was a brief silence, and then—"I imagine she must be unwell. Nevertheless, I will speak with her." It was *his* voice—Mr Thornton.

Margaret sat up and dashed the fresh tears from her cheeks.

"She is seeing no one," repeated Dixon. Margaret could imagine how Dixon was likely crossing her arms to block the towering manufacturer's way.

"I am afraid it is a legal matter, Miss Dixon," Mr Thornton replied flatly. "I have not the leisure to wait upon the lady's ailments."

"Have you no decency, sir?" Dixon cried.

Margaret could not understand Mr Thornton's next words, for they were murmured low and in clipped tones. She did hear the familiar old creak in the floor when Dixon stepped back.

"I still say you must come back tomorrow," Dixon mumbled resentfully.

"Tomorrow will be too late. It may already be. If you have a care for Miss Hale—"

Margaret rose with hasty decision and went to the door but paused at a small looking glass on a side table. Her eyes were puffy, her cheeks frightfully pale, and her hair in such a state as would have made her mother hang her head in shame. She pressed uselessly at the dark circles below her eyes, tried to liven her cheeks a bit, and opened the door to the hall.

"—don't care if you are the only magistrate from here to London!" Dixon was protesting. "Miss Hale is grieving. I cannot let you—"

"It is quite all right, Dixon," Margaret rasped. She cleared her throat as discreetly as she could and looked only at Dixon. "I will speak to Mr Thornton if it is a legal matter."

Dixon looked at first as though she meant to challenge Margaret over the matter but reluctantly excused herself. Margaret turned to Mr Thornton yet could only bring herself to look at his hands as she beckoned him into the sitting room. "Sir?"

She heard him draw a breath. "Thank you, Miss Hale."

He allowed her to precede him, then closed the door. "Forgive the manner of my intrusion today."

"Of course, sir. I understand it must be of utmost importance." She paused, half-turned away, but finally raised her eyes to his when she sensed that he was studying her. He was pale, his lips and cheeks more drawn than she had ever seen. Those dark eyes of his seemed almost black with intensity, and his shoulders—always before so straight and powerful—were rounded as if anxiety and care had bent him at last.

"Are you well, Miss Hale?"

The gentle, sincere question startled her. She blinked. "I-I am... bearing up, sir."

A flicker passed over his expression, then his features hardened once more to the familiar mask of the businessman. "As you are presently in mourning, I see no need to prolong matters. You must know why I have come."

She nodded, her eyes fixed unseeingly on his waistcoat. "Mr Leonards is dead and you must investigate it as a homicide."

He was silent for a moment and, when he spoke again, there was a curious catch in his voice. "May I ask your business at Outwood Station two nights ago?"

Margaret looked away.

"Miss Hale, I came alone today, without the police inspector, because your father is my friend. I would spare you what mortification I may, but I cannot do so without your cooperation."

The tears were stinging and she blinked ferociously. She could not cry now, not in front of *him*! "I was escorting a...a friend to his train. That is all."

"And this...friend. Does he have a name?"

Margaret lifted her chin about to face him squarely. "Naturally."

Mr Thornton raised a brow.

"Dickenson. A Mr...S-Samuel...Dickenson."

"Miss Hale," sighed he, "I had been accustomed to think of you as truthful. Whatever else you are, you are a poor liar."

Margaret bristled. "That is the name he goes by."

"And how do you know him? By what name do *you* call him, and who is he to you?"

Her chin hitched still higher. "I do not see how that is germane to the affair at hand. You came to ask after my involvement in Leonards' death, and I can only tell you what I know. He attacked a person, was repulsed, and then he went away. I do not know how he died."

Mr Thornton took a threatening step closer. "*How* was he repulsed? With mortal violence? And *whom* did he attack?"

She set her teeth and stared back into his glittering eyes. His figure seemed to waver, to sway, and then his hand fell softly upon her arm. "Miss Hale, did Leonards attack you?"

Her lips parted—how she longed to tell him all! To tell *someone*... someone who might find a way clear of the desolation that had become her life. But Mr Thornton! No, she could not tell a magistrate, one who saw matters only in black and white, about Frederick's crimes. Her fate was her own to suffer.

"*Did he?*" Mr Thornton demanded. "If you but say the word, I will close the investigation at once. I have seen the body and spoken with the doctor. Leonards was sick...may have already been dying from a degenerate stomach and wasted liver. If attacking a woman can also be added to his sins, I will call it divine justice and let the matter be at an end. Did he touch you?"

She felt herself nodding against her will. "Y-yes."

His hand eased upon her arm and he tilted his head as if examining her all over again. "Are you unhurt?"

"I am well in body." As the words left her mouth, she bit her tongue. What had made her confess so much?

"And the rest?"

His voice was low, almost tender, but a shiver overtook her. It was too much! He was too near, too gentle, too...something. She stiffened away, and his hand fell from her sleeve.

"Mr Thornton, have you any more questions? As you have said, I am in mourning, and I should like to look in on my father. He has taken my mother's death very hard."

But Mr Thornton did not stir. He gazed at her, his look full of doubt, pity, and something else she dared not name. "I am sorry, Miss Hale."

She swallowed. "Thank you."

He lingered another moment, then slowly turned. She watched him go—the shuffling steps, the broken line of his typically rigid spine. A wild, insensible longing came over her to call him back, to pour out the entire truth, and to beg for his help, plead for his understanding. He might be the only person who could...

His hand touched the latch, and he stopped. "One more question, Miss Hale." He looked back, and there was a hollow ache in his eyes that she knew from another day—a wretched day. "Why Hamper?"

Margaret clenched her eyes. "I wish I could say, Mr Thornton."

"Do you mean that you do not know, or that you will not tell me?"

Her throat was closing up again. "Both." The word sounded like a helpless squeak and she hated herself for such a display of weakness.

He was at her side again in a moment. "What could make you agree to such an engagement? What power does Hamper hold over you?"

She gazed up at him, her breath short.

"Why? In God's name, *why?*" he begged. "You are protecting him—that man at the station. Is that it?"

"I...yes. Please, Mr Thornton, I cannot tell you all. The secret is not mine!"

"Still, you protect him?" he hissed. "After he compelled you to walk out, risked your reputation, and left you alone in the night with Leonards still about? You would shield him rather than give him up—to the point of marrying a man more than twice your age for whom I know you have no kind feelings?"

A quaking from within threatened to crumple her, and she bowed her head into a knotted fist. "You do not understand!"

"Aye! I do not!" He drew a sharp breath, tightened his voice, and bent low near her ear. "But I wish to. Make me understand... Margaret. Please."

She lowered her hand. A mere tip of her chin, and she could feel his breath hot against her cheek. Something in her core trembled, urging her to step back, away from the edge of danger, but it was too tempting...too comforting to have him close.

"Do you care for him?" Mr Thornton's voice quavered.

"For Mr Hamper!"

"Hamper can rot," he snapped. "The other—whatever his name is. Do you love him?"

"I...of course." She drew in her lower lip, clamping it between her teeth. "Please, Mr Thornton, do not seek him as a murderer. He did nothing wrong!"

Mr Thornton closed his eyes, his head bobbing faintly as if he were struggling for words. "I will not. But it is he who is responsible— he who should...Miss Hale, you cannot marry Hamper."

"Do you not see? If I refuse Mr Hamper, the scandal could expose Freder—" She broke off with a gasp and covered her mouth.

"And Hamper is your cure for this evil! What power or knowledge does Hamper have that I do not?" he cried. "Better that you should wed this blackguard you care for. Frederick, is it? I will seek the man myself, if I must. I will drag his miserable carcass back here from London, or wherever he has gone, and make him marry you on pain of a trial, if need be. And if that failed, I would—"

"Please, Mr Thornton! It is impossible—everything you say. If you sought him, it would be his death!"

He was panting now. He drew back, staring in bewilderment. "How? Tell me, Miss Hale."

She sniffled, choked back a sob, and angrily dashed a tear from her cheek. "Mr Thornton, if the honest carriage of your duty permits, if you ever considered my father a friend, do him this service. Please do nothing. Others have suffered in doing their duty—now I shall do mine."

"Your father? What has he to do with this?" He shook his head. "I will not stand for it. You cannot throw yourself away on Hamper because of some misguided sense of loyalty. Let me help!"

Misguided? Had that word not slipped from his tongue and betrayed his true sentiments, Margaret might have found herself vulnerable to his pleas. He thought her foolhardy—always had. And he could never understand, surely he could not, how vital was her resolve and her need to protect Frederick. Weak, she was already. Beaten, and desperately in need of an ally. But it could not be *he*...no matter how she might long for it.

"Mr Thornton," she pronounced crisply, "if you would help, then do nothing. I will say no more on the matter."

He released a long breath and turned to the door. "Then I suppose congratulations are in order, Miss Hale. Good day."

∽

"Ah, Thornton!" Hamper rose from his desk with a jerk of his shirt cuffs. "I was just about to stop by your office. I trust that business with the dead man is all settled."

"Far from it," John growled.

"What? You do not mean that it was anything but a coincidence!" Hamper laughed. "I told you how it all happened, Thornton. No one did more harm to Leonards than he himself did."

"Leonards died of an internal haemorrhage brought on more by poor health than any blow," John confirmed. "But you said he attacked Miss Hale. What did he do to her?"

Hamper tucked his thumbs into his waistcoat. "Well now, that was a slip of the tongue. The lady was not involved."

"Hamper," John warned, his voice dropping dangerously. "Was she forced to defend herself?"

"Oh, very well. I suppose you are hardly the man to gossip about a woman's reputation and, if it helps the investigation, then so be it. I saw the wretch trying to grasp her boot, and he pulled it from under her until she fell. A shocking state she was in—I am sure I need not tell you what happens to a lady's petticoats—"

"Hamper!"

"Oh, Thornton, stop being so righteous. She kicked Leonards in the face with her boot, and that was the end of it. I helped her to her feet and saw her home."

"And what of this strange man Leonards attacked? You saw him, did you not?"

"Aye, everyone did. Young fellow—about six or seven and twenty, I should say. Handsome features, moderate build, not over-tall. Dressed like a gentleman. But from what everyone tells me, he did nothing more than break free of Leonards' grip. No one saw him strike in malice. Come, now, Thornton, do you mean to charge the man with murder or not?"

John clenched his fist as he paced across Hamper's office. "No. But I would know who he is. What do you know of him?"

"Oh! Some admirer, I suppose. Mr Hale knew all about the fellow, so I cannot think the young lady was doing anything unchaste."

"Mr Hale knew?"

"Well, he seemed to. He fell very quiet when I recounted the evening and how I came to be engaged to his daughter. I asked the same as you, you know—politely, of course, as I assumed that any man betrothed to a daughter of the house ought to have the right to. He only said the youth was some old Hampshire neighbour who had come to pay his respects to Mrs Hale and could stay no longer. I supposed that to be a bit of a falsehood but, as Miss Hale seems to hold no expectation of his return, I shall merely presume that it was a passing attraction and is at an end now."

"Miss Hale has not a capricious nature. You do the lady a disservice, Hamper."

"Did I say she was capricious? But neither is she a fool. She knows well the advantages a steady, established husband could provide. Far better than an impoverished lover! Moreover, she needs someone to marry her after all the gossip, and who else would so readily overlook such a scandalous incident?"

"A man who thinks only of his own interests," John sneered. "You are old enough to be her father. It is disgusting, Hamper."

"Ah! And this, the fellow whose eighteen-year-old sister is presently receiving calls from Miles Watson? The man is forty-five if he is a day. Be careful you do not sound the hypocrite, Thornton."

John ground his teeth. "Miss Hale is not my sister. Her interests, her motivations are not the same."

Hamper permitted a curve to his lips. "Indeed! A ball of fire that one is. I shall have to check that tongue of hers—but you seem to know my future bride rather well, Thornton."

But John would not rise to the provocation. "How did you threaten Miss Hale into an engagement? Do not persuade yourself that no one else will think the same as I. Miss Hale is Southern gentility and has no love for Milton manufacturers. Everyone knows it."

"Well, I'd say that *you* certainly do, at least."

"Her father is my friend."

"Indeed, he is! And you must have spent many an hour taking tea with his wife and daughter. Quiet evenings round the family hearth? Perhaps it is *I* who ought to be asking *you* the nature of your relationship with Miss Hale! Do you fancy her, Thornton?"

"Do not change the subject, Hamper. What do you hope to gain?"

Hamper snorted. "What every man hopes to gain upon marriage. Do you begrudge me a handsome young wife? Do you know, I'd only a vague notion of ever marrying again but, after thinking on it some while, I am rather enamoured of the idea. You ought to consider it for yourself, Thornton. The winters are long and cold, but Miss Hale— why, that lass is a right inferno." He finished with a wink and a smirk —a suggestive waggle of his eyebrows and a low chuckle.

John felt ill. He stalked near and hissed into Hamper's face—"You are indecent and vulgar, Hamper! No lady ought to be spoken of so crudely."

"And most especially not Margaret Hale? Come, admit it, Thornton! For once, I have what you can only dream of gaining. I never thought the day could come."

"You are mistaken. In fair and equal circumstances, Miss Hale would never have me, but even less would she have you. Were you not so conceited, you would see the injustice you do her by presuming an engagement."

"Injustice! I am helping the lass!"

"And did you bother thinking of *her*? Do you think she will consider herself grateful for all your supposed pains on her account when she is bound to a man she hardly knows and cannot esteem?"

Hamper crossed his arms. "By Jove, I have finally done it."

"Done what?" John spat.

"Found your weakness. There is no sense in denying it. By next week I will have broken you at last. Nay, I am not crowing my victory like a fool. We need each other, our mills do. We have always stuck together, have we not? But always, you had the upper hand and lorded it over us underlings. It is a curious feeling to have that reversed."

John felt his shoulders heaving as he simply stared at Hamper. "Let her out of this sham of an engagement. Now, before more harm is done!"

"Let her out! Do you hear yourself, Thornton? She has no choice, and it was not my doing. What, do you mean to sweep in on your white charger? Marry her yourself if I will but stand aside? Not bloody likely. But I will tell you what I will do; I will keep matters quiet. No public announcement yet, though I daresay every day that goes by casts more shame upon her. However,if you have such qualms about my marriage to Miss Hale, perhaps I will give you a day or two more to accustom yourself to the idea. 'Tis the least I can do for an old friend, eh?"

John glared at his counterpart—a man with whom he had shared whiskey and cigars, a man who had sided with him in every Union conflict and sent flowers to his mother when a distant relation had died. All this, and he barely knew the man. "What game are you playing, Hamper?"

"No game. But if it *were* a game, I should say that I just won."

"Oh, it's yo', Miss."

Margaret rose from the table where she had been helping Mary cut vegetables for the family's supper. "Nicholas, how do you do this afternoon?"

He sagged into a chair and began to tug at his boots, disregarding

Margaret's quick and embarrassed turn of the head. "Wear' from goin' on tramp."

"You still have not found work?"

"Nay, and it's thine ould friend 'hoo's ter thank."

Margaret's ears heated. "Mr Thornton is hardly my friend."

"Thornton! If 'twere Thornton, I coul' tell yo' straight-like what I think on him, and he'd fight me like a man. But Hamper!"

She slowly resumed her seat, a pit forming in her stomach as the reality she had tried to ignore this last hour rose up to confront her. She had hoped Nicholas had not heard, but the man seemed to know every whisper in the whole city. And he was indignant.

He shook his head and his gaze hardened in glittering resentment. "Dinna think yo'd be like a' the rest."

"What can you mean by that?" she asked hoarsely.

Higgins snorted and ignored her. "Where's my soup, Lass?" he demanded of Mary.

Mary hastened to bring her father something, and both pointedly looked away from Margaret. She felt her shoulders hunching consciously as she gazed between them. She had thought that here, at least, she might still be welcome, but...perhaps not. "Nicholas," she mumbled, "It is not what it appears."

"Oh! 'Tisn't, 'tis it?"

Margaret caught his eye, then glanced at the Boucher children gathered at his feet. "Just as you have made choices to protect others and do as you felt was right, so must I."

He snorted and shook his head. "So that's how it's to be! What did I say, Mary? I allus said yo'd one day set up for one o' the masters, but Hamper? Yo've sold out, Miss, and I'll n'a say 'nother word on it."

Margaret toyed with the edge of her sleeve. "Mr Hamper is eligible as any other. He is willing to offer his protection—"

"Why don' yo' say it, Lass? Yo' like his fancy house and his purse. Aye, yo'll be well set up as the mistress. A blood-sucker, Hamper is, claimin' wha' he don' merit."

"It is not like that," Margaret insisted—in vain, she could see, for Nicholas grunted and looked away. "I hope we can still be friends."

"Friends! You'll n'a be for coming to see us anymore, an' I won' darken Hamper's door. A cur an' a swine he is."

"I thought you reserved such vitriol for Mr Thornton," she said with a weak smile.

"'Least Thornton's a man I co' respect, and none too bad a catch if yo' take my meanin'. But Hamper—don' know wha' yo'd be thinkin'. Where's my bread, Mary?"

Margaret subsided in humiliation and excused herself only a few moments later. Nicholas refused to speak with her any further despite the sympathetic looks he was casting her way as she bade a good evening to the children. She said a word of thanks to Mary for her hospitality and braved the streets.

Everyone seemed to be watching her. She could not quite decide how utterly that sentiment resulted from her own guilty conscience. Yes! She felt guilty—in guarding Frederick, she had betrayed herself and all who knew her. How could she not reproach herself? The one mercy was that, so far, Mr Hamper had displayed some delicacy for her state of mourning and had not forced her to acknowledge the engagement openly, but there it was. She must accept him or surrender Fred.

Her respite, it seemed, must come to an end. Mr Hamper was right —the more time passed before the engagement was known, the more her own reputation was damaged on the streets. A secret lover, a late-night rendezvous only hours before her mother's funeral! A trollop and a fancy piece for some wandering gentleman—that was what everyone thought of her. Why, even Dixon could confirm the rumours, for the family servant could not go to the market without being assailed by those plying her for gossip.

Margaret blinked uncomfortably away as she passed four young ladies on the street. The way they tipped their heads together and cast sidelong glances at her was enough to persuade her that her name had just been in the air. Her cheeks burning, she hitched her chin higher and walked on.

Safely inside her own door once more, she made straightaway for her father's room. No one else could counsel her so tenderly! But he was not himself just now and, need him though she might, he needed her still more. Margaret paused with her fingers resting on the door and looked on in pity.

Mr Hale's head was bent over his desk, his hand outstretched as if he held another's. He was speaking in that dream-like way that had been his of late. "When spring comes, Maria, I will take you out for that picnic. Do you remember the picnics we would have in Helstone? Down by Potter's Glen—you would have the fresh biscuits and butter packed, and we would sit on that old quilt my mother made. Do you recall the roses in the hedge? How fine they looked in your hair! We shall ask Margaret to bring her paints and frame a pretty likeness for your room."

Margaret thinned her lips and gently knocked upon the door. Her father's head jerked up, and he sought his spectacles. "Margaret? You've come back."

She eased into a chair near him. "Yes, Father. I was only out to see Mary Higgins."

He tilted his head anxiously. "Something troubles you, Margaret. Is there more talk?"

She sighed. "I am afraid it is to be expected. Too many people saw…"

"But…Frederick *is* safe," he confirmed. "You said he boarded the train and was not followed."

She smiled gently and patted her father's hand. "Yes, Fred is safe."

His expression dropped, and he regarded her over the rim of his spectacles. "Then we must see to it that he remains so. I do not believe I trust Mr Hamper's word should he learn all."

"He never shall," Margaret declared. Her jaw was fixed, and there was a hardness to her tone that made her father draw back. "We shall never tell him, and there were no others who knew of Frederick."

"But how could you keep it a secret? You said that Leonards shouted his name, and you were clearly recognised. Any curious man would make inquiries of his wife's affairs, and I fear that Mr Hamper is more curious than he will say."

"Which is why I *must* marry him." Margaret blinked back the sudden rush of tears that scalded her eyes when she choked on those words. "That way, no matter what he does learn, he will still be obliged to protect his lawful brother rather than to give him up."

Mr Hale shook his head, his already pale complexion taking on a sickly hue. "Oh, my child, I pray you rethink this notion. Surely, Mr Hamper will never suit! I cannot think of you bound to him—why, he is not at all worthy of you! And I think he is the same age as Mari—" Hale faltered, and Margaret squeezed his hand as her father bowed his head.

"Do you know, Margaret," he managed after a moment, "I believe what I regret the most is all that your mother and I never did."

She caressed the worn old fingers. "What do you mean?"

His mouth worked as his watery eyes lifted—avoiding her and seeking the thin grey light of the window. "Everything I never gave her. I have never been a wealthy man but, do you know, Margaret, it was not riches or finery she desired. It was more of *us*. That was what she really wanted, but she wept over the material things because, after we lost Frederick, she gave up on me and on what might have been."

His throat bobbed and his chest seemed to quaver but, after some time, he gave a slow, steady nod. "Margaret, I cannot lose another child."

"But you have not lost me, Father. I am here—even if I marry, I will be near and I will see that you are well-cared for."

He shook his head vehemently, as a recalcitrant child who cannot make himself understood. "No, no, Margaret, it will never do. Have you not heard Nicholas speak of Mr Hamper? He is deceitful and hard. I dare not trust him with either of my children but especially not you. You deserve a man who can understand you...who can appreciate his good fortune! I would see you matched in the heart and never discontented or settling for less, as your mother and I did. Is there—there must be some other way! Can you not simply speak with him and ask him to release you from the engagement?"

Margaret gazed sorrowfully at her hands. "I have tried. I care not for the gossip, but I am afraid of what he could do, and he was most insistent upon it. I believe he finds it to be some advantage that he does not care to lose. Whenever I exhibited the least reluctance, he would deliberately ask me more information about Frederick. I would not tell, but he could see that I was not being truthful and how his interest frightened me. He knew just how to silence me."

"And so it is!" Mr Hale mourned. "My dearest child to be bound to a monster who would claim her as a thing to be possessed! But surely, Margaret, the man can be worked upon." Then, as if pricked by a sudden thought, he suggested, "I shall ask John. Yes, that will do. I will send him a note to see if he might stop by. Perhaps he can help."

Margaret's inner parts turned to ice. "Oh, no, not Mr Thornton! Please, Father! We ought not to trouble him—"

"But what else would a friend do but offer aid at such a time? We must tell him everything, of course, but I feel certain that he can do what no other can. Yes, I shall speak to John at once," Mr Hale decided.

He rose quickly, his movements powered by an urgency and a resolve Margaret had only seen once—the day when his conscience had driven him out of his comfortable Helstone and into the unknown. He sought something to write with, pausing only a moment when he discovered a portrait of his late wife beside his notepaper. Margaret held her breath, prepared for tears and despair, but her father gently pushed aside her mother's portrait and touched Frederick's. He drew a shaken breath and nodded firmly to himself, then searched for a pen.

Dear John, he wrote, then the pen trembled in the air as he stared at the paper.

"But what shall you tell him?" Margaret protested. "Surely, you cannot tell *him* about Frederick. What will he say? He is a magistrate, Father. Moreover, he..."

Mr Hale turned round. "He what?"

Margaret's mouth moved, but the words were reluctant. "He...that is, he and I are...not good friends."

"No, but you are hardly enemies any longer, are you? He has always spoken highly of you, and you have said yourself that you admire his ethics and cannot fault his honour."

"But to tell him about Fred! It is madness. Why, how should we trust even him? There must be another way."

Mr Hale pursed his lips and drew a few unsteady sighs as he regarded her. "No, Margaret, you are wrong. Apart from Bell, who is too far away at present to be of help, I believe Mr Thornton might be the only man I *can* trust where the safety of my children is concerned. In fact, I ought to have told him of Frederick sooner, for I think he has heard something of it already and is rather offended that I have said nothing."

"Heard something?" Margaret stiffened. "Yes, of course, he was the magistrate involved in Leonards' death. How I wished I could have spared you that knowledge, Father!"

But Mr Hale was waving her off and dipped his pen again. "No, no, I believe Bell may have spoken. He might have, you know, when he first wrote to John about my coming to Milton. I am sure of it for, since Frederick was here, John has seemed rather distant. Surely I have offended him. I ought to have said…" He stopped again as he fumbled about the desk for something to blot his paper.

"Father, please consider!" She came to him, caught his elbow, and pleaded. "I can bear my future. Truly I can! But I could not bear it if Frederick were exposed. What is a lesser life for myself when his could be taken? No, Father!"

"Margaret," he murmured in a low tone, "I shall ask you only this: which man is known for saying one thing and doing another?"

Margaret set her jaw. "Mr Hamper."

"And which conducted himself with mercy and justice after the riots?"

She closed her eyes. "Mr Thornton."

"I shall send John a note. I do hope he can come this very afternoon."

JOHN SCARCELY LIFTED his head at the knock on the door. If he ignored it, whoever it was would probably go away. His letter was far more critical than any mill crisis. He dipped his pen again.

The knock sounded once more. He frowned, then completed the line he was composing.

A third knock echoed.

"Very well, damn you," he grumbled and rose from his desk. He thought to catch his coat but, if the intruder was so impertinent, he would bloody well receive them in his shirt sleeves. "Come in."

The first thing he saw was the lady's gloved fingers on the latch, and he knew. *Margaret.* He hastened to the door.

"Miss Hale!"

She hesitated, her eyes widening faintly when they fell on his informal attire. He retreated quickly for his coat, but not before he noted the delicate blush to her cheeks.

"Forgive me for interrupting you, sir."

"Not at all. Will you be seated?" He gestured to the chair before his desk but was secretly relieved when she coloured again and declined. Had she taken the seat, he would have been obliged to do the same and his work-covered desk would have stood between them.

Margaret bent her head and withdrew a note from her coin purse. "My father wrote this for you and asked for it to be delivered, but Dixon and Martha were out. He felt it urgent."

John took it with a sceptical frown. "And you substituted yourself for an errand boy who would have brought it for a ha'p'orth?"

Again, those chiselled cheeks darkened. "It is a matter of some delicacy, as I am sure you must understand."

He grunted and slowly read Mr Hale's cultured script...then stopped cold. Lifting his eyes again to Margaret, he found her fidgeting with her glove tips and trembling. "What is this mystery your father speaks of? Shall I guess?"

"I doubt you could," she returned flatly.

"Nevertheless, I shall try. Your father objects to his gently bred daughter being betrothed to a manufacturer. He has corresponded with this...er...*admirer* of yours, and there remains some obstacle to your safe betrothal to the man. Perhaps he is not free to marry or is in need of money or has run afoul of the law. Or perhaps he is unwilling, and your father is begging of me to threaten him into an engagement by reopening the murder investigation?"

She cast her eyes to the ceiling and snatched her father's note back. "My father is not one who readily yields sensitive intelligence on any matter, and you mock him when he begs for that privilege?"

He held up his hands. "Forgive me, Miss Hale, but I am only acting the bitter, calloused brute that you no doubt expect."

She studied him—a fine line appearing between her brows and her lips drawn into a thoughtful rosette. She startled him by her gentle, almost remorseful tones when she spoke. "I am sure you could cast the blame for that at my feet. I have been unkind and unfeeling, but you have done better than I. Whatever else you have been, you were always honest with me."

He opened his mouth for a ready retort but failed to utter it. Swallowing, he heard his voice crack. "Perhaps, Miss Hale, you will do me the courtesy of accepting my apology."

Her rigid posture relaxed somewhat, and she drew a long sigh of apparent relief. "If you will accept mine, sir." She put out her hand—a gesture previously foreign to her ways that spoke much of her sincerity.

He clasped it eagerly and held it somewhat longer than was proper, but she did not pull away. Instead, she steadily met his gaze with eyes rimmed by moisture. "Mr Thornton, I need your help."

"Anything, Miss Hale."

"The truth is—" she turned away to pace and visibly repressed a shudder as she continued brokenly—"I do not wish to marry Mr Hamper."

"I knew that. What made you agree to it? Will you trust me with the truth this time?"

She looked back, a soulful, aching expression in her eyes. "It is one thing to trust someone with my own life. It is quite different to trust someone with another's life."

He followed her across the room and reached boldly again for her hand. "Your life! Miss Hale, I am already indebted to you for *my* own

life. Have you so readily forgotten? You may not count it an obligation, but I do, and I bless you each day I draw breath. Aye, I have
confessed my heart to you—you cannot claim ignorance, but know
that I cherish your happiness above my own. Though it cost me all, if
you ask anything, I would do it."

She had grown pale; the curve of her nostrils flared in astonishment and her fingers slackened in his own. "Mr... Mr Thornton, I..."
She gently cleared her throat and tried again. "Sir, I cannot know
what to say to such a speech."

He gazed steadily down into her face, wishing to burn that impression into his memory for the rest of his years. "Ask what you will. Tell
me what you must. But please do not go yet." If only he could savour
this nearness, this vulnerability for a lifetime!

Her eyes rounded and, for a moment, he thought she would become
faint. But then something even more extraordinary happened. A tear slid
down her cheek...and then another. It was as if a tide had been unleashed,
and she began to shiver, to quake, and dipped her head before him.

"Miss Hale—Margaret," he called softly. She attempted to lift her
head, but a gasp escaped her, and she gripped his hand with a
desperate fervour.

His heart pulsed and ached. Daring, he held his breath and grazed
his fingertips over her cheek, brushing away the tears. "What are you
so afraid of telling me?" he asked, his voice as gentle as he could make
it. How he longed to gather her against his chest! She was listing,
tipping unsteadily as if some magnetic allure drew her close, but still
she tottered in uncertainty.

She gave one more strangled sob, bowing still more as her hair
nearly touched his shoulder. Then she sucked in a few short draughts
of air, making a visible effort to straighten. His hand fell away, and she
seemed to glance at it in some regret before swallowing and looking
into his face. "Mr Thornton, I—I must trust you...what I mean is that
no matter your true thoughts, you have ever been good."

"Good? I have been a fool. Had I been less prideful, I might have
bent more easily—might have made a friend of you."

"But you *have* done so," she insisted. "And I could not have trusted one who was any less..." Another gasp—the remnant of tears—shook her anew and she put a hand to her face.

"Permit me," he offered, and touched his own handkerchief to her cheek as her grey eyes gazed up in silent wonder. "Margaret, you know I could never let any harm come to you. Aye, I would sweep you away and make you my own if I could but, if I cannot, then at least know that much. Tell me how I can help."

She drew her upper lip between her teeth and studied him for a second or two before bracing herself. "I have a brother," she blurted all in a rush.

"What?" He shook his head. "A brother? How?"

She closed her eyes and swayed slightly. "It is hard to...please, may I sit a moment?"

He led her to the chair, but rather than distancing himself in a seat of his own, he crouched at her knee, retaining her hand for himself. "Frederick...Hale," he murmured. His brow pinched. "I have heard that name somewhere before."

She bobbed an unsteady acknowledgment. "If you did not hear it from your witness statements, you may have read it in the paper. Fred went to the navy when he was young. He was accused of mutiny six years ago and has been an exile ever since. It was my mother's dying wish to see him again, and so he came." She bit her lips together and stared expectantly—as if waiting for him to denounce her. "This is my father's great secret—he wished to trust you with it. He is waiting even now to tell you of it."

"And so...rather than give your brother up or let word of his presence on English soil spread, you took the scandal upon yourself? How did Hamper enter into this?"

"He heard Frederick's Christian name when Leonards cried out—or perhaps it was my own cry. He certainly saw Frederick's face, nearer than any other did. If I allow gossip and curious talk to spread of some rumoured lover until someone begins repeating his name or, worse, offend Mr Hamper, who can identify him, then Frederick is lost. Mr Thornton, my brother is innocent, and I would make a pact with the Devil himself to save him."

"I believe you have found one of his messengers, at least," John growled. "Hamper knows what he is about, blackmailing you as he is doing. Before you ask, I have already spoken with him and he proved rather immovable."

She looked crestfallen. "I see," she answered, her tones fragile. She stared blindly for half a moment, then bent to gather her skirt. "Then I shall trouble you no more."

"Margaret, wait."

The familiar name had slipped from his tongue again, but this time the haughty indignation of former days gave way to gentle awe. Her expressive brow furrowed, and she stilled, gazing at him in such a tender, broken manner that his heart seemed to seize. Slowly, he dared to claim her other hand.

"Margaret," he repeated, "I did not say I was without hope, nor that I meant to yield easily to Hamper's intentions."

He watched her throat tremble as she began to blink rapidly. "But what is to be done? I have no means of persuading him, nothing but myself to offer."

"'Tis too high a price! I know Hamper—know him well. Despite your present experience, you must understand that he is far from a sadist. He does not cause pain to give himself pleasure but rather to bring pressure to bear—to seek his own ends."

"But what does he want? I have nothing, can do nothing for him."

"There, you are wrong. I expect his first thought was that he had won himself a handsome young gentlewoman for his bride—a prize, indeed, for nearly every single man of new wealth longs for such a feather for his cap. However, I think he still might have been persuaded to forget the scheme had it not been for me."

"For you?" She drew a sharp breath. "I have said nothing to anyone of—"

He squeezed her hand. "You did not need to. It was all my own doing. I acted the brash idiot, blustering my demands and thinking I had the right to issue orders, all because of my offended pride.

Hamper devoured the whole scene—why, I imagine it was the greatest thrill he had known in years, knowing he had bested me and that I was undone by it."

She lowered her gaze to their hands, and her thumb brushed lightly over the back of his knuckles. "You are far nobler than I deserve."

"Noble! What were my actions but those of a jealous fool? I expected to hear you chastise me, and you would have every right. Aye, I did interfere—and I mean to do more, but I shall keep my head about me. I'll not disgrace you again by making a scene, but I cannot stand by and let you marry Hamper."

"But what is to be done?"

He smiled and lifted his hand to caress her cheek once more, thrilling in the way she closed her eyes and seemed to melt into his touch. "I had already thought of something. In fact, I was working on that notion when you came in and, with your blessing, I shall bring the matter to Hamper. But please do not ask me what it is—not yet."

She blinked, then lowered her face into his palm with an expression of surrender. "I will trust you, then."

~

"THORNTON, I never thought I would see the day." Hamper rose from his desk, his eyes still on the letter in his hand. "Lost your head, you have."

"My head I can do without," John clipped. "Are we agreed?"

Hamper folded the letter once more and gave it back. "You truly mean to send this? You will give up the Regimental contract and all that easy income? What, oh great and mighty Thornton, do you think your hands will have to say on that?"

"Marlborough Mills is secure enough without the contract," John lied. "So long as there is work, my hands will be content."

Hamper permitted a half-grin. "Don't worry, Thornton. When you fail, I promise to hire your best workers."

"I trust you will not find that necessary." John tucked the letter into his breast pocket. "I will post this at once. About Miss Hale—"

Hamper snorted. "I shall forget I ever knew the lass. But that is just the trick, is it not? For I expect I shall encounter her frequently, if you have any say in the matter."

John narrowed his eyes, then turned to collect his hat. "Good day, Hamper."

~

"COME, now, Miss Margaret, you're naught but skin and bones," Dixon clucked. "You must eat something."

Margaret stood resolutely by the window, her hands clasped quietly and her figure straight and tall. Her inner being, however, was in turmoil. Her heart was hammering in her throat and every nerve tingled with a sick kind of dread and longing.

"Dear me," Dixon muttered as she came closer, "You look like a ghost, Miss."

"Do not be concerned for me," Margaret managed unsteadily. "How is Father?"

Dixon shook her head. "Says he won't rest till Mr Thornton comes. I told him—"

Margaret stiffened and put out her hand. Her eyes had never left the window, and a familiar shape—a figure that inspired as much comfort as bewilderment—had just passed by. She tilted her head to follow the cut of his shoulders for another step or two, then drew back. "Dixon, we have a caller."

An instant later, his firm hand echoed upon the door, and Dixon left to receive him. *Had that knock sounded confident or vexed?* Margaret dashed to the looking glass and sighed in frustration when she beheld her own pale countenance. She swallowed, passed a trembling hand over her skirts, and then braced herself for the door to open.

Her first glimpse of his face told her all. His jaw was relaxed, his brow smooth, and the line of his mouth easy. There was a searching in his eyes, a hopefulness that had marked them once before. This time, she would rather die than to crush him again.

She went forward, her hands extended, and he took both with a light, reverent touch. "All is well," he reported.

His words broke some kind of reservoir, and her whole body shuddered in relief. She closed her eyes for composure and, when she opened them again, he had drawn nearer. "How did you do it?"

One side of his mouth pulled up. "Hamper and I each had something the other held dear. I offered him what he most desired, and he is content."

She regarded him carefully, her breath tight in her chest. "And you?"

His expression became at once guarded and vulnerable—hesitant but sanguine together. "That remains to be seen."

"Can you be in any doubt?" she asked softly. "How could I be anything but grateful? I owe you—"

"No." He shook his head vehemently. "You owe me nothing. I will not have your gratitude, Margaret, just as you would not accept mine once before. I did what I felt I must. Let there never again be talk between us of debt or obligation."

She permitted the shadow of a smile. "Then what may I say without giving offence? Shall I speak of scandal? For you must know, I am not untouched by rumour. What is said of me on the street—"

"I care nothing for that. You know I would offer you my protection, but that is not why I came."

She glanced down at their hands, still joined, and tightened her fingers. There was something so natural in his touch...so *whole*. And for the first time, she discovered that she understood him as she could understand no other. His was no simple character—the depths of his ways might take her years to fully comprehend and they would never agree on all matters. But what they did share, that which they held kindred, was more powerful than misapprehension and more foundational than opposing perspectives.

He was waiting; his chest seemed tight with restrained breath, his eyes intense. Boldly he had come, and now boldly she would answer.

"Mr Thornton?"

"Margaret?"

She smiled—fully and easily this time. "John—will you marry me?"

His eyes widened in astonishment. He gasped, nearly laughing, and caught her around the waist. "Good heavens, Woman, you insist on catching me off my guard! Yes, again and again. With my last breath —yes."

At last she was free to let go, free to laugh, and she did. His arms tightened around her, and there was nothing to do but to rest her hands on his shoulders, then slide them up to cradle his face. As he lowered his head, she touched her brow to his and simply held him.

"Margaret," he breathed, almost as a mantra. "Love, I can scarcely believe it is true."

She brushed her thumb over the proud line of his cheek and her smallest fingers tickled the tender flesh below his ear. "How can I convince you that I am perfectly in earnest?"

Those dark eyes seemed to speak, to ask. His head lowered still more, he drew one last breath, and his warm lips caressed hers. She gave herself wholly to his embrace—forgetting for a moment where her self came to an end and his began.

John—her own John—pulled her gently closer until she pressed against his heart. Every sigh, every pulse they shared, even as his mouth left hers to nuzzle her cheek. A shiver coursed over her skin. There was so much she would say to him! So much to be spoken over, to be brought into the light. But for now, it was enough to describe feeling without words, to breathe the same breath and dwell in the same essence.

A creak from the floorboards drew her back to the present, and she lifted her head to look over John's shoulder. Her father stood there, his hand to his mouth.

John turned—one hand fell away, but the other remained possessively at her waist. Margaret met her father's eye, her own arm still wrapped round John as she raised her chin.

Mr Hale blinked and trembled as he looked from one to the other...and then he wept tears of joy.

~

Nicole Clarkston is a book lover and a happily married mom of three. Originally from Idaho, she now lives in Oregon with her own romantic hero, several horses, and one very fat dog. She has loved crafting alternate stories and sequels since she was a child, and she is never found sitting quietly without a book or a writing project.

Nicole Clarkston's books include *No Such Thing as Luck, Northern Rain, Nowhere but North, Rumours and Recklessness, The Courtship of Edward Gardiner, These Dreams, London Holiday, Nefarious,* and *Rational Creatures (Anthology).*

LOOKING TO THE FUTURE

Nancy Klein

"I have not the slightest wish to pry into the gentleman's secrets,' he said, with growing anger. 'My own interest in you is—simply that of a friend. You may not believe me, Miss Hale, but it is—in spite of the persecution I'm afraid I threatened you with at one time—but that is all given up; all passed away...I see we are nothing to each other. If you're quite convinced that any foolish passion on my part is entirely over, I will wish you good afternoon.' He walked off very hastily." - Chapter XXXIX, North and South

~

*N*ot long after Margaret and Mr. Bell concluded their trip to Helstone, Dixon arrived in London from Milton, ready to resume her post as Margaret's maid, confidante, and protector. Her morning arrival caused a flurry of interest in the house on Harley Street, the city being thin of company. In an unheard-of display of courtesy to a servant, Aunt Shaw asked Dixon to join the women when she brought in the tea tray so that Margaret could hear all the news from Milton.

Dixon entertained them with snippets of Milton gossip, key of which was her ebullient enthusiasm over Miss Thornton's wedding. From her lookout on a side street near the church the day of the wedding, and supplemented by information from the Thornton's housemaid Martha, she was able to provide elaborate descriptions of the bridesmaids, flowers, and dresses.

'The lace—I have never seen so much lace on one gown. It was all the women could talk about! Miss Thornton's dress cost a pretty penny, as did the breakfast—so much food, and of such quality! Not just the usual breakfast fare, but ham and venison and pigeon—and all sorts of accompaniments. And an iced fruit cake! Many said it was much too grand a wedding, considering the losses suffered by Marlborough Mills during the strike.'

Dixon paused to allow her listeners to pose questions but, to her great disappointment, none were forthcoming. Aunt Shaw sniffed, as if the discussion of the affairs of Milton people left a disagreeable odour in the parlour, grand wedding notwithstanding. Edith smiled vaguely, trying to decide which dress to wear to dinner that evening— Henry was coming and no doubt bringing the latest up-and-coming politician to grace her table. Only Margaret, bent over her needlework and a complicated set of French knots, seemed mildly attentive. Unbeknownst to Dixon, Margaret burned with interest to hear any news of Milton and its inhabitants, although she refrained from asking any direct questions. She had heard much of Fanny's affairs, but what of Fanny's brother? She longed to hear that he was well and had hope of recovering his prospects.

Having exhausted her trove of information about the wedding, Dixon moved on to the topic heavy on her heart—how little money articles of furniture owned by the Hales (and cherished by Dixon) had fetched at the auction.

'I consider it a downright shame when you consider how wealthy Milton folks are. Mrs. Thornton—now, she's a sharp one—she came and snatched up several bargains. But, don't you worry, Miss

Margaret—Mr. Thornton came the next day and paid too much! He bid against himself several times, anxious as he was to acquire what he had set his eye upon—that little sewing table of your mother's! Imagine that! How the crowd did laugh and jeer at him for his absentmindedness! So, Miss, if Mrs. Thornton paid too little, Mr. Thornton paid too much, and all came out well at the end.' Dixon finished her tale with a great smile of satisfaction at having bested the Master of Marlborough Mills.

Margaret reddened with chagrin at this news. How little she understood him! Spending money on a sister's lavish wedding was one thing, but bidding on objects from her parents' house to supplement their small income while his prospects suffered was intolerable. And the sewing table, which he must know had been dear to her mother—and of little use to him!—showed a tender side to his otherwise iron character. She had come to realize over those last months in Milton that she had grievously misjudged him, growing to appreciate him only after she had given him reason to despise her.

Dixon's recital heaped burning coals upon her head. How she wished she could meet him once more to thank him for this small kindness—and to judge if Mr. Bell had been to Milton and imparted the news about her brother!

To turn her mind from this question that plagued her incessantly, she asked breathlessly, 'And what of Higgins, Dixon? Any news of how he and Mary fare? And the Boucher children?'

Dixon sniffed. Her bias against the working class in Milton made her memory vague on this point. 'Nicholas was well, or so I heard. He came to the house several times asking for news of you, Miss—the only person who did ask, except once Mr. Thornton. And Mary has gone to work at Mr. Thornton's mill because her father wants her to learn to cook, whatever that means. I'm sure I can't puzzle it out.'

Clever Nicholas, Margaret thought with a smile. He has gotten his lunchroom for the workmen and a livelihood for Mary. Well done. And well done, Mr. Thornton. Perhaps his feelings toward the hands were softening.

If only his feelings towards her would undergo a similar transformation—but why should they? Her refusal of his proposal, capped by what he thought he had witnessed at the Outwood Station, had sunken her forever in his eyes. She had lied about what happened that horrid night, and he knew it. She felt cold and sick at the remembrance, ashamed of herself and yet uncertain what she might have done differently. *You might have trusted him,* her conscience suggested, but she knew that was dangerous, given Frederick's situation.

Her thoughts broke off as she realized everyone was looking at her expectantly. Dixon cleared her throat. 'I asked if you had received any word from Mr. Bell. I can't make heads or tails of what he wants of the poor master's books.'

Margaret shook her head. 'I have had little news from him. He was never a great correspondent, but his last note was brief and full of complaints. I had written him inquiring after his health, which seemed to displease him.' She sighed. In expressing her concern, she had roused his irritation. 'So I shall write him no more until we meet again. I believe he means to come to London sometime soon.'

'He is a singular man, and no doubt his many years as a bachelor have made him jealous of his privacy.' Aunt Shaw arose from her seat, indicating with a significant look that conversation was at an end and Dixon was free to return to the servants' quarters.

As Dixon reluctantly left the parlour, Aunt Shaw addressed Margaret. 'Henry will be coming to dinner tonight, Margaret. I asked Dixon to freshen up your best gown.'

Margaret did not meet her aunt's gaze. 'I daresay Henry is familiar with every gown I own—he has been to dine in this house four score times since I arrived and has seen the entire extent of my wardrobe.'

Aunt Shaw frowned. 'Do not pretend you do not understand me. I believe Henry has been showing you particular attention. Given his success at law and his rising place in society, it would be foolish of you not to encourage his suit.'

Margaret nearly snorted, an unladylike sound that would rain yet another lecture down upon her. Henry had been anything but particular in his attentions; he had displayed an icy civility in all of their encounters. He was a brilliant young man suited to his place in society, but she could tell from the glint in his eye and the coolness of his smile as he bent over her hand that she was not forgiven for her rejection of his proposal in Helstone when she was but a girl. He was a man of great pride, and she had wounded that pride. He set a high store on his value, and she had shown little regard for him by saying no.

It was little matter that she was too young then to know her heart or mind—she knew it better now, but it was not Henry that she bitterly regretted rejecting.

If only Mr. Bell would go to Milton! With a few words of explanation, perhaps he could clear away the mists of uncertainty and restore some manner of good opinion that Mr. Thornton once held of her. She would never be dear to him now, she knew; he had made that clear. But at least if he understood that Frederick was her brother and not some strange man, perhaps he might not think her character so black.

Well! She must be patient and hope for some restoration of friendly feelings, even if they might never meet again. That thought brought on a mood of such bleakness, not even a quiet afternoon playing with Edith's boy helped to expel it.

EDITH HAD RECENTLY SHARED with Margaret a fragment of conversation she recalled having with Mr. Bell where he revealed he intended to accompany Margaret to Cadiz to pay a visit to her brother and new sister-in-law. Upon hearing this, Margaret had sharply questioned Edith until her cousin declared there was nothing more to remember. As Edith recalled, Mr. Bell half-thought he should go and hear Frederick's account of the mutiny, which would also enable Margaret to become acquainted with her new sister-in-law.

Edith begged Margaret not to leave them, fearing she would be wooed away by the romance of Spain and the joy of reuniting with her brother. Margaret reassured her that she was content with her current situation, though the thought of travel to Spain did enchant her. She knew enough of Edith's feelings to keep her pleasure to herself.

While she dressed for dinner the evening of Dixon's return, she asked Dixon if she would not like to see Master Frederick and his new wife.

Dixon expressed the concern topmost in her mind. 'She's a Papist, Miss, isn't she?'

'I believe so,' replied Margaret.

'And Spain is a Papist country?'

'Yes.'

Dixon sighed in resignation. 'Then I'm afraid I cannot go. As much as I love Master Frederick, I would be in constant terror of being converted.' Seeing Margaret smile, she added tartly, 'Well, I would. And you should not put yourself in temptation's way, either, lest you lose your soul.'

'It is just an idea,' said Margaret. 'I do not know for certain that I will go. But if I do go, I am certain I could manage on my own and, in that way, you may remain here and keep your soul quite safe, dear Dixon.'

But in the contrary way she had once she had gotten her way, Dixon immediately doubted her choice. She did not like the thought of being left behind while her young mistress had adventures. And to see Master Frederick again would lift her spirits inordinately. After carefully clearing her throat, as if to show her willingness to do away with difficulties, she asked Miss Margaret whether she thought that, if she took care never to enter a church or clap eyes on a priest, there would be little danger of her being lured to Catholicism.

Margaret maintained a sober mien, not wanting to laugh and injure Dixon's pride. 'I believe you would be safe. But we should not let our fancies run away with this plan of travelling to Spain, given Mr. Bell's capriciousness of late.'

Margaret sighed in resignation. The thought of Spain, an exotic land that she imagined consisted entirely of sunshine and blue water, helped divert her mind from her fervent wish that Mr. Bell would explain all to Mr. Thornton. *What a bright escape such a trip would be from the monotony of my present life and my treacherous thoughts of what might have been!*

~

WHILE MARGARET HAD no desire for Henry Lennox to renew his suit, she recognized that his presence at Harley Street added an agreeable aspect to daily life. His intellect and wide knowledge of the world served to redirect the otherwise insipid conversations centered on fashion and gossip.

Margaret suspected him of disapproving of his brother and sister-in-law's mode of life, which he appeared to consider frivolous. She often heard him speak to his brother in a sharp tone as to whether he meant to give up his profession. On Captain Lennox's offhand reply that he had quite enough to live on, Mr. Lennox would shake his head and say derisively, 'And is that all you live for?' He would then suggest other avenues of employment where Captain Lennox might better direct his energies and talents. Despite their differences in temperament, the brothers were attached to each other as long as Mr. Lennox led, and Captain Lennox was content to let him do so.

Edith loved nothing more than to throw dinner parties that consisted of beautifully dressed guests conveying large dollops of gossip leavened with smatterings of intelligent conversation on topics of the day. These topics were guided in part by the luminaries that Mr. Lennox brought to the table— politicians, bankers, lawyers, and men of science—who helped sustain a rapid flow of conversation.

Margaret found these dinners tedious. The conversation was never serious, but rather amusing and brittle. Every topic was open for discussion and a target for ridicule. Margaret thought these friends of Henry shallow and chafed at the time she must spend at table and in the drawing room. Nothing was of substance; all was superficial. Everything in London seemed too bright and colorful to Margaret. All seemed too beautiful without having purpose. She missed the sepia tones of Milton, the sound of the mills, even the tinge of smoke in the air—though she was reluctant to admit it.

Because her face was a tolerable indicator of her thoughts, Henry knew she was not happy during these dinners. One evening, when the men joined the women in the drawing room, he surprised her by drawing near and speaking directly to her. Previously, he had only spoken to her when prompted by Edith or Aunt Shaw. Now he drew close to her upon the sofa and remarked in a low voice, 'You were not pleased at what my friend Shirley said at dinner.'

'No? My face must be very expressive,' replied Margaret.

'It always is.'

Margaret hesitated before her words tumbled out. 'I did not like his way of advocating what he knew to be wrong—even in jest.'

'But it was very cleverly done.'

'Yes.'

'And you despise it. Pray, do not deny it.'

'I do not care for joking about a topic that deserves serious consideration—' she stopped short, reddened, and turned away.

He said in a low voice, 'If you dislike my tone or mode of thought, will you do me the justice to tell me, and so give me the chance of learning to please you?'

She turned back to him in surprise. His serious demeanor and steadfast gaze gave her pause. Perhaps her aunt was right—perhaps he had grown to care for her again.

She shrank from the thought of having to disappoint him once more, for his suit was no more acceptable to her now than it had been in Helstone. Then she was a young girl and did not understand love; he had frightened her with his avowals. Now she believed she better understood what it meant to love someone, even when it appeared all hope had gone.

As summer passed to the early days of autumn and brittle leaves began to fall from the trees along Harley Street, Margaret despaired of receiving any intelligence of Mr. Bell traveling to Milton. He had spoken of it at Helstone as a journey he would shortly undertake, but

Margaret concluded that he must have transacted his business in writing.

She could not be angry at him; he did not comprehend the great importance she pinned on such an explanation that could only be given face to face. Margaret tried to tamp down her disappointment and put aside her aspirations with some degree of grace, but it was hard.

On a wet September morning, Margaret received a letter from Wallace, Mr. Bell's servant. Margaret and Edith were at the breakfast table, lingering over their cups of coffee, when a servant brought in the letter.

Breaking the wafer and spreading the sheet before her, Margaret read with rising alarm that Mr. Bell had been seized with an apoplectic fit. Wallace wrote that he had sent for the medical man at once, but the doctor did not believe he would survive the night. The frightened servant feared that, by the time Miss Hale received this letter, Mr. Bell would be dead.

Margaret turned pale as she read the dreadful news. Dropping the page upon the table, she left the room. Edith snatched at the letter to discover what had so disconcerted her dear cousin and was shocked. Mr. Bell dead—that hale and hearty man? It was inconceivable.

Edith began weeping loudly; never had death touched her so closely. Her husband, hearing her noisy lamentations, came to discover what had happened; upon hearing Edith's halting tale, he did not know what to do or say. He patted her shoulder awkwardly and entreated, 'Edith, you must not cry so—you will frighten our child. Where is Margaret—how has she taken such news?'

His continued consolations at last quieted her, and he reminded her that someone else was grieving, too. She left the breakfast table to find her cousin and found Dixon packing a small valise, while Margaret hastily donned her bonnet with hands trembling so that she could hardly tie the strings.

'Dear Margaret!' Edith exclaimed, 'You are not going out? Do you want us to send a telegraph?'

'No, Edith. I am going to Oxford—indeed, I must. There is a train in a half hour. I must see Mr. Bell again—he may have recovered and need assistance.' Seeing the look of dismay on her cousin's face, she added, 'Don't try to stop me, Edith. He was there for me in my time of need, and so I must be for his.'

'But I must stop you.' Edith wound her arm about Margaret's waist. 'I know you want to help Mr. Bell. Even as a little girl, you always did the right thing. But Mamma won't like it. Come and let us ask her about it.'

Edith's insistence overcame Margaret's reluctance, and so she missed the train. As Edith had suspected, Mrs. Shaw became incensed at the idea of Margaret travelling alone to a bachelor's quarters.

But Margaret was not to be swayed, and her firmness overcame the weaker objections of her aunt and cousin. After ceaseless discussions on propriety, it was decided that Captain Lennox would accompany Margaret to Oxford.

As evening fell upon London, she found herself sitting in a railway-carriage opposite Captain Lennox, praying that Mr. Bell's servant had exaggerated his diagnosis and that Mr. Bell was simply unwell. However, when they arrived at his rooms, Wallace met her at the door with the news that Mr. Bell was dead.

In later days, it was a comfort to her that she had gone though it was only to hear that he had died in the night. She saw the rooms that he had occupied and associated them ever after most fondly with the memory of her father, who had loved him so faithfully.

Margaret shed many tears that day for her friend and was reluctant to leave, but she had promised Edith they would return that night if, indeed, Mr. Bell had died. Margaret took a long, lingering look around the room where her father had taken his last breath and gave a silent farewell to the friend who had supported her so in her time of need, who had loved her father, and who had given her time at her precious Helstone.

As she prepared to leave, Wallace entered the room, his face lined with grief and care. Margaret asked him what he would do now and received the reassuring news that he had a place with another Oxford don who had been friends with his master.

He lamented that so few people seemed to know Mr. Bell and that but a handful had visited him his last days. 'But that was the way my master wanted it—he were very private. But there was that manufacturer from Milton who spent a day here.'

Margaret's heart gave a leap. 'A manufacturer?'

'Yes, a great, tall fellow—the man who was Mr. Bell's tenant.'

'Mr. Thornton?'

'Just so, miss.'

Margaret's spirits fluttered—perhaps Mr. Bell had found a way to tell Mr. Thornton about Frederick!—but no. He was dying. It would have been the last thing upon his mind at such a time. There would have been no bedside revelations from Mr. Bell.

But, oh, how she honored Mr. Thornton for coming to the sick man in his hour of need! It revealed a firmness of purpose, a kind intent, and a nobleness of soul that made her glow with pleasure. She was ashamed anew for having judged him so harshly.

Captain Lennox fell asleep on the return journey, allowing Margaret the luxury of crying at leisure and reflecting upon this fatal year with all its accompanying woes. She recalled similar times spent at train stations and in train compartments. There was her melancholy first trip to Milton, leaving sunny Helstone for the dark mill town. She only vaguely remembered the trip to London after her father's death, so wrapped in misery that she had barely registered her surroundings. And she thought of the fateful night at the Outwood Station with Frederick, when Mr. Thornton had spotted her in her brother's embrace and thought the worst.

And why shouldn't he, Margaret thought, swiping yet another tear from her cheek. *What have I done to make him think well of me?* She felt almost feverish in her desire for Mr. Thornton to know the truth, to wipe away the worst thoughts he held about her. But with Mr. Bell gone, that would never occur. She was ashamed that her grief for her friend was eclipsed by her grief that the Master of Marlborough Mills would never know she was not as depraved as he believed.

~

SHE FOUND solace in Harley Street that night in the sight of the well-lit rooms that greeted them as they approached the house. As she was engulfed in the tender ministrations of her aunt and Edith, with the weight and warmth of little Sholto on her lap, Margaret felt the heavy mantle of hopelessness slip from her shoulders, and began to feel that life held some hope of happiness. She had Edith's place on the sofa, and Sholto carried Margaret's cup of tea carefully to her. By the time she went up to dress, she was able to thank God for sparing her dear friend a painful illness.

When night came and the house was quiet, Margaret sat at her window gazing down at the silent streets and out upon the beauty of the night sky on a summer evening—the purplish light about the moon and the soft clouds floating in the clear moonlight. Margaret's room had been the nursery of her childhood, where she and Edith had taken their lessons. As a child, she had read wondrously romantic stories and vowed to live as brave and noble a life as any heroine in her books.

How easy it had seemed! It was only upon adulthood that she realized how difficult it was. Trusting only in herself, she had stumbled and sinned—the concealment of her brother and subsequent lies told had culminated in the dreadful incident at the train station.

Moreover, she had learned how false her own ideals were. Her childhood home in London had seemed idyllic. Upon Edith's marriage, she had returned to a Helstone dearer to her for all her longings and imaginings. When she was uprooted to Milton, she had been filled with resentment and prepared to despise everything she found there. But her memories had betrayed her. London now held little attraction for her with its glittering superficialities, and her golden memories of Helstone had proven to be dross during her visit.

Milton was where her thoughts flew now, to its noisy mills, busy streets, and industrious people. She missed Nicholas and Mary. She missed her ramblings above the town. She missed many things—and certain people.

She shifted on her seat, uncomfortable in these recollections and the melancholy that they aroused in her. The past was done and the future cloudy. She had only the present and must learn to live within that space.

Her suffering was just recompense for her sins, she believed, and the time to offer excuses to the person in whose opinion she had sunk the lowest had long passed.

She stood face to face at last with her sin. Her anxiety to have her character excused in Mr. Thornton's eyes was a petty consideration compared with the death of her friend. She must accept the consequences of her actions. She prayed fervently for the fortitude to speak truth and live honorably from that day forward.

NOT LONG AFTER Mr. Bell's death, Edith began speculating upon whether Margaret might be his heiress. To her knowledge, the old gentleman had no other family and, given his close relationship with Mr. Hale and his deep fondness for Margaret, it stood to reason (at least for Edith) that Margaret might inherit whatever constituted his estate.

Captain Lennox tamped down her high expectations, explaining that a Fellow from a small college at Oxford would not possess much of an estate to bequeath. Edith sighed, and her pretty dream of Margaret as a wealthy woman turned to ashes.

A week afterwards, however, she pounced upon her husband as he left his library. 'It appears I am right after all! Margaret has had a letter from Mr. Bell's lawyer, who writes that she is to receive legacies of two thousand pounds. And the remainder is forty thousand or thereabouts, which is the present value of the old gentleman's property in Milton.'

Captain Lennox was astonished. 'How did she react to this news?'

'Oh, she knew she was his heiress but had no idea of the size of his estate. She says she's afraid of it, but that's nonsense. I left Mamma to console her.'

Aunt Shaw and Edith insisted that Margaret must have a legal adviser now, and they considered Mr. Lennox the logical choice. She had no knowledge of business, and so she took the matter of her estate to him for his advice. He selected an attorney and was happy to discuss the myriad mysteries of law, although her interest waned early on in such conversations. It was apparent to her that Edith saw this as the first step to draw her under Henry's protection. While she had no intention of succumbing, she was too exhausted to correct this assumption.

Edith feared that Margaret's inheritance would give her the means as well as the motive to travel to Cadiz, but Spain did not materialize for Margaret that autumn. Instead, she contented herself with time spent by the seaside at Cromer with her Aunt Shaw and the Lennox family.

They had all wished her to accompany them, and her present languid, depressed state did not offer another alternative to her. Perhaps, she thought, the seaside would provide the rest and return to health she so sorely needed.

Few hopes remained to her: her brother was far away and her friends in Milton lost to her, given the upper-class mindset of the Harley Street residents. As for Mr. Thornton, he was lost to her as well. A dozen times a day, her heart ached with longing for him to know the reason behind her rash actions at Outwood Station. But this longing was in vain. She knew she must resolve to move ahead and make the best of her life.

At Cromer, she sat long hours upon the beach, gazing as the waves foamed on the pebbly shore, hypnotized by the roar and retreat of the sea. She was soothed without knowing how or why. She sat there, unmoving, while her Aunt Shaw shopped, and Edith and Captain Lennox rode in an open carriage about the countryside. When the family gathered at dinner-time, Margaret was so silent and absorbed that Edith declared that she was moped and lamented that they had not asked Henry to join them at the seashore in order to entertain Margaret.

However, this time of quiet and reflection helped Margaret frame her present circumstances and her future. The hours by the sea-side were not lost, and Mr. Henry Lennox noted the improvement upon their return to London.

'The sea has done Miss Hale an immense deal of good,' he confided to Edith. 'She looks ten years younger than she did before.'

'It is the bonnet I purchased for her!' Edith exclaimed in triumph.

Mr. Lennox looked at her askance, a smile of faint amusement on his lips. 'I believe I know the difference between the charms of a bonnet and those of a woman. No bonnet would make Miss Hale's eyes so bright or give her face such color.' He paused before continuing in a quiet voice, 'She looks more like the Margaret Hale I first knew.'

He was enthralled once more and determined to try his suit with her again. He admired her beauty and believed that, in time, he could bend the strength of her mind to follow his own. Her fortune was advantageous to his situation, but he would have taken her without it. Having travelled to Milton to assess her property, he realized that it was of great value and would yearly accrue more in such a prosperous and growing town. Surely their present relationship of client and legal adviser would gradually evolve into one of intimate intercourse, given her gentle manners and his ardour.

For her part, Margaret appreciated that he spoke of Milton in judicious tones with none of the contempt voiced by Edith. Mr. Lennox appreciated Milton and its inhabitants, and admired their energy and power. When other subjects bored her, and she gave short answers to his questions, Henry Lennox found that he could animate her expression by asking about some Darkshire quirk of character.

When they had first returned to town from the seashore, Margaret announced her resolution to take her life into her own hands. Edith feared that she would establish her own household, but Margaret set her worst fears to rest, telling her she had no immediate plans to leave them and only wanted to make her own decisions about her person.

'Then you will let me buy your dresses for you?' Edith enquired with eager smiles.

'No, I mean to buy them for myself. You may come with me if you like, but I shall determine what I will buy and wear, just as I shall determine how I shall live and where.'

'Promise me you'll not dress in drab brown or mousy colours as you were wont to do in Milton.'

'I'm going to please myself, Edith,' was her reply. 'If I wish to dress in drab colours, or stay home in the evening rather than attend a dinner, or walk by myself in the park rather than be attended by a maid or footman, I shall do so.'

After much discussion, Edith and Aunt Shaw determined that these plans of hers to remain in Harley Street for the interim would help Henry Lennox win her at last. In a misguided effort, they avoided inviting friends with eligible sons or brothers to dinner and advised Henry to not invite any bachelors to Harley Street. They were heartened by Margaret's apparent avoidance of her previous admirers, and, if Henry thought her absentminded in her thoughts, he attributed it to her change in circumstances rather than her longing to hear from one particular person.

It was a warm evening near the end of summer when Edith came into Margaret's bed-room dressed for dinner. She found Dixon laying out Margaret's dress on the bed but Margaret was not there.

Edith could not help but exclaim, 'Oh, Dixon! Not those blue flowers with that gold gown. How horrible! Pomegranate blossoms are what are needed to set off such a shade.'

'It's not gold, ma'am. It's straw and everyone knows that blue goes with straw.'

Dixon was insulted, but Edith was determined and shortly returned with a handful of scarlet flowers which she held against the gown. 'There, that's perfect. But where is Miss Hale? She really must give up the rambling habits she acquired in Milton. A well-bred lady should never go out without a servant.'

Put out by the refutation of her taste, Dixon replied shortly, 'Miss

Margaret is not such a fearful, fanciful creature as you suppose her to be—'

'Oh, Margaret! At last! I have been looking for you this past hour or more. But how flushed you are, poor child! I dare say you have been wandering up and down the avenues.' Edith was at her most caressing.

'Edith, I have just spoken with Captain Lennox. Is it true that Mr. Thornton is to dine with us this evening?'

Edith huffed in displeasure. 'Henry has exceeded a brother-in-law's limits tonight. I had my numbers done up beautifully to accommodate his Mr. Colthurst, and he has the effrontery to ask if he may bring that Mr. Thornton, pleading that he is your tenant and in London on some business. It quite spoils my numbers!'

Where Margaret had been flushed before, she was now white. 'Do not mind your numbers—I shall not come down to dinner after all. Dixon can fetch a tray for me here, and I will come down to the drawing room after I have had a chance to lie down.'

Edith was astonished and affronted. 'Not come down to dinner! Henry would be most disappointed. You must come, Margaret. Never mind me. I shall cope with the numbers. You do look pale, but it is exhaustion from your walk. Rest for a few moments, and Dixon and I will help you dress. You know we had planned for you to talk about Milton to Mr. Colthurst, and now he might speak with Mr. Thornton as well. Mr. Colthurst can ask him questions about all the subjects in which he is interested, and Mr. Thornton's opinions may help shape Mr. Colthurst's next speech in the House.'

There was no help for it; Margaret understood she must go. Glancing at the bed, however, she made a gesture of repulsion. 'I cannot wear that gown—it is too fine. Dixon, I want the sage green gown, the one with the ribbons about the neckline.'

Dixon was astonished. 'What, that old thing? You haven't worn it since the night of that dinner at Marlborough Mills—'

'Never mind. It will suit me for this evening.' *Let him see me in something familiar,* she thought, *rather than dressed as a grand dame he would despise. Let him recognize me as the same daughter of a parson who lived in*

Milton for a time. Let him not hate me so much that he will not even speak to me this evening.

Her hands shook as she placed her bonnet and reticule on the bed.

Edith chattered away in happy expectation, blind to Margaret's agitated spirits. 'I asked Henry if your Mr. Thornton was a man one would be ashamed of, and he got quite angry with me. So I suppose he is able to sound his h's, which is not a common Darkshire accomplishment—is that so, Margaret?'

'Mr. Lennox did not say why Mr. Thornton was in town?' asked Margaret in a subdued voice.

'His business has failed, or something of the kind—what was it? Oh, Dixon, that's lovely—that gown may be a bit dated, but the colour is perfect on her, and highlights her skin. And the blossoms will be perfect in your hair. Miss Hale will do us great credit this evening. I wish I were as tall as you and as slender. But I daresay you will lose your figure too when you have a child—'

'Edith,' Margaret interrupted, 'What about Mr. Thornton?'

'Oh! Henry will tell you all about it. He did say that Mr. Thornton is very badly off and a respectable man, so I must be civil to him. Come, go with me and rest on the sofa for a quarter of an hour. You do look quite ill—as I feared, that walk did you no good.'

MR. LENNOX ARRIVED EARLY and was surprised when Margaret approached him at once, her cheeks reddened as if by strong emotion. She posed the same questions concerning Mr. Thornton that she had asked Edith, anxious for clarifications to Edith's unsatisfactory responses.

'He has ventured to London to inquire about sub-letting Marlborough Mills and the house and adjacent properties. He cannot hope to keep it in his present penury, and deeds and leases must be reviewed and agreements signed. Edith was rather put out by the outrageous liberty I took in inviting him, but I thought you would like to have some attention shown him, given the terrible breakup of his fortunes.'

'Yes, of course,' Margaret replied hastily. 'But, is it indeed so very bad? Must he give up the house as well as the mill?'

'Yes. As it stands, he hasn't two pence to rub together. Shame, really, for such a promising man of industry.'

He stepped away from Margaret at a sound from the hall. 'Oh, here he is now!'

Margaret's former feeling of weakness was nothing to what she felt now, as the object of her trepidation crossed the parlour threshold and held out his hand to Mr. Lennox. She felt hot and cold at once, by turns elated and terrified of his reception of her. Would he be cold or merely polite? She was not sure which would be worse. She clasped her hands until the knuckles whitened.

While Henry introduced Mr. Thornton to Edith and Captain Lennox, Margaret studied him and was struck by the quixotic idea that he was exactly as he had been and yet totally different. It had been more than a year since she had last seen him. She thought he looked older and worn by cares, but his carriage was erect and his dark hair thick. He held himself with the same noble mien she had previously termed arrogant. She knew better now; he had much to be proud of, and she was glad to see he carried his cares like the strong, confident man she knew him to be. Her eyes swam with tears. While she had endured much, so had he—the strike, the loss of her father's friendship, and now the mill and his home.

She blinked rapidly. She would not have him see her in such agitation. She noted he was in evening dress, and she was struck by the blaze of crimson at his neck. She recalled of a sudden coming unawares upon him at the Great Exhibition. He had worn such a cravat then, and she remembered how handsome she had thought him.

His eye scanned the room as he exchanged pleasantries with his hosts until he pinned Margaret with his brilliant gaze. She saw his expression ignite with pleasure, and he took an unthinking step toward her before halting. His lids came down over his eyes and the glint was gone, and she feared herself unforgiven. Henry led him toward her, and he came up with the regulated manners of a distant acquaintance which wounded her more than she thought possible.

'Miss Hale, how do you do? I am sorry for the loss of your old friend, Mr. Bell. My mother wished me to convey her condolences.' He held out his hand in the familiar gesture of old, and she slid her fingers into his warm palm. Her mouth went dry at the feeling of his skin against hers. She felt lightheaded for a moment. When he released her hand, her composure returned.

'Thank you, Mr. Thornton. I understand you visited him in his final illness?'

'Yes, but I reached his lodgings too late. He had slipped into a deep sleep before I arrived.'

A crushing disappointment overcame Margaret, and she fell silent. So, there had not been time to divulge the truth about Frederick. She knew she was being irrational and heedlessly selfish, but she had held onto that slender reed of hope. Tears burned her eyes once more, and she could see Mr. Thornton gazing at her quizzically.

It fell upon Henry to advance the conversation.

'Does not Miss Hale look well?' he asked. 'Milton did not seem to agree with her for, when she first came to London, I thought her drawn and pale. To-night, she is radiant and has so recovered her strength that she can walk several miles, as she did last Friday evening when we walked to Hampstead.'

Margaret thought that Mr. Thornton looked displeased, and she felt a prickling aggravation at Henry and his exaggerated gallantry. Her spirits sunk even further at the thought that Henry's dismissal of Milton had injured their guest's innate pride in his home.

Before she could speak, Mr. Colthurst was announced, and Henry herded Mr. Thornton toward the guest of honor.

Mr. Colthurst was a rising Member of Parliament with a quick eye at discerning character and little patience for fools. Over dinner, it was obvious that he was impressed with Mr. Thornton's knowledge of the north and manufactures. He appeared familiar with Mr. Thornton's name and reputation, and he spent a greater share of his time at table talking with him on subjects of mutual interest.

All during dinner, Margaret watched Mr. Thornton's face, trying to decipher his expression. He never returned her gaze, absorbed as he was in Mr. Colthurst's narrative, so she was able to study him without notice. On closer examination, he looked tired and despondent. Only when he laughed at some quip of Henry's did she see a flash of his old humour in the brilliance of his eye and the gleam of his smile. One time, at a lull in the conversation, his glance met hers. But when their eyes met, his smile faded and he became grave again. That was the last time he looked at her during dinner.

In the drawing-room, Margaret had no desire to join in the various conversations among the ladies, and she took up her needlework to occupy her anxious hands. It seemed to her that the men lingered longer over their brandy and cigars this evening—would they never appear? When the gentlemen finally entered, she was disappointed that it was Mr. Lennox who came and sat next to her.

He was in an amiable temper. 'Your tenant is such an agreeable fellow. He is up on any number of topics and has been able to answer all of Mr. Colthurst's questions on industry. How in the world did he come to botch his affairs so badly?'

'Not everyone has the backing and friends that you do, Henry,' Margaret replied. She could tell he was displeased with this answer but was in no mood to cater to his vanity.

As they sat in a strained silence, she heard Mr. Colthurst say to Mr. Thornton, 'I heard your name frequently mentioned during my short stay in Milton. Everyone to whom I spoke said you were a leader among the Masters.'

Mr. Thornton laughed, but the sound was humourless. 'If they spoke of me in that way, they were mistaken. I am not quick to take up new fads or projects and I do not make friends easily. I thought I was on the path to success and, since the other masters had similar objectives, I gained the acquaintance of many. All of us benefited by learning from each other.'

'You say you *were* on the path. Don't you intend to stay the course?'

Mr. Lennox arose to intervene, but Mr. Thornton replied with a simple air of dignity. 'I was unsuccessful in business and have had to give up my position. I am currently looking for a position in Milton where I may work under someone who will appreciate my experience and let me manage affairs to my liking. My only wish is to be allowed to interact with the hands to devise improvements to manufacturing the cloth and managing the mill. Unfortunately, the masters I have met with so far shake their heads and look doubtful about the experiments that I should like to try.'

'You call them experiments,' said Mr. Colthurst, his kindly face radiating interest and respect. 'Why so?'

'Because I do not know what the outcome might be—but I still believe they should be undertaken. Working men are closest to the machines and have a more thorough knowledge of the methods of manufacture. Masters need to harness this knowledge and fire their workers' enthusiasm to devise new and better methods.'

'And you believe this will help avoid strikes?'

'No, but it may help us understand one another better so that the strikes won't be the source of such bitterness. If I were more hopeful, I might be able to envision masters working side by side with the hands.' His voice trailed off. 'But I am no longer a hopeful man.'

Margaret's heart was pierced by the simplicity of his words and the look of sorrow on his face. Glancing up, he noted her expression of concern and crossed the room to stand before her. 'Miss Hale, my men presented me with a list of those who would be willing to work for me if I were ever in the position to employ men again on my own behalf. I suspect it was Higgins' idea. That was good of him, wasn't it?'

Margaret's heart beat so thickly she could hardly speak. 'Yes, I am glad of it, for your sake,' she whispered. He had to lean toward her to hear her words and, for a moment, towered over her. Her words were inadequate, but the glance she gave him was full of warmth and admiration, and it seemed to strike him to silence. They gazed at each other, neither willing to break the enchantment that held them immobile, until Mr. Lennox appeared at Mr. Thornton's side to announce that Mr. Colthurst was leaving and requested the pleasure of his company.

Mr. Thornton gazed at Margaret for a moment more, as if uncertain what to say. Then he sighed and a rueful smile played about his lips. 'I knew you would like it,' he replied. 'Good night, Miss Hale.'

He turned from her, and Margaret had the strongest urge to stop him from leaving—when would she see him again? Would these be their parting words? She felt almost wild in her despair and longing as she watched him leave the room. She wanted to run after him, to grasp his sleeve and tell him to come back, to come and see her again, to never leave.

'Henry!' she exclaimed, 'Could you come to see me tomorrow? I have a business proposition I wish to put before you.'

Henry stared at her. 'A business proposition? What is this about, Margaret?'

'I have a business proposition which I wish to put before...Mr. Thornton. Will you come tomorrow?'

His eyes brightened with interest. 'Certainly—will ten suit you?'

She nodded and bade him good night.

Mr. Lennox left in exultation. She looked upon him as her closest adviser and confidante. Surely, her dependence on him would pave the way very soon for a deeper understanding!

EDITH LOITERED outside the drawing room the next morning, anxious to hear any happy news. Henry had come so early and seemed so happy. But the morning passed without any sight of Henry or Margaret and, shortly before the midday hour, they were still shut up about some mysterious business. Too agitated to write letters or settle in the parlour, she paced the length of the room, imagining wedding gowns and floral arrangements.

The slam of a door and footsteps interrupted her reverie, and she arrived at the hallway in time to see Henry rush by on his way to the door. She had to call his name twice before he halted his progress.

'Well, Henry?'

'Well, Edith?' he retorted.

'Come into the parlour!'

'No, thank you. I have no more time to waste.' He consulted his pocket watch.

'Oh! Then nothing is settled between you and Margaret,' Edith pouted.

'No, and it never will be settled, if matrimony is what you mean—at least, not between Margaret and myself.'

'But it would be so advantageous for us all,' pleaded Edith.

'Miss Hale would not have me. And I shall not ask her again. So give that notion up.'

'Whatever have you been talking about all this time?'

'Investments,' he replied succinctly, impatiently beating his hand against his leg. 'I really must go—I must ask Mr. Thornton to come meet with us tomorrow.'

'Mr. Thornton! What has he to do with Margaret?'

'He is Miss Hale's tenant and means to give up his lease. Margaret has concocted a scheme that will let him keep it. That is all. I only ask that you let us have the back drawing room tomorrow morning and that you ensure we will not be disturbed.'

He turned to leave, hesitated, and turned back. 'Do not tease Miss Hale about this, Edith. It is between her and me, and really none of your business.' With these cutting words, he departed.

THE FOLLOWING MORNING, Margaret received word from Dixon that Mr. Thornton awaited her in the back drawing room, but Mr. Lennox had not yet arrived. Margaret wrung her hands, reluctant to start without Henry. She needed Henry to explain her plan to Mr. Thornton. He must have been detained—she would wait.

But an hour later, Mr. Lennox had still not appeared and Margaret knew she could not keep Mr. Thornton waiting any longer. Sick with anxiety, Margaret entered the room.

She had dressed carefully that morning, wearing a day dress in her favorite green, and had surprised Edith by asking if her maid would dress her hair. She was distinctly off kilter, wanting to appear beautiful for him one moment and despising herself the next for such foolishness.

Mr. Thornton stood before the hearth, his back to the room, but turned at the sound of her footsteps. If she looked tired and pale, she thought, he appeared utterly downcast by a crushing load of care. She had thought last night what a blow the loss of Marlborough Mills had been to him, given his early losses as a boy—his father, his family status—and the years of hard work and sacrifice required to raise his mother and sister up from poverty and earn his place as Master. She remembered Mrs. Thornton's proud words: 'Go where you will—the name of John Thornton of Milton is known and respected amongst all men of business.'

Once she had thought the idea ludicrous. Now, she believed that his mother's proud words did not do him full justice. Mrs. Thornton had spoken of the respect men of business had for him, but Margaret believed that every person of worth would note and admire his spirit, his intelligence, his humility, his sufferance in sorrow, and his innate kindness. No, she had not done him justice and would regret it to the end of her days. She admired him—nay, she loved him. It was long overdue for her to admit it—even though she believed he would not have her now.

Still, she had it within her power to help him in his time of need and would not shirk from putting her idea before him.

'You asked me to come this morning, Miss Hale.' His voice was strong and assured, in total contrast to her unsettled and quivering tone.

She rushed in her explanation. 'I am so sorry Mr. Lennox is not here. He advises me in business affairs and would explain all much better than I could—'

'I am sorry that I came, if it gives you grief. Let me go to Mr. Lennox's chambers and I will try to find him.'

'No!' she exclaimed, holding up her hands as if to physically prevent his departure. 'No, please, do not leave. I wanted to tell you how grieved I am to find that I shall lose you as a tenant, to hear of your situation and the ills that have befallen you. Mr. Lennox tells me that things are sure to brighten—'

'Mr. Lennox does not understand,' replied Mr. Thornton, a note of bitterness creeping into his voice. 'Why should he? He is just starting out on his own path to success and full of hopes of obtaining all he desires. Half my life is gone, and what do I have to show for it? Miss Hale, I would rather not hear Mr. Lennox's opinion of my affairs. He does not understand—how can he? He has not suffered failure or reversal.'

'Mr. Lennox may not understand, but he has great faith in your abilities. As do I,' she said and raised her luminous eyes to his. 'I have a proposition for you. Please, do not speak until I have finished explaining it.' In great agitation, she walked over to the desk and began rummaging among the papers strewn across its surface.

'Oh—here it is! Henry drew me out a proposal—' She saw his face darken with disapproval. Thinking he objected to discussing business with a woman, she pressed on, determined to make her point. 'I wish he were here to explain it, he would do so much better than I should. But, he is not here.' She held the paper out to him, brandishing it like a sword. 'This shows that if you borrow some money of mine—eighteen thousand and fifty-seven pounds, lying just at this moment unused in the bank, and bringing me in only two and a half per cent—you could pay me much better interest and could go on working Marlborough Mills. So, you see, it is a business arrangement, and it would be all to my advantage—'

'Miss Hale.' He cut across her rambling speech, compelling her to silence. He took a cautious step closer, ignoring the papers she still held out. 'I understand from several acquaintances that congratulations are in order for you and Mr. Lennox. Mr. Colthurst told me the banns were all but complete.'

'Oh!' Margaret cried, her cheeks flushing in agitation. 'Why can't people mind their own affairs? Why must they thrust their noses into mine?' She dropped the papers on the desk and wrung her hands, close to vexatious tears.

'Is it true?' he pressed her, coming closer still. She glanced quickly at him and saw he was as discomposed as she, frowning in disapproval.

'No, it is not true.' She mastered her emotions and resumed her search for the papers he must sign to make their arrangement official.

To her surprise, he moved purposefully around the desk to stand beside her. 'And is that all you want from me—a business arrangement?'

'Yes, it would be a business arrangement. You would not be obliged to me in any way....'

She held out the terms of the agreement to him once more, and he took it from her hand. Instead of reading it, he set it aside and with slow deliberation took her hand in his. His thumb caressed the back of her hand in slow, hypnotic strokes.

She glanced up at him and dropped her eyes, unable to hold his passionate gaze. A wild longing rose within her and, with a reckless gesture, she raised his hand to her lips and kissed it.

'Margaret.' He had never before said her name, and certainly had never addressed her in such a tone of wonder and tenderness. 'Margaret!' he exclaimed again, relentless in his pursuit. 'Look at me.'

She shook her head, incapable of speech. Her heart was too full of strange and wondrous emotion, but the blush crimsoning her neck and face told him all that he wanted to know.

He raised her chin until her gaze met his. 'Take care—if you do not speak, if you do not tell me to leave, I shall claim you as my own. My feelings have not changed. Since almost the first I saw you, I have loved you—'

With a small gasp, she moved into his embrace, standing on tip-toe so that she could press her face against his. He felt her lips upon his cheek, and he pulled her into his embrace, turning his head swiftly to kiss her sweet mouth.

After a prolonged moment of delicious silence, Margaret murmured, 'You cannot have forgiven me, Mr. Thornton. I know I am not good enough for you—you told me as much that day when you said any passion on your part was done—that you were looking to the future.'

'I spoke a great deal of nonsense. I was angry and heart-sore, and I wanted to wound you as you had wounded me. I know now how wrong I was to suspect you, but I did not know at that time that your silence was to protect your brother.'

She started and raised her head to meet his loving eyes. 'You know? Oh! I did not think that Mr. Bell was able to convey the truth to you.'

'It was not Mr. Bell but Higgins who told me—and to whom I owe a debt of gratitude.'

While she absorbed this news, he caressed her cheek. 'If I were to ask for your hand once more—would you answer me differently than that day in Milton?'

'Yes.'

'Will you be my wife?'

'Yes.'

He kissed her again, a sweet, lingering kiss. 'Margaret, I have loved you almost from the first moment I met you. I feared after you refused my proposal that you were lost to me forever.'

'Oh, don't remind me of that day—how unkind I was—and confused. When you left the house, I had the strongest impulse to run after you, to tell you to come back. I did not know it then, but I must have cared for you.' She trembled but bravely met his eyes. 'As time went on, I realized how good you were, how kind and caring, and how I admired—and loved you.'

He took her hand and kissed her palm, a swift and loving kiss. 'Your refusal of my proposal made me reflect on my behavior as I never had before. It made me consider those who worked for me, and to try to understand them better and strive to work with them for our mutual success.'

'Will you accept my business proposition?'

'Yes, I will accept your generous offer and use it to reopen the mill —I would be a foolish man to say no. But reopening the mill is nothing to the gift you have given me today. You are the prize, Margaret.'

She could think of nothing to say, but clung to him and he could feel her tears on his cheek. 'Nay, lass, do not cry. Our tears are at an end now that we are together.' He gently disengaged her arms from his neck and exclaimed, 'Look here! I have something to show you.' He drew out his pocket-book from which he removed some dried petals. 'Do you know these roses?'

'They are from Helstone!' she exclaimed, 'Where did you get them?'

'I found them in the hedgerow. You'd have to look hard.' He smiled and placed the petals in her hand.

'You have been there? When were you there?'

'I went there on my return from Havre. I wanted to see the place where my Margaret grew to be what she is, even when I had no hope of ever calling her mine.'

'But I am yours now,' she gently chided him.

He smiled ruefully. 'What a lovesick lad you must think me, to treasure up blossoms when all hope seemed gone.'

'Would it help if I told you I had kept an article of yours since the day of your proposal?' When he gazed blankly at her, she moved around to her reticule and removed a pair of worn leather gloves that he recognized as his own. 'You left them, and I have kept them by me ever since. I did not understand why at first, but now I know.'

He held out his hand for the gloves, but she shook her head. 'You must pay me for them,' she teased, and he gladly acquiesced.

'How shall I ever tell Aunt Shaw?' she whispered, after some time.

He laughed. 'And how shall I ever tell my mother?'

She took his hand and threaded her fingers between his. 'We shall tell them together.'

'And you will marry me?' He moved closer and whispered in her ear, 'And use my Christian name?'

'Yes, Mr. Thornton—John,' she amended, blushing. 'I shall wake up on a Sunday morning, put on my favorite dress, and walk to the church, as I have planned since I was a child. Now that I know what it is to love, I shall marry. But no one but you.'

∾

NANCY KLEIN: I have been writing fiction for quite a few years now, and surprise! I find I love it. I owe a huge debt of thanks to Trudy for reading what I write and offering incredibly helpful insights (and wonderful friendship). I am a writer and editor by trade, so I enjoy beta reading for other writers. Besides playing in Milton and Nottingham, I enjoy finding treasures at yard sales and auctions, running/hiking and race walking, working with dog rescue, listening to NPR (especially This American Life and Wait, Wait, Don't Tell Me), travelling, singing Broadway scores, reading, drinking good wine, and hearing a good joke.

NANCY KLEIN's other book is *How Far the World Will Bend*

ONCE AGAIN

Trudy Brasure

"He had known what love was—a sharp pang, a fierce experience, in the midst of whose flames he was struggling! but, through that furnace he would fight his way out into the serenity of middle age,—all the richer and more human for having known this great passion." —Chapter XL, North and South

He train jostled its passengers for a moment before returning to the rhythmic clack and sway of the steady journey south. Mr. Thornton glanced up from his paper to look out the window. Gone were the idyllic green expanses. The train now passed through a closer jumble of houses, shops, and byways that he knew signaled their proximity to London.

He had been to London several times for business. It was not an unfamiliar routine. But this time was utterly different. This time he would sign papers that would close his official relation to Marlborough Mills forever. All his years of unrelenting work—his self-sacrifice, intellect, and economy—had come to this.

The temptation to wallow in bitterness welled up inside of him. He thought of that terrible morning weeks ago when his steadfast mother had rebuked God for forsaking him. Even this morning, as she had sent him off on his solemn journey, he had seen in her eyes how much her heart still suffered sorely for him.

But he refused to be an object of pity for anyone. He had accomplished much—he had built up his mill to be the leading cotton factory in Milton. He had learned, only too late, how vital it was to work with the mill hands—to treat them as equals.

He let out a breath of helplessness as he thought of Higgins and all the others he knew by name who were now out of work. He felt his responsibility to the men keenly. He had done all that was in his power to keep the mill running, to keep their families fed, but he could find neither a loan nor investors to support his operation.

He had little hope of finding such investors in London. He would set his efforts to approach several of the great men of business who honored his name and discover if there might be manufacturing ventures to which he could play a managing part.

He looked down again at his paper and tried to read but could no longer focus on the words.

The last time he had travelled this way, Margaret was still living in Milton. The time she had lived in his world had been the most precious weeks and months of his life. His heart, even wounded as it was, had beat with a fervor that only her nearness could evoke. Nothing in Milton had been the same since she left.

When her carriage had pulled away from his yard that unspeakably black day, she had taken a part of his heart with her. It had been over a year now. Yet that aching longing to see her—to be near her again—had not truly abated. He had merely dulled the pain of her absence by working long hours and throwing all of his efforts into saving the mill from financial ruin.

With the mill now closed, his days were empty—his nights even more so. It was at night, when the house was still, that all the thoughts and images he had pushed aside came rushing back to fill the gaping void.

He stared blankly out the window as the ever-more grey scenery of man's creations passed by. Such was the view surrounding his own home: colorless, drab. All the color and zest of life had drained from Milton now that she no longer lived there.

He had little to hope for concerning his future but to keep his mother comfortable and to find for himself a position of interest so that he might forget...no...not forget. He did not wish to forget her, else he would have put away the book that he kept at his bedside—the copy of Plato she had given him. It was not alone for the tender memory of her father that he kept it in sight, although he often told himself so. He knew otherwise, for sometimes he would open it to the frontispiece where she had signed her name, and he would stare at the word just above it. A word she had written for his eyes—*Yours*.

It was a strange comfort to have the book near. It was the only thing he had left of her. That, and the flowers he carried with him.

His hand went to his breast pocket. He pulled out the pocketbook that held his prize and gazed for the thousandth time at the dried flowers he kept within it. He had gathered the roses from her child-hood home on the very day that Mr. Bell had told him the terrible news of Mr. Hale's death. He sighed aloud at the memory of the awful event which had taken her away from him. Left fatherless and moth-erless in a town that had given her so much trouble, she had fled to London to be with family—the only family accessible to her.

Mr. Bell had told him of Frederick, an exiled brother who lived in Spain. But it was Higgins who had finally chased away all the unset-tled doubt about Margaret's relationship to the man at the train station. It had been heavenly relief to realize his simmering jealousy had been for naught. The man she had embraced was only her brother!

He put the dried flowers away and checked his pocket watch.

He knew it was not wise to let his thoughts dwell on her for long. He had done well to read some and ponder the possibilities of his future during the time spent traveling. He even believed that he was not greatly affected by this journey thus far but, as much as his mind endeavored to put the thought of her away, in truth he felt every mile travelled was a mile closer to her.

~

Mr. Thornton's first order of business after checking into his hotel was an appointment with Mr. Lennox about the lease to Marlborough Mills.

He had heard of Henry Lennox from Mr. Bell. And he was not at all eager to meet a man who hoped to court Margaret—a man who, as Mr. Bell had bluntly revealed, had only been kept back before by Margaret's want of fortune. His jaw tightened, and he clenched his hand. The knowledge of this gave him a great distaste for the London man.

It was only the necessity of business that propelled him onward to the Temple, a classical construction in massive stone that embodied the weight of centuries of steadfast English law.

He walked down a long marble hallway to Mr. Lennox's chambers. The heavy wooden door was half open, inviting him inside. A high ceiling matched the air of dignity and the lofty purpose that the building itself imposed upon each visitor. But on the floor below, where mortals worked the grand ideals of law in ink and paper, Mr. Thornton walked into a room with two desks, each occupied by a gentleman bent over a pile of documents.

It was a relief to Mr. Thornton that Mr. Lennox shared his chambers with another. London barrister though he may be, Mr. Lennox was not a man significant enough to have a room of his own.

Mr. Lennox looked up from his papers. "Mr. Thornton," he said, standing to offer his hand with curious enthusiasm. "I'm very glad to meet you at last. I'm sorry it could not be on more acceptable circumstances. I understand that you had some trouble with a strike which ultimately caused your enterprise to collapse," Henry began, wearing a look of sympathy appropriate for his profession.

Mr. Lennox's glance swept over the northern manufacturer's tall frame. Mr. Thornton was younger and more distinguished-looking than he had imagined. Had he been dressed in more dashing attire, the Milton industrialist might well pass for a Londoner.

"There are a great many factors that accumulate to cause either success or failure—the price of cotton, extended investment in equipment, American competition, and the general state of the financial houses. The complexities of running a business are great, Mr. Lennox —as are the risks involved," Mr. Thornton replied, appraising the London lawyer before him as a man who had not yet seen fortune turn against him. Mr. Lennox's smiles came easily, as they would to one who had every dream in life still to expect.

"I regret very little," Mr. Thornton continued. "All my decisions, I believe, were sound. But from what I have learned in these last two years, I would practice business in a manner which might have mitigated the radical acts of the workers."

Henry studied the man before him with a different air. He had not expected such eloquence from a Milton master. Indeed, the calm dignity with which the failed businessmen composed himself was something of a surprise. Henry had been to Milton, with its bustling energy and noise. He had imagined Mr. Thornton would be a passionate, vociferous, and perhaps distraught character out of his element in the more refined atmosphere of London offices of great import.

"Have you any obligations for dinner this evening?" Mr. Lennox asked, suddenly stricken with an idea that might enhance his own social standing.

"No, I…"

"Then you must join me at my brother's house. There will be a member of parliament there—a Mr. Colthurst—who is very interested in Milton industry. I cannot think of anyone better to speak to the subject than yourself," Mr. Lennox implored.

"Thank you. It would be an honor to accept," the northern visitor answered with a mechanical smile.

"And I am obliged to you for coming at such an opportune time.

This really exceeds my former plan. You will be far more knowledge-able about Milton than Margaret," Mr. Lennox responded.

Mr. Thornton's heart skipped a beat. *She would be there, then.* A thrill of expectancy surged through him even as a conflicting stab of dread warned him of the pain it would cause him to see her happily situated so far away from him.

"Now then, let's get to business, shall we?" Mr. Lennox began, seated once more at his desk and pulling a few papers from his stacks. "You've come to discuss the terms of the lease. I'm confident that Margaret—excuse me, I mean to say, Miss Hale, as I'm sure you know her—would be happy to forgo a month or two of payments for the sake of an old friend."

The sting of jealousy silently thundered in Mr. Thornton's breast. Did he presume to know her better than he? Had he ever seen how her eyes flashed fire when she spoke of injustice? Had he ever stood side by side with her in the face of danger? Had he ever felt her arms around his neck, or noticed how her lips trembled when she spoke of her dead parents?

"Perhaps you could find a way to stabilize business in a matter of a few months enough to continue on," Mr. Lennox proposed.

"I appreciate the offer to defer, but I have already closed my doors. Trade is down, and banks are not lending. I don't expect I shall re-open them. However, I am here to pursue all possible avenues."

The two men discussed the probability of finding a party to sublet Marlborough Mills for a short time more.

"Dinner is at seven. Ninety-six Harley Street. I look forward to the pleasure of seeing you again this evening, Mr. Thornton," the barrister concluded, shaking hands with the former mill master before the northern visitor stepped out once more into the marble hallway and then out into the hazy sunshine of a humid city.

THE TALL WINDOWS had been thrown open in Hannah Thornton's bed chamber, but no breeze stirred the late afternoon heat. The silence from the empty mill shrouded the house with a palpable gloom.

The maid stopped to wipe her brow with the back of her hand before proceeding to wrap the porcelain and silver items from the vanity table in cotton as the mistress had dictated.

Hannah pulled out the few remaining garments hanging in the dark walnut armoire and laid them carefully on the white matelassé coverlet of her bed. She had not many clothes, but what she did have was of high quality—a symbol of her son's great accomplishments. She would wear them proudly wherever they would live next.

As she began to roll the clothes for their removal to an unknown destination, she told herself again that it did not matter where they lived. She possessed an unwavering conviction that John would rise again to greatness, whatever he did. She did not worry about herself. She had lived a long life—with her own portion of sorrows and happiness. She counted herself blessed among all mortal mothers to have been given a son such as she had.

It was the thought of him that taunted her motherly anxieties at every turn. Would John find satisfying work? How long would he wear that look of melancholy, the one he thought she did not see?

Chance and circumstance had torn from him the position in business he had worked hard to achieve. Her sense of justice raged against this indignity, although she knew he would achieve it again—in time. But nothing was more agonizing to her than to think of what time might never heal.

She walked to the window a moment to look out at the abandoned mill yard.

She had long been aware—and had been rightly wary of—John's attraction to the old parson's daughter. Something in the way John spoke of her and in the flicker of his eyes had warned her from the very first that this girl had woken something new in him.

Thoughtless, stupid girl! How could she have thrown away the love of the best man who lived on this earth? She would never find a better!

Her anger piqued at the far-away girl, although she knew it could do no good. Love was a mysterious power which often struck unevenly—leaving the unlucky to live in the torment of loving without a return of affection.

Did the girl know the suffering she had caused her son? She doubted it, although she reluctantly admitted that Margaret had also borne a great deal of suffering. There had been a soft humility about her the last time she had seen her. Yet, for all that, Hannah was exceedingly grateful that Margaret was removed from Milton so that her son might heal.

It troubled her that John was again in close proximity to her in London. She fervently hoped there would be no opportunity for the two to meet. It was best not to reopen old wounds.

She shook herself from these thoughts and returned to her task. Stooping to empty the compartments at the bottom of her wardrobe, she pulled out a package wrapped in faded cloth and satin ribbon. Her face softened at the recognition of the forgotten stash of letters and mementos.

"Jane, you may go down for tea. We will continue our packing later," she told the girl, and she sat down with her treasure once the room was hers alone.

She unwrapped the package with a sacred gentleness, knowing that within were things which her husband had once touched.

One by one, she read some of the letters George had written to her before they had married. Tears came to her eyes as all the sweet earnestness and hopeful confidence of her husband's spirit tore at the ancient wound of his unspeakable death. The horror of his end had scarred her deeply, but she had survived it all—for John and Fanny's sake.

She had learned to stifle sorrow and self-pity with a diligence to duty and self-reliance. She had been determined to keep her honor and to embed in her son the type of character that all men must revere. He was a prince among men. Her heart burst with the fervent love she held for him, her firstborn.

She sifted through a few her husband's sketches. He had had a keen eye for the artistic form of everyday objects. His talent was simple, but she had not been able to part with all of his drawings.

Her breath stilled as she came across a pencil sketch infinitely precious to her. Her husband, thoroughly fascinated by the perfection of his newborn son, had drawn the sleeping face and tiny curled fists of their baby. She traced the penciled lines of John's infant cheeks with her fingers as tears began to slide down her own wrinkled cheeks.

To see her husband's fall was bitter enough to bear. But to witness her stalwart and good son suffer loss both in business and in love tempted her faith in the Almighty's righteousness. God must give her son his faithful reward erelong. He must, for she could not endure seeing John's days filled with endless toil and quiet sorrow.

Her daily, fervent prayer was to see John happy once again.

As the sun's intensity began to fade with the approach of evening, Mr. Thornton returned from unfruitful meetings with a few London contacts to his solitary hotel room. He slid off his coat with a breath of relief and peeled off the white cotton shirt clinging to his body. He poured the pitcher of lavender-scented water into the porcelain basin and leaned over to splash water on his face. Cool water dripped down the expanse of his bare chest as he stood to reach for a towel and wash the grime of perspiration off his skin.

It was a refreshing luxury to remain half undressed for a time in this private space. But he had not long to linger here. Soon he must dress for dinner. In another hour, he would see her.

The seed of anxiety that had been sown inside him since he had received the invitation began to grow. How would she receive him?

He examined his face in the framed mirror on the wall. The morning shave in Milton had been long ago. He could see the faint shadow now appearing along his cheek and jaw. It could not be helped. He was but a rough and unpolished fellow, after all. He believed he saw the lines of age beginning to etch themselves on his face. It would be no surprise to him if it were so, for he had never felt so worn in his life—so drained of hope and promise—than these past few weeks.

But he would carry on. He had been through deep waters before. He raised his chin and turned away from the mirror. He was not a vain man. He would appear to her just as he always had—an honest man with no pretensions about his social standing. He knew his own worth; he did not need the approval of others to verify his place in the world.

The only judgement he cared about was hers. He longed for her to see him as far more than a manufacturer who treated his workers with disdain. If only she knew how much he had changed! The yearning to prove himself to her still burned inside him, as it had the first day she had walked into his life.

Perhaps she might hear him speak tonight of some of the developments that had taken place at Marlborough Mills since she had left town. It would settle something in his soul if he could only know that she approved of how he had improved his relationship with the hands. He knew he was a better man because of her.

He picked up the burgundy cravat he would wear. He had worn it to tea the first time he had been a guest—not a paying student—in the Hales' Crampton home. He chastised himself for creating any significance over what he would wear tonight. She would not remember or pay attention to his particular attire. Besides which, he had no fashionable array of dress clothes from which to choose.

He had not expected to see her. It was a blessing and a curse to have been asked to join her company. He could never resist the lure of seeing her, even if it were fraught with danger. He knew his mother would think him unwise for going.

As he rode to the destination in the cab, ever closer to her, persistent images of what he most dreaded tormented his thoughts: that he should find her closely companioned to Mr. Lennox. He had no right to let such a relationship disturb him, for she had made it clear long ago that she did not care for him—a man who would use policemen to repress starving men.

He told himself that he would be satisfied if only she would receive him with the warmth of one who had been kind to her family—to look on him as someone worthy of her remembrance.

The walk to the front door from the street was short, but he took long breaths to settle himself. No matter what transpired, he would retain his calm demeanor.

The instant he stepped into the house, his body tingled with the suspense of meeting Margaret again. As he was ushered into the elegant drawing room buzzing with chatter, he caught a glimpse of her sitting at the far end of the room. She was listening intently to something Mr. Lennox was saying, as they leaned close together in some intimate tête-à-tête.

His smile evaporated, and he felt the sudden impulse to turn and leave. But Henry Lennox caught sight of him at that very instant and sprang up from his seat to usher the Milton guest around.

Edith smiled charmingly at being introduced, although Mr. Thornton saw the glint in her eyes that revealed her wariness as to whether a manufacturer was worthy enough to be a guest here. He could not help but think of his sister Fanny, who also set herself above most others. He took no umbrage whatsoever at Edith's judgment.

At meeting Margaret's aunt, Mr. Thornton looked for the resemblance to her deceased sister but noted only the disparity between the plump and pampered woman before him and the wan, depleted figure who had been Margaret's mother.

He successfully kept his attention to the round of guests he met, although all he really longed to do was let his eyes stray to the corner where he knew Margaret was standing.

And then Henry led him nearer to her. He recognized at once the elegant green dress she had worn to his dinner party, the night their hands had met for the first time. His pulse skittered madly, part in wakened desire and part in mild alarm at how her nearness affected him.

All the latent longing he had repressed for months came rushing forward to crack the steely surface of his self-control. Had he forgotten the intense power she had to rouse him? Her queenly bearing, the tendrils of hair just brushing her neck, her rounded shoulders and voluptuous shape made him ache inside. He swallowed and stepped forward as expected.

"Miss Hale, I am glad to see you again. I trust you are well," he uttered in perfectly regulated deep tones and extended his hand in greeting to confirm her remembrance of the old Milton ways. He kept well-hidden the tremor of sensation that ran through him as she slid her slender hand in his. The handshake that he knew must mean little to her, he would store among the treasured memories of this evening.

"Mr. Thornton, I'm pleased you have come," she answered, though scarcely looking him in the eye. "How are your mother and your sister? I hear she is married. Your sister, I mean, of course…"

Her flustered manner disappointed him. He sensed her reluctance to engage him in conversation. He spoke a little of his sister and answered her inquiry concerning Higgins and the Boucher children, but their conversation was formal and caused her to be visibly uneasy. Soon others she knew well came up to receive her attention, and he fell to the background, where he belonged.

Henry returned to Mr. Thornton's side. "Does not Margaret look well? She has regained her strength since coming back to London. Milton did not agree with her at all. Last Friday we walked all the way to Hampstead and back, and yet she was as strong as ever on Saturday."

Mr. Thornton gave a grim smile in reply, but his eyes flashed with envy when the barrister turned aside. Mr. Thornton did not at all agree that London had improved Margaret's looks. Although she could command the stars with her beauty, he thought she appeared frailer and that her cheeks were a little hollower. There was a tinge of sadness in her eyes which he attributed to the loss of her family and Mr. Bell.

Although Mr. Thornton did not speak to her again until much later, he was aware of where she was at every moment. At dinner, he was pleased to see her seated across from him but at a distance too far for easy discourse. If dinner had been a quiet affair, he might have been tempted to let his gaze drift often in her direction. However, as the guest from the strange and distant North, he was called into much of the conversation.

"My wife and I travelled to Milton once," Mr. Colthurst related. "Why, you could see the smoky cloud hovering over the town from quite a distance. I must say it sobered me to think of what it must be to live in such a place. Mr. Thornton, do you spend all year in Milton? Surely, you must travel to more...scenic venues from time to time."

"I'm afraid my mill required my strict attention. I have travelled from time to time, but for purposes of business. I should like some day to see the ancient ruins of Greece," he revealed.

"Ah yes, to walk the same ground where Socrates and Plato once walked is quite something. You must indeed go," Mr. Colthurst replied.

"The skies in Greece are unlike anything I've ever seen," Edith chimed in. "Clear and blue as far as the eye can see. I'm certain it would be a magnificent sight for one who lives...well, for one who lives where you live, Mr. Thornton. However, I cannot say I am one to admire dirty old relics," she admitted.

"But Mr. Thornton," Captain Lennox began, still perplexed by the northern industrialist's schedule, "You may not have the opportunity for travel, but Milton men cannot spend all their time upon things of business, can they? What is done for leisure in your town?"

"Ah, but you must not use the word 'leisure' to the Milton dwellers," Henry interjected. "It is an altogether different word in their parlance, I'm sure. 'Leisure' to them would be to construct a new machine or devise a new routine for saving time so that they may be even more industrious!"

Mr. Thornton smiled broadly at the jab. Instinctively, he sought Margaret's sympathy.

Their eyes met. But there was no mirth in Margaret's face. For one brief moment, they bonded in this silent exchange. He saw in her eyes that spark of compassion and strength that lay within her—as well as all the strife and secrecy, bitterness and sorrow that had engulfed their turbulent relationship.

She would never walk in his world again. The realization hit him with almost violent force. His stomach clenched in sickening agony of what would never be. All that he desired lived and breathed in the very room with him this evening, but never again. She would never be his own. And although he loved her with a passion that drove him half mad, she would someday belong to another man.

He felt all hope of happiness drain from him. Darkness, loneliness closed in around him like a heavy cloak. He could not breathe.

He looked away to the other end of the table, fighting to keep his composure. He resolved to not look her way again.

It was a relief to him when the women began to leave the room. As the gentlemen continued their discussions, Mr. Thornton cast furtive glances at Margaret's retreating figure—drinking in the tortuous vision of the curve of her neck, the sway of her walk, and the milky skin of her bare shoulders.

Once the door was shut, he threw his attention to the talk of industry, politics, and management—of which he was well able to share his experience and challenges with the London men surrounding him. Mr. Colthurst plied him with many questions to satisfy his curiosity about the pace and effect of industry on the entire Lancashire county.

When the men finally emerged into the drawing room, the conversation about his management of the mill continued. Mr. Thornton saw that Henry Lennox walked straight to where Margaret was and began to speak to her privately while he himself was constrained to remain by the fireplace, supplying Mr. Colthurst with explanations of how he had attempted to improve the lives of his workers through mutual ventures.

"You seem to indicate that your experiments—as you call them— with your workers are now at an end. Have you stopped such experiments or...?"

Henry Lennox appeared at this juncture to interject a topic that would veer the conversation into a different direction, so as to save Mr. Thornton the mortification of declaring himself a failure. But as soon as the new subject had exhausted its course, Mr. Thornton returned to the previous inquiry.

"I have been unsuccessful in business and have had to give up my position as a master. I am on the look-out for a situation in Milton, hoping I may meet with employment under someone willing to let me go along my own way in such matters as these. I wish to have the opportunity of cultivating intercourse with the hands beyond mere methods of inducing profit." As he spoke, Mr. Thornton was eager to know whether Margaret could hear their discussion from her vantage point.

"And so to find ways to gain the trust of your men by an interest in their well-being or circumstances?" Mr. Colthurt asked, searching for a logical motive.

"Not only their trust. If communication between master and men is open, there is more opportunity to involve the hands in improving operations that they themselves initiate with their ideas. And, having their own ideas heard and implemented, they thereby become themselves invested in the success of the business."

"Do you believe that such methods would prevent the laboring class from rising up to strike?" Mr. Colthurst continued.

"I have no expectations that all disagreements between men and masters can be resolved in such a manner. I only know that I have found it mutually beneficial to operate in this way. The hands trust me more, and I rely on them with more confidence in their abilities. I would like to hope that this will aid in avoiding bitterness between the two classes from rising up as it has formerly."

Suddenly, he broke away and took two or three strides to where Margaret sat.

"Miss Hale, Higgins gave me a list of men who wish to work for me, if ever I was in a position to employ men again on my own behalf. That was good, was it not?"

"Yes. Just right. I am glad to hear of it," she said, looking up to meet his searching gaze.

He saw for a moment the spark of intelligent interest in her eyes. But she dropped her gaze quickly. Her frightened retreat from engaging with him reminded him again that he held no particular significance in her life.

He sighed and turned away, believing that the simple words of approval she had given were the most he could expect from her.

When he departed later, it was only with a formal "good-bye" to Margaret. Even this brief parting was awkward, for she appeared to want to say something of deeper import but withdrew from her impulse to instead merely utter the empty words of propriety.

It hurt him to feel her nervous retraction from him at every point. She had not forgotten all that had passed between them. His very presence caused her distress; he knew she must wish him far away.

He turned to pass through the mirrored hall leading to the front door, acutely aware as he stepped over the threshold into the night that he was leaving her presence for the last time. He would not see her again.

As he walked to the waiting cab, he told himself that he had done well. He had been in the same room with her again; he had looked into her face and had proved to himself that he had dominion over his feelings. He could be satisfied now that he was capable of letting her go, as he knew he must.

But as the cab jerked forward and the wheels began to turn, taking him away from her, his heart sank lower. The settling doom of perpetual loneliness drew him into a black night of despondency.

In a moment of surging despair, he imagined springing out of the coach and bounding back up those granite stairs to burst into the room again and see her surprise. He would sweep her into his arms and hold her tightly to him, so that she might know the strength of his devotion.

His forehead creased in concern for his own sanity. What kind of self-control was this? It would never do to allow himself to conjure such visions of fantasy. It was vain to imagine that anything he could do would win her affection.

She was lost to him. Forever. Indeed, she had never been his. And he would do well to learn to live with this truth and build his life on a foundation of service to others. He himself would never know great joy.

As he climbed the steps up to his hotel room, he struggled to find the strength of will that he normally relied upon. Alone once more in the confinement of his own private space, he took off the stiff garments of formality and stood once again in the bed chamber in his drawers.

He sat down and picked up the day's newspaper for distraction but then set it down as useless. He glanced at the list of prospects he had written up in Milton. It would do no good to attempt to think of business purposes now.

He tried to fend off the impending gloom that began to seep into the crevices of the room. But the vision of her every movement that evening played in his mind, torturing him. He bolted up from his chair and paced the room in his helplessness.

Her hair, her skin, those lips! He let out a cry of despair. How foolish he had been to ever have thought that she could love him. But he had been mesmerized by the memory of her touch—those soft arms had wrapped around his neck once. He had felt her body pressed against him, her heartbeat next to his.

It was this torturous memory that nearly drove him to delirium with the desire to hold her in his arms once again. Her touch had been as fire to his soul. And he wanted to feel that flame—he wanted to show her what she meant to him—not just one moment more, but every day and night that he drew breath on this earth.

He stopped his pacing to lean in desperate agony against the mantelpiece.

He knew how she would love, with a deep and tender passion and fierce loyalty! And he knew he was not worthy of such as she. But— oh, selfish man that he was!—he did not believe that Henry Lennox could be such a man worthy of her at all. He was ashamed to feel a certain hatred for the man who lived daily within her sphere.

That sociable and self-assured barrister did not truly know her. Not one of them saw her in all her true magnificence. No one could cherish or appreciate all her damnable and exquisite attributes as he did. No one else could love her the way he would.

The thought of her in another man's embrace was more than he could bear. And for this reason, he would reject a London position if one were offered to him. For he knew with absolute conviction that he wished never to see her as a married woman.

He moved away from the fireplace and sank down upon his bed.

His mother had been the wiser one. Seeing Margaret again had been a torment. It had only engraved deeper in his mind that which he already knew: that there was not, and never would be, any woman like Margaret. And yet, the one woman he wanted for a wife did not love him. It was this plain and irreversible fact that cut him to the core.

The only comfort he could wring from the wretched despair that crashed over him through this long night was that he would be in the same city as she tomorrow, much as he had lived those few precious years she had lived in Milton.

HE WOKE EARLY, as was his custom. But there was no mill to tend, and his mother was not waiting to join him for breakfast downstairs.

He did not rise. He cast his gaze around the dim room and traced the faint pink light illuminating the yellowed wallpaper to the open window. The clop and creak of a passing wagon and a murmured exchange of voices somewhere outside carried the mundane sounds of civilization to his ears.

He was alone in this teaming city. Today was the first day of many that he would not see her. He would rise every day of his life the same way as this day: alone. Already images of her began to swarm his thoughts and fill him with a sinking gloom.

He cast off the sheet he had slept under and rose from his bed in decision. It would do no good to dwell on his unhappiness. He had come for a purpose—to pursue his next position in the business of this country. And he would be better served if he got right to work looking up the contacts as he had intended. He dressed and took a simple breakfast in his room before heading out the door.

After he had spent the morning meeting with men who might help him find work, he sought respite in seclusion—someplace where there would be no need to maintain a pleasant visage or hopeful manner.

He walked along the unfamiliar streets of the city where none of the passing faces knew his name or took any notice of him.

The wealthy and powerful bankers and traders of London that he had met this morning accorded him all the respect due a once-flourishing and commanding mill owner. They had known him, and recognized the reputation for integrity in business he had acquired over many years. But to no avail. Not one was comfortable investing the capital required to restart the mill—the outcome he desired most of all. And in asking about any possible management positions in ventures already established, he had received the same response: "We'll keep your name in mind."

He let out his breath in disgruntled disappointment as he climbed the stairs to his hotel, eager to return to his room. There would be time for him to retreat for a while before meeting with yet one or two more connections this afternoon. Perhaps he would decide to leave London on the last train this evening, if no good prospects appeared.

As he passed the concierge's desk, he heard his name called out.

"Mr. Thornton—a message for you."

At once hopeful, he retreated a step to take the folded paper and took it to his room, where he broke the unfamiliar seal to read the clipped and cryptic note.

MISS HALE REQUESTS *your presence at 10 in the morning tomorrow at Harley Street to discuss a final business matter.*

Henry Lennox

THE JOLT of surprise was at first pleasant. But at once, doubtful dread began almost to eclipse the undeniable privilege of seeing her again.

He wanted to believe that she meant to do him some final deed of kindness, if nothing but for her father's sake. But any logical man—such as he had once been—would perceive that she wished to be free of any tie to him. There was little doubt that she wanted to terminate his lease so that she would no longer be required to see him or hear his name again.

This final anguish—that she would cast all memory of him away—weighed like a heavy stone on his heart.

Nothing, however, could ever take away the sacred experience he had gained from knowing her. He had known what it was to truly love. He had known how it felt to be fully alive.

And he would bind up his weary heart as he had before and train it to treasure what he had learned of love. And someday, perhaps not too distant a day, he would think of her only with a warmth of feeling without the fresh scars of pain.

MR. THORNTON ARRIVED the next morning at the appointed time and was ushered into the back drawing room to await Miss Hale. He was perplexed but pleased to find himself alone, for he had expected Mr. Lennox to be in attendance at this business proceeding. He relished the quiet opportunity to absorb the atmosphere and study the surroundings of the world she lived in. The tick-tick from a porcelain clock set above the marble fireplace was the only sound.

The house looked even more elegant in daylight. The high ceiling and delicately patterned papered walls gave the room a bright and airy feel. The rich Persian carpet underfoot nearly spanned the breadth of the room. Fresh roses overflowed from a wide vase on a cherry wood sideboard. Gold-tasseled draperies of velvet and damask framed the tall windows. The ornaments of luxury could be seen in every corner: a painting of a scene in Corfu; a white marble sculpture from Italy.

This was the home she had known for many years. The elegance and beauty of it was a piece of Margaret. It was indeed a stark contrast from the Hale's dingier home in Milton.

And yet, he missed the Crampton abode with its simpler embellishments of daily living, where piles of books and bowls of fruit invited wholesome indulgence. The country curtains and faded furniture from Helstone spoke more of life and love than all the stolid and polished finery set here in perfect display.

And although he felt she deserved to live in luxury and elegance, he could not help but think that she might tire of a life confined in such a sphere of perfection. How did she fill her days? He imagined she would find some cause or situation that needed her aid and her passionate sense of justice. She would not be satisfied to waste her life upon self-indulgence.

He glanced at the ticking clock and checked it against the watch in his pocket, for it had been forty minutes since he had arrived. But the wait did not trouble him. He was in no hurry. It was a pleasure merely to be in the same realm as she.

He wondered if she used this room to write or to read. It was difficult for him to imagine her being permanently sheltered in such a still and formal environment. Her life as a refined heiress, secluded from the rougher classes, was a far cry from the struggles she had seen and endured living among the jostling crowds of Milton.

Was she happy here? He was saddened to see how changed she had appeared at the dinner party. All her former fire seemed extinguished. She had been quiet and spoke only when spoken to. Had her grief changed her thus? Was this the effect that a life of ease had upon her, or was it his presence alone that had made her so subdued and withdrawn?

He longed to know if she could be happy here. He wished it for her, even though he would never be a part of making it so.

He turned around at the rustling sound of someone's approach. Margaret entered the room, her head downturned. Her eyes flickered and met his for a sole moment but swiftly turned their gaze about the room, looking for something—someone?—who was not there.

Her presence staggered him. She had not yet said a word, but her very silence commanded his attention. He felt at once as he had the first time he had met her—awkward and unworthy. His heart beat erratically while he took this moment to worship her every feature, engraving his mind with the image of her for the long years ahead.

"I'm very sorry Mr. Lennox is not here," she uttered as she arrived at the corner desk.

Mr. Thornton thought to himself that he would be happy if he never saw Mr. Lennox again. "Do you wish me to seek him at his chambers?" he asked.

"No…no…there must be a reason he was unable to come. I only… it's just that we drew up some figures yesterday…" she answered, hastily sorting through papers set upon the open secretary. "If only Henry were here to explain…"

"I'm certain you don't need Henry to explain," he replied in a deep, soothing tone. It pained him to see her dependent upon any other man. He took a step forward as if to aid her.

"No!…don't…" she exclaimed with a faint tremble in her voice. "I'm certain it is here…I need but a moment."

Her response startled him. Was he so abhorrent to her that she wished him to stand apart? Her frightened manner confused and wounded him.

"I have a business proposition which I hope will be agreeable to you," she nervously announced as she continued to rifle through the papers. "Mr. Lennox felt certain it would be most agreeable."

"Mr. Lennox knows nothing of what it is to lose all that one has built or striven for. Mr. Lennox has every happiness to look forward to. He can know nothing of what I would find agreeable," Mr. Thornton replied with a bitterness he could no longer hide. His hands clenched and unclenched restlessly by his sides.

"You do him a disservice, then," she returned. "For I, too, have reason to believe you will be pleased with…oh, here it is!"

She grasped the paper with a shaking hand while she stood to make her presentation. "I have, at present, money in the bank which is earning only two and a half percent interest. Mr. Lennox says that if I should invest in Marlborough Mills, you could provide me with a much greater return. So, if you will take my money—eighteen thousand and fifty-seven pounds—I might get a better return and you could re-open the mill…oh, there was another paper from the bank…"

And with this, she anxiously turned again to search through papers, her cheeks aflame with color.

Eighteen thousand and fifty-seven pounds!

Mr. Thornton froze in stunned silence as tremors of comprehension began to shake the very foundation of his stifled existence. No financial advisor would propose such an odd sum. And at this moment of caution in the trading houses, no wise counsel would condone such tremendous faith in one man's venture. But she...she trusted him with every last cent in her account!

His heart beat thick and fast as he stared at her—her nervous posture and blushing face now revealing a wholly different picture. All the assumptions of her disdain that he had built to a towering wall came crumbling and crashing down. One clear truth now stood before him: she cared for him!

"Margaret!" he heard himself utter, his voice hoarse in accelerating wonder.

She stilled and then collapsed into a chair, covering her face with her hands.

His body quaked and his heart pounded even more furiously, for her very reaction confirmed the revelation that was still crashing over him in wave after wave of disbelief. How had he not seen it before? Fool that he had been!

"Margaret!" he called out to her again, in agony to know once and for all that she would save him from this perpetual misery of longing.

She lowered her face to the desk, still covering it with her hands. But he would not leave unless he knew the truth. If she felt but a portion of what he felt for her...! Did she truly wish to leave this luxury and make her home with him—in Milton?

He crossed the room to her side and knelt to speak close to her ear.

"Take heed...if you do not speak," he panted, "I will claim you in some strange and presumptuous way! Send me away at once if you must...Margaret!"

All was still for a moment, and then she quickly turned to bury her face on his shoulder.

He clasped her close, letting out a slow breath of incredulous rapture to feel her soft form pressed to him. *She was his!*

He trembled inside as he held her, breathing in the scent of her, afraid she would withdraw. He wanted to hold her in his arms forever. But she did not move, and they both stayed silent in this first embrace until their heartbeats slowed into a comforting symphony of rhythm as every passing moment gave sweet assurance that this was indeed reality—that nothing would part them from this time forward.

He gently pulled her up to stand beside him. He was almost dizzy in his new-found joy. Was this all a dream? Was she now his to caress and hold as his own?

He placed her arms around his neck—just as he remembered she had done once before—to feel again that press of her arms about him that he had longed to feel since she had clung to him that fateful day.

"Do you remember, love?" he murmured. "And how brashly I spoke to you the next day in return!"

"I remember how cruelly I spoke to you— that is all!" she cried.

"Shh... look," he coaxed, drawing out his pocketbook to show her his devotion. Carefully, he pulled out the dried roses he kept there. "Do you know these flowers?"

Curiosity and confusion clouded her face for a moment until recognition cleared the creased brow and lifted her eyes to his. "They are from Helstone! Have you been there?" she asked, astonished.

"I went there to see where my beloved had come from. When I had no hope at all of calling her mine," he relayed.

"They have the deep indentation around the leaves... you must give them to me!" She reached out to take them, but he snatched them away, placing them behind his back.

"You must pay me for them," he said, with a devilish smile.

She blushed as she comprehended his request but met the gleam in his eye with acquiescence. And as he stepped forward, she lifted her chin and closed her eyes.

He gently took her face into his hands, trembling inside to distill three years of hungering longing into this caress. The first brush of his lips against hers sent pulses of sensation through every nerve ending. This was a bliss he had never known. He could spend all afternoon in a paradise such as this. With every touch of her lips, he felt the promise of her affection dissolving all his bitterness and pain.

The ache now growing inside of him was a pleasurable agony of repressed passion, for he desperately desired to show her how much he needed her. But he would not frighten her, and so—gently, and with utmost care—he tempered his fervency with reverent tenderness, knowing that he had a lifetime to love her.

A SHORT TIME LATER, Mr. Thornton emerged from the back drawing room and bounded down the carpeted hall with long youthful strides of radiant jubilation.

It was all decided. They would wed as soon as the banns had been read. She would stay in London to arrange the wedding. He would return to Milton to round up the men and prepare to open the mill.

This time, when he crossed the granite threshold of ninety-six Harley Street into the noontide sun, he could not suppress a beaming smile. The world around him had never looked so gloriously bright. The woman that had once sorely rejected him would be his wife. *She loved him!*

HANNAH THORNTON SAT at the long gleaming table in the dining room. A great leather Bible lay open in front of her as she pored over favorite verses from the Prophets to comfort her restless mind. She heard the brusque rattle of the front door below and froze to listen for the familiar ensuing sound of quick steps. She got up at once to receive her son, who appeared in the drawing room in a matter of seconds. Her heart leapt in perplexed surprise to see the corners of his mouth lifted in a joyous smile.

"Mother, I have good news," he announced as he took her hands and brushed her cheek with a kiss.

"What is it, John? Have you enterprising work?" she asked, endeavoring to read the answer in his eyes.

"Do no more packing. I am opening the mill again!" he announced as he walked over to the long window to gaze over his kingdom with a swelling eagerness to begin his life anew.

"What? You have found a loan? From whom?" She pressed, following him to the middle of the room.

He turned to answer her, with a smile that could not be repressed. "From an unlikely source. One that I believe may astonish you," he cautioned.

"Tell me," she demanded, flummoxed by his warning and his glowing joy.

"It is Miss Hale!" His eyes flashed out now in his delight in surprising her.

"Miss Hale!" She faltered, sinking down into a chair. "I thought you had gone to sever all connections to that woman! Why should she suddenly wish..."

"Mother," he called out with a firm gentleness that startled her.

The tender earnestness of his entreaty went straight to her heart, silencing her. She watched with growing trepidation as her son drew close and dropped to one knee in front of her.

"She wishes to give all she has to the mill, Mother. She wishes to come home to Milton—to come home to me."

Consternation and a sinking recognition crossed her face as she listened to his words. She hung her head, shrinking from this news. She had not been prepared to give him up! She would need time to adjust to such a startling change.

"Mother," he said softly, reaching to take her hands into his. "You know this is what I have long wanted."

Ashamed of her selfish concerns, she lifted her head to look into his pleading face.

"She cares for me, Mother!" The utterance of it reverberated its truth into his being. "I cannot ask for anything more. I have gained all that I thought was lost to me," he said, his voice trailing off into a hoarse whisper as he felt tears begin to gather in his eyes.

Mrs. Thornton took her son's face into her hands. *"I will restore to you the years that the locust hath eaten...and ye shall eat in plenty, and be satisfied, and praise the name of the Lord your God, that hath dealt wondrously with you: and my people shall never be ashamed."*

He bowed his head, nodding, and they were silent for a few moments with clasped hands and closed eyes.

When he lifted his head and looked to her again, her heart melted at his boyish hope—and she thought back to those years when they two had struggled long and hard together. He deserved every happiness in the world. And if this girl could bring such happiness to him, then so be it.

"She's seen your worth at last," she consented, brushing her hand along his cheek. "If she makes you happy, John, I might learn to like her."

He brought her hand up to his lips and kissed it, taking her words for a blessing. Then he rose up and turned to leave.

"Where are you going?" his mother called out in surprise at his haste. "It's nearly time for dinner!"

"To tell Higgins and the men about the mill," he answered with a wide grin, for he could not contain his joy. "The day is nearly over, but there's still time..." And with that explanation, he left her to contemplate the great turn of events.

As Mr. Thornton strode down Marlborough Street, many were the passersby who blinked in surprise at the Master's jubilant face and took a second look to determine if it was indeed the mill master well-known for his impenetrably stern gaze.

Mr. Thornton threaded his way through the backstreets and alleys of the Princeton District, knowing well the way to Higgins' home. As he passed listless children sitting in the streets and straggled women hanging up laundry to dry in the warm air, his heart pounded with the excitement of conveying news that would affect the lives of hundreds.

As he neared the Golden Dragon, he spotted his friend in a small huddle of men, all without work on this late afternoon. Several of the men he knew by name—they had worked in his mill.

The group ceased their talk as he approached.

Mr. Thornton nodded to the men as a greeting but sought out Higgins.

"May I have a word with you, in private?" he asked the jaunty union leader.

"Only because the mischief in your eyes is a blasted mystery!" he retorted, forcing a breathy laugh from his former employer.

The two of them walked the short distance to Higgins' house, where Nicholas opened the door to allow the Master to enter first.

Higgins had barely shut the door behind him when the younger man spoke.

"I've just come from London."

"Aye…and?"

"I have found the means to open the mill again!" the Master announced with a beaming grin.

Nicholas tore his cap from his head and slapped it against his thigh. "I knew if there were any man tha' could find a way to start 'er up again, it was yo'!" he exclaimed with a grin to match the Master's. "When do we start? …I've got to tell th'others!" He started as if to go, but checked himself.

"As soon as we can gather the men and materials," Mr. Thornton replied with a great sense of satisfaction. "But I have a few changes in mind."

Higgins cocked his head in curiosity, boring his gaze upon his employer.

"I'd like to make you overseer, if you'll take the job. Mind you, the position requires a good deal of brains and a fair amount of brass. Are you fit for it?" Mr. Thornton asked with mock solemnity.

"Blast yo'! Dunnit play with me now! I've half a mind to take yo' for your word," he shot back in dumbfounded confusion, trying to read the Master's face.

"I am in earnest," Mr. Thornton replied, softening his demeanor to convey his sincerity. "Williams has found work elsewhere, and I am glad of it, for I have thought for some time now that you are the right man for the job."

Higgins turned his face away a moment and then wiped a sleeve across his eyes before stepping forward to clasp Mr. Thornton's hand in both of his. "I thank yo' for yo' trust in me."

"You have earned it," his employer—and friend—said firmly as he placed his other hand over Higgins'.

"There are more changes. I have not yet told you the best of it," Mr. Thornton revealed, an unmistakable twinkle in his eyes.

"Not the best of it…" Higgins echoed in disbelief, still reeling from the onslaught of good tidings.

"Miss Hale is coming back to Milton," he said, a twitch of a smile playing on his face.

"Miss Marget? Her hoo's been in London?"

"The very one. Only she will no longer be Miss Hale," Mr. Thornton hinted, wearing a beaming smile now. He watched his friend carefully as confusion and then recognition crossed his face.

"What? Ah! Am I to offer yo' congratulations?" Higgins exclaimed, with a widening grin.

Mr. Thornton answered with a shy smile.

"Ah-ho! I see yo've both finally come to your senses! I couldna be happier to hear it. Congratulations!" he said taking the Master's hand to shake it heartily. "She's not a common lass. Yo'll treat 'er well," he intoned, placing his hand on Mr. Thornton's shoulder in a fatherly manner.

"I am the most fortunate man of all who walk the earth. I'll not squander the blessing bestowed on me," he answered with reverence.

Higgins clapped his friend's shoulder in satisfied approval.

The door behind them rattled and scraped open. Mary stepped into the house. Strands of hair hung loose from her head wrap. She wore a haggard expression from a long day of fustian cutting.

Her father called out to her with a ring of joy meant to wipe away her weariness. "Mary, Mary! There is such good news!

Trudy Brasure's curiosity about life in past times and her fascination with the Victorian Era have been part of her since she was a small girl considering the ruins of her grandfather's barn in rural Pennsylvania.

She began her own personal romance story with a whirlwind courtship. Her married life started in a picturesque colonial town on the coast of Massachusetts. With the addition of three children and several dogs, she currently lives in California.

As a hopeless romantic and a fervent enthusiast for humanity's progress, she loves almost nothing more than to engage in discussion about "North and South."

TRUDY BRASURE's books include *A Heart for Milton* and *In Consequence*

FINIS

IN APPRECIATION

The authors wish to thank the following for their generous contributions and support for this project.

Cover Artist: Janet Taylor
  Proofreader: Deborah Brown*
  Promotions: Rita Deodato

~

Above all, we are humbly grateful to Elizabeth Gaskell for her immortal tale.

*Excepting *Passages in Time* and *Loose Leaves from Milton*

NOTES

CINDERS AND SMOKE

1. 1 1 For more on dobby looms and the Jacquard device, please see
2. 2 2 https://en.wikipedia.org/wiki/Dobby_loom
3. 3 3
4. 4 4 *Social Darwinism* would be more fully articulated by Herbert Spencer and Joseph Chamberlain in the 1880s as a comforting philosophy to explain the correctness of the exploitation of labor by capital.
5. 5 5 Much as the Amalgamated, the steelworkers' union, was destroyed after the violence of the Homestead strike against Carnegie Steel in 1892.
6. 6 6 In this universe, Jacob Marley and Ebenezer Scrooge were well-known in financial circles throughout Great Britain. Charles Dickens published a biographical sketch, *A Christmas Carol,* in 1843. Please see my comments on *solipsism.*
7. 7 7 *The Fifth Love* was first articulated by Mrs. F. L. Bennet in 1947 to her husband. Later, sometime after Mr. Bennet's death in 1815, Mrs. Bennet discussed both the *Fifth and Sixth Loves* with her youngest daughter, Mrs. Lydia Bennet Wickham.

Made in the USA
Middletown, DE
30 November 2020